MW00808156

MAX FEND BOOKS 1-2

GLIDEPATH & THE OSHKOSH CONNECTION

ANDREW WATTS

POINT WHISKEY PUBLISHING

Copyright © 2017-2018 by Point Whiskey Publishing.

All rights reserved.

No part of this book may be reproduced in any form or by any electronic or mechanical means, including information storage and retrieval systems, without written permission from the author, except for the use of brief quotations in a book review.

ISBN: 978-1-64875-026-7 (Paperback)

ALSO BY ANDREW WATTS

Firewall

The War Planners Series

The War Planners

The War Stage

Pawns of the Pacific

The Elephant Game

Overwhelming Force

Global Strike

Max Fend Series

Glidepath

The Oshkosh Connection

Books available for Kindle, print, and audiobook. To find out more about the books or Andrew Watts, visit

AndrewWattsAuthor.com.

GLIDEPATH

A MAX FEND THRILLER

The Cold War may be 'over' for the West. For the Soviets it has entered a new, active and promising phase.

— Anatoliy Golitsyn, KGB Defector

1

"Have you met Mr. Morozov before?"

"No. But I know the type," Sergei said, sweat on his brow, shielding his eyes from the bright sunlight shining off the Mediterranean.

Sergei was a midlevel manager in one of the most powerful Russian mafia organizations on the planet. Born in Moscow, he had come to France a decade earlier to run his family's business dealings there.

Mikhail and Sergei sat on a small porch overlooking the marina, ten floors up. Below, tourists lined up for ferry rides and deep-sea fishing trips. Seagulls glided in the air, searching for discarded food.

"When you speak with him, make sure you are respectful and to the point. Mr. Morozov does not normally meet with men like you."

Sergei waved his hand dismissively. "Maybe I don't normally meet with men like *him*."

Mikhail took a final drag from his cigarette and then pressed it into the glass ashtray on the porch table. *If that's how this arrogant little prick wants to play it, fine.*

He'll soon learn.

Mikhail had seen enough of this new generation. The ex-Spetsnaz soldier was getting older, but he still was a foreboding presence. He had cut his teeth in Afghanistan as a member of the Red Army. Mikhail didn't care for men like Sergei. He would just as soon have snapped his skinny little neck for disregarding his advice like that—but working for Morozov required total discipline.

And Morozov wanted to talk to Sergei.

"Can you shut that thing up?"

Sergei's terrier was yapping at Mikhail's feet. The dog hadn't stopped barking in the five minutes since he'd entered. An earsplitting, high-pitched yelp. Over and over and over.

"He likes you. He's a friendly dog."

Mikhail glared at the animal, then looked down at his buzzing phone.

"He's coming up."

Sergei shrugged. He glanced down at the gun holstered on Mikhail's right side.

"You like that piece? I can get you something better."

Mikhail ignored him.

Minutes later, Pavel Morozov entered with two security guards in tow. Mikhail's men. They were younger, but well trained. They closed and locked the door behind them and remained near the entrance of the small vacation condo.

Morozov stepped out onto the patio and took a seat. He was fit for a man of his age—nearing sixty-five. And his tanned skin hinted at a comfortable life in the sun. His expression was stoic. But behind his eyes was the distinct look of a man who had experienced decades of power. The look of an oligarch who expected nothing less than pure obedience. Behind those confident eyes was a master spy—one who had seized power through treachery and violence after the collapse of the Soviet Union.

Sergei hadn't stood as he'd entered. And the tiny dog only intensified its bark—now aimed at Morozov.

Sergei made a clicking sound and the dog hopped up on his lap, now emitting a low growl at the guests.

Morozov looked at Mikhail with one eyebrow raised and then gave a thin smile. Mikhail pulled out a chair for his boss and positioned himself behind Morozov without saying a word.

"Glad you could make it," offered Sergei.

"Tell me what I came to hear."

Sergei said, "I have information that you will be most interested in. My associates and I would like to provide you with the first bid."

"What are you offering?"

"Access. Access to the Fend Aerospace data center. Every document they have. Their designs for aircraft. Their software. Their classified military programs. I can get you into their system."

"How?"

Sergei leaned back and smiled, looking satisfied.

Morozov glanced back at Mikhail and then said to Sergei, "Fend Aerospace is a multibillion-dollar American corporation. They will have very good IT security systems in place. I find it unlikely that a man in your position would come into something like this without outside assistance. So...who is getting you into their system?"

"Max Fend." Sergei petted his dog and stared into the eyes of Pavel Morozov.

"Max Fend? Charles Fend's son?"

"Yes."

"How do you know him?"

"We have done business together."

"What kind of business?"

Sergei ignored the question. "Mr. Morozov, as I understand it, you have been interested in Fend Aerospace for some time. Word is that you have been fishing for a way into their network. I can give it to you. For a price."

The tiny dog was showing its teeth at Pavel Morozov. Sergei made a shushing sound to quiet it down.

Morozov rubbed his chin. "Why?"

"Excuse me?"

"Why would you offer this to me?"

"I was told that you would be interested. And with your work...you would be the best person to help monetize this. My family doesn't normally deal in this area, as you know."

"Yes. Your family deals with prostitutes and drugs." Morozov looked as if he was contemplating something.

"Only the best prostitutes, and the highest-margin drugs." Sergei chuckled.

"Tell me, Sergei, why am I hearing about this from *you*?"

Sergei shifted in his seat. "What the hell does that mean?" The dog began growling again.

Morozov took the tone of a school principal speaking to an unruly student. "Why not one of your cousins in Moscow? I've dealt with them personally in the past. I have a relationship with them. Do they know about this?"

Sergei swallowed.

"Look, if you are not interested, I can go—"

"Oh, no. I *am* interested."

"Then what is the problem?"

Morozov said, "Tell me, who would the buyer be? In your most experienced and professional opinion."

Sergei shrugged. "If you are worried about the liquidity, don't. You wouldn't have to sell this stuff to a big aerospace company. I would think that you could sell the different pieces separately. Any technology company would be interested in the technology. Fend Aerospace is a treasure trove. You are familiar with their new automated flight program?"

"I am."

"My sources tell me that the right person could make billions with this."

Morozov crossed his legs, looking out over the Mediterranean Sea.

"Sergei, are you familiar with the significance of my namesake?"

Sergei rolled his eyes. "I am not here to talk about your name."

Morozov shot the young Russian a look.

Sergei winced. "I'm sorry, Mr. Morozov. I just...what does this have to do with what we are here to discuss? I want to talk about a business proposition. You—"

"I don't care what you want. When I tell you something, you listen."

Morozov snapped his fingers.

Mikhail walked over and gripped Sergei's neck in one hand, twisting his left wrist behind his back until Sergei let out a squeal of pain and pressed his head down firmly against the overhang. Sergei was now bent over, his smushed face looking towards Morozov, partially protruding over the edge. The street was ten floors down.

The little dog barked furiously and then grabbed onto Mikhail's pant leg, pulling.

Morozov uncrossed his legs and stood. He grabbed the tiny animal by its neck.

"What are you doing? Let me go. You know who my family is. This is not the way we do business—"

Mikhail punched Sergei in the kidney. With the size of Mikhail's arms, it was quite painful. "Be quiet and listen—or you get more."

Sergei shut up, his eyes wide. The dog kept barking, suspended in air by Morozov's left hand.

With his free hand, Morozov took out a knife from his pocket. He flicked it open and rammed it twice into the dog's throat. A quick, sickening squeaking sound emanated from the dog's mouth. Morozov released his grip and the animal fell to the ground with a thud.

Morozov's hands were covered in blood. One of the guards came over with a damp towel, and Morozov began cleaning himself. He left the dog's carcass on the ground.

Sergei's mouth was open, releasing a slow, painful gasp. His eyes were moist with anger and fear. Spittle dribbled from his lips.

Morozov moved his deck chair closer to the edge, so that his face was mere inches from Sergei's own.

"Let's try again. The name Pavel Morozov—my name—are you familiar with its story in Russian history?"

Sergei's voice was strained. "Yes. Of course."

"The more commonly known name is Pavlik. Pavlik Morozov. A Soviet boy. What is he known for, Sergei?"

Sergei's eyes were looking down over the ledge, ten stories below. He then looked back at Morozov. "He turned his parents in. To...to the Communists."

"Yes. Pavlik Morozov was thirteen when he did that. A peasant. Born in a small village in the country. He was a good Communist. But his father was not. His father had broken the law, forging documents and selling them to criminals. So Pavlik did what any good Soviet boy should have done—he turned his father in to the political police. What happened next?"

Sergei had stopped fighting but was still being forced down at an awkward angle.

"The boy was killed—by his relatives."

"Something like that. Pavlik Morozov turned his father in. His father was sentenced to ten years in a labor camp and then executed. But then Pavlik's family took their revenge. They did not appreciate disloyalty. Little Pavlik's uncle, grandfather, grandmother, and cousin murdered him in cold blood. And they killed his younger brother too, for good measure."

Sergei winced in pain. Mikhail's thick fingers still dug into his neck, Sergei's forehead scraping against the plastered overhang.

Morozov whispered, "Then the Soviet political police—found out about the horrific murders. So they went into town, rounded up the perpetrators, lined them up, and executed all of them by firing squad."

"The people of the Soviet Union were aghast at what happened. Pavlik became a martyr. A symbol. Statues went up. Songs and poems were written. Poor young Pavlik's school became a memorial where children all over the Soviet Union were sent to pay tribute to his great sacrifice."

Morozov looked up at Mikhail and nodded. Mikhail placed Sergei back on his chair but remained standing behind him. Sergei was bleeding from his forehead, where it had ground into the rough stone wall.

Morozov said, "So my parents named me after this great example of Communist bravery. What do you think, Sergei? What do you think of my name?"

Sergei said, "I don't know...I think it is good, I guess."

"Do you know what I think?"

Sergei shook his head, looking down at the floor.

"I think it is all propaganda bullshit. The Communists fabricated that story. It was the most perfect Russian tragedy you could imagine. And my poor parents bought it. Now I have to walk around with this goddamned lie of a name."

Sergei just stared back, eyes lowered.

"But you know what, Sergei? The story does have a good lesson. But it is not the lesson that the Soviets wanted us to take away. Do you know what I am talking about?"

Sergei shook his head rapidly.

Morozov got in his face, speaking through gritted teeth.

"Family members are often a great source of vulnerability. They are blind spots. Take Max Fend. Max Fend might be his father's undoing. And what about you, Sergei? Are you the weak link in your family?"

Fear shone in Sergei's eyes.

"Like I said, Sergei, I am used to dealing with your family. *Not you.* So when you called, guess what I did? I called your uncles. And I told them something that they did not know. Your uncles don't want to have a rat in the family. That is a problem for them. A problem that they would very much like to go away."

Mikhail came back into Sergei's view again. He was twisting a silencer onto the barrel of his gun, his eyes on Sergei.

Morozov smiled. "I make problems go away, Sergei. I'm very good at it."

"Mr. Morozov, please just—"

"I want you to tell me everything you know about Max Fend. And then I want you to tell me exactly how you propose to gain access to the Fend network."

"You are going to shoot me." Sergei's voice sounded defeated.

A thin-lipped smile. "Tell me what I want to know, and I promise you that I won't shoot you."

* * *

Twenty minutes later, the sounds of the marina were interrupted by screams. The screams began ten stories up and changed pitch as the source hurtled downward, ending in an abrupt smack as Sergei's body smashed onto the pavement.

2

National Air and Space Museum
Washington, D.C.
Five Days Before the Fend 100 Flight

Charles shook his head. "How did they get through our firewall?"

"I just spoke with our IT security team. They still don't know."

"And you're sure that they weren't able to access the Fend 100 software?"

"It appears that way, but they have the aircraft design, including the wing. If the investors find out..."

"They're going to find out, Maria, there's no way around that. The best thing we can hope for now is to manage the message. You've notified the authorities?"

"Yes, Charles. We did that when it happened. But we're just now learning how serious this was."

"I'll have to fly to New York and speak to some of the investors. The NextGen contract isn't complete yet. They'll be nervous."

Maria Blount nodded in agreement. She was one of Charles Fend's top executives and head of the Fend 100 autonomous flight program. She had just broken the news that a cyberattack had penetrated many of their most precious company files. They had known about the breach for several weeks. But until today, the Fend Aerospace leadership had been under the impression that their cybersecurity had prevented any important data from being stolen. This was bad news at a critical juncture in the company's schedule.

"The *Today Show* is ready for you, Mr. Fend."

The camera crew was setting up right under the National Air and Space Museum's exhibit on commercial aviation. A DC-3 was suspended in the air overhead, and the giant front end of a Boeing 747 protruded from the wall.

"Excuse me, we will have to discuss this more later," Charles said and walked onto the set.

The production team hooked a microphone to his shirt and handed him an earpiece. Bright lights illuminated the area. The crowd of museum tourists that had gathered around him hushed, seeing that *the* Charles Fend was about to go on live TV.

Charles could hear "the talent" in his ear, carrying on with their morning news update. Then came the voice he assumed belonged to the producer, instructing them to cut to Washington for Charles Fend.

The large black camera rolled up in front of him, keeping the museum's aircraft in the frame. A tiny TV screen next to the camera showed the host saying, "We're now joined by the illustrious Charles Fend—aviation pioneer and owner of Fend Aerospace. He's coming to us live from the National Air and Space Museum in Washington, D.C. Charles, would you care to tell everyone watching how the Fend 100 project is going so far?"

Charles smiled, his white teeth and gray hair recognizable to the viewers from many years of wide publicity.

"It's going great, thank you for asking. In five more days, the Fend 100 will be airborne, and I wanted to thank you for having me on your show to talk about it."

"Can you tell our audience what to expect during the flight next week?"

"Sure thing. The Fend 100 will fly its first passenger flight just like any other commercial airliner, with one key difference. The Fend 100 Artificial Intelligence Pilot System will be doing all the work. The computers will completely take over for the pilots. The Fend 100 will fly up and down the Florida coast for a few hours, allowing our passengers to experience what real airborne luxury can be like, and then the Fend 100 will return for a safe landing back at our headquarters near Jacksonville."

Charles looked around the room, beaming. "I can't tell you all how proud I am of the men and women on the Fend 100 project team. They have each put a great deal of hard work into this. Decades of research and development have led to this moment. It is truly the dawn of a new era in aviation."

The TV host said, "Mr. Fend, what do you say to those that are worried about flying on pilotless aircraft?"

Charles nodded and smiled. "You know, there was a day not too long ago in our history when people rode on elevators, and they couldn't imagine the possibility of not having a bellboy there to expertly control it for them."

The crowd around him gave a muffled laugh.

"Today," Charles continued, "we think nothing of walking into an elevator and pressing that little button. That button sends you traveling through the air, thanks to a bunch of computers and electronics. There was a time when pilots used to control aircraft mechanically, through yokes attached to cables. You needed muscle power to move the elevators and ailerons. To manipulate the surface of the wing, which would move the aircraft into a turn. Aviators needed a wealth of knowledge to navigate and solve problems while flying. But those days are long past. We have computers in our phones that are exponentially more powerful than anything we had in the early days of aviation."

The TV show host said, "So you're saying that computers can do it all now?"

"Let me ask you a question. Have you gone on an airplane in the past few months?"

The TV host smiled. "Yes, Mr. Fend."

"How long was your flight? Probably a few hours, right? And do you know that the pilots on your commercial airliner were probably only touching the flight controls for about two minutes out of the entire flight? Aircraft can *already* do everything by themselves. On a foggy day, they even land themselves. Why? Because computers make fewer mistakes than people. In truth, mankind has been ready to take this step for quite some time. And, despite what the newspapers say about me, I'm a human being...not a computer."

The crowd around him laughed again. Louder this time. That was good. Keep them happy. People needed to believe in this.

"I... believe it or not, I understand the unease that some might feel at the thought of a pilotless aircraft flying them around the world. But science and statistics prove it...computers *are* safer. The majority of advancements in aviation over the past few decades have been incremental introductions of automated flight. Airspeed control. Altitude hold. Different computerized functions that most of you laymen would simply lump into the term 'autopilot.' But each one of these improvements was another step towards allowing a computer to more fully control the airplane. It is worth mentioning that these improvements have saved countless lives. Now, with artificial intelligence, we have machines that can learn, just like a pilot. And that is really the groundbreaking technology that we're going to provide. We want to make flying even safer and more efficient than it is today."

The TV host said, "Will you still have pilots as a backup? In case anything goes wrong?"

Charles Fend looked over at Maria and then back at the camera. She had told him to be ready for that question.

"We have built in that capability. And we will continue to work with the FAA and other regulatory agencies on best practices as we look to integrate this into the commercial aviation industry. Fend Aerospace has meshed the latest in AI capability with autopilot software. This creates a proprietary feature that enables safe and effective pilotless commercial flight. It's really quite extraordinary—and it will make flying both safer and cheaper."

"Mr. Fend, I think we can all agree that those are both improvements to look forward to." The host thanked him and transitioned to the next segment.

Cheers and claps from the crowd around him.

* * *

Brunch was at Sequoia, a restaurant on the shores of the Potomac. White tablecloths and a glitzy atmosphere.

"Are you excited?" Max said.

"Thrilled," his father answered, although he didn't sound it. Max and Charles Fend sat across from each other at an outside table. "This automated flight program has been more than ten years in the making. It will be nice to see it through before my retirement." He took a drink. "So your classes start in a few weeks?"

"Orientation. It's just a weekend. The classes start in August. I think I'll be the old man of my cohort."

His father shook his head. "I can't believe you're going to Georgetown. It hurts my heart. You know you don't need it for a resume. I'll give you the job anyway. That's a privilege of owning your own company."

Max smiled. His father had gone to Boston College, a rival Jesuit institution, for his undergrad degree back in the day.

Max had decided to get his MBA at Georgetown prior to starting his new career. His twelve years of prior work experience would qualify him for an elite subset of jobs, but those jobs were unrelated to managing an aerospace company.

"Well, we'll have to start betting on the sports games," his father said.

"Deal."

Max forked another bite of his "Chesapeake eggs Benedict"—a delicious hollandaise sauce dribbled over lump crab meat, a poached egg, and an English muffin. His father sipped on his bloody mary, looking up at the dreary gray sky.

"So you're sure about the retirement, then?" Max asked as he chewed.

"Mr. Fend, good morning!"

A woman strolled along the walkway near the restaurant's outdoor seating area.

"Maria. You can't get away from me, it seems. How are you, my dear? Care to join us?"

"Oh no, I couldn't."

Max realized Maria must have been in the group of executives that had flown on the corporate jet up from Jacksonville the day before. They were doing a full court press publicity tour in the run-up to the Fend 100 flight. Max's father had been on TV more often in the last few weeks than in the past decade. And for a man as in the spotlight as he was, that was saying a lot.

"Are you sure? We don't mind," said Max's father.

Maria came up to their table, sliding awkwardly through a large set of potted frond leaves.

"No, thank you, though. I was just doing a little shopping before we head back." She smiled at Max. "Max, I'm surprised your father didn't send you on the *Today Show* in his place yesterday. Now that you'll be joining the company and all."

Max gave a humble grin. "I hope he has more common sense than that. After spending the past few weeks with you all in Jacksonville, I've realized just how much I still have to learn."

Maria pushed a lock of her red hair back over her shoulder. "Max, you will do just fine." She smiled widely and looked back at Max's father. "Every time he comes down to Jacksonville, he's always asking such good questions."

"Well, I've always been interested in flying. Just need to learn more about the business, I suppose."

"Oh yes. I recently heard that you're a pilot. Is that right, Max?"

"Just for fun. I have my private pilot's license."

"What aircraft do you fly?"

"I've flown a few of them, but I'm partial to the Cirrus aircraft. I keep telling my father that Fend Aerospace needs to get into the general aviation market."

Charles laughed. "Maria, this is the part that worries me. If I give him too much of a leash, he'll turn the company into his own hobby center."

Maria smiled politely. "That's the sign of a good executive, Charles. Someone who's already interested in the work."

"Excellent," Charles said. "Well, you don't need to waste time on us. Anything more on that thing we were discussing yesterday?"

"No, I'm afraid not."

"Very well. I'll see you later today."

"Max, it was a pleasure as always. Charles, I'll see you on the plane."

Maria departed and walked away, along the brick walkway next to the Potomac River.

When she was out of earshot, Charles said, "A lovely woman. She has exceeded my expectations. You'll do well to shadow her when you join us full-time."

Maria had been hired by Charles Fend personally a few years ago, out of London. Max had gotten to know her relatively well, as she was one of the few people he interacted with when he would visit his father. She was one of Charles Fend's most trusted advisors.

Max lowered his voice. "So you were saying you think you're ready to scale back a bit?"

His father looked at him and nodded. "Yes. It's time. I'll still keep involved. I'm staying on as chairman of the board. I can step in if I see anything out of sorts. But all the day-to-day decision-making will be handled by a new CEO."

"And who will that be?"

Charles shook his head. "That's months away. I need to get us through this Fend 100 project first. Once we get that finished, my real work will be complete. The Fend 100 program will set Fend Aerospace up for the next few decades."

Max raised an eyebrow. "I don't mean to be selfish, but your retirement does make me curious about how I might be affected."

His father smiled. "That doesn't make you selfish, just human. Nothing will change for you. I'll see to that. You'll be employed with the company, as long as that's what you still want. You can finish your master's program here at Georgetown and then start working full-time after that."

Max sat back in his chair, mulling it over. His whole life, he'd been running from his wealth. His father had a controlling interest in one of the largest aerospace companies in the world. Everyone had heard of Fend Aerospace. When Max was growing up, most people that he met assumed that he was some spoiled rich prep school kid. And he *had* gone to all the best schools. They'd never been short of money. His father had taken him around the world on fabulous vacations.

But he'd always had a chip on his shoulder. Max wanted to forge his own path. He hadn't gone on to work on Wall Street or as an investment banker, like many of his classmates at Princeton. Instead, he had chosen to take a job that allowed him to see the world, live an exciting life, and do something fulfilling.

It just wasn't the type of occupation that he could talk to people about. In that field, talking about your work was the quickest way to ending up dead in a ditch.

But he was no longer *in* that line of work, he had to keep reminding himself. Whether he wanted to or not, now it was time for him to move on and try something new. Time to learn his family trade—and in doing so, accept an opportunity that few received.

The family business was worth close to twenty billion dollars. Fend was one of the largest airplane manufacturers on the planet. For years, Max and his father had an ongoing joke about how Max would one day take over as CEO. At least, it *had* been a joke. Until that walk on the French Riviera, when Max had asked his father if he might be able to come to work for Fend Aerospace.

Max said, "I don't feel like I've earned it."

His father took a bite of his bagel, a smear of cream cheese and smoked salmon on top.

"You *haven't* earned it. But *I* have. That's capitalism, son. To the victor go the spoils. One of mine is being able to name whomever the hell I want as my successor. And another is being able to place my son in management, if I so desire."

"I don't like getting handouts."

"It isn't one. You'll work your tail off, won't you?"

"Yes."

"I know how smart you are." He hesitated. "Your mother would have been proud of the man you've become, Max. I mean that."

Max flushed. "Thank you." He had trouble looking his father in the eye after that one. Compliments were sometimes hard for him. He changed the subject. "So what's next for the Fend 100?"

His father's face lit up. Max knew that he could talk all day about his work. "The FAA is going to evaluate the first passenger flight the week after next."

"And they don't mind that you're going to have a big show about it?"

"The FAA has all but granted us the contract as the sole supplier of autonomous flight technology for the NextGen program. They want us to succeed, and to generate enthusiasm among the public."

"And you don't have any reservations about it? Safety-wise, I mean."

"No, of course not. We've tested everything a million times. This is a dog-and-pony show. For the investors, for the trade, and for Washington. The FAA and those who are making the decisions with NextGen want to see consumer confidence in the product before they grant us final approval for the contract."

"So you'll have this first passenger flight..."

Charles said, "Yes."

"And that will get you the contract?"

His voice lowered. "Essentially, yes. That's what I'm being told. After that, the FAA will approve Fend Aerospace as the contractor for all US autonomous commercial flight software and networking. And then...I'll be looking at taking more vacations."

Max didn't respond. He was distracted by a young couple sitting at an umbrella table on the far end of the restaurant patio. They weren't talking. They both had sunglasses on. And Max was almost positive that they were conducting surveillance on him.

Why would anyone be surveilling him now? He hadn't been in Europe for a few months. And who were *they*?

Max tried to keep up his conversation with his father without appearing distracted. "Any thoughts on where you'd travel to first?"

"I liked Japan very much the last time I was there. There are some great spots in the mountains. Peaceful spas. Great food. Friendly, respectful people. I very much like the Japanese culture."

"That certainly sounds nice."

He spotted two more inside the restaurant. Max guessed that they were probably US federal law enforcement. They each wore a very small, almost imperceptible earpiece. And they looked nervous, like they were trying too hard to play it cool. Definitely not interested in what they were ordering, or in talking to each other.

For a moment, he thought that they might be there for someone else.

Perhaps even his father, the way the man was obviously glancing in their direction.

No. They appeared to be watching *him*.

They never looked at him *directly*. Their glances were always at someone or something *near* him. Just like they were trained, Max knew. Just like *he* had been trained.

Max's mind kicked into high gear. He began thinking about an exit strategy. Vehicles. Doors. Weapons. No—weapons were out of the question. Better to just roll with it and trust that his father's lawyer would be able to handle whatever misunderstanding there might be.

But what if he was wrong? What if they *weren't* US law enforcement? What if they were some less talented foreign intelligence service? (The talented ones wouldn't be so obvious.) What if they were contractors? Lawyers might not matter to those types.

Max spotted a dark SUV with tinted windows in the street. The door opened only for a second, but it was enough for him to see a dark blue jacket—just like the raid jackets that federal agents wore.

He wracked his brain to think of what this might be about. His father was still speaking. He had moved the conversation on to Max's new corporate training plan.

"Come to think of it, I may have Maria schedule some time to go over the company's priorities for the next fiscal year. It would be good for you to get a head start of sorts. To learn about the company's big bets and priorities while you're still in school. You'll have a steep enough learning curve as it is."

Max tried to remain in the conversation. "Alright. Anything else I should do to prepare?"

His father took another bite of his bagel and washed it down with ice water. "Yes, actually. I think it's about damned time you learned how to fly."

"I *know* how to fly, Dad."

"I'm talking about one of these bigger aircraft. You can't very well be expected to lead a company that makes jet airliners and not have any idea how to pilot them."

"You mean get my multiengine or jet rating? Sure. I can do that.

Maybe I can schedule some lessons up at BWI? There's got to be a multi-engine instructor there."

"Max, we have our own school. It's top-notch. We can train you. You'll just need to find the time."

Another SUV pulled up and parked just in back of the first. What were they doing, bringing in the whole agency? He was one man, and unarmed. He wasn't going to fight them. Not to mention that *he hadn't done anything wrong.*

The couple at the far table both cocked their heads at the same time and looked at each other. Someone had just given them a command via their earpieces.

The man rose from his seat. Then the woman.

They began walking toward Max, hands down near their waists. The two at the table inside were headed his way as well now, walking through the restaurant exit and out onto the patio.

"Dad."

"Yes?"

"I think I may need you to call your lawyer."

3

The agents were actually quite polite. They asked Max if he would voluntarily accompany them. He wasn't under arrest; they just had some questions. Max was amenable. His father was not.

"This is ridiculous, disturbing us here like this," his father said.

"We're sorry, Mr. Fend, but this is an urgent matter that we need to resolve."

Max tried to calm his father down, but that proved to be a tall order. After arguing with the agents and threatening to sue, Charles was on the phone with his lawyer. Max wasn't sure what his father would sue for, since he was voluntarily following his FBI escorts. But he knew that his father was just embarrassed and maybe a bit scared. He was always overly protective of Max.

Still, Max knew this wasn't normal, the FBI showing up like this. He tried to think of why they might have done it. Something time-sensitive, perhaps.

Or maybe they wanted to catch him off guard. Before he had the chance to lawyer up. If Max was running this little op, he would want to get as much out of the guy as he could, as soon as he could.

The FBI probably realized that as soon as one of Max's father's high-powered attorneys came into play, he wouldn't be saying a thing. Max wondered if they knew about his background. *No. That's not possible.* If anything, they knew about his cover. Now *that* could be a problem. Maybe that was it, then.

Max reverted back to his training. In the US, federal agents would need probable cause to arrest him. They could detain him no more than about twenty minutes without placing him under arrest. But if he voluntarily went with them...that changed the dynamics of the relationship. Still, it would be hard for them to use anything in court if they didn't play it by the book.

The FBI was all about what they could prove in a court system. That wasn't an issue for men like Max. In his former occupation, they only cared about getting accurate information, no matter how it came out.

Max and his FBI escorts walked up to a line of dark government SUVs parked on the curb of Rock Creek Parkway. The doors opened, and a few men stepped out of the cars, "FBI" emblazoned in bright yellow on both sides of their blue raid jackets. People on the street stared. It must have looked like a scene out of a movie.

"Mr. Fend, my name is Special Agent Jake Flynn. We'd like to speak with you for a few moments, please."

Max looked at the group, a grin on his face. "All of you?"

"Could you come with us, please, sir?"

Max said, "Sure thing."

A few moments later, Max sat in the middle seat of the Suburban. Two big FBI agents on either side. The vehicle drove fast through the streets of D.C.

The SUV stopped at a townhouse on Eighth Street in Northeast.

Max gave the FBI agents an odd look. "What's this?"

"It's an off-site residence that we use sometimes. It's easier than taking you all the way down to the D.C. field office in Manassas. Unless you'd rather be stuck on I-95 for three hours today. If you can answer all our questions, we might be out of here in under an hour."

"I'll do my best."

An agent at the door collected his phone on the way in. "You'll get it back once we're done. Security."

They walked up to the second floor. Max kept going over things in his head. With this many agents here, Max figured that whatever they were working on must have been pretty high-profile. Maybe that was just because his father was Charles Fend. Maybe it was something else.

"Have a seat." Special Agent Flynn extended his hand to a simple white desk, surrounded by a few chairs. Max sat.

"Can I get you anything to drink?"

"No, thanks," Max said.

"Do you know of any reason why we might want to speak with you today?"

Max shook his head. "I don't."

Agent Flynn stared back at him for a moment, letting the question hang.

"Can you tell me where you were on the fifteenth of last month?"

Max thought about it. "I was in Jacksonville, Florida."

"Where exactly?"

"I was with my father. Touring the Fend Aerospace plant and headquarters."

"Touring the Fend Aerospace plant and headquarters?"

"That's right."

"Did you access the computer network at the Fend headquarters?"

"Can I ask you something? Do I need a lawyer?"

"Not if you didn't do anything wrong."

"I didn't."

"Then we can keep this informal, if you want. It'll be quicker. Did you access the computer network at the Fend headquarters?" His voice was melodic. Casual.

Max didn't have a good feeling about this. Why were they concerned about the Fend computer network? He thought about his former line of work. If the right person had access, they could have done a lot of things with corporate network access like Max had.

Max said, "I think I might have used one of the company computers. Maybe to type a few emails. That sort of thing. But that was several weeks ago. It's hard to remember."

"It was three weeks ago."

"Okay, it was three weeks ago."

"So you had access to the Fend network?"

"Yes. I'm becoming an employee there. They've granted me access."

"What type of employee?"

"Excuse me?"

"What will your job title be, if you don't mind my asking?"

"My father owns the company. He's training me for a managerial position."

A few of the agents raised their eyebrows, smiling. "Must be nice," one of them said. Max reddened.

Flynn said, "While you were there, did you email anyone who resides outside of the country?"

Max frowned. "I don't know. I doubt it."

"You doubt it, or you did *not*?"

"I don't remember."

"You don't remember?"

"It was almost a month ago. Do you remember everyone you emailed exactly one month ago?"

"Did you email anyone in Syria or Iraq?"

Max frowned. "No."

"Have you ever had contact with a foreign government, its establishment, or its representatives—whether inside or outside the US?"

"I worked for a European consulting firm. We did a lot of business with a variety of clients. Some of them were foreign governments."

"Any from any of those countries that I mentioned? Syria or Iraq?"

"I don't think so, no."

"Have you worked with any government or nongovernment organizations that were involved in criminal or terrorist activity?"

"No, of course not."

"Were you involved with any nongovernment organizations from any of the countries I previously mentioned? Or maybe somewhere else in the Middle East?"

"Probably not."

"*Probably* not?"

"What do those countries have to do with anything?"

"Could you please answer the question?"

"I thought we were having a friendly discussion."

"We are." Flynn gave a forced smile. "See?"

"Some of our clients were from Saudi Arabia, I believe. And I think at least one was Syrian. But I worked with businessmen from just about every other country in the world. So it's not like I was just working with Syrians and Saudis the whole time. Although last time I checked, Saudi Arabia was a pretty staunch ally."

Flynn frowned. "Did you communicate with any of those clients from the Fend network on the fifteenth?"

"What clients?"

"The *Syrians*."

Max shook his head. "No. I do not have a continuing relationship with any of my *former* clients. I don't send any of them emails. I'm changing fields."

"Are you aware of a Fend network security breach last month?"

"No."

"Did you know that a foreign entity attempted to steal information from Fend Aerospace?"

"No, I didn't know that."

"Do you know how much someone would pay to access the Fend Aerospace servers?"

"I wouldn't know."

"Don't you find it interesting that this security breach happened on the fifteenth, right when you were there?"

Max stayed quiet. Was the FBI agent telling the truth? He certainly looked like it. So how was it that Max *didn't* know about this, if it was true? Why would his father have kept it from him? Perhaps the agent was misinformed? Or maybe it was a minor incident, and they were blowing it out of proportion. If it was something routine, Max could see his father not telling him about it. Would the FBI be questioning him if it were a minor incident? Unlikely...

Flynn waited for a response but got none. Then he said, "Mr. Fend, you will understand when I tell you that this security breach has raised some very serious questions. Fend Aerospace has some pretty big government contracts in the works. Some of them are defense-related.

Some of them aren't, but still affect the safety and well-being of many Americans."

The agents were watching him closely.

"How can I help you with this Agent Flynn?"

Flynn said, "We have reason to believe that on the day of the incident, someone provided an external source—likely originating from one of the countries that I mentioned—with access to the Fend computer network."

Max moved in his seat. "That is concerning."

"It *is.*"

No one spoke. A dog barked outside. An ambulance siren was going off in the distance.

"You understand why I'm asking you about your foreign connections now, don't you?"

Max said, "I think I see where you're going, yes."

"My team of specialists think it's possible that someone from the inside granted access to this hacker group. The hacker group then attempted to steal highly confidential corporate secrets from Fend Aerospace."

"That's incredibly disturbing," Max said.

"Yes, it is. And do you know what *else* is disturbing?"

"What?"

"The hacker group had connections to one of your former business associates in Europe."

"Well, I wasn't—"

"And the account that granted them access was *yours.*"

* * *

They continued to question him for almost an hour. The longer it went on, the more uncomfortable Max got. There was definitely a trail of evidence that pointed to Max.

Multiple cyberintrusions on the Fend network over a two-day period. Each through Max's account. Each from some group that was supposedly connected to someone Max knew in Europe. They wouldn't say who.

"Are you sure there isn't more that you'd like to tell us?" Flynn said.

"Because to me, it looks like you could be connected to a cybercrime. You know people that were likely involved, and you were at the location of a crime at or about the time it occurred."

"Special Agent Flynn, respectfully—I can assure you that I had no knowledge of any hacking that went on at my father's company."

"And?"

"And you must agree that I have no obvious motive. You have a few bits of information that are implicating me, but the obvious hole is this: why would I want to harm my father's company? I have a good relationship with my father. And I would never want to harm him, his company, or our country. Look, I'm happy to continue to answer any questions you might have—I will cooperate fully. But please know that I didn't do anything wrong."

The room was silent. One of the agents glanced at Flynn, who looked uncertain.

The doorbell rang. Max could hear one of the agents as he marched down the stairs and spoke to someone at the door.

"Flynn?"

"What?"

"The father's lawyer is here."

Flynn whispered. "You gotta be shitting me. How'd he know where we were?"

The agent shrugged. "What do you want me to do?"

Max tried not to appear pleased.

Flynn said, "Let him in, of course."

A tall, thin black man wearing a suit jacket walked up to the floor where Max was being questioned.

The lawyer scanned the room in silence. He seemed completely comfortable as he looked each one of the agents in the face. His gaze landed on Flynn.

The lawyer said, "What in the *world* are you doing?"

"He voluntarily came with us. He—"

"Do you have PC?" *Probable cause.*

Flynn clenched his jaw. "Not at this time."

"Then he doesn't need to answer questions. Let's go, Max."

Max stood. The lawyer began walking out.

Agent Flynn cleared his throat. "We aren't *finished*. We really could use about twenty more minutes of your time, if you'll give it to us, Mr. Fend."

Max looked at the lawyer questioningly. He guessed that the lawyer would say no, but Max didn't want to appear as anything other than cooperative. Let the lawyer be the bad guy.

Max said, "If it will help clear up this mess..."

The lawyer stopped and turned, hands folded across his chest. He sighed. "If Mr. Fend wants to continue to answer your questions, we can finish this at my office. *Tomorrow*. I need time to confer with my client."

The FBI men looked at each other. One walked away with his phone to his ear, whispering into it.

"Fine," Flynn said. "We'll finish up tomorrow."

Max could see the other agent on the phone in the kitchen area. He was making eye contact with Flynn. He held up two fingers.

Two minutes.

Special Agent Flynn nodded back to him.

What was happening in two minutes?

Max got up and the group of agents escorted him down the stairs. Flynn said, "Give him back his phone and personal items."

One of the agents leaned in close to Flynn. Max tried to read his lips but couldn't. It looked like he uttered the phrase "press charges." As in, "*Do you want to press charges?*" Max knew that if one of the agents was asking that, then they were probably close to that threshold of evidence they needed to place him under arrest.

They *couldn't* have that. Not unless there was something they weren't telling him.

He didn't hear Flynn's reply. But he saw Flynn looking right back at him, shaking his head. The group continued to walk outside the building.

A maroon Lexus sedan was parked on the curb. The lawyer opened the door for Max. "We'll be in touch," he told the FBI agents.

Once Max was inside with the doors closed, the lawyer looked Max in the eyes. His expression changed.

Max heard some commotion outside the vehicle. The FBI agent that had been on the phone was running down the front steps of the townhouse. Holding up his hand, calling something out to Special Agent Flynn.

In the side mirror, Max could see them talking. Flynn turned and looked at the sedan. He held out his hand and yelled, "Hold up!"

The doors in the sedan locked and Max looked at the lawyer in confusion. The lawyer placed his hand on Max's shoulder. "Listen to me." His eyes were deadly serious. "I'm not a lawyer. And I've never worked for your father."

A sinking feeling grew in the pit of Max's stomach.

The driver said, "Someone set you up. That's why the FBI is questioning you. And it won't get any better."

A knock at Max's window. Flynn stood there, giving him a signal to roll down the window. His voice sounded muffled from outside. "Max, please step out of the vehicle."

Max looked up at him. A group of agents were behind him. One was going around the driver's side. Flynn's hand began reaching down toward his holster.

The lawyer said, "Max, whatever information they just received, it's *false*. But it's something that could lock you up for years, and place your father and his company in peril. You need to get out now, while you can."

"Right. Question—can you go back to the part where you—"

"Max, I need your consent. This will be your only chance. Come with me now, and I can give you a shot at freedom. You'll have a chance to find out who set you up, and stop them. But you need to tell me now that you're in. Otherwise, my orders are to release you back to the FBI."

Max looked into the face of Agent Flynn. He didn't look happy.

Max said, "Let's go."

"Strap in. We're going to try and lose them."

"Oh, hell."

The lawyer slammed on the gas and peeled out, his Lexus tearing down the road. They left the FBI agents openmouthed and panicked.

4

At first, Special Agent Flynn had thought the lawyer was just a pompous ass. Coming in like he owned the place, happy to throw his weight around and force the FBI to play by the rules.

Flynn had been stuck between a rock and a hard place. He had taken a risk, asking Max to voluntarily come in to answer questions before the second arrest warrant was issued. The first warrant had been recalled as they were moving in to arrest him.

The Cyber Division had sent them evidence that morning, and his team had a location on Max Fend. A judge issued the warrant, and they began moving.

The evidence was obvious enough at first glance. Fend looked dirty. The Syrian hacker group on the other end certainly was. The electronic forensics data connected Max to the cyber intrusion. The Cyber Division had cross-checked it with their partners at the NSA, who in turn had shown it to the DNI's office as a courtesy.

That's when the trouble started. After the warrant was issued, the lawyers from DNI and the NSA had informed the Justice Department of some irregularities in the data. Flynn had seen this show before. The judge would recall the warrant. But by that time, his team was walking toward Max Fend and had likely been spotted. Pulling them back meant that they would be alerting Fend that they were on to him, and giving him a chance to flee.

Sure enough, the judge decided to cancel the warrant. Flynn's team was already moving in on Max. He had to think fast. So he told them to see if Fend would come in voluntarily.

But Flynn needed corroborating evidence. So he reached out to the DST—the French domestic intelligence agency. They had responded to a request for information on Fend earlier. The French had records of Max taking meetings with men connected to the suspected hackers. Flynn needed those documents sent to the judge.

Flynn's team received the evidence from the French and were taking it up the chain. They would have an arrest warrant within the hour. In the meantime, Flynn would ask Max Fend a few questions. If they were lucky, he might get spooked. Maybe he would admit allowing the hackers into the Fend computer network. If not, the French evidence would provide what they needed to place Fend under arrest before they had to let him go. That was the plan.

The Fend lawyer had changed everything.

Once he entered the picture, Flynn began to worry that any case he had would be thrown out because of procedural mistakes. He had stuck his neck out, and now his head was about to get chopped off. Flynn had attempted to take down wealthy guys like this Fend character before. Their lawyers always got them off on technicalities. That's what the money paid for. Greatest judicial system in the world.

So Flynn went along with the lawyer's suggestion to meet down at his office tomorrow. Better to play it by the book at this point and live another day. If the lawyer wasn't going to raise a stink about taking Fend to the safe house for questioning, that was a good thing. The judge's office was due to call back any minute.

Special Agent Flynn didn't know what would make someone like Max Fend get involved with organized crime rings out of Eastern Bloc nations. But that's what his file said. Fend had taken meetings with people who were involved in arms dealing, drugs, and human trafficking. He had close ties to some less-than-reputable Middle Eastern businessmen. Some were even on terrorist watch lists.

He was also plugged in to the young elite European crowd. Wealthy twenty- and thirty-somethings not unlike himself. Lots of flashy cars and pretty girls. Fend liked to have a good time, apparently. He worked as some type of high-end consultant—wheeling and dealing and living the high life in the South of France. Why he cavorted with criminals, Flynn didn't know.

When the FBI asked Special Agent Flynn to investigate the potential hacking incident at Fend Aerospace last week, he would never have guessed that it would lead back to Charles Fend's own son. But that's what the evidence was telling him. The Cyber Division was dependable. They could really work some magic with their computers. And the more Flynn read up on Max Fend, the more it all fit into place.

Flynn had come so close to arresting him.

But now, as the brand-new Lexus rounded the first corner—and out of sight—the veteran FBI agent began to panic.

"Let's move!" he yelled.

The group of agents piled into the SUVs and chased after them. A few seconds later, they could see the Lexus, racing through the streets of D.C.

Flynn rode shotgun. "There! They just took a turn."

"I got 'em, I got 'em."

He flipped on the blue light and siren and called it in to the D.C. police and US Secret Service, since they were driving right near the White House.

"Suspect is a white male, about six feet tall, medium build. Driving a maroon Lexus sedan...now turning onto..."

"Constitution," the other agent said.

"Constitution Avenue. Request immediate backup and pursuit."

The D.C. dispatcher relayed the message, and the Washington streets came alive with police and federal agencies. Two minutes later, a Maryland State Police helicopter was en route.

Flynn smiled.

What a piece of work. Who the hell thinks he can run from the FBI in the middle of Washington, D.C.?

* * *

Max was pressed back into his seat at the unexpected acceleration.

The lawyer glanced in his rearview mirror as he drove.

"Who are you?"

"That's not important. This is: don't let yourself be taken into custody again, understand? They might not have enough to arrest you with right now, but they will. That's what I'm being told."

"Told by whom?"

He didn't answer.

The Lexus's engine roared as the driver swerved through the busy D.C. traffic. Max held on to the door handle and his seat, tensing his legs against the floor for stability. He could see blue flashing lights both in front of and behind them.

His body jerked to the right as the driver took a hard left turn on Fourteenth Street.

"Why is someone trying to set me up?"

"We don't know yet."

The driver reached in the backseat and threw a small backpack on Max's lap. "Here. Put this jacket on. Make sure you leave your phone and any electronic devices in this vehicle. You know the drill." The man smiled.

With the smile was an unspoken acknowledgment that he knew about Max's background.

"Got it," Max said, a twinge of apprehension in his voice.

He unzipped the backpack. Two phones. A gun, with several magazines taped together. A Ziploc bag filled with cash, prepaid debit cards, and false IDs. All with Max's face. He examined one of them. It was quality work. Must have taken a while. How long had they been planning this?

The driver took a hard right on Constitution Ave. The Washington Monument was out the left side of the window now. The speedometer read over eighty miles per hour, the slow-moving traffic whipping by as the sedan zigged and zagged in between lanes.

He was a good driver. But also a little lucky. They barely missed hitting a woman crossing the street. She had been looking down at her cell phone.

"Put this on."

The man handed Max a large black motorcycle helmet. Tinted visor. Max did as he instructed.

By the time they took the circle around the Lincoln Memorial, the police cars were pretty far behind them. But Max wasn't worried about the ones behind them. He could see blue flashing lights and halted traffic on the bridge crossing the Potomac.

Max said, "Tell me you aren't going for one of the bridges."

"Not yet."

The Lexus swerved around the circle and jerked to the right, going off the road at over fifty miles per hour.

"Wait," Max said, realizing where they were going.

The ground in front of them dropped off into a steep incline. Max couldn't see what was beyond.

"*Hey...wait...*"

It looked like they were about to go off a steep drop-off in the road, heading towards the Potomac.

"*Hold on,*" said the driver.

The Lexus launched over the long concrete set of stairs that led down to Ohio Drive, twenty feet below. The sedan crunched into the bottom of the stone steps and skidded into the ground as the driver turned left and braked.

It wasn't enough to stop the collision. They hit a Mercedes sedan first. Sideswiped it while going about thirty-five miles per hour. Max jolted around in his seat. He clenched his teeth so that he wouldn't bite his tongue in the crash. Another car bumped them from behind, its driver pumping her fist.

Drivers slammed on their horns as the Lexus momentarily came to a halt. The man in the Mercedes started to get out of his car, furious and swearing. But Max's driver just put his car in reverse and backed up a few feet, shoveling the car to the rear. It cleared enough space for them to break free. He drove forward, leaving the angry drivers behind.

They raced to a spot only fifty yards away, under the bridge.

"Alright, listen up. You have a heads-up display on the inside of your helmet. Do you understand what that is?"

Max couldn't believe what he was hearing. "Yes."

"It's going to project turn-by-turn navigation onto your visor. That will tell you where you're supposed to go. The other bikes are going to leave you and rejoin you at various spots. That will ensure that you can't be followed."

"Other bikes?"

"Yeah. Now get out."

Max opened his door and stepped out under the overpass formed by the Arlington Memorial Bridge. The Lincoln Memorial was just behind them. Cars' tires thumping overhead on the bridge.

He now wore the black leather jacket and a black motorcycle helmet, visor down. The sedan driver was dressed the same. So were two others, already waiting in the shadows of the bridge. They straddled identical black Ducati motorcycles.

Max's heart beat faster as he saw the two empty bikes.

One of the bikers yelled, "Bloody hurry up. We've only got a few seconds before the police arrive. Whatever you do, make sure you keep up."

* * *

The Maryland State Police helicopter flew over the Potomac just as the Lexus barreled into traffic.

The pilot looked down through his chin bubble—the glass window by his feet. "That's them, right?"

The copilot said, "Looks like it. Idiot just wrecked his car, and he's still not stopping."

"Can't see him anymore. He just drove under the bridge tunnel. Hold on, I'm coming around left."

"Roger, coming left."

As they maneuvered, four black motorcycles shot out from underneath the bridge and began speeding down the road that paralleled the Potomac River.

"You *see* that?" said the pilot. He stayed over the river, turning the aircraft to follow the motorcycles.

"Yeah. Those guys are really moving," said the copilot.

The pilot said into his radio, "Dispatch, Maryland State Helicopter 223 is just west of the Lincoln Memorial. We have four black motorcycles heading north at over seventy miles per hour and are pursuing them. Recommend—"

"Hey, they just took the exit..."

The pilot watched as three of the bikes took the bridge. But one of the motorcycles continued heading west.

"Shit. Now what do we do?"

"I'm following the three. We'll stick with the group and see if we can get a squad car to follow the other." Dozens of blue lights were converging on the scene. The pilot veered left to stay over the group of three racing bikes.

"Dispatch, Maryland Helicopter 223...one of the motorcycles is now headed west on Ohio Road, but three of them have taken the Roosevelt Bridge and are now on...uh...stand by..."

"Another one broke off."

"Yeah, thanks man. I can see that."

"Dispatch, make that *two* bikes are on the George Washington Parkway. One has continued south on...stand by..."

"Now they're all going in different directions."

"Well, shit," said the pilot. "What the hell...?"

"Which one are we supposed to follow?"

"I don't know. I'm coming up. There are too many tall buildings over here."

"We're gonna lose them."

The motorcycle he was following turned into a side street and then took another turn out of view behind a tall building.

The pilot looked at his copilot. He shook his head.

"Bud, I think we already did lose them."

* * *

It had been a while since Max had ridden one of these, but it came back fast enough. His trouble wasn't riding the Ducati. It was keeping up with the other three riders. They were lightning on wheels. The engines blazed into a fierce, high-pitched whine, the traffic zooming by so fast it felt like Max was traveling in a fighter jet.

Each rider had a set path. It took a moment for Max to get used to the turn-by-turn navigation being painted up onto his visor by a set of lasers. Max had to train his eyes to continuously flip between the transparent map and the actual outside world as they raced down Ohio Drive, only feet away from the Potomac River.

Max had done some riding in France. He'd even spent time at a race-track in Italy once. He wondered if they knew that. They must have. This kind of riding would have been a death sentence to the uninitiated. None of this was a coincidence, Max realized.

He followed the pack of other bikes, weaving in and around traffic. But as three of them took an exit—which was what his turn-by-turn navigation told him to do—one of the motorcycles peeled left and kept traveling along the road next to the Potomac. They were separating.

He took a chance and glanced up at the helicopter overhead. It all made sense now. This was the only way they were going to escape so many police, and an aerial pursuit.

Each route must have been preplanned for this exact situation. They hit speeds over one twenty on the straightaways, the engines making a deep guttural sound. His chest rattling, heart pounding. The high-speed turns forced Max to remember how to hold his body. He leaned forward, his legs straddling the seat, knees bent at a sharp angle, only inches away from the ground.

The three motorcycles raced over the Theodore Roosevelt Bridge, weaving in and out of traffic. They bolted around a lone police cruiser, its lights flashing. If he hadn't been holding on for dear life, he might have laughed at the blurred expression of shock on the police officer's face as they whizzed by. Max felt sorry for him. He was only trying to do his job.

But so was Max. And him getting thrown in jail wouldn't help anyone.

They sped down Wilson Boulevard, and Max could feel the air pounding against his black leather jacket. His stomach fluttered as he accelerated even faster, the engine screaming. People stared at them as they raced past. But only for a split second. After that, they were gone.

They were moving so fast that there were no police cars in the area now. Another of the bikes turned and it was just two of them. They raced through Clarendon and then slowed to a mere forty miles per hour as they turned a corner.

Minutes later, the two other bikes had re-joined them for their entrance into the lower parking garage of Ballston Mall.

They drove at a normal speed up through the garage, turning and climbing higher and higher, up through the levels of parked cars. The lead bike stopped in the corner of the top level. Very few cars up this high in the garage, and no people around.

Everyone began taking off their helmets and outerwear. Removing their gloves. Moving fast. No one would look the same when they left. The bikes were parked in a row, lined up neatly next to each other in the corner. No fingerprints or other biometric evidence. Just four black racing bikes in one of the few blind spots in the garage.

Each of the other three riders left in a different direction. None of them so much as spoke to Max. One of the riders, now wearing a sweater vest and khakis, left via the parking garage stairway. Another rider—a woman in sunglasses and a bland dress—took the elevator. The last rider was the man who had pretended to be the lawyer. He looked completely different now, as he walked through the double glass doors into the Ballston Mall. Hands in the pockets of his denim jacket. A Nationals baseball cap on his head.

Max stood waiting, watching the only other vehicle nearby. An Audi Q7 SUV that was parked next to the bikes. Tinted windows. Engine running. When the three others were gone, the door opened, and a man got out.

"She's all yours, mate," he said, with a British accent.

"Thanks."

"Do me a favor. Try not to blow this, eh? As I'm not sure you'll get another chance."

Max knew his face. He'd worked with him on an operation in France once. What was his name?

Max spoke quietly, his voice a whisper. "You're MI-6, right?"

The man smiled. "I wouldn't know what you're talking about."

"That was an interesting exit strategy."

"One of my personal favorites, now that you mention it."

"Who asked you to do it?"

"Mum's the word, chap."

"So you're not going to tell me what this is all about?"

The man took out a piece of paper and handed it to Max. "Call this phone number tomorrow. Six p.m. Eastern. Repeat that back."

"Six p.m. Eastern. Tomorrow. Who am I calling?"

"She's one of ours. She'll help you from here on out. And do us a favor and don't go asking her what you just asked me. You know better."

The man patted him on the shoulder and walked through the double doors of the Ballston Mall.

Max got in the Audi and drove.

5

"How did this *happen*?"

Special Agent Jake Flynn had never been in the office of the deputy director of the FBI before. Honestly, he'd expected it to be nicer. But it was just as cramped as all the other shithole office space in the J. Edgar Hoover building. Every year they talked about how they were going to start construction on a new FBI headquarters in Maryland or Virginia. But that would require the government to agree on something.

And the only thing that anyone in the government could agree on right now was that Flynn had screwed up *royally*.

"Sir, I apologize. I take full responsibility. We had no reason to believe that Max Fend would flee. A man pretending to be his father's lawyer came to the safe house where we were questioning him, and—"

"Why were you questioning him there? Why were you questioning him at all? My understanding was that the NSA and DNI feedback was that the evidence wasn't strong enough."

"Sir, after speaking with the Cyber Division and our counterparts in the French government, we were confident that the updated evidence they were about to provide us would be enough to grant a warrant for Max Fend's arrest. We were already in the process of moving on Fend. I thought there was a chance we might end up charging him with something, so I decided to ask him to voluntarily answer questions at our safe house in D.C...."

"Wait. Hold up. You're saying this man claiming to be a lawyer arrived at one of our D.C. safe houses?"

"Yes, sir."

"As you were questioning this Fend kid?"

"Yes, sir."

"That didn't strike you as odd? That he *knew* your exact address?"

"In hindsight, sir, it is a bit strange..."

The deputy director dug his tongue around his lips, breathing out his nose. Flynn figured that he was probably trying to sort out whether to kill him quickly, or slowly.

"Mr. Flynn, you have made a mess of this. Some guy that you brought in for questioning runs away from you? Fine. Go get 'im. Bring him back in and charge him. But this...this is out of control."

He held out his hand, gesturing towards the TV screen in the corner of his office.

The cable news channels had run nonstop coverage of the footage. Everyone loved a good car chase. A car chase in D.C.? Even better. Throw in four black motorcycles? Now *that* was viral video gold.

Since D.C. had countless cameras and tourists with smartphones taking pictures, there was ample video for the networks to use. They kept showing footage of the Lexus sedan getting air as it jumped the concrete stairs next to the Lincoln Memorial. Then the driver and passenger jumped onto four identical black motorcycles that were waiting under the tunnel overpass. The Fox News banner still read, "Car Chase of the Century." The subheadline read, "Criminal masterminds make their motorbike escape from the FBI."

It was humiliating. And nothing pissed off the front office of the FBI like humiliating headlines.

The deputy director said, "So the lawyer shows up to an FBI safe house. An *unlisted* FBI safe house. Then what happened?"

"The lawyer says that the only way he'll allow further questioning is if we conduct it at his office the next day. He says he needs to confer with his client. As we're all getting into our vehicles, I get the call from the judge that the updated evidence is in and we have his approval for an arrest."

"You didn't follow proper procedure there. DNI's going to be pissed that you went around them because you didn't like their answer the first time. This is a mess."

"Sir, respectfully, what the hell was the DNI's office thinking?"

"They get input from other intelligence communities, Flynn. You figure it out. Keep going. Tell me what happened next."

"So I tried to get Fend out of the car. I was about to place him under arrest, when the lawyer peels out and speeds away. At first I thought it was some type of joke. Him showing us up. That kind of thing."

The deputy director just shook his head in disapproval.

"So then the sedan drove off and my men began to pursue."

"Back up. Tell me about the original evidence that made you decide to arrest him."

"We have a team from the Cyber Division that's been down in Jacksonville. They've been working with CIRFU."

CIRFU was the FBI's Cyber Initiative Resource Fusion Unit. The group was a combination of FBI and private sector cyberexperts, as well as Carnegie Mellon's Computer Emergency Response Team, and the FBI's Internet Crime Complaint Center.

"What did they find?"

"They were able to piece together electronic data that links Fend to the hackers. It's highly probable that this Max Fend kid granted access to a foreign entity. And he had a business associate—a Russian. Sergei Sokolov. We think the Russian had been working with a criminal hacker group. We believe that the hackers broke into the Fend network and tried to download a bunch of their data. Fend also does defense contracting. Usually these hacker groups try to sell the technology or hold it for ransom."

The deputy director said, "So you're telling me that the owner of Fend Aerospace—Charles Fend—his own son is the bad guy here? Why would he do that?"

"I don't know. We're looking into it. He's been working as a consultant in Europe for the past few years. The reports we got on him say that he's been associated with some questionable people over there. It's possible he's been compromised."

"Compromised by whom?"

"The data that we got from the Cyber Division says that the hackers were located in Syria—but that they were probably working with Russian or Eastern European cyberexperts."

"Jake, listen to me. You need to be careful. Charles Fend has been around for a long time and has a lot of friends in this town. His lawyers have been calling us nonstop. You can't just go arresting his son without stone-cold evidence."

"I understand, sir. I'm sorry this happened this way. I was afraid we were going to lose our chance."

Flynn expected to be removed from the case. But it didn't appear to be going that way...yet. Maybe they wanted to save that card for when they really needed a scapegoat for the press.

The deputy director said, "Okay. Here's how it's going to go. You'll stay on the case for now. I'll brief the director on what you told me. In the meantime, keep this quiet. The press still hasn't said his name. Let's keep it that way. Don't let anything out about Max Fend beyond our own agency. Is that understood?"

That was odd. Charles Fend's son would be a high-profile fugitive. Flynn was surprised that Max Fend's name wasn't already in the news. He figured it was only a matter of time until one of the networks picked it up. That would help massively with the search. Tips to local law enforcement could locate him within twenty-four hours. Why on earth would the FBI not want Max Fend's face on a billboard everywhere they could get it?

"Sir, it would really help our search if..."

The deputy director shook his head. "No. Did you just hear me? Absolutely not. Let me be clear. Do not speak the name Max Fend to anyone in the press."

Flynn shifted his weight from one foot to the other. "Sir, excuse me, but why is that?"

"The director has had enough embarrassment. It was suggested to him from above that we should keep the Fend family name out of this until we are one hundred percent sure that the facts support our case against him."

"But he evaded us—"

"Did he? A few moments ago, you told me that he was going to voluntarily answer questions."

"Yes, but—"

"And you never officially placed him under arrest."

"I was about to."

"Flynn...maybe you aren't getting this. Read between the lines. We're being asked to keep the Fend name out of the press for now."

Flynn stared at him, visibly frustrated.

Seeing this, the deputy director said, "And there may be other factors that you aren't yet privy to."

Flynn didn't know what to say. "Sir, you want me to find Max Fend, but not tell any member of the public that we're looking for him? And you think that the press isn't going to pick up that it was him escaping on one of those motorcycles?"

"That's what we're being asked to do, yes. Listen, Flynn. Sometimes it's better just to put your head down and follow orders. Okay? Now I've got to go brief the director."

The deputy director walked through the side door of his office that connected to the FBI director's own office.

Jake Flynn walked out of the room, glad at least to be done with the ass-chewing. He wasn't sure what had just happened. *Something doesn't add up.* Yeah, sure, Charles Fend was wealthy and had friends in high places. But why was the FBI willing to give him cover after running away like that? Max Fend's occupation was listed as consultant. Last time Flynn checked, consultants didn't run away on motorbikes like they were in some damned James Bond movie.

Just who the hell *was* Max Fend?

* * *

For now, Special Agent Jake Flynn was still the senior agent assigned to the Fend Aerospace case.

In the past few weeks, he had learned more about the type of aircraft and how automated flight worked than he had ever wanted to.

Agent Flynn looked over his notes again, at the profiles of the main team members.

There was the senior engineer for the project, Bradley Karpinsky. Flynn had learned that Karpinsky had been passed over for the project lead position. One theory was that he harbored a grudge, and maybe he had offered to sell secrets to a foreign group. But nothing Flynn had seen led him to believe that Karpinsky would have purposefully tried to sabotage the aircraft.

Another theory suggested that a competitor had hacked into the system. Their aim may have been to expose safety flaws, in order to reopen the government bidding for the lucrative automated flight network contract in the FAA's NextGen program. But careful investigations by the FBI on all major competitors had turned up very little.

Foreign governments and organizations conducted cyberhacking attacks on US companies and government websites every day. It was a low-risk, high-reward crime. Most hackers were petty criminals. Low-level scum that tried to use phishing techniques to try and gain access to email or network passwords. From there, they could try to discover more and more information, until they found something truly valuable and either sold it or put it to use.

But this hacker group was very professional. Flynn knew that because of the facial expressions on the FBI Cyber Division's chief investigator.

"I've only seen this level of sophistication a few times," the man had told Flynn. "And both times, it turned out to be Russian state-sponsored activity."

Flynn decided to take another look at Max Fend's personnel file.

Princeton University, class of '02. A football player. Wide receiver. Graduated in the bottom half of his class. Then he went to work for the Department of Defense in D.C. right after college—some entry-level job. He then quit that role and moved to Europe to become a consultant.

Flynn figured that after realizing what real work was, Max Fend must have gone whining to his dad to get him some cushy job on the French Riviera.

But now Agent Flynn had new facts to inform him. What had he seen? How had he behaved in the interview? Calm. Polite. Confident, but not overly cocky. He seemed to resent any suggestion that his father's money got him a job. He was respectful and his answers seemed honest. None of this fit with the personality sketch of a spoiled rich kid turned international white-collar criminal. Max Fend had carried himself with the same swagger Flynn had seen in many of the FBI agents that he worked with.

Something wasn't right. Had Flynn made a mistake?

Flynn looked at the TV screen. The news was playing the car chase over and over again. The screen cut to the motorcycles, crossing the bridge, one of them peeling off by itself down Ohio Street.

He did a Google search on Max Fend. There was a smattering of articles. Mostly low-end "most eligible bachelor" type stuff from years ago, when he was at Princeton. Heir to one of the largest private companies in the United States. There wasn't much on him after he graduated college.

Flynn decided to double-check his FBI file. It took him a few moments, but he found what he was looking for.

Max Fend had gone to work for the Department of Defense right out of college and worked there for nearly two years. That meant that he had a Single Scope Background Investigation on file. The investigation was required for anyone trying to get a government security clearance in the United States.

After leaving the DoD, he had lived in Europe, working for a US-based consulting firm there.

Flynn used his FBI computer to gain access to Max's latest Standard Form 86. It had last been updated in 2003. Nothing interesting.

He decided to contact the Department of Defense and see if anyone there who had worked with him could provide any extra information.

Flynn found the reference on Max's security clearance form. He dialed the number, wondering if the man still worked at DoD, or if he used a different phone number now.

"Hello?"

"Hello, my name is Special Agent Jake Flynn, with the FBI. I was hoping to speak with you about one of your former employees. A man by the name of Max Fend. Are you familiar with him?"

Silence. "Uh, yes, sir. I remember him. He's the son of the airplane billionaire, right? How can I help?"

"Yes, that's him. Were you his supervisor from 2002 to 2004?"

"That's right."

"Listen, I'm going to be down near your office this afternoon. Would you have time to speak with me? Say around one p.m.?"

"I have a meeting. Can we make it two?"

"No problem."

At two p.m. sharp, Jake Flynn was sitting in a private meeting room at the DoD manager's office.

"What type of work was Max Fend involved in when he worked with you?"

"Standard stuff. Accounting, mostly. Some procurement for defense programs. He was a new guy, so it was entry-level stuff."

"And are you familiar with where he went to work after that?"

"I've got my suspicions, yes."

Flynn sat up straighter in his seat.

"What do you mean by that?"

The DoD manager squirmed. "You are FBI, right? So I guess it's fine to talk to you about this. We see a few Max Fend types every year. Not billionaires' sons, mind you. I mean guys like him. I think someone in Langley's human resources department must have my section flagged. I've been here nearly thirty years, and it seems like we're always seeing them."

"Langley's human resources?"

"Yeah. You know, Langley. Like the CIA."

"I'm familiar. What's Max Fend got to do with the CIA?"

The man cleared his throat. "Well, every couple of years, we get a few of their new guys. We're asked to find something for them to do for a year or two. They tend to stash them here before they ship off."

"What do you mean, ship off? You mean like go to a new DoD job?"

"I don't think it's with the DoD. But who knows? I could be wrong. Look, man, I just hear things, okay? I don't want to get in trouble."

"What kind of things?"

"Well...one of my employees, she has family down near Williamsburg. So she goes there a lot. She says that she's seen a couple of these guys down there over the years. Almost always right after they leave their job with me."

"In Williamsburg?" He scribbled on his notepad: *Max Fend—CIA???*

"Yeah. There's a bar there that they all hang out at, I think. But this girl who works for me, she goes there, and she's run into a few of them. I probably shouldn't be saying this."

Flynn fought the urge to roll his eyes. "Sir, you are helping an investigation. Please speak freely."

"I heard that they go to Williamsburg and start their training. The Langley guys probably use the time working for me to do their in-depth background checks or wait for new classes to start."

Flynn frowned. "And this is in Williamsburg?"

"Yeah, you know. The Farm."

* * *

Flynn found that in times of uncertainty, it was best to speak with trusted friends. He decided to give his buddy Steve Brava a call. Steve had started off in the FBI with him but had transferred to the DNI's office when that organization had been created. The man would shoot straight with him. He could get access to information that others couldn't. And most importantly, he could be trusted.

"Jake, good to hear from you."

"Steve, you too."

They exchanged pleasantries for a few moments.

Steve said, "You see all this car chase stuff on the news?"

"Yeah...actually, that's part of the reason I'm calling," Flynn said.

"Really?"

"Yeah. Listen, this has got to stay quiet."

"Say no more. What can I do for you?"

"Hey, I'm looking...unofficially...at a man by the name of Max Fend."

"As in Fend Aerospace?"

"Yes."

"Okay."

"I got a tip from someone recently that the CIA sometimes stashes guys within the Department of Defense before they go off to start their training at the Farm in Williamsburg. Does that sound right to you?"

"Yeah, sure. That's possible. Probably gives them time to do a full background check. And places like the Farm have to schedule classes just like any other big government school. So it might take guys a few months before they're ready to class up. So what?"

"Is there any way you could check out Max Fend, and see if he was one of those guys?"

"Sure, I could do that. But, Jake, why don't you just go ask the CIA?"

"I will. I just like to check multiple sources."

"Alright, I'll see what I can dig up for you."

6

Max Fend's first stop was at a storage center in Leesburg, Virginia. He drove in at night, wearing baggy clothes and a golf visor pulled down low over his forehead. He typed in the code and heard the beep, the chain fence sliding over to one side. He drove along the rows of storage units and parked in front of his rental.

He fidgeted with the lock until the right combination was entered. It snapped open, and Max lifted up the sliding garage door. It stopped with a bang. Max then flipped the light switch, illuminating two trunks in the center of the otherwise empty storage space. A stale smell hung in the air.

The rented-out garage had been his own personal decision. After operating as a field agent for over ten years, he didn't trust anyone. He had his own plan to disappear, if need be. A "break glass in case of emergency" plan that no one else knew about but him.

Max closed the garage door behind him and found himself alone with his stash. He moved quick, his hands and eyes racing from item to item. He knelt on the floor as he worked.

Max emptied the contents of the first trunk and then closed it to serve as a surface to work from. He placed a laptop on the closed trunk, plugged it in to a large portable battery, and powered it up.

He took the phones, IDs, and prepaid debit cards that the MI6 agents had given him and threw them all into the empty trunk. Max would use his own items.

He took out his own prepurchased phone and entered the number he was supposed to dial tomorrow night at exactly six p.m. He named the contact SECRET AGENT. No reason he couldn't have a sense of humor about it.

Max connected the computer to his phone and used it to access the Internet. He accessed a secure cloud drive and opened a spreadsheet file. The file was his little black book. People whom he had known and worked with over the years. Max paid a virtual assistant—a very capable and trustworthy one—quite a good sum of money to keep this list up to date. Should he ever find himself in a certain place, in need of someone who had a particular skill, he could rely upon this list.

There were several hundred names on the spreadsheet. He could sort by column: name, country, state (if in the US), and skill set.

He needed someone close. He didn't have the time or the inclination to travel far right now. He set the filter for the eastern half of the United States. All within range. And all had rural areas that he could fly into easily.

Next he sorted for skill sets. He had decided on just five skill categories. Procurement. Tactical. Tradecraft. Transportation. And cyber. Each person had multiple columns. Some people on his list had multiple skill sets.

He filtered for cyber. A half dozen names came up. While they were each listed as living in the stated locations, he knew from looking at several of the names that most would be out of the country. On assignment.

One name stuck out. Renee LeFrancois.

Max hadn't seen her in years. He clicked on her name and looked more closely at her updated file. His virtual assistant was expected to keep each personnel file current. It was costly, but Max had the means.

He read over her file. One thing surprised him. She had been married. He hadn't known. Then again, it wasn't like she would have invited him to the wedding. Her file said she'd gotten divorced two years earlier. She now lived alone and did contract IT security work. No obvious red flags.

Max still didn't like the idea of going to her. She didn't have experience in this type of thing. Her computer skills were off the charts, but who knew how she would react when she found out that he was a wanted man?

Not to mention their personal history. Things hadn't ended badly for them, but they hadn't exactly ended well, either. He tried to think of the last time he'd seen her. It must have been at least eight years ago. Princeton reunions, he thought. Drinking together on the dance floor under a massive tent. Screaming into each other's ears, trying to have a meaningful conversation over deafening music. That meeting had been bittersweet.

Max pushed out any personal feelings he might still harbor. He needed to be clinical about this decision.

He once again looked over the list of personnel who were located on the East Coast of the US. Most were "Tactical" experts. Those were the types of men who specialized in weaponry and warfare. They weren't on the list for their knowledge, but for their skill. They were the black bag job boys.

Max didn't need people like that. He had already prepared for something like this. For running and hiding. He had supplies, transportation, and money all lined up. Some people prepped for a future Armageddon; Max prepped for the day when someone might come after him.

What Max really needed was someone who could help him investigate who had done this to him, and what he was up against. Someone who could understand the world of cyberespionage. That field was a mystery to Max.

That left two names.

One was actively employed by the National Security Agency. Max didn't want to go to him. There was too much risk. Max was being pursued by the US government. Most of the people on his list got their paychecks, in some way or other, from Uncle Sam.

He sighed, frustrated by the painful realization. That might cross off ninety percent of his contacts.

He would have to try Renee. She was trustworthy, and in relatively close proximity. She wasn't, nor had she ever been, employed by the US government. And when she was able to access a computer, she was magic.

Max closed up his laptop and slid it into the backpack that contained his prepared items. His own false IDs, weapons, and cash.

There was a good chance that everything the MI6 team had passed on to him was perfectly usable. But he hadn't procured it himself. What if the IDs were flagged? What if the phones were being tracked? Even friendly operatives made a habit of doing that. No, the best way to stay alive was to assume that everyone and everything else might be compromised.

Five minutes after he'd entered, Max walked out of the garage and locked it behind him, got into his car, and drove to the Leesburg Executive Airport.

* * *

Max left the Audi in the parking lot across the street from the airport. He pulled the backpack tight on his back and then hopped the fence, landing in the grass.

Leesburg Executive Airport was small by most standards. It was mostly used by general aviation and private aircraft. One of those planes was his.

Washington, D.C. airspace restrictions were notoriously onerous—there were precise rules that general aviation aircraft had to follow in order to get in and out of the area. But Leesburg Executive had a special triangular cutout in the Air Defense Identification Zone around D.C. That would help make things a bit easier.

Max doubted the FBI knew about his plane. Max's virtual assistant had used a shell company to make the purchase and pay for the maintenance and hangar fees.

It was a single-engine piston. A Cirrus SR-22T. He had hired a local operator to take care of it and lease it out every so often to one of the local flight instruction companies, just to make sure that it was working. Until today, he had never flown it personally. He would always rent the same type of aircraft from other locations.

He climbed in and threw his bag in the passenger seat, sliding the seat belt through one of the straps and clicking it in place. He loved this aircraft. The Cirrus interior was similar to that of the finest luxury automobile. And it flew like a dream. The plane would travel at over 200 knots without breaking a sweat.

Max filed his flight plan under an alias and flew west out of the D.C. airspace, using visual flight rules. He then canceled his flight plan while he was airborne over Front Royal, and turned off his transponder. If and when investigators looked up his flight path, they would expect him to have landed there.

It wasn't much of a diversion, but it might throw them off the scent for a bit. More likely, they wouldn't expect him to be traveling this way at all.

He then turned south and flew to Charlottesville. The Blue Ridge mountain air made the flight a little bumpy, but it wasn't too bad.

An hour later he made a night landing on the cool blacktop of the Charlottesville Albemarle Regional Airport. The tower was already shut down for the night.

Max tied down the aircraft and placed the chocks in front of the wheels. No one else was out this time of night. The only sound was of summer crickets. Lightning bugs glimmered in the sky.

He walked toward the Signature Flight Support building and checked his watch. It was getting late. Almost eleven p.m. The automatic doors opened up, and a rush of cool air came over him. The air conditioning felt good. A girl stood behind the front desk. She looked as if she was about to close up shop for the night.

"You need fuel, honey?"

"Yes, please. Top it off if you would."

"Will do. May I have your card?"

"Actually, I'll use cash if you don't mind."

"Um...okay, sure."

Probably didn't hear that too much. Fuel cost for planes could be in the thousands of dollars. Much higher, even, for the jets. But Max wanted to leave the smallest trail possible.

"You need a cab?"

"That would be great, thanks."

"Where you going?"

"Local area."

She smiled at him. "You know, I'm about to get off. If you don't mind, I'd be happy to give you a lift." She was cute. And interested, by the look in her eye.

"Sure. That would be great." She called the fuel truck. Max could hear its engine grumbling outside and its brakes squeaking as it came to a stop next to his plane.

She took him to her car, apologizing as she cleared off trash from the cramped passenger seat. He had her take him to the Double Tree Inn. She parked in the parking lot.

"So...you want to have a drink or something?" She twirled her hair, chewing her gum.

Max had two voices in his head. The voice of reason told him that he had been stupid to have her drop him off. That he needed to keep a low profile, and even right now his face might be on the news. The other voice sized up her measurables and provided him a firm thumbs-up.

"As much as I would love that, my girlfriend is supposed to come by later..."

"Oh. Sorry." She giggled.

"Appreciate the ride." He ducked under the door and swung it shut. Max waited for her car to leave before whipping out his phone and dialing the number.

"Hello?"

"Renee," Max said.

"Who is this?"

"Renee, it's Max...*Fend*. I need your help."

Silence on the other end. Shock, perhaps. He had expected that. This would be a lot to ask of her. To drop everything, and risk her career—not to mention legal troubles—to assist him. But he needed someone he could trust.

* * *

Princeton, 2000

. . .

They had met at Princeton. Max was a minor celebrity there. The sons and daughters of some of the most famous people in the world walked the campuses of elite Ivy League institutions such as Harvard, Yale and Princeton. Indeed, some of the students at those schools were already celebrities themselves. Actors and actresses. Olympians. Budding stars in the tech industry.

Max was well known because of who his father was, and barely a day went by that he wasn't asked about being the son of Charles Fend.

Cap and Gown was one of Princeton's eating clubs—sort of a cross between dining halls and coed fraternities. Prospect Avenue was lined with large mansions, each one home to one of the eating clubs. On nights like this, warm Saturday nights during football season, they erupted into massive parties. Celebrations of life.

Max loved the parties. But it also meant that he had to answer the same question over and over again. *Are you really Charles Fend's son?* Yes. *Oh my God, that's so amazing.* Yup. Sigh.

The deck had a nice wide view of the backyard. He had walked out onto that second-floor wooden deck, hoping to take a break from it all. A Dave Matthews cover band played on the stone patio below. At least three hundred people were at the house. The girls on the field hockey team were already dancing in front of the band.

He stopped when he saw her sitting alone on the unlit wooden balcony. Crutches at her side. A cast on her leg. Leaning back and looking up at the clear night sky. Stars twinkling. She looked peaceful, but lonely.

She heard his footsteps on the wooden planks and glanced up at him. A guarded look.

"Good evening," said Max.

"Hi."

"How'd you hurt yourself?"

"A field hockey accident."

"Ouch. Sorry. Anything I can get you?" He was just being polite. He had expected her to say no.

"God, yes. A beer would be great. Be a dear and bring two, if you wouldn't mind."

Max laughed. "Sure."

She was his kind of girl. The right priorities. And a proper planner. He hobbled down the creaky wooden stairs of the mansion and made his way through the crowded basement. The sophomores were manning the beer kegs. He waited about five minutes and was then handed several full plastic cups of cold beer. It sloshed and spilled a bit on his way back up the stairs. But she was grateful when he arrived with them.

A big smile, which he suspected was a rare thing for her. Dark hair. Strong cheekbones.

"You're a lifesaver." And an accent.

"Where are you from?"

"Montreal, originally."

"What's your name?"

"Renee."

"I'm Max, Renee," he said, sticking out his hand.

"I know." She shook it.

"Mind if I join you?"

"Be my guest."

"Those your teammates out there dancing?"

"They are. Normally they would try to get me out there. I despise dance floors, so the crutches are a nice excuse. But I'd give anything to be playing still. I'm afraid I'm done for the season."

"Sorry to hear that. But happy for my luck."

She flashed a wry smile and raised her plastic cup in a toast.

They spent the rest of the evening talking on the balcony. It would be the first of many evenings that they spent together. While Max had dated many women, Renee would be the only one he really would characterize as a serious girlfriend. Their on-again, off-again relationship was all at once passionate, comfortable, and painful. They made a "clean break" upon graduation. In all, they dated for nine months. She was a year younger, and—given the field he was entering—it didn't make sense to continue on. He had never explained to her why he had broken it off. That only made it harder.

* * *

Present Day

Renee and Max agreed to meet the next morning. He used one of his prepaid cards to pay for the room at the hotel and then spent an hour scanning the news.

The lead story was about the G-7 conference that was being held at Camp David in a few days. It would include Russian attendance for the first time in a few years. The Russian president was attempting to mend relations in the West. The bloc of nations would become the G-8 again in a special ceremony.

The rest of the coverage was about the motorcycle chase.

The talking heads were going crazy about the car chase in D.C. But surprisingly, Max wasn't mentioned. Now why was that?

He could think of only one reason. Someone in the government didn't want Max Fend's name put out there.

That was a good thing for Max. If he just had to avoid law enforcement, he could do it. But if he had to avoid going out in public...that was another thing entirely.

Max wondered how long this gift of anonymity would last. With the right spin on it, this could really be a big news story. Rich playboy son escapes from FBI in high-speed motorcycle chase through the streets of D.C. That was the way he would write it up, if he were trying to make headlines. The news would plaster his face on every TV and electronic device in America.

Max was already known to a lot of people who read the gossip columns, thanks to his father—and maybe his own extravagant lifestyle. That had been a necessary evil. But being involved in this motorcycle chase would skyrocket his reputation into the stratosphere.

He sighed as he thought about his father. What must he be thinking? What was the FBI telling him? Max doubted his father would believe that he would sabotage Fend Aerospace. But the fact that he had run away from law enforcement—that would likely plant a seed of doubt in his mind. And the nature of the escape would raise even more questions.

There was nothing Max could do about it now. He did a quick calisthenic workout, took a shower, and went to sleep.

* * *

The night had been a disaster for Renee. She had gone out to dinner with a client. He was older. Late forties, but not bad looking.

They were barely halfway through dinner when he had crossed the line. Suggesting that he could come back to her place for drinks. Maybe Renee was smiling too much? Maybe she had dressed too provocatively? She hated herself for thinking like that. And the worst part was that Renee had actually considered it. He wasn't anything special, but it wouldn't have been that bad to have male companionship once in a while. It had been too long.

But there was something about him that didn't sit well with her. He was too pushy. She excused herself and went into the bathroom, taking out her phone. One thing a married cheater should never do is try to date a hacker.

Renee found out everything about the man within a few minutes. The disgusting pig had been lying to her about his personal life. He must have taken the ring off before they had dinner.

Renee should have known. Clients didn't normally come to see her. But he'd said he was going to be in the area for business. And her contract was up for renewal soon.

When Renee had gone back to the table, she said, "May I see your hand?"

"Excuse me?"

"Your hand. Please let me see it."

The man frowned. He started to, and then thought better of it.

"What's wrong, Renee? Did I say something? Look, if you don't want to have drinks, that's fine—"

"You've been married for fourteen years. And you have four kids."

His face went white...and then red. Eyes narrowing. "You checked up on me while you were in the bathroom? Who the hell do you think you are? Look, I don't think we can do business. I can't work with someone I don't trust."

"Neither can I."

She stood, glaring at him. Then she walked away, not bothering to let him say any more.

For a moment, she had thought of threatening him. She could demand that he switch her account to a different buyer, or she would... what? Ruin his marriage? Hurt his children? Better to walk away. Hopefully, he wouldn't spread nasty rumors about her to other potential clients. She sighed. She didn't need the money that bad.

What was it about that type of man? It was like they were drawn to her.

She kept telling herself she didn't need anyone else in her life. But it was hard doing everything alone. And she worried about growing old and not finding anyone. And she wanted to have kids, before it was too late.

After college she'd had one serious relationship that lasted for six years. He had been in pharmaceutical sales. She had moved to follow him to Charlottesville for his work. They'd married after a year of dating.

When she thought about it now, she didn't know why she had said yes. She didn't really love him. It had just seemed like the thing everyone was doing at the time. All of her girlfriends were getting married. It was like musical chairs, and no one wanted to get left out.

She had wanted to travel. To compete in road races. To meet new and interesting people. To get drunk at concerts. To hike the Appalachian Trail. She wanted to live life. To have the adventure.

All her ex wanted to do when he was home was sleep and watch TV. He had wanted her to be his housewife. To stay at home and make meals, and to take care of the kids they were going to have.

Thank God she hadn't gotten pregnant with him. If she had, she probably would have stuck with him, even after she'd found out he was cheating on her. Bored out of her mind and faking it for the sake of the kids.

Kids. The word made her want to cry. She was almost forty. And while she would admit it to no one, she desperately wanted to have children.

But he had taken her for granted. It wasn't just the cheating. She could forgive that, if it were an honest mistake. It was the lack of passion in him. She was a romantic, and he was...a mistake. She'd felt guilty for feeling that, until he'd cheated on her. Then, truth be told, she'd felt relief. She had an excuse. It had been time to fish or cut bait, as the expression went.

He wanted to keep fishing. She cut bait.

The sad part now was that her life hadn't gotten much more adventurous. She ran road races, and had done a few mini-triathlons. She tried to schedule one big vacation to somewhere fun every year. But her love life had been pretty nonexistent. She usually worked from home. The only places she really went were the gym, church, and the grocery store. None presented her with great opportunities for meeting people.

Work was at once an escape and a worry. It took her mind off the worry that her life wasn't progressing as planned. But the work itself wasn't exactly curing cancer. Still, the job paid well, and it gave her freedom and control. Renee's clients didn't care when the work got done. Most of the time, they didn't even understand what it was that she was doing. Corporate IT security. She was an anti-hacker. She liked to joke with her niece, who adored Harry Potter books, that she was like a witch who specialized in the Defense Against the Dark Arts.

Renee had started off after college in one of the big multimillion-dollar corporations. Now they were her competition. *They* didn't see it that way. They didn't know she existed. But she had a book of business. About six figures a year. Nothing to scoff at, but it could dry up in a heartbeat. And she always felt the pressure.

And loneliness. And guilt. She was thinking about seeing a psychologist or a psychiatrist—whichever one didn't give you medicine. She didn't want medicine. Just someone to tell her how to get her life back on track. Maybe a life coach? No. She had read that many of them were people who'd been laid off.

Renee kept telling herself that in another year or so, things would finally change for the better. She would get a new big contract and would have more time to get things done. It would be easier then. She would then read more, work out more, and travel more. She would call up her best friends from college and demand that they go hike the Appalachian Trail with her. She had so many adventures that she wanted to have, before she grew too old, and before her life began to fade away into memories.

Memories.

It was funny how strong some of them could be, when they came back and slapped you in the face. Renee hadn't thought of Max in quite some time.

"Who was that on the phone?"

"No one, Mom."

"It didn't sound like no one." Renee's mother came to visit every six months or so. And whenever she did, she always gave Renee advice that she didn't want.

"Just an old friend, Mom."

"A boy?" Nosey.

"The friend was male, yes."

"Does your old friend have a name? Tell him to take my daughter out. She needs a man in her life."

Renee walked into the living room, where her mother was knitting and watching a home-buying show with the volume down low.

"Enough, please," Renee said.

"You're much too young and pretty to give up on men now."

"*Mother.*"

"Well, I'm only saying. What happened with the nice man who took you out tonight? You came home early."

"He's a client. I won't be seeing him again."

Her mother looked up from her knitting. "Well, that's a shame."

"I'm going to my room, Mother. I need to get a little work done. What are your plans tomorrow morning—do you need the car? I have something in the morning."

"No, dear. I'll be fine. Goodnight."

"Goodnight."

Renee went into her bedroom and sat on her bed, bringing her computer onto her lap. Time to find out what Max Fend had been up to over the past few years, and what kind of trouble he was in.

7

Four Days Before the Fend 100 Flight

The next morning, Renee was there waiting for him in the lobby of the hotel, a laptop resting on her knees, and a cup of steaming coffee lying on the hotel rug next to her chair. She put the computer down next to the coffee and stood, extending her hand.

"Hello, Max."

A quiet, steady voice. That same lovely French Canadian accent. She'd changed her hair up a bit. It was shorter. And he saw that she'd added a long flower tattoo that wound down her milky-white leg.

"Renee. It's good to see you again." A quick embrace.

"Why don't we go somewhere we can talk, Max?"

He took her back to his room.

Max and Renee sat on two opposite ends of the room's ugly couch.

She began. "You're in trouble."

"How much do you know?"

"As much as I could find out, before speaking in person. I looked at everything I could get my hands on last night after you called."

Renee held dual Canadian and US citizenship. She had always been very good with computers in college, but while there, she had mostly been concerned with playing field hockey. The tech companies had come at her hard her senior year. She had gone to work for a cybersecurity firm after graduating.

When they'd last seen each other at a reunion party in 2008, Max had asked her about her job. She had been coy, saying only that she worked for a small Canadian firm. Max knew how to spot a lie. The answer had piqued his interest, and he'd used his resources to look into Renee's work the following week.

Max was surprised to discover that Renee had gone to work for Canada's Communications Security Establishment in Ottawa for a few years. The CSE was Canada's version of the National Security Agency. From what he could decipher, she was one of their cyberwarriors. Then she'd left and had gone to work for herself...probably about the same time she'd met her ex-husband.

Max had thrown her name into his little black book spreadsheet.

"Are you guilty?" she asked.

"Of what, exactly?"

"The FBI thinks that you gave some foreign cybercriminals access to your father's company network. This allowed them to steal information"— she looked down at her notes—"something about an autonomous test flight. I haven't read up on that yet. But I'm sure you are more than familiar."

"Well, to answer your question, then, no." He shook his head. "I'm not guilty of that."

She raised an eyebrow. "What are you guilty of?"

"Good looks. A voracious appetite for life."

She tried not to smile. "I've missed you. But you don't need to put on your little show for me. Remember, I know who you really are."

"And who's that?"

She shrugged. "Not this act that I've read about."

They stared at each other for a moment. Each trying to unmask the other.

Max shrugged. "I hate it when my reputation gets ruined."

"If you were the little brat the gossip columnists make you out to be, I wouldn't be talking to you. But I knew you before you went away to Europe and got put in the magazines with your shirt off."

"You saw those?"

"Oh, yes. Quite the heartthrob to the tweens and moms who read that sort of thing."

"Moms and their daughters have always loved me. What can I say?"

Renee didn't respond.

"I checked you out. Your work in Europe seemed..."

"Interesting?"

"Controversial."

"What do you want to know?"

"How did you get involved with all those people?"

"Which ones?"

"Max, the things I read about...the FBI file says that you've been mixed up with several groups...well, they aren't the types of people I would expect you to know."

Max leaned forward, his elbows resting on his knees. "Let's get this out of the way now, because you'll need to know. Renee, when I was in Europe, I wasn't just a consultant. That was a cover. A nonofficial cover."

"What do you mean, a nonofficial cover?"

"Intelligence agencies have two types of operatives. Ones who are official government employees...and ones who aren't. The official cover agents are the ones who work in the State Department or some other section of government. But really, they serve multiple masters. You might have seen news stories about how Russia will send home several of our diplomats, claiming that they're spies. And then we send home several of their diplomats, claiming the same thing. Those people are under official covers. They get diplomatic immunity. Protection."

"Wait, are you saying that you worked for the intelligence community?"

"Yes."

"As in...like...you were a spy?"

"Yes, Renee. I was an illegal. I had no diplomatic immunity. And my posting was unrelated to any government agency."

"You were a spy, Max. I'm still trying to wrap my head around this."

"I understand."

She blurted out, "I worked for the CSE. In Canada."

He laughed at her expression. As if she'd been holding it in for years and had finally found someone she could admit it to.

"I mean, the work was pretty boring. Nothing like being a spy. I was trapped in a windowless room all day for a few years. But it was all super hush-hush." The words flew out of her mouth, like she was trying to match confessions.

Max smiled. "Actually, I know."

"You *know*?"

"I'm familiar with your professional background. That's part of the reason I've reached out to you."

"Hmm. And I thought you missed me."

"I do."

Her voice was excited. "So who did you work for? The CIA?"

"DIA. The Defense Intelligence Agency."

"Since when?"

"Pretty soon after I left college."

"That long?"

Max nodded.

"So is that why you were running around with all those bimbos in France? It was a cover."

"Some of those bimbos meant a lot to me..."

Renee rolled her eyes. "Fine. Maybe we should just get down to business, shall we?"

Max said, "Very well. I want you to come work for me. I want to hire you. I need help. Someone with your talent. Someone I can trust. And someone who won't turn me in, because they believe me when I say that I'm innocent."

Renee pursed her lips, not speaking.

"I understand if you have to say no. But you saw what the FBI thinks. Someone's after me."

She cocked her head. "How long would the contract be for?"

"Until this mess is cleared up." Max smiled, his wide, charming smile.

"Yes, well. If you want me to drop everything and come work for you, you'll need to make it worth my while."

"Nothing is off the table."

"What's the pay?"

"I'm not sure if you're aware of this, but I'm painfully wealthy."

"I am aware. Although last time I checked, those who are running from the law face problems when accessing their bank accounts."

"I've got my own stash under the mattress. Turns out Grandpa was right after all. Besides, if you do your job well, I won't be running from the law for long, right? How much do you make now, annually?"

She told him.

"Consider it tripled. Next?"

She tried not to look too pleased, which was difficult. She said, "I will need job security. You're on the run. If I help you, and we're caught, I'll be considered an accomplice."

"Doubtful."

"That they wouldn't consider me an accomplice?"

"No. That we would be caught." He winked.

"You're almost famous. Your father is famous. What happens when people start finding out that it was you racing out of Washington on a Ducati racing bike yesterday?"

"It wasn't a racing bike, it was the model—"

"*Max.*"

"We won't be caught. We'll just need to move fast. And send what we find to the Feds. There seems to have been a dreadful misunderstanding, is all."

"I know, but still. You can't very well expect me to leave my other contracts on a whim like this without knowing that I'll be taken care of. I've got a life, after all."

"I'll do whatever it takes to give you peace of mind. But we can't stay here. If you decide to help me, it will require travel. I don't yet know who or what I'm up against. So I think that it would be best if we...if we were able to disappear for a few days. Is that possible for you?"

Renee thought for a moment. "My mother is in town. She won't be happy, but I can tell her that I have a work trip. Yes, Max, it's possible."

Max nodded. "So, are we good? You'll agree to help me?"

She pretended to think about it. Truth be told, she wanted nothing more than to get away for a few days. This sounded like interesting work. And a good friend was in need. Beneath Max's wild act, she knew that there was a decent man there. She had to help him.

"Alright. Let's get started."

"Let's."

"Tell me your story, Max Fend. And let's try to figure out who might be after you."

Max recounted the last twenty-four hours. He had given her hints on the phone last night, but this was more in depth. It took him about fifteen minutes to catch her up. Most of it she was already aware of, having made the connection that he was the one who had escaped law enforcement the previous day. But she did stop him several times with questions.

"Wait. You said you were going to go to work for your father? At his company?"

"Yes."

"So you don't work for the DIA anymore?"

"Correct."

She looked at him in disbelief. "So when did you stop working for them?"

"Last year."

"So if you're no longer in, how were you able to escape law enforcement in D.C. like you did?"

He smiled. "That's the other part of the mystery. I don't know who set me up, and I don't know who helped me escape. But I have my suspicions."

Her jaw dropped open. "So you're saying that you didn't know the people that rode the motorcycles with you out of D.C. before you took part in all that?"

"They obviously planned it, but I didn't know it would happen. I recognized one of them. He was MI-6, I believe."

"British intelligence? Like James Bond?"

"Yes. I met him in Europe several years ago. An operation I took part in there. But I don't know the man's name. Just the face."

"So you *think* MI-6 broke you out of the FBI's custody? That's insane."

"Technically, I wasn't in custody at the time."

She gave him a questioning look.

"They hadn't placed me under arrest. I voluntarily went in to answer questions. Although, I'm pretty sure that they were about to arrest me. The guy outside my window was yelling and reaching for his gun. Never a good sign."

"If they didn't think that you were guilty then, they certainly must think you are guilty now."

"Because of the car chase?"

"Yes."

"Well, OJ was still presumed innocent after his car chase."

"I don't think that should be your standard of excellence, Max."

"You're probably right. See, I was smart to hire you."

"So why did you run?"

"MI-6—if that's indeed who they were—leads me to believe that there was more to come in terms of evidence against me. The man who helped me to escape warned me not to let myself get taken into custody. He informed me that someone was trying to set me up. Knowing that I was innocent, his advice seemed of high quality. Plus, I tend to believe folks like that."

"Folks like what?"

"Spies with elaborate motorcycle escape plans."

"Ah. Them."

"Someone's set me up to take the fall in this Fend Aerospace hacking thing. I wasn't even aware of a problem. Some sort of network intrusion involving Russian hackers. My father must have known, though."

"And he didn't tell you?"

"No, actually. It's very unlike him to keep things from me, but perhaps he didn't think I needed to know. But the people who helped me get away implied that there was more incriminating evidence to come. So—I would like you to help me find out who did it, and why they did it. Can you do that?"

"I can certainly try," Renee said.

Max held up his phone. "The MI-6 team gave me a phone number. I'm supposed to call it at six p.m. tonight."

"And who will you be speaking with?"

"A woman. A member of their team, I presume. They said it was someone who would be able to help me out."

"Let me be there when you make the call," Renee said. "I'll set some analytics software up. Perhaps we can learn more about who's on the other end."

"Excellent. Thanks." He stood up. "Renee, there's something else that I'll need help with."

"What?"

"Do you know a good bakery around here? I'm famished."

8

Fend Corporate Jet
30,000 feet over Atlanta, Georgia

"Mr. Fend, we'll be landing in another forty minutes," the stewardess said.

"Thank you."

The stewardess disappeared back towards the front of the aircraft.

Charles sat across from Maria Blount. Her red hair was pulled back. She had been discussing the hacking incident. He hadn't told her anything about Max. Charles thought that it was best to keep that to himself for now.

"Should we work with the FAA to postpone the Fend 100 flight?" Maria said.

Charles shook his head. "No."

"But if..."

"This is only going to increase the pressure on us, I'm afraid. If we don't put on a good show next week, the different stakeholders might get spooked."

"But the cybersecurity investigators said that they weren't able to penetrate all of our firewalls."

Charles looked out the window of the jet as he spoke. "You went over the data they stole. What do you think?"

Maria looked glum. "They have the Fend 100 aircraft blueprints. Those alone are worth a lot to us. But they weren't able to access the servers that held the AI program."

"So? What's your prognosis, doctor?"

"If our aircraft design gets into competitors' hands, that would be bad. And Wall Street will punish us if we don't secure the FAA's NextGen contract. That's the most important thing to us now. We need that government contract finalized."

Charles tapped his fingers against his armrest. "Our corporate cybersecurity experts tell me that these hackers are like Somali pirates. They'll seize our precious information and hold it hostage for an indefinite period. Or like you suggested, sell it to the highest bidder. We can't postpone the Fend 100 flight. If we delay that flight, we give the hackers and our competition more opportunity to hurt us. Delaying the Fend 100 flight would delay the finalization of the NextGen contract with the FAA —or worse, put it in jeopardy."

"That would be awful for the company."

"Yes, it would."

"So what do you want to do, Charles?"

"We need to ensure that we improve our cybersecurity efforts. The FBI tells us that the hackers attempted to steal our AI technology, but they were unsuccessful. Fine. But they also warned us that they would keep trying. I want you to make sure that we are improving all of our security. Under no circumstances will we allow someone to steal the Fend 100's AI program."

"I understand. Who would do this sort of thing?" Maria asked.

Charles continued to look out the window. "The leeches of the earth. The Fend 100 flight must go off without a hitch. The sooner that happens, the less vulnerable we will be."

The stewardess walked back down the aisle. "Mr. Fend, you have a phone call, sir."

He thanked her and walked to the front of the jet, where the corded satellite phone was plugged in.

"Hello?"

The voice on the other end was one that he hadn't heard in quite some time. "Hello, Charles."

Charles closed his eyes, tightening his grip on the phone. "I had hoped that we were finished."

Charles could see Maria trying not to be too obvious in her attempt to eavesdrop on the conversation.

The voice on the other end said, "We *were* finished, Charles. We were. But it seems that our old friend has renewed his interest in you and your company. And now there is another consideration, I'm afraid."

"And what is that?"

"Your son."

9

Camp Peary
Near Williamsburg, Virginia

The fact that Max Fend had been working for the CIA wasn't a problem, per se. But the fact that Max had lied about it to the FBI during their investigation—well, to Jake Flynn, that *was* a problem. Maybe that was standard procedure for them. Flynn didn't know. But he needed to find out.

Flynn drove down early in the morning. He could have gone to Langley. But if Langley was anything like the FBI headquarters, Flynn preferred to stay as far away from there as possible. The farther away you get from government headquarters, the more people smile, and the looser their lips become. Although he wasn't quite sure if that would apply in this case.

The Farm, as it was known, was the CIA's training ground near Williamsburg, Virginia. Officially, the place was known as the Armed Forces Experimental Training Activity, or Camp Peary. The land was owned and run by the US military. But much of the base was used to train officers in the CIA's Directorate of Operations. He'd had to get special permission from both the FBI and CIA to gain access to the base. His interview was set up with someone the CIA thought would best be able to help him out.

The CIA man's name was Caleb Wilkes. By the looks of it, he was in his late forties. Maybe early fifties. Thinning gray hair. Suit jacket with no tie. Top button undone.

"You comfortable? Can I get you anything?"

"No, I'm fine, thanks," replied Flynn.

Wilkes closed the door and sat down across from Flynn. "We were surprised that you called us asking about Max. Mind if I ask what led you to believe that he worked for us?"

"Sure. I'm looking at Max Fend as part of an ongoing investigation into Fend Aerospace. When I was looking at Max Fend's background, I came across his Defense Department security clearance form. He worked for the DoD for a few years after college. So I talked to his contact that he had listed on his security clearance for when he worked at the DoD."

The CIA man listened but didn't speak.

Flynn went on. "So the guy gets talking, and he tells me that he thinks that they get a few people a year stashed there by CIA's personnel department, awaiting further assignment. He said he thought Max was one of them, but couldn't be sure. The more I thought about it, the more his job overseas seemed like a good cover for CIA employment. I think the fact that we're both sitting here tells me that I'm warm."

Wilkes nodded. "Is that it? Anything else I need to be aware of? You understand the sensitivity here. If there's a way that we can improve our process, I'd like to get that feedback."

The CIA man's voice was impassive. Flynn wondered if he already knew about Max Fend fleeing in a car chase yesterday.

Flynn said, "That's it."

"And the reason you're investigating Max Fend? What's his connection, if you don't mind my asking?"

"We're just looking into a recent Fend Aerospace incident, involving their automated flight system."

Caleb Wilkes stayed still. "I see."

Flynn flipped open a small notepad and clicked his pen. "Mind if I take notes?"

"Actually, I'd rather you didn't. This is a courtesy discussion. And I'm afraid it will be a short one. Normally we never discuss former employees, but we'll make an exception to help aid your investigation. You see, Max Fend actually didn't work here for very long. Your friend at the DoD was probably right. I'm afraid that we do stash people there—and in various other jobs within the government—while we're running background checks. We can't be too careful."

"So you're confirming that Max *did* work for the CIA?"

He held up a finger. "Yes, but not for long. He washed out of the program."

"Why?"

"Performance. He just wasn't up to our standards, I'm afraid. But I implore you—keep this to yourself. We don't normally provide information on *anyone* who has been to this school, and that includes washouts."

Flynn lowered his voice a little. "You mind if I ask you a question? Is this place really what everyone says it is? It's really a spy school?"

Caleb smiled. "It's not exactly a well-kept secret. They have many books and TV shows about it. But most of them aren't very accurate." Flynn noticed that he didn't really answer the question.

Flynn nodded. "But you *are* sure that Max Fend never worked for the Agency beyond being here?"

"Correct."

"And how long was he at this...*school*?"

"I would have to check the record again. Sorry. I only glanced at it just before you arrived. I think it was a matter of weeks. Maybe a month, tops. It's quite rigorous training."

The FBI agent tapped his pen against his blank notepad.

"And to be clear, Fend is no longer employed by the CIA?"

Caleb Wilkes's smile looked fake now. Annoyance in his eyes. "Again, that's correct. He's no longer with the Agency."

"Why did you guys recruit him, if he wasn't up to your standards?"

"We recruit a lot of people. Sometimes you don't know who can handle the pressure until you put them in the cooker. A lot of them don't make it through. But we funnel most of those to other CIA roles, if they're fit for those types of assignments. It would be a waste not to. Security clearances are expensive, and take a long time."

"But you didn't do that with Fend?"

"What? Send him to another CIA role?"

"Yes."

"No. Not with him."

"Why not?"

"He wasn't suited for other roles."

"Why not?"

"He just wasn't." Wilkes's eyes narrowed.

"When's the last time you spoke to Max?"

"Years ago. Just before he left our employment."

"And what exactly is *your* position here?"

"I can't say."

"How is it that you remember Max Fend so well if he was only here for a month, over a decade ago?"

Caleb tapped his temple. "Memory like a steel trap. It's a gift."

Flynn wasn't getting anywhere. He decided to take a chance. "Can I ask you a question? Did you happen to see that motorcycle chase—the one in D.C. yesterday?"

"Of course," Wilkes said. "It's been all over the news."

"What did you think of it? Like, as in, what is your *professional* opinion?"

Wilkes stared at Flynn for a moment and then said, "It was a competent group. Professionals. They were able to evade law enforcement in one of the most highly secured areas in the world. Then they disappeared. I couldn't have planned it better myself."

Flynn stared into Wilkes's eyes. His investigative instincts were colliding with his sense of interagency propriety. The FBI agent in him won out.

"*Did* you plan it?" He watched Wilkes's face carefully during the response.

Wilkes laughed. "No. I definitely did *not*. While I said that I couldn't have planned it better, and that might be true, I would like to think that I'd have planned it *differently*."

"How so?"

"I wouldn't have made the escape so...*public*. That's against everything we teach here. If we make the news, we're doing something wrong."

"So you think the people who did that wanted Max to make the news?"

"Perhaps." He shrugged.

"Do you know if Max Fend ever worked for any foreign governments? Foreign companies? Or acted as a foreign agent in any capacity?"

"No, I told you. He was only here for a month."

"What about after the CIA?"

"You are asking about what Max Fend went on to do after his time here? That, I wouldn't know."

While this CIA guy may have been a well-trained liar, Flynn had been a federal investigator for over twenty years. He had a great built-in lie detector, and he was pretty sure that Wilkes's last answer was a whopper.

"Look, Wilkes, I'm just trying to make sure he wasn't involved in anything that I need to investigate further. We had an incident at Fend Aerospace that involves billions of dollars in technology. And there's evidence of foreign interference—as in industrial espionage. It might even have national security implications. There are foreign nationals who'd *love* to get their hands on that technology."

"And you think Max Fend was helping them? The son of the owner of the company?"

"You'd be surprised how often family is involved in crimes against each other."

Wilkes said. "No, I wouldn't, actually. But look, I'm sorry. I just don't have anything for you. I've told you all I know. Max Fend did *not* work for the CIA."

Flynn rubbed his chin. "Alright. Between me and you, I thought it was a long shot anyway. I see no reason to keep digging. Thanks for your time."

"Of course."

They stood, and Wilkes walked him out to his car.

"I appreciate your help today."

"No problem. Always glad to help the FBI."

* * *

Special Agent Jake Flynn drove west along I-64, towards Richmond. From there he would take I-95 north and head towards the FBI's Manassas office. Flynn planned to make a quick stop there before catching a flight to Jacksonville in the afternoon.

He went over the interview in his mind, getting more and more frustrated as he replayed it. Flynn had met guys like Wilkes before. Spooks. Some of them really thought they were better and smarter than everyone else. Like they were the only *real* cowboys, and everyone else in law enforcement was just pretending.

Guys like Wilkes thought they had license to manufacture a false reality when it suited their needs. It became hard to tell what was real and what wasn't. They were good at it. After all, it was what a professional spy did for a living.

If the CIA had Wilkes teaching at the Farm, he probably had decades of field experience. Every lie he told was likely mixed in with just enough truth to convince Flynn to believe him.

But Flynn *couldn't* believe everything he had just heard. He didn't believe that BS line about having the memory of a steel trap. What kind of asshole says something like that? Wilkes had a certain level of familiarity and interest in Max Fend that was *way* more than he should have had. There's no way a guy like Wilkes would have wasted his time talking to the FBI about some washout. Max Fend was more than Wilkes was letting on. Flynn could feel it.

His phone rang. He looked down at the caller ID. Steve at the DNI's office. Perfect timing.

"Jake, it's Steve." His voice sounded funny, like he didn't want to talk too loud.

"Hold on, let me pull over." Flynn pulled off at an exit and parked in a gas station. "What's up?"

"I looked into what we had been discussing yesterday."

"Yup. And?"

"Something isn't right."

"Really? Can you go into it?" He didn't want to say the name if it was that sensitive.

"In person."

Flynn looked at the clock. He would have to forego his planned stop at the FBI's DC field office in Manassas.

"I've got to catch a flight this afternoon, but I've got a little bit of time. Can you meet me for coffee? I can be up there in a few hours."

"Text me when you get here."

The drive took two hours. I-95 was backed up around Dumfries, but no more than usual. They ended up meeting at a little coffee shop in Springfield, Virginia.

Steve said, "So I checked the personnel file for Max Fend—or I started to, anyway."

"And?"

"The system that the DNI network uses will trigger alerts if I look at things I'm not supposed to. But I know this much: he worked for one of the intel agencies. If Max Fend had never worked in the intel world, I wouldn't have found anything on him. But there's definitely a DNI personnel file on Max Fend."

"What was in it?"

"I don't know. But I could see the classification level of the file. And in this case, it was above what I'm allowed to access. *Way above.*"

"What does that mean?"

"I'm not sure. I'm afraid if I dig any further it'll trigger an audit on me. We don't want that. I'll get in trouble...or get both of us in trouble."

"Let me ask you this—would you have seen that file if he'd worked for the CIA for a month and then washed out of their training program?"

Steve thought about it and then shook his head. "Nah. I don't think so. The file would have looked different, or there may not have even been one for him."

"Okay. Listen, Steve, I just came from Camp Peary. I met with a guy down there who represented the CIA. He just completely denied that Max Fend ever worked for them. He said he was in training for a month, and then washed out."

"That's what they told you?"

"Yeah."

"That seems strange, considering the classification of his personnel file."

"Yeah, I'm not buying it either."

Steve said, "Well, maybe he just works for another agency."

"What do you mean, like who?"

"A lot of the agencies have spies, Jake. It's not just the CIA out there in the field, you know."

"But the guy down at the Farm said—"

"Jake, I gotta tell ya, in my experience—a lot of these CIA field agents are like politicians, but with different motivations. You can tell when they're lying by whether their mouth is moving or not."

"You think he would lie to an FBI agent conducting an investigation on one of his men?"

Steve shot him a skeptical look. "Come on, man. You know how it is."

Flynn sighed. "Well, what can I do?"

"Let me talk to someone else at my work. It's okay, I'll be careful what I say. And he's trustworthy. If I find anything else out, I'll call you. It might be a few days."

"Call me whether you find anything out or not. I want to know."

"Got it."

"Thanks, Steve."

"You bet."

Flynn looked at his watch. He needed to be on a plane to Jacksonville soon.

10

Max and Renee stopped off at her home so she could speak to her mother and grab her things. Max waited in the car for ten minutes until she was done.

They ate their breakfast in the MarieBette Cafe and Bakery in Charlottesville, Virginia. The place was crowded with a mix of locals and University of Virginia students. Max had a penchant for good French pastries, and MarieBette made some of the best ones he'd tasted in the States.

"I have a house in Georgia. I'll fly us there this morning. It's out of the way. No one will see us. We'll make our call at six tonight and see what we can find out. And you'll have time to do your thing."

"Sounds good."

Max wiped his mouth with a napkin and stood. "Okay—I'll wait in the car. If you don't mind paying? I'd prefer as little interaction as possible."

"Sure." Renee closed her laptop and placed it in her bag. She ordered two cups of coffee to go and a few more croissants, and paid for their food.

A few minutes later, they walked through the Signature Flight Support building at Charlottesville Albemarle Airport. Max wore his aviator sunglasses and kept his head facing away from the man behind the counter, who was paying much more attention to the cling of Renee's shirt than to Max. That was fine. If the FBI questioned him later, he would be that much worse of an eyewitness.

Max untied the plane and threw the chocks back inside the storage compartment, along with their travel bags. He got into the cockpit and helped Renee strap her seat belt on and plug in her headset. Then he went through his checklist.

He held open the aircraft door, yelled, "Clear prop!" and started up the 315-horsepower engine.

Max checked the weather one last time on his phone. Severe clear all the way down to Brunswick. He called ground control and began to taxi, holding short of the runway. He then told the tower that he was departing to the south using visual flight rules, and they cleared him for takeoff. Max smiled to himself as he saw Renee tense up out of the corner of his eye, her thighs flexing and her hands grabbing the seat as the aircraft vaulted forward down the runway.

Then he pulled back on the stick ever so slightly, and the Cirrus was airborne. It was a smooth climb out. A little left stick and they were headed toward the south horizon.

* * *

"Can you hear me okay?" Max asked Renee over their pilot headsets.

They were flying southeast now, sitting side by side in the cockpit, green pastures and farmland beneath them. Renee was on her laptop, using her satellite connection to get work done while they traveled.

"I can hear you fine. I'm reading an article on you. On your father, actually. But it mentions you. It's a write-up about the Fend 100, and a profile on him."

Max looked over at her and then back out the windscreen of the aircraft.

She quoted, "While Charles Fend is known as a pioneer in the aviation world, his son Max has yet to make his mark. Max Fend has lived in the lap of luxury in the South of France for the past decade. He is best known for throwing decadent parties at his villa in Saint-Jean-Cap-Ferrat, located in a region of France known as an exclusive vacation spot for the ultra-rich. He often hosted celebrities and the wealthy elite from around the globe. Controversy erupted last year when two men were found dead on the premises. While rumors swirled regarding Max Fend's connection to the crimes, he was never charged, and was reportedly out of the country when the deaths occurred."

Renee looked at Max again. "I've been meaning to ask you about that."

"I've promised you honesty. Ask me anything."

"Did you kill those two men?"

The drone of the plane engine was the only sound for a few seconds.

"Yes, I did."

"Why?"

"We had a disagreement."

"Over what?"

"How to treat a lady." Max glanced at her. "Have you flown in a small plane like this before?"

Renee frowned at the obvious change of subject. "Actually, yes. In Canada. When I was younger, my family spent a lot of time on the West Coast. North of Vancouver. Have you been there?"

"Yes, actually. It's quite beautiful. Lots of great hiking and fishing."

"Yeah. My father has a cabin there. It's pretty remote, so sometimes we would get there by float plane. That was a lot of fun."

"A float plane, huh?"

"Yup."

"Always wanted to try that. This one can't land on water, but it does have its own parachute."

Renee made a face. "Are you messing with me?"

"No, I swear." Max pointed up at the ceiling. A black oval covering with a bright red and white warning label was above them.

"What is that?" Renee was reading it now. "Oh my. You *are* serious. This plane actually has a parachute?"

"I figured with all of the trouble I get into on the ground, it's best that I take the proper precautions when I'm in the air."

She smiled at that. "Have you ever used it?"

"The parachute? No. You would only use it in a dire emergency. But I must admit, I've always wanted to try it. It has an exceptional safety record."

"If it's all the same to you, let's just land normally."

Max laughed. "Not a problem, my dear."

* * *

The aircraft touched down on a tiny runway near the shores of southern Georgia. Jekyll Island. The airport was nothing more than a long strip of black pavement, with a few Cessnas parked next to a small shack.

The island was part marshland, part golf course. On a secluded strip of beach were a scattering of vacation homes, one of which Max owned.

A rental agent was waiting for them with a car. Max had had Renee order it while they were flying. They'd provided false information and paid using one of Max's prepaid cards. The rental agent tried to make small talk in the airport parking lot, but they kept it to a minimum.

They stopped at a small grocery store and picked up some essentials, then drove to Max's property. The house didn't look like much, but it was quaint. A dated two-bedroom ranch underneath a low-hanging weeping willow. More sand than grass in the yard. A few leaning palm trees.

Max said, "The view in back gets better."

It certainly did. While the house was old and beat up out front, the backyard was a narrow sandy passage right down to the beach. Rows of perfect tube waves rolled into the shore. It was mid-afternoon, and the sky was a deep blue. After throwing their bags in separate bedrooms, they went outside and sat on two wooden beach chairs, facing the water.

Max cracked open two beers and handed one to Renee. He stared off towards the Georgia shore, a few hundred yards away, a cool sea breeze rustling the trees in the yard.

"I got this place a few years ago," Max said. "I was home for a month, visiting my father, and I wanted somewhere I could go to get away from it all."

"Do you buy a lot of property on a whim?"

"It's relaxing here. The neighbors are far enough away that we don't see each other. The beach is relatively undiscovered. And most of the year, the weather is warm."

"It's very nice." Renee opened her laptop and began typing. Without looking up, she said, "Why did you start down that path?"

"What do you mean?"

"Your father being who he was, you could have had any life you wanted. But you chose to be in the intelligence world. Why?"

"Honestly? Probably because it sounded exciting. Like an adventure."

"And was it?"

"I think the hope of an adventure is what attracts a lot of us at first. But you find out pretty quick that it's not like they portray it in the movies."

"What is it like?"

"You have to pretend a lot. Some might call it acting. And you have to document and pass on everything. In a world where so much is accessible by computer, the intelligence agencies are more reliant on human sources than ever."

"That seems counterintuitive. Why?"

"Because cyber data is too easily tracked. A lot of the best spies and terrorists stay off phones and Internet. So the best way to track them ends up being old-fashioned tradecraft."

"Did you like the work?"

"Sometimes. Sometimes not."

"So why did you stay on?"

"Because people need protecting. It's a noble cause. You did work for the CSE. And you work in cybersecurity now. You must know as well as I do that there are evil men in this world. I don't know how they got that way, and I've given up trying to find out. But I saw it enough to want to fight them."

"So you joined for an adventure, and stayed on to protect us from bad guys?" She was smiling.

"And probably 9/11, if I think about it. September eleventh changed everyone, I think. I was in New York City when it happened. I had actually skipped class to go visit my father. I never did anything like that—skip class, I mean. But I hadn't seen him in a while, and it was early in the semester. I planned to make it back for football practice. My father and I ended up watching the smoke from the first building when the second airplane hit. That was the moment—when the second aircraft struck. People were still trying to figure out what was going on when it was just one smoking tower. But the second aircraft hitting—that was when the world changed."

Renee looked up from her computer as Max spoke.

"I remember seeing the people who jumped off the burning towers. Their bodies falling through the air. Their choice was to stay and burn to death, or jump off. Maybe it wasn't a choice. That was the most terrifying thing I've ever witnessed. When you see something like that, and you know that there are these men out there who intended for it to occur—men who celebrated when it happened—it makes you realize that there is good and evil in this world. And I guess I just wanted to fight for good."

"Sometimes I think it takes a truly shocking event to wake us all up out of our slumber." Renee paused. "So, you see yourself as...what exactly? A knight?"

He smiled. "I guess. Something like that."

"So why the act? Why do you pretend to be the spoiled rich boy, if that's not who you really are? Does the DIA tell you to pretend to be that character?"

Max shrugged.

"Come on, Max, give me an answer."

"Are you psychoanalyzing me now? Should I lie down?"

"If it would help." The wind blew a few strands of her dark hair across her face. She stroked it out of the way with her fingers.

"Because if people think I'm the cliché of a rich billionaire's son, they're expecting to see certain things," Max said. "I give them what they expect. It's a convenient mask. And then they don't see anything else I might do."

"It allows you to be anonymous?"

"It allows me to be sneaky."

"And the act didn't get too distasteful for you?"

"No. I'm good at pretending. I feel like all my life, I've pretended. When you get good at it, the act requires less effort. And if they think you wake up at dawn, you can sleep till noon. Or in my case...if they think you're sleeping till noon, no one knows that you might be sending intelligence to your handler at dawn."

She touched his arm. "So if you were satisfied being a spy, then why did you decide to get out?"

"I didn't decide to get out. They *forced* me out." He started to say something else and then bit his lip. "We can talk more about that later. Right now I need you to find out as much as you can before our call with the MI-6 agent."

"Sure. That's fine." Renee began typing. She shot him a curious glance as he got up and walked away.

11

Jacksonville, Florida

The Fend Aerospace business center was a tall metal-and-glass structure that rose up just west of the St. John's River. It housed a sizable chunk of the managers in the company - those involved in finance, purchasing, marketing, and sales. Charles Fend and the c-suite executives had their offices there, along with a select group of project managers and R&D scientists.

The view was excellent. From the eighteenth floor, one could see the St. John's River winding through the city. The football stadium stood to the north, and Naval Air Station Jacksonville was to the south. Multiple bridges cut across the shimmering river.

Special Agent Flynn sat across the glossy conference table from the senior Fend 100 program manager. She looked nervous, which was understandable considering that she was talking to the FBI. Most people Flynn spoke with were nervous.

Flynn looked at his notes. Maria Blount.

Charles Fend had personally hired her away from a London-based competitor. Maria had gotten to know Max Fend informally in the two years that she'd been with his father's company. Red hair. A nice smile. And very smart. Aerospace engineering smart. Not that Flynn was a dummy, but these people were all brainiacs. She'd graduated near the top of her class at Cambridge and had turned down a job at NASA to work on this project, for God's sake. Flynn would have to bring his A game.

"I appreciate you guys blocking off your afternoon for me."

"Of course."

"Tell me about Max Fend," he began.

Maria blinked. "Max? Well, I've known him for a number of years through his father. He's a good soul, Max. A little bit of a comedian, I think, but sharp, and eager to learn. He'll fit right in."

"Do you have any reason to believe that Max Fend would be angry with his father?"

She was taken aback. "No. No, of course not. Why do you ask?"

"Have you seen any suspicious behavior? Talking to anyone that you didn't know? Or perhaps asking questions that were unlike him?"

Maria thought about it. "He was asking a lot of questions about the automated airliner. The Fend 100. But *everyone* has been asking questions about that. And it's completely appropriate for Max to ask those sorts of questions. He'll be coming to work for Fend Aerospace, as you know."

"Yes, I'm aware. What kinds of things was he asking?"

"I don't know," Maria said. "The basic questions. How it worked. Who controlled the aircraft at different phases of the flight. That kind of thing."

"Did you see him using the Fend computer network the day of the network breach? Or at any time leading up to that incident?"

"What do you mean, the Fend computer network?"

"Did you see him use any company computers on the fifteenth of last month?"

"Yes, I think so. But again, that's completely appropriate and normal behavior."

"I'll decide that, thank you."

"Very well. I apologize."

"It's no problem. Confirm for me this—you had a computer network breach, right?"

"Yes."

"And the day after, you had a test flight for one of your Fend 100 prototypes, right?"

"Again, that is correct."

"Was there a risk there? Was the Fend 100 aircraft affected by the hacking incident?"

"No."

"You sound very sure of yourself."

Maria frowned. "Look, I understand that it's your job to investigate this computer security incident. But in my opinion, it's silly to think that someone logging in to the Fend network's email system could gain access to the datalink that controls the Fend 100 remotely."

"Why do you say that?"

She rolled her eyes and sighed, exasperated. "Do you mind if I bring in Bradley? He's better at explaining this type of stuff."

"He's the chief engineer on the project?"

"Yes."

"Sure. Please bring him in. I'll wait."

Bradley Karpinsky entered a moment later. Flynn said, "Mr. Karpinsky, I was just talking to Miss Blount here about the external computer breach that occurred on the Fend network."

"Okay." Karpinsky shrugged.

He was going to make Flynn do all the work. Flynn hated guys like this.

"Miss Blount was telling me how she thinks it's implausible that anyone could have gained access to the Fend 100 aircraft through the company's computer network."

"I would have to agree with her on that," Karpinsky said.

"Would you mind elaborating? Using laymen's terms?"

"Well, for one thing, the system that remotely controls the Fend 100 is a closed system. There is no connection to the company's main computer network."

"But our Cyber Investigation division has identified that your company's computer network was penetrated by foreign entities."

"So we heard," Karpinsky said. "So what?"

"I'm just trying to cover all my bases. I want to figure out what the hackers were after. Some of my cyber experts raised the question that the aircraft itself could have been tapped into. I would like to hear your opinions on that theory."

Maria whispered, "They think it was Max."

Flynn frowned. "Excuse me. I never said that."

"Well, you were asking all those questions about him. It doesn't take a rocket scientist to see where you're going."

Flynn realized that she actually *was* a rocket scientist.

Karpinsky let out a snort. "Max Fend? Look, don't repeat this, but that kid is more interested in buying a new boat or whatever it is rich folks do. And I doubt he would have the skills needed to gain entry into our computer network."

Agent Flynn said, "I take it you don't have a very high opinion of Max Fend?"

"Not really, no."

"Why is that?"

"His father's setting him up with a comfortable job here when he's done with school. But the kid's done nothing to earn it," Karpinsky said. "Meanwhile we're all busting our asses so that his dad can make history."

"*Bradley*. Come on," Maria said.

"Well, it's true. You know it is."

Flynn watched the exchange. What Flynn didn't bother to mention was that Max Fend himself didn't need much skill to open up the Fend network to criminal hackers. He just needed *access* to the Fend Aerospace computer network. Inserting a preprogrammed thumb drive, or clicking on the right external link, would create a hole in the firewall—the hackers would do the rest.

Karpinsky's comments raised two questions in his mind. First, was it really implausible that the Fend 100 had been accessed through the company's separate network breach? Flynn made a note to ask his cyber team about that. He had taken their word for it. He would have to dig there.

The second question in Flynn's mind was whether Karpinsky held a grudge against Charles Fend, because he felt that Max was getting favorable treatment.

Flynn decided to change up the questions. "Mr. Karpinsky..."

"Please, call me Bradley."

"Bradley, if you were going to seize control of the Fend 100, how would you do it?"

"I wouldn't."

"But if you *had* to—do you see any possible way for a criminal organization to do so?"

Karpinsky rubbed his chin. "I mean—hypothetically—and I mean this is *way* out there—but if someone was able to access the actual aircraft...maybe then they could mess around in there and—"

Maria shook her head. "I doubt that's possible. We have so many security measures."

"Yeah. She's right. I mean, we have teams of engineers crawling all over the aircraft every day. We treat it like a NASA rocket launch. We check everything eight different ways to make sure there are no defects. That's why I told your FBI investigator that I don't think this computer network breach is a safety concern—more like a corporate security issue. Hackers trying to steal the design and software code. That is my worry."

Flynn said, "You're saying that the hacking incident isn't a safety concern because no defects showed up on your tests?"

"Right."

"Look, this might sound crazy, but I've gotta ask this," Flynn said. "I've heard reports about people on commercial flights hacking into the aircraft's controls through the onboard Wi-Fi network. Does the Fend 100 have any security flaws like that? Something that hackers could have taken control of?"

Maria looked at Karpinsky and they both shook their heads.

Maria said, "No. That's not possible. I think I read an article in *Wired* magazine about that. Some engineer claimed to have changed the aircraft's trajectory. But that's just not realistic."

"Why not?"

"Oh, I remember this one. We looked into that," Karpinsky said. "We think the engineer in the article was able to access that aircraft through the IFE system."

"IFE?"

Karpinsky sighed the way IT people did when talking to "non-computer" people. "The in-flight entertainment system. He probably used the port in his seat to get into the IFE system. Then, on his computer, he saw some data that he thought was the avionics system data, and he tried to manipulate it."

"The article I read said that he *did* manipulate it."

Karpinsky rolled his eyes. "That's not possible. The data is routed through a different bus."

"So then how—"

"Okay, let me put it this way. My daughter has a pretend steering wheel on her car seat. When we go to the grocery store, she turns the wheel and she thinks she's moving our car, but she isn't. That's what happened with this guy. The data bus we use on commercial airliners is a secured, closed system. It is not possible for a passenger to hack into it."

"And the security breach didn't affect the Fend 100 that was flying that day?"

"Correct," Karpinsky said. "We analyzed the electronic data stats for hydraulics, avionics, electrical and mechanical controls, along with their built-in redundant systems and fail-safes. Any interference with the normal signal would be detected and flagged to us. We're clear to proceed with our test flight."

"And when is that flight?"

"Four days from now."

* * *

They took a break around five-thirty p.m. Sandwiches and drinks were brought in from a local place down in San Marco.

Flynn asked to speak to one of the test pilots who worked on the program. They brought in a guy named Tim Hutson. Karpinsky stepped out for a meeting.

"So are you going to be flying the Fend 100 during the big test flight in four days?"

"That's right."

"And you used to fly for the Air Force?"

"That's right. C-141s, among others. I was a test pilot before I retired and started working here."

"Excellent. I saw a bunch of Air Force jets at an air show once. What do they call them? The white ones that fly together?"

"The Thunderbirds?"

"Yeah. That's it. They were incredible. Wow. Hey, thank you for your service."

"Thanks."

Flynn looked at Tim. "Can I ask you something? As a pilot, what do you think of all this automated flight stuff?"

Tim said, "I think it's going to put guys like me out of business."

"Really?"

"Sure. I mean, autopilot functions have been around for decades. And they're getting better and better. Hell, now any kid can buy their own quadcopter drone and control it with a smartphone."

"So you're saying that the technology is already there."

"Yeah, has been for years."

"So then what gives? Why is everyone making such a big deal out of automating commercial airliners?"

"This is more than just a few safety measures. Your car has cruise control, right?"

"Sure."

"Okay, well, think of today's autopilot in planes as being the equivalent of cruise control in cars. The Fend 100 autonomous flight is like those driverless cars you hear about all the tech companies testing out. We're actually using some of the same technology. There are very sophisticated computers on board that will—potentially—be able to completely replace the pilots."

"From the tone of your voice, I'm picking up that you're a bit skeptical?"

Tim said, "Most people want to know that there's a human being up front, making sure everything goes smoothly. An expert, ready to take charge if anything goes wrong."

"Do you think pilots are still needed?"

"Right now I do, yeah. I think with any new technology, you're gonna have bumps. And flying is an unforgiving business. Small mistakes have big consequences. I would want a pilot on board."

Flynn ate a potato chip. He looked at Maria, who was shaking her head in disagreement. "Maria, what are the arguments for automated commercial airliners?"

"I mean...aside from the massive profits, and it being part of our company's main growth strategy?"

"Yes. Aside from all of that."

"Safety. Cost efficiencies. Do you know how many car accidents there are in the United States every year?"

"A lot, right?"

"Yes. Over thirty thousand people die in road crashes every year. Thirty thousand. Think about that number. Not only that, but another two million are injured. *Two million people.* That's almost one percent of the entire population. Every stinking year. Compare that to aircraft accidents. The fatalities are in the hundreds."

"What has this got to do with robot pilots?"

"Her point is going to be that robots make fewer mistakes than people," Tim said. "She's saying that bringing autonomous driving and flying to market will save lives."

Maria nodded. "It *will* save lives. Lots of them."

Flynn looked at Tim. "You seem skeptical. You still don't trust a robot to do your pilot job."

"That's because he's a dinosaur." The gruff voice of Bradley Karpinsky, who stood in the doorway, wearing his light blue lab coat.

Maria looked at her watch. "Your meeting go okay?"

He plopped down at the head of the conference table. "Yes, thanks. Maria's right. Computers are smarter than people. It's not even close. Tim here"—he pointed at the pilot—"is going to get tired. He's going to drink alcohol. He's going to forget things. He's going to have to pee. He's going to get sick. Distracted. Sometimes, he'll underperform."

"Never," said Tim. "Except maybe the part about getting drunk. But not while flying."

"A computer—or a robot, if you will—will never get tired, sick, hungry, or have to go to the bathroom," Bradley said. "It will be ruthlessly efficient. Do you know that even today, if you're flying on a commercial airliner, the hardest landings are given to the computers? Did you know that?"

"That's not entirely true," Tim said.

"What does he mean?" Flynn asked.

"He's referring to the fact that—depending on the airline and the type of aircraft—if weather minimums get bad enough, the pilots are required to have autopilot fly the landing," Tim answered.

Flynn stopped chewing. "Are you serious? What do you mean weather minimums—like if it gets too windy?"

Tim gave him a funny look. "No, sorry. I mean ceiling and visibility. If the clouds get too low...the best way to think of it is when it's really foggy out. That gets the visibility way down. So in that scenario, when the cloud layer is basically zero, and the visibility is zero, then a lot of airlines require that their pilots use an automated approach. In essence, the computers will fly the landing."

"No shit. Wow. I had no idea."

"Most people don't."

Flynn said, "What if the computers mess it up?"

"The pilots are right there, ready to take the controls. But in reality, with the improved navigational equipment on board and the reliability of the automated flight software, the computers never make a mistake."

Flynn said, "So is your Fend 100 as simple as that? You guys just hit the autopilot button and the pilot leaves the plane?"

"There are three modes of operation in the Fend automated flight software," Bradley said. "Type one—normal, pilot-controlled flight. Nothing out of the ordinary. Type two—remote-controlled flight. A pilot from the ground controls the airplane. This is the way the military controls its drones. Finally, we have type three—this is the really innovative stuff. This is where machine learning and artificial intelligence come into play. And it's where Fend actually adds to the value chain."

"Bradley's never had trouble talking up his own program," Maria said.

Karpinsky frowned. "Fend's type three automated flight means that the computers inside the aircraft are doing everything. They handle all the communications to and from ground controllers, tower controllers, and all other air traffic controllers throughout the flight. Much of this is through data exchanges. But there's an actual voice action-response mechanism that'll supplement the pilot. And the machines are *learning*. Getting better every day with the sum learning of the entire system."

"So how does a computer know what to say like a pilot would?"

"That part is pretty easy. It's just a bunch of code. A bunch of if-then statements, so that it knows what to do in every scenario. For instance, before it goes into class bravo airspace, it knows that it has to establish two-way communications with the class bravo air traffic controller. So it won't enter that airspace until it does."

"What if the radio failed, and it could never establish communication in the first place?"

"Then it would keep going through the if-then statements until it got to the correct course of action. Tim, as a pilot, what would you do?"

Tim said, "It depends—but if all else failed, I could set the transponder to 7600 and keep making my radio calls in the blind. Then basically keep flying the approach and land on the runway and hope they can hear you."

"And that is what the computers would have the aircraft do," Bradley said. "It would automatically know who to talk to, what to say, where and how to fly. No humans required. And it would be taking in data from a variety of sources, *including* the radios. If the air traffic controller called up the aircraft and told it to turn, our computers would follow orders—as long as there wasn't a more pressing need, like a fuel emergency. And this is just how a human pilot would behave. Right, Tim?"

"That's the theory."

Bradley frowned. "Tim's a purist. He believes that all planes should have people in them."

Tim said, "Bradley, let me ask you something. Have you ever used the voice-to-text feature on your phone?"

"Yes."

"And did it transcribe everything perfectly? I doubt it. I once told my mom I was going to get her a birthday cake, but instead my phone told her that I got her birthday crack."

"I understand your point."

Tim said, "Same example—but with typed text messages—if the auto-complete feature on your phone messes up and changes what you meant to type, it might give your text message a completely different meaning. Those are two separate technologies. Voice transcription, and text auto-complete. Billions of people around the world use those technologies. Yet everyone knows of stories where they have failed, leading to unintended consequences."

"This is true," Bradley said. "Voice recognition is challenging. But it's constantly improving. And your phone needs to be able to interpret anything. We're able to cut down a lot of errors because of the standard-ized terminology in aviation. Pilots and controllers are expected to use precise terms and phrases."

"My point isn't that voice-to-text is a weak link here," Tim said. "It's that when you replace a complex human worker with a robot, you're probably going to have a lot of errors that the human would never make. Because humans are critical thinkers, and we can use all our senses and experiences to help make decisions."

Jake Flynn listened as the pilot and engineer went on arguing their points to each other. He wondered how it must feel to know that computers were about to make your job obsolete.

* * *

After a brief break, they came together again so Flynn could finish up his questions to the Fend 100 project team. It was well after business hours now, and Flynn could see that he was wearing out his welcome. "Okay, talk to me about your upcoming test flight."

"We're calling it a final approval flight," Bradley said. "The type certifi-cation has already been granted by the FAA, but this is more about the contract. The FAA wants to make sure our first passenger flight goes well, and they're going to evaluate us while it happens."

"So if it goes well, what happens?"

"We get the NextGen contract for autonomous flight. You're familiar with NextGen?"

Flynn shook his hand back and forth. "I've read about it. But refresh me."

Bradley looked at Maria, who smiled politely. She said, "The Next Generation Air Transportation System. NextGen. It's the new national airspace system that the United States will adopt over the next ten years. The plans will transform the way planes and air traffic controllers navigate and communicate, and the way the industry manages flights in the United States."

"What are the major changes?" Flynn asked.

Maria looked at her watch. "How much time do you have? How about I give you the high-level version? Today the US air traffic control system primarily uses radar and radio communications. NextGen will change that to use more GPS and data transfers. It allows planes to shorten their routes by going directly to the airports, instead of using inefficient navigational beacons. The data exchanges will reduce how much time it takes to get information back and forth between the planes and the controllers. Think of it as using text messaging instead of voice communication. Texting saves time, right?"

"Right."

"Before, controllers had to read out long chains of instructions. The pilots would then read it back. That took up a lot of valuable time. Mistakes were sometimes made. The data exchange method is quicker and more precise."

"So that's it? That's NextGen?"

"There's a lot more to it than just that," Bradley said. "But those changes *are* major changes. It might sound simple, but making it happen is a massive amount of work."

"So how does Fend Aerospace fit into the NextGen plans?"

"Many companies are part of it. I mean, it's transforming the entire commercial aviation industry," Bradley said. "The commercial *airline* industry alone is almost ten percent of the US GDP. And it's growing fast."

"Wow. I didn't realize it was that big."

"Prior to NextGen, automated flight wasn't permitted," Maria said. "There are still a lot of regulatory hurdles, but we're lobbying hard, and things are looking up. As long as everything goes well during our FAA final approval flight in a few days, we think there's a very good chance that Fend Aerospace will be the main contractor for automated flight when that part of NextGen comes online."

"Won't other aircraft manufacturers just make their own technology?"

"Well, that's why this is so important to us as a company," Maria said. "Fend Aerospace isn't building technology just to be used in its own planes. We're creating the hardware and software that allows aircraft to be preprogramed, and—if need be—controlled remotely. *All* aircraft in the NextGen Automated Flight Program would use this technology."

Karpinsky said, "Our strategy is to own the entire autonomous flight software *platform*. All the major aircraft manufacturers and airline companies will become our customers. Think of the Fend 100 as our iPod. But we're also creating iTunes. So if the FAA decides to use the Fend 100 platform, everyone will buy from us."

Maria said, "It would be the standardized brain for every aircraft that wants to fly using automated flight in the NextGen aviation system—so all commercial flights, as well as logistics flights. Like FedEx. There are a lot of those, too."

"So what's the problem?" Flynn asked.

"Competition. Right now Fend has a leg up. We earned the bid for the US program. But European and Asian markets are modernizing their airways as well. Ideally, we would form the global solution. But that's probably not going to happen. We would probably create a licensing agreement with the leading European and Asian companies to share the tech. But first, we have to prove that it can work in the US. Everything culminates in our FAA final approval flight in a few days."

"I didn't realize this flight was so important."

"Oh, yes. If this flight goes well, we'll advance to the next tranche of funding. And our fifteen-year contract with the government will go into effect. That's everything for Fend Aerospace."

"Let me ask you a question. What would happen if all your technologies were given to your competition? Say, through a cyberattack?"

"That would be catastrophic for the company," Maria said. "But we've made sure that can't happen. After the cyberattack last month, we've really upped our IT security standards. The data for the Fend 100 is in the Fort Knox of IT security. And it isn't accessible through the Internet."

Flynn nodded. "Good to know."

12

Max and Renee spent the afternoon doing research and waiting for their phone call with MI-6. After two hours of Max watching Renee type, she sent him out to get some food.

Max returned and cooked her the best frittata she had ever eaten.

"My God, you're a good cook. Where did you learn that?"

"Europe. But the secret to this was the ingredients. Roast tomatoes and onions from the local farmers' market. I have to admit this is one of the better ones I've made."

She smacked her lips, finishing every bit of the dish.

Max and Renee sat in the living room of the beach house talking and working until six p.m. He had just gotten off the phone with the local fuel truck owner. The man was filling up his Cirrus now.

"It's time." Time to call the female MI-6 contact.

She nodded, sliding over on the couch. "Here. Sit."

Renee had connected her computer to Max's phone. It would run a series of programs designed to gather more information about who they were talking to.

At precisely six o'clock, Max dialed the number. Renee sat close enough that she heard everything.

The person on the other end answered, "Hello?" A woman's voice. So far so good.

"I was given this number to call." Said Max.

"Did that person give you a car?"

"Yes."

"What type?"

"An Audi." A minor identity check.

"I'm glad to see that you are out on your own."

Max said, "Can you tell me why you assisted me with my problem?

"Our organization attempted to find a mutually agreeable solution with our counterparts in US government. But they weren't interested. Due to the nature of the emergency, we took matters into our own hands."

Max pressed the mute button and looked at Renee. "So what does that mean? Counterparts in US government? As in the CIA?"

"That's what it sounds like, yes."

"So she's saying that MI-6 contacted the CIA regarding me, and the CIA wasn't interested in helping me out?"

"I think that's what she's saying."

Max unmuted the phone and said, "What do you mean by 'the nature of the emergency'? What emergency?"

"I can't go into it in too much detail in this format. I'll need you to come meet me."

"Where and when?"

"Key West. Tomorrow evening. Can you make it?"

Max looked at Renee, who shrugged. He said, "I can make it. What are you doing in Key West?"

"Look up Sailing Vessel Bravo. You'll see."

Renee typed a few keystrokes into her web browser. Max could see that *Sailing Vessel Bravo* was the name of a massive sailing yacht owned by a Russian billionaire, Pavel Morozov. Last spotted off Key West, Florida, a few days ago.

Max hit the mute button again as he looked at her screen.

"Morozov," Max whispered.

"You know him?" said Renee.

"I know of him."

"And?"

"Not a nice guy."

He could hear the woman on the phone say, "I need to go."

He unmuted the phone, "Where will I find you?"

"The Southernmost point. Sunset."

Max heard a beep and saw that the call had ended. He looked at Renee.

"Were you able to get anything useful?"

"A little. The transmission definitely came from the Florida Keys—that's where the cellular data was routed through. Other than that, not much."

"Okay. At least we have a lead. Let's find out everything we can about Morozov, and how he might be related to me or my father's company."

* * *

They were both on their computers for the next few hours, researching Pavel Morozov and his crew. While they had found out a lot about him, it had yet to reveal an obvious connection to Max or his father.

Max let out a sigh of frustration. "Anything?"

"Be patient. Your conversation with the MI-6 contact helped me identify potential computers and IP addresses to dig into. I have programs running right now that should give us more information, but it'll take time. When shall we go to Key West?"

"I figured we'd fly there first thing in the morning."

She looked at her watch. "It's getting late."

"I'm going to take a walk on the beach. I need to clear my head."

"Okay. I have my phone if you need anything," said Renee.

Max took his phone and placed it in the pocket of his cargo shorts. He walked barefoot past the small grove of palm trees in his backyard and out along the hard-packed sand beach. He fought the urge to contact his father. Nothing would be stupider, he thought. But he hoped that the old man wasn't taking this too hard.

He walked for a good twenty minutes, the cool saltwater lapping the fine white sand off his feet. A nice breeze blew against his face, a sliver of moon rising over the horizon. He loved coming here. A shame it had to be under these circumstances.

* * *

While Max was gone, several of Renee's sources in the hacker community began to return her messages. They were contractors, mostly. While Renee worked almost solely for nongovernmental organizations these days, she knew people who were plugged in to the state-sponsored cyber-security world. Unlike the way pop culture portrayed the intelligence agencies, the community was not a tight-lipped vault of top-secret information. Private contractors had permeated just about every crevice of the modern intelligence apparatus. One of the results of that trend was that, for a price, Renee's contacts would be able to provide her information on just about anyone or anything.

Her first order of business was to confirm that it was actually MI-6 they were dealing with. Renee's paranoia worried that it could be some elaborate trick, designed to look that way to Max.

So far so good.

Word on the street was that it was indeed an MI-6 team that had been responsible for Max's motorcycle escape out of D.C. No one knew *why* they'd done it, but it was very likely members of that specific British intelligence agency. The team who had executed the operation had gone underground. No one had seen or heard from any of them in the past forty-eight hours. A dead end.

Renee's second order of business was to reach out to someone she knew on the FBI's Cyber Forensics and Training Alliance. She wanted to find out more about what had prompted them to investigate Max in the first place.

Her source was able to provide her with what the FBI knew about the Fend Aerospace network intrusion, and the evidence that linked it to Max.

The hackers had stolen some data on the new Fend 100 aircraft, but they were unable to access the most secure information on the Fend 100's AI program.

The FAA had agreed with Fend Aerospace that there was no safety concern with the aircraft test scheduled for the next week.

Then why so much interest in Max Fend?

Renee's source told her that the FBI had received information from Interpol about Max's ties to Eastern European and Middle Eastern criminal enterprises. While Max's shady dealings might have piqued the FBI's interest, it was his association with a Russian mobster that put Max at the top of the suspect list.

The Russian mafioso was a man by the name of Sergei. Sergei had taken a leap off a building only a few weeks ago. The French government had provided the FBI with Sergei's communications records. They showed that Sergei had been working with a cybercriminal group that was operating out of Syria.

Furthermore, Sergei's communications implicated Max as being complicit in the Fend Aerospace cybertheft. The communications had been sent only hours before Sergei's death in Gibraltar.

But this information had been delivered electronically. Easily faked, Renee thought. The FBI thought that Sergei's death had been ordered by the Syrian hacking group he'd been working with—tying up loose ends and increasing their share of profits.

Renee's work in the cybersecurity world had exposed her to many of these criminal hacker organizations. They were white-collar criminals. Murder usually wasn't part of their skill set. Sergei's death smelled of something different, Renee thought—a ploy.

The FBI's working theory was that Max intended to sell access to Fend technology to the highest bidder. The technology could be worth billions.

Renee wanted to point out the flaws in this theory—namely that Max was the son of Charles Fend, and already filthy rich—but she decided to stop asking questions. While her contact wasn't an agent, and she trusted that he would keep her inquiry confidential, one never knew. Dig too deep, and she might trigger the FBI to look into her.

Lastly, Renee wanted to check up on Max's departure from the DIA. His story didn't quite add up. He seemed happy with his work there. His explanation of how his cover had been blown didn't seem like a fully adequate explanation for why he would have to leave. She would ask him more. But first, she wanted to try and find out what she could on her own.

After a few moments, Renee was conducting an encrypted chat with one of her former counterparts in the Canadian cyberintelligence organization, the CSE. There was a small video window so that she could see her friend as he typed, and her friend could see her. It was a security measure, to make sure that the conversation was actually with the intended person. The CSE folks were just as paranoid as she was. That was where she had learned it. She was surprised at what she read.

Renee: What do you mean?

Anon: It says that Max's cover was blown.

Renee: How?

Anon: Something involving a Russian arms deal. He was supposed to help facilitate the sale of weaponry from a Russian supplier to a buyer in northern Africa. But something went wrong.

Renee: What happened?

Friend: Max ended up killing the Russian arms dealers. The DIA and CIA decided that his cover was blown. There are phone records that indicate the Russians knew he was an American operative.

Renee: How would his cover be blown if both of the Russians were killed?

Anon: Don't know.

Renee: And so the DIA just let him walk away? They don't use him at all anymore?

Anon: Apparently.

Renee: Seems unusual.

Anon: Agreed.

Renee: So who does the intelligence world think is after him? Were you able to find that out?

Anon: There are two theories. One is that it is related to the people that he killed. The Russian group settling old debts.

Renee: And the other?

Anon: The other theory is that Max is dirty. That he might have been turned while in Europe. That would also explain why the DIA wanted him out of their organization, if they suspected that.

Renee: They wouldn't just ask him to leave. They would investigate him, right?

Anon: Maybe they couldn't prove anything, but didn't want to take a chance keeping him.

Renee: So what, then? People think he really gave someone access to his father's company? Why? Money? He's as rich as a Saudi prince.

Anon: No idea. Don't shoot the messenger.

Renee: Okay, thanks.

Anon: Renee, be careful. I don't know what's going on, but if this Max Fend guy is wanted by this Russian mercenary group, he probably isn't a good person to be around.

Renee: Understood. Send me what you can on the Russians.

Anon: Will do. And I don't have to tell you that if theory #2 is true— you better watch your back.

Renee: Thanks, goodnight.

Renee closed the chat window and made sure to delete the conversation history. She leaned back on the couch. The lights were off in the living room of the beach house. The dim computer screen illuminated her face. She looked out at the dark beach. She could hear the waves. Max was walking out there somewhere. Was it really just to clear his head? Or was he calling someone else?

She shook her head. She had known him for a long time. Before he had gotten involved in the espionage world. He was a good man. Right?

* * *

Max came back in, wiping the dry sand off his feet. The screen door shut with a snap behind him. "Anything new?"

"I just reached out to a few people. That MI-6 team has gone underground."

"Okay. Well, we don't need them anymore anyway. We know we have to go to Key West."

"I also looked into the evidence the FBI has on you."

"And?"

"A lot of it's circumstantial. But there's an Interpol report that ties you to several organized crime syndicates in Europe and the Middle East." She filled him in on what she knew.

"Sergei? That little Russian bastard? He was nothing. Just a regional... and he's dead?"

Renee nodded. "Any idea what information he might have had that led to you?"

Max's eyes darted from side to side as he thought. "He was plugged in to the type of people who make money off ransomware. But it was petty stuff. They would lock up a thousand people's computers and make them each pay like three hundred bucks to get back their files. It was a volume game. You must know more about that stuff than I do."

Renee nodded. "That's what most of the small-time groups do. High-volume, low-dollar ransoms. The bigger fish go for corporations and can ask for millions of dollars. But those targets are harder to hit. And the penalties are worse if you're caught."

"You think Sergei thought I might be a good target?"

"Either he or someone he was connected with. It makes sense."

"Looks like my past is coming back to haunt me. Nothing I can do about that now, I guess."

"Were those connections related to the work you did for the DIA?"

"Of course." Max frowned. "Why else would I have associated with those types?" He walked into the kitchen. "I'm going to make something to eat. You hungry?"

"A little."

Max dug around the freezer. A few minutes later, he walked back into the living room with paper plates of steaming microwaved pizza.

"Anything else?"

"Are you really going to keep asking me that every few minutes?"

He put a plate of pizza in front of her. "Sorry. Just anxious."

She blew on it and took a small bite. "It's okay. Here's what I'm doing right now. Some of the software programs I've been running have returned information that I can use. They've identified computers that were in close geographic proximity to the device the MI-6 agent was using to communicate with you. So now I'm sending back pings to those computers, to see if any more information turns up. I have to be honest—I don't think we'll learn anything. But it's worth a shot."

"Yes, it is."

"So how did you start off in the intelligence world? Like…how did they hire you?"

Max chewed his pizza and took a swig of sweet tea. "It started when we were at Princeton. My senior year. That's when they first approached me. I was at a career fair. Looking at sales jobs. I wanted to make money on my own. I've always had an aggressive streak. Not sure if you've noticed."

"Maybe a little."

"So we had quick little interviews at this career fair. You probably went to some of them, at those big conference hotels near town. They conducted separate interviews in each of the hotel rooms, all going on at the same time. At least a hundred other students came. I thought I was interviewing for a financial sales job. I'd been through two of those interviews already that day. But my interviewer wasn't part of a financial sales firm. He was a DIA recruiter. It took me a while to figure that out, though."

She nodded.

"So he asks me a series of questions. Everything's normal. They were all behavioral questions. Tell me about how you would respond in this situation. Tell me about a time you led a team. That sort of thing."

"Then what?"

"Then he asks me about my mother's death. She died in a car accident when I was just a child. But I hadn't told him that."

"He asked about that?"

"Yeah. I mean, you know I was very young when it happened. I didn't really know her. But still, it was unexpected."

"So because the interviewer brought up your mother—you knew that they knew more about you than normal."

"Yes. At first, I assumed they must know about it because they knew about my father. I wasn't famous at the time." He winked. "That came later."

Renee rolled her eyes. "I think you have a complex."

"Yes, I'm quite complex."

"You misunderstand."

"You're French Canadian," Max said, "it's probably getting lost in translation."

"I speak better English than you."

"That's up for debate."

She pouted.

He grew more serious. "Anyway, my father was famous then. Still, it wasn't common knowledge—my mother's death. So when the interviewer asked about her, it caught me off guard. But more than that, it was the question itself that was strange."

"What did he ask you?"

"He asked me—hypothetically, if I found out that a criminal had been responsible for my mother's death, would I be comfortable killing that person, if I knew that I wouldn't be caught?"

"What did you say?"

"I didn't hesitate," Max said. "I said yes."

"Interesting interview."

"Then he said, what if there was a job where you could save people's lives by fighting the worst types of people in the world—would I be interested?"

"And you said yes."

"I did. Then he asked if I would be able to keep secrets, and lie, and commit acts of espionage, and things like that. Obviously, I kept giving him the answers he wanted."

"The interviewer asked you if you would be able to commit acts of espionage?"

"What? Oh. Hmm. Yes, that is a little too obvious for a first interview, isn't it? My memory fails me. Somewhere in the series of interviews they threw that one in. I had to go through several interviews. But really, once I figured out it was them, I was in. They had just released a Jason Bourne movie in the theaters. And I didn't want to go into the real world."

"Peter Pan syndrome?"

"Maybe."

"That was around the time that we broke up."

Max looked back at her, a flash of guilt on his face. "Renee..."

A beeping sound emanated from her computer. Renee sat up, looking at the screen. A frightened look crossed her face. "Shit."

She began typing.

"What is it?" Max asked.

She hit a series of keys and then powered down her computer. "Dammit. Shit. Shit. Shit." She punched a pillow on the couch.

"What?"

Renee looked at him. "Give me your phone."

Max narrowed his eyes. "What is wrong?"

Renee was looking around the room. "I think we should leave."

"What? Don't be silly."

"I mean it, Max. I think we should go. First give me your phone."

Max sat up straight. He handed his phone to her. "Renee, how worried should I be right now?"

Renee hooked his phone up to her computer. "I have a program on my computer that alerts me when someone is—well, the best way to describe it is when someone is 'looking' at me. And someone was definitely checking me out. They know where I am. They know where *we* are."

"How?"

She was typing. "Shit. They accessed your phone. When we made the call, they were able to use its GPS signal somehow. Max, I'm sorry. I was careful. I don't understand how they were able to do this..."

"*Who* knows where we are?"

"I'm not sure, but I think..."

"Renee, *who*?"

"I'm assuming the people who wanted to set you up. Someone used your call to the MI-6 agent to track us down."

"How is that possible?"

"The techniques they used were very sophisticated. I'm sorry. I wasn't expecting it."

Max said, "Okay. Well, we're in the middle of nowhere. Your alert just went off, right? It would take a long time for anyone to get here—"

She was shaking her head, frowning. "No."

"What do you mean, no?"

She let out a stream of French profanity. "That was so stupid of me."

"Renee. Calm down. We've got time."

"No. *We don't.* The timestamp was for two hours ago."

"Two hours ago? That's when they first had our location?" Max looked a bit more concerned. "Maybe you're right. Maybe we should leave."

As he spoke, the power in the house went out.

* * *

The four Russians were all former Spetsnaz. Mikhail was the most senior. He wasn't in the same shape he used to be in, but he was still deadly. The others were all younger. Fit, athletic, and capable, these three had been part of the Forty-Fifth Guards Detached Spetsnaz Brigade. Air assault troops.

For the past few years, they had each been working for Morozov. He paid well and always had interesting work.

They'd gotten the call while waiting in their hotel room in Jacksonville. They had located the Fend boy. Morozov expected Fend to show up near his father. He was only an hour or so away from Jacksonville, where Mikhail's team had been waiting.

It took them ten minutes to get to Craig Airport. Morozov's pilot was already in his helicopter, rotors turning.

Once the aircraft took off, the team began putting on their night vision goggles and checking their weapons. Mikhail spoke to the pilot on his headset.

"How long?"

"About thirty-five minutes. I'll put you down on the beach. Send me a message when you are finished and I will pick you up from the same spot."

Mikhail texted Morozov's computer men on the yacht. They were the ones who'd alerted him of the opportunity.

Mikhail texted: *Kill or capture?*

The response was immediate.

Will shut off power when you arrive. Kill any personnel in the house.

* * *

The only lights that had been on were the kitchen overhead and the bathroom light in the master suite. Both lights went out simultaneously. Someone had intentionally cut the power.

Now Max had two choices: hunker down and fight, or try to make it to the vehicle and run. He didn't know where his adversary was coming from. Helicopter noise was coming from the beach. But what if some were arriving by car? What if some were circling around the property? If they were out in front of the house, they might just be waiting for him to walk outside towards his car so they could pick him off.

"How are you with firearms?"

Renee shook her head. "No. Max, I don't want—"

"Follow me." It was dark, but the light from the moon shone in through the windows.

Max took Renee into one of the bedrooms and threw the mattress up. There was a storage chamber underneath, which he opened. It held weapons and tactical gear.

"Oh my God. What, are you prepping for doomsday?"

"I like to be ready. Just in case. Quick, put these in." He took some earplugs and handed them to her.

"Why?"

"Trust me. And take this."

He handed her an MP-5.

"No. Max, I don't like guns."

"Renee, I'm sorry, but we don't have time. Take the gun. There. Now the safety's off. It's in single-shot mode. You just point and shoot. And make sure you aren't pointing it at me."

The Eurocopter hovered just above the beach, and all four Russian mercenaries hopped off. The helicopter took back off and circled overhead.

The Russians had been told that there was likely only one target. He would be well trained. And the fact that the helicopter had just dropped them off meant that he would be expecting them. They sprinted down the beach.

"Here!" Mikhail shouted when his GPS told them that they had reached the right location. He gave a command and they fanned out into a line, about five yards between them. They scanned the backyard of the house and looked for movement in the windows.

"There," one of the Russians said. The man depressed a button attached to his AEK-919K Kashtan submachine gun, emitting a green laser that was visible to all of them through their night vision goggles. It pointed to a room on the northern side of the house.

Two of them approached the back door. Another crept around the side of the house, keeping his Saiga 12-gauge semiautomatic shotgun pointed at the window in question. Mikhail stayed back, on a mound of sand in the backyard, keeping his weapon trained on the house and searching for any sign of the man inside.

There was no movement. No flashlights. No voices. Doubt crept into Mikhail's mind. He didn't like how still it was.

* * *

Max watched the attackers approach from the living room window. He hunched over behind the couch. Renee was on the other side. There were four of them. He could see their silhouettes making their way over the small sandy mound in his backyard, their weapons trained on the house. A laser pointer shot out from one of them, pointing at Max's bedroom.

Max risked a whisper. "Can you take the one on the left?"

"I don't know, Max." Her voice was quivering.

"Relax, Renee," he whispered. "It's going to be okay. Just point and shoot—when I say three, shoot. After that, we go to my car and head for the airport. Understood? Whether we get them all or not, we'll make a run for it. Okay?"

"Understood."

"One...two...three."

He fired two three-round bursts. The rattle of the MP-5s rang out in the night air. Empty shells fell onto the hardwood floor. Bullet holes appeared in the walls. Splinters of wood and chunks of plaster flew through the dark room.

Max watched his two targets drop to the ground. Then he turned towards Renee's side. She was frozen, her finger off the trigger. Damn.

Max took aim at a section of the wall where he thought Renee's target might have been, then he fired at the remaining silhouette that had stayed back near the beach.

He saw the dark figure fall down in the sand, and more bullet holes began to appear on the eastern wall of Max's home—the attacker in the backyard was firing at them.

Max flattened himself on the floor and dragged Renee down with him.

"We need to get out of here."

"I'm sorry," she said, her voice muffled by his earplugs. In the moonlight, he could see her eyes, wide with fear and anguish. Household items exploded around them as an attacker fired into the home.

"Let's go." Max quickly looked back up and fired several more bursts from the MP-5, until his magazine was empty.

"Come on!"

He grabbed Renee's arm and they both ran out to the Toyota in the driveway. Max emptied his magazine and reloaded another. They were both treading backwards, aiming their weapons around the house in case anyone jumped out.

They got in and Max started the vehicle and slammed on the accelerator. They sped off down the road, the sound of a helicopter looming overhead.

* * *

"Who were they?" Renee asked, her voice near hysterical. She was in the passenger seat, looking behind them.

"I don't know. But I heard one of them say something in Russian."

Max turned right and floored it, speeding through the closed gate of the Jekyll Island airport.

"Who would be able to come after us this quickly?"

Max slammed the brakes and the car came to a halt. "I have some ideas. Were you able to bring your laptop?"

"Yes, I got it," Renee said, patting her messenger bag.

They both exited the vehicle and hopped the airport fence. Max looked back in the direction of his house. It was about a mile away now. He could still hear the sound of the helicopter. He couldn't be sure, but he thought it was a little louder now.

"This is our plane. Get in." Max threw the bags and weapons into the back cargo hold and then thought better of it.

"Here." He handed Renee one of the MP-5s and an extra magazine.

She took it with both hands, not asking questions.

Starting up the aircraft went quick, but taxiing seemed painfully slow. When the helicopter buzzed them for the first time, Renee let out a yelp.

This was what Max had been afraid of.

If he got airborne, there was no way a helicopter could keep up with his fixed-wing aircraft. The helicopter would max out around 150 knots. His aircraft would leave it in the dust. But that was only after he took off and climbed out. Right now, he was vulnerable.

It was dark, and they could barely make out the helicopter as it looped around and headed back in their direction. They were still on the taxiway, but there was a lot of flat pavement in front of them.

"Hold on," Max said. "I'm going to try and take off here."

"Are we on the runway yet?" Renee said, looking at him with incredulity.

"No, we're on a taxiway. But I think I can make it. If I take off now, the helicopter might get one more pass in before we take off. Then we'll lose him. If I take the time to taxi all the way down to the runway, he'll be able to keep shooting at us the whole way."

"But?"

"But we might not have enough runway to take off..."

"What did you just say?"

"Never mind. I'll tell you later."

Max pushed the throttle forward and the engine let out a fierce whine. They were both pressed back into their seats as they moved faster along the pavement.

"Here they come again."

Max could see the nose of the helicopter dipping down as it raced towards them from the left side.

He looked at his airspeed indicator. Forty knots. Fifty knots. *Come on...* He could see little yellow bursts of gunfire coming from the helicopter's rear cabin.

A bullet burst a hole in the Plexiglas window on his left-hand side.

"What should I do?" asked Renee.

"Fire back."

Renee took a deep breath. She reached over him and aimed her MP-5 out his window, firing three shots towards the hovering helicopter. The gunfire was very close to Max's face, and he reflexively turned away. He could smell the odor of the spent rounds and felt the shells dropping on his lap.

"*Careful,*" Max yelled, his ears ringing. "That's enough. Just have a seat." Perhaps Renee might be better as an observer.

Renee sat back in her seat as the helicopter sped overhead.

There. Takeoff speed.

Max pulled back on the yoke with his left hand. The airflow through the broken window was intense, but otherwise, there was no sign of damage.

They quickly gained altitude and Max turned south, along the beach. The moonlight illuminated the surf. Renee was still looking behind them. The helicopter lights grew more distant.

"Relax. They won't be able to catch us."

Renee's chest was heaving. "Where to now?"

"Key West."

13

Three Days Before the Fend 100 Flight

Special Agent Jake Flynn arrived at Jekyll Island, Georgia, the next afternoon. The local news reported it as a burglary gone wrong, thanks to the local police. The FBI had a great relationship with local law enforcement around the country.

Many local police had attended the FBI's National Academy in Quantico, Virginia. The National Academy allowed local police to improve their law enforcement standards, knowledge, and training. It also forged strong bonds between the FBI and local police for when cooperation in the field was needed.

And it was needed today.

Flynn had first seen the report of the Jekyll Island incident in a bulletin when he'd logged on to the FBI email system from his hotel in Jacksonville that morning. He hadn't thought much of it at first. Three men, dead. The location was strange, but he figured it was probably drug-related. Some meth deal gone bad.

Then his phone rang.

"Hi, I'm looking for Special Agent Jake Flynn. This is Special Agent Mike Gagliardi. I'm the SAC with ATF down in Brunswick, Georgia."

"Mike, this is Jake Flynn. What can I do for you?"

"You the one looking for this Max Fend guy?"

Flynn sat up in his chair. He wondered how the ATF knew he was looking for Max Fend. But hell, he would take all the help he could get. Any further pretense was pointless.

"Yeah. Why?"

"Well, we're working with local police on this Jekyll Island thing. Have you heard about it yet?"

"I was just reading up on it, actually. It says three dead. That right?"

"Yeah. Forensics is looking at it now, but they were 9mm rounds. They think they were all fired from MP-5s. And the dead guys at the scene were carrying Russian-made weapons. The type that Russian special forces use. We've been running their prints but haven't found anything yet. We're working with Interpol now to see what they have. Looks like a professional hit went wrong."

Flynn was intrigued. "*Really?*"

"Yeah. First time they've ever seen anything like this down around here."

"So what's it got to do with Max Fend?"

"Fend's fingerprints are all over the house. The owner is an LLC. Still tracking down someone to speak with there. Looks like it might have been some sort of safe house. If I had to guess, Max Fend was the one being attacked, and he and at least one other person killed these three guys."

Flynn looked at his watch. "Alright. Let me figure out transportation. I'll be there as soon as I can. Mike, thanks for the heads-up."

"No sweat."

Flynn checked the directions and called his office to let them know where he was headed. A few hours later, he was pulling up to the crime scene.

The Jekyll Island Police Department was more than happy to help them keep the news media and local gawkers at bay. The ATF forensics team had finished their initial evaluation by the time he got there. The Russian hit team had been using AEK-919K Kashtan submachine guns and some type of semiautomatic shotguns. Both weapons were types favored by Spetsnaz commandos and Russian mercenary groups.

"Jake, you'll want to see this."

One of the local FBI agents took him into one of the bedrooms. The mattress had been flipped up. Underneath were opened trunks. One of them was filled with cash. Stacks and stacks of twenties. Most were in US dollars, but there were tens of thousands of dollars' worth of foreign currency as well.

The other trunks were filled with equipment. Guns, mostly. And silencers, ammunition, eavesdropping equipment. Passports, IDs, night vision goggles. Knives, medical equipment, and phones.

"This guy looks like he was ready for something. Either he's dirty, or he's..."

"James Bond?" one of the men offered.

Flynn nodded. "Right. So which is it?"

He decided that he needed to pay another visit to the CIA.

* * *

"Special Agent Flynn, this is Maria Blount, the program manager for the Fend 100 aircraft."

"Yes, of course, Maria. How are you?"

"You asked me to call and update you on the upcoming test flight."

Flynn sat in his hotel room in Georgia. He was going over his notes from the crime scene on Jekyll Island. Not something she needed to hear about. He needed to switch gears.

"One moment, please. Just trying to find my notes."

Jake Flynn kept meticulous notes on his laptop. He usually brought a notepad to interviews and when investigating crime scenes. He would then transcribe it all into a Word file later. That way he could search for keywords and have a more durable record of everything he found.

"Okay. Go ahead."

"We're still on schedule for the Fend 100 flight to proceed in three days' time," Maria said. "We've gone over everything with the FAA approver who's been working with us, and they've signed off. The FAA has no safety concerns about the computer network intrusion that was detected."

Flynn didn't think the FAA was the best one to make that judgment, but he didn't say that to her. He was getting the distinct feeling that there was a lot of push from Washington for this flight to occur.

"Maria, let me ask you a question. What would happen if they were to postpone this flight?"

"Oh my. That would not be good. We've been working on this product launch for some time. Billions of dollars have gone into it. And not just our company. Many of the airlines—our potential customers—are waiting for the Fend 100 system to get approved by the government so they can start making their orders. Like we talked about when you were here, this is a major building block in the future of commercial aviation. A lot of people, and a lot of money, are depending on it."

Flynn frowned. "Okay. But you are feeling good? No safety concerns?"

"If you're asking if I feel pressure to have this flight go on as planned, yes, of course I do. But we would never approve it on our end if we thought it was unsafe."

"That's good to know."

"Will you be coming down for the big day?"

"We'll see. I kind of doubt it. But I wish you the best of luck."

"Thank you, Special Agent Flynn."

They hung up.

The gears in his head were turning.

14

They landed in Key West just after dawn. Both of them were exhausted. He kept his sunglasses and a hat on and tried to keep his face pointed away from anyone who might be watching.

The fuel truck pulled up to their plane. "You guys want fuel?"

Max had Renee do the talking. "Yes, please," she said, "fill it up."

"Okay." The man looked the plane over. "Say, it looks like you guys got a broken window. How'd that happen?"

"Bird strike," Max said.

"Must have been a big bird."

"It was."

Max walked through the FBO lobby and hailed a cab. Renee paid for the aircraft parking fees and asked to see if they had someone who might be able to fix the window while they were in Key West. More funny looks when everything was paid for in cash. But no hassle.

Renee then walked outside and got into the waiting cab. Max stood next to her, his baseball cap pulled down low over his head.

"Where to?" the cabbie asked.

"Know anywhere we can find a rental on short notice?"

"I know a guy, sure."

The "guy" was mopping up the inside of a bar on Duval Street. It was early morning, and the only people outside were the walkers and joggers. Renee negotiated a price, and they were able to rent out a two-bedroom cottage a few blocks away from the center of town.

Max collapsed on the couch shortly after they got in the door. Renee went into one of the bedrooms and did the same. They hadn't slept all night, and the adrenaline had long since worn off. They both slept for several hours.

Max awoke in the late afternoon. He walked through the home and out onto the tiny back deck. The small area was surrounded by green tropical plants. A quaint blue swimming pool. Three wicker deck chairs.

He changed into a pair of running shorts—the most appropriate thing he could find in his bag—and walked out to the private pool area. He placed his phone on the outdoor table and slid into the cool water. He dunked himself, got out, and lay down on one of the deck chairs. He grabbed one of the colorful folded towels that had been laid out by the property manager and used it as a pillow. Max took his phone and started catching up on the day's news.

The incident in Georgia wasn't being reported accurately. The local papers were calling it a burglary. The *Atlanta Journal-Constitution* mentioned something about a possible meth gang. While the news stories didn't give him much information, the pictures did.

Special Agent Flynn, the man who had questioned him in D.C. two days before, was photographed on the scene, wearing a navy-blue FBI raid jacket.

Renee walked out onto the pool deck. "Enjoying the vacation?"

"I hate to waste a chance to relax." He gripped her shoulder. "Are you alright? After last night, I mean?"

She stood close to him. Nodding ever so slightly, she whispered. "Yes. I think so. I've never seen or done anything like that before." He could see how upset she was.

"Like I said, you did well. Thank you. Look, if any of this gets to be too much...I'll understand if you need to stop."

Her expression changed, determination flashing in her eyes. "You need my help."

He nodded.

She sat on the chair next to him and opened up her laptop. Max watched her type for a few moments. He admired her bravery. It couldn't have been easy for her.

After some typing, Renee said, "I just started looking at the tracking data I was able to collect last night. The hackers who located us—when they did that, it allowed me to collect some of their electronic identification info. I know more about them now."

"And who are *they*?"

"I think they're connected to an outfit called Maljab Tactical."

"I know that name." He searched his memory. "How do I know that name?"

"Tell me about the Russians that ended up dead at your home in France," Renee said.

Max looked up at her. "They were part of an arms deal."

"Were they connected to the Russian mobster that got killed in Gibraltar? Sergei?"

"Sergei set up the introduction, but they weren't Russian mafia."

"How were you involved with Sergei?"

"I ran him. He was an informant and an asset. Because of his mafia affiliation, he was well plugged in."

"Did you trust him?"

"I never trust any informant as far as I can throw them. Informants get to where they are by being either too dumb or too morally corrupt to know better."

"So Sergei introduced you to the two Russian arms dealers, and then you killed them? He must have been pissed off at that," said Renee.

"He didn't give a shit. Sergei was paid off. Cash cures all kinds of heartache in that line of work."

"You paid him as a way to say sorry?"

"That's the way things are done. The Russian arms dealers I killed weren't part of his organization, so he didn't care as long as it didn't get him in any trouble. We made sure it didn't point to either of us. Officially, I was out of town."

"When did you kill those two men?"

"The incident happened about a year ago."

"And you were pulled out of France when?"

"Shortly after."

"A year ago."

"Yes."

"So that was the last time you were in touch with Sergei?"

"Yes."

"So then he gets in touch with a hacker group and what...remembers his old rich friend Max?"

"Maybe he saw an article about the Fend 100 and thought of me?"

"Okay, so let's play that out. So they come up with a plan to hack into the Fend Aerospace Company and steal all their data. They might sell it to the competition. They might hold it for ransom and have the company pay them off. That's the way those things normally work. But when you go after big fish like that, a company like Fend Aerospace...they usually can afford to bankroll their own white hat or black hat hackers. People like me. People who can track down and upend the ransomware."

Max rubbed his temples. "So what are you saying?"

"None of this makes sense yet. It doesn't make sense that Sergei would find a hacker group all by himself and come up with this plan. And it also doesn't make sense that they would frame you."

Max said, "Well, we know it isn't Sergei's family mafia business that's after me anyway. They wouldn't have killed him."

"What about the two arms dealers?"

"You think that's what this is about?" Max asked.

"The men who attacked us in Georgia and the arms dealers are both Russian, for starters."

"Yeah, but those two were low-level nothings. The people who just attacked us in Georgia were professionals, Renee."

"Tell me more about how it happened in France," she said again.

Max sat up, eyeing her. "The DIA had me facilitate a meeting between the Russian suppliers and one of our assets in northern Africa. Libya, I believe. I was essentially just a matchmaker. A middleman. I would help connect people who were looking for certain hard-to-get items with the type of people who could procure them."

"And?"

"As you're aware, the rule of law is not quite as strict in different parts of the world. So while most of the matchmaking I did was legit, much of it was not."

"How did you not get in trouble with French authorities?"

"The DIA took care of that. The French government knew enough not to get in my way."

"And these small-time Russian arms suppliers—these were men that the DIA instructed you to set up a deal with?"

Max nodded. "The agent was embedded with a terrorist group in Libya. He needed to prove to his group that he could get them access to arms. We were trying to help him set up that deal."

"Why didn't you go through another channel? Why use this Russian group?"

"Part of my job was to continuously make new contacts. In this case, I was trying to establish a connection with the Russian group. It was two birds with one stone. I figured they'd supply the arms, and the DIA agent in Libya would get what he needed."

"But it didn't work out that way."

"No, it didn't."

"I think I'm starting to see a connection. The hackers that found us in Georgia were part of Maljab Tactical. Maljab Tactical worked all over the Middle East, including Syria. And they specialized in cyber operations, among other things."

Max raised his head. "Very good, Renee."

"Maljab Tactical is the subsidiary of a larger Russian mercenary organization—Bear Security Group. I'm curious if those 'small-time' arms dealers you were with might have been connected to Bear Security Group as well."

"I know Bear Security Group. They're huge. They're the primary Russian mercenary group in Syria and Crimea."

"Right," said Renee.

"So what is Maljab Tactical? Remind me."

"Maljab Tactical is a small subsidiary of Bear Security Group. Do you know who they sell to?"

"Who?"

"To Muslim extremist militias. One of their biggest clients is the Islamic State. Maljab is basically a Russian-owned mercenary group that trains jihadist fighters. It's made up of mostly Uzbek fighters—along with other mercenaries from Muslim-majority Russian Caucasus republics."

"So they're Russian private security consultants who work specifically for jihadists?"

"Pretty much. There's a lot of money flowing into these groups from wealthy radicals in the Middle East. Hiring companies like Maljab Tactical is seen as a great return on investment, rather than just giving the money to the groups directly."

Max said, "Because a professional defense contractor like Maljab makes these groups much more effective."

"Exactly."

Max nodded. "Yes. Now I remember them. Maljab Tactical was in Syria and Iraq. They improved Islamic State's recruiting numbers by managing their social network outreach—they made ads similar to what you would see from a Fortune 500 company. And they improved their combat effectiveness by giving them top-notch weapons training."

Renee said, "And Maljab Tactical is part of Bear Security Group. Bear Security Group is owned by a wealthy Russian named Pavel Morozov. You said you know of him. What do you know?"

Max said, "My work over the past few years has primarily been in Europe and the Middle East. As CEO of Bear Security Group, Morozov is head of one of the largest private armies in the world, and the largest mercenary group in Russia. They do all the Russians' dirty work in places like Syria and Ukraine. I encountered Morozov only once, but it was enough. It was in Syria."

"What happened in Syria?"

"I did some work with a US military task force there. Special Forces types. Whenever we did work in Syria, we had to be careful. We didn't want to get into a shootout with the Russians who were operating there. They were well trained and well armed. And starting a gunfight with them could have led to bigger and worse fighting between Russian and US forces. Oftentimes Bear Security Group was working alongside the Russian military. We had to treat them the same."

"What were you doing there?" Renee said.

"A meeting. Making an introduction between a rebel group and an arms dealer. The US wasn't willing to *officially* sell arms to this group, but we still *wanted* them armed. My man was seen as the workaround. But this Syrian rebel group was unstable. A junior varsity team." Max sighed. "When it happened, we could see a lot of it from the windows."

"When what happened?"

Max nodded. "So one day when I was there, a few local fighters who were in this rebel group—they were nothing more than teenagers—made the mistake of going head to head with the Russians."

Renee raised an eyebrow. "I can't imagine that ended well."

"It didn't. Bear Security Group was there—embedded with the local Russian military unit. They took turns going out with the Syrian military when they did security patrols. Morozov himself was in the country, visiting his operational commanders.

"The teenage fighters from the rebel group took one of the Syrian security patrols hostage. Only three hostages, but they were *soldiers*. Shortly after, a few more of the rebels came in to reinforce the two idiots who started it all. I don't think they really wanted to be there, but it was too late at that point. Two of the hostages were Syrian Army. But *one* of the hostages was one of the Russian mercenaries. *Big mistake.*"

"What did the Russians do?"

"Morozov moved dozens of his men into the area, clearing out all the civilians for blocks around. The Syrian Army showed up and tried to take control, but Morozov told them to piss off. He didn't want anyone to see or interfere with what he was about to do."

"Even the Syrian Army?"

Max took a sip of his water. "Even them. When the rebels saw they were surrounded by well-armed men, they sent out a list of demands. They thought they could negotiate. I don't think they thought they would be dealing with the Russians. They expected Syrian Army or government representatives to come."

"So what happened?"

"Morozov had his men sweep the local area. He got the names of the rebels—the men who'd taken the hostages. Then he had his men find their *families*."

Renee shook her head.

"Morozov instructed his men to begin cutting off limbs of family members and sending them inside to the Syrians."

Renee gasped and placed her hand over her mouth.

"The Syrian rebels started *pleading* to negotiate. Never a good sign. They sent one of the hostages out for nothing in return, hoping it would be a sign of good faith. They told the Russians they would lay down their weapons and release everyone else. They were begging the Russians to let them surrender."

"What did Morozov do?"

"He accepted. Then he waited until they came outside and laid down their arms. I remember seeing the Syrian rebels standing there, unarmed and dumbfounded. Waiting. Morozov stood twenty feet away, flanked by his commandos. Then he walked up to the group of *hostages*—the two Syrians and the one Russian—and executed them. The Syrian rebels just stared at him in disbelief. Morozov shot the *hostages. Including his own man.*"

"What? *Why?*"

"He said it was a message to anyone else who worked for him, never to put themselves in that position of weakness. He then killed all but one remaining family member of each of the Syrian rebels. The rebels were forced to watch. When Morozov was finished, he let the rebels leave, unharmed. He told them that if they ever did anything like this again, he would finish the job and kill the remaining relative. I heard from someone else once that leaving a single family member alive was a sort of calling card. He believed it was the great deterrent. Anyone thinking of seeking revenge on him would just have to look at their one living family member, and they would stand down."

"He is...*evil*."

"Yes, Renee. He is."

* * *

Max got up and sat at the edge of the pool, dipping his feet in. "Okay. Thinking out loud here. Walk me through this. So far, you've linked the cyber group that located us in Georgia to Maljab Tactical."

"I believe so, yes."

"And Maljab Tactical is a subdivision of Bear Security Group."

"Right."

"Bear Security Group is the big one. Pavel Morozov's outfit. The largest Russian mercenary organization, filled with Russian ex-military special forces types."

"That's correct."

"And we just got attacked by guys who fit that description. Russian ex-military."

"Yes."

"And you think these people are related to that small-time outfit that tried to kill me in France? The two men."

"All I have to go on is that they're Russian, they're dirty, and they tried to kill you—but I'm picking up a definite theme here. Are you?"

"Bear with me," Max said. "Sometimes I need to be hit on the head by a hammer to see it. This is all helpful, Renee, but it doesn't answer a key question—*why*?"

"Why are there Russians trying to kill you, or why did they try to set you up for sabotaging your father's company?" Renee asked. "Because assuming that we are talking about the same entity, they seem to have changed strategies. They don't seem to want you alive anymore."

"I guess I need both questions answered, really."

"Let's start with you telling me why two Russian men tried to kill you in France."

Max looked up, remembering. "There were a group of people over that night. Lots of booze. Several dozen of my clients. The Russians were invited. It was my second meeting with them, and I wasn't sure what to expect. And...well, let's just say we had a disagreement about how to treat a lady."

"What do you mean?" Renee said.

"There was a young French woman there at my place that night. Early twenties. Blond hair. Beautiful figure."

Renee raised an eyebrow. "Was that description necessary?"

"What? She *was* beautiful. Great birthing hips. You know how I love those. There's nothing wrong with me pointing that out."

"I see your sense of humor still has poor timing."

"Don't ruin the story, Renee. Anyway, the two Russians were there and the girl brought a few friends. But the Russians were just getting way too drunk and obnoxious. Major buzzkill. So the girl's friends decided to leave. She stayed because she was interested in me, I believe."

"Of course."

"What? I can't help it. My good looks are both a gift and a curse."

"Please just continue."

"So I was hoping to get what I needed from the Russians and send them on their way. I went into another room to make a phone call—working on another deal. The girl was pretty drunk. She was alone with the Russians only for a moment. They were trying to get her into one of the bedrooms. She said no. I heard the commotion and got off my call. I told them to leave. They didn't. One of them grabbed the girl and started dragging her into the bedroom screaming, and the other Russian just stood there smiling, typing on his phone."

"Typing on his phone?"

"Yes. In the after-action report, the DIA showed me an intercept from their phone records. The guy had sent a message to someone. We never found out who, but I assume it was his boss."

"What did it say?"

"It said something about me being an American agent."

"And then you killed them?" Renee said.

"Well, I tried to work it out peacefully, but they left me no choice."

"And so that's how your cover was blown? You stood up to them when they attacked the French girl? And from that, they knew you were an agent?"

"It seemed like they were testing me. I think they wanted to see what kind of things I would let slide. Hell of a litmus test."

Renee shook her head. "You think Morozov sent those two?"

"Why? That was a year ago. Why send them to blow my cover back then, and then kill Sergei only a few weeks ago?"

"I'm not sure. There's still something missing here."

Max stood. "Well, you keep digging. That's what I'm paying you for. In the meantime, I've got a hot date with an MI-6 agent. Maybe she'll be able to help."

Max threw on a navy-blue polo shirt and khaki shorts and began walking down Duval Street. He stayed on the side streets mostly, trying to keep as low a profile as possible.

The sun was low in the sky, and the Key West shops were lit up with bright lights. The surface of the road was wet from a recent rain. Lush green trees overhung many of the stores and restaurants. Happy tourists, many of them liquored up from their rum-based drinks, walked along the street. Live music blared out of many of the bars.

Max walked down the full length of Duval Street and finally arrived at a waterfront bar and restaurant with outdoor seating. Orange barstools. A mix of patrons wearing bathing suits and floral shirts. Street entertainers in the courtyard, one playing guitar quite well. Two others walked along on stilts, juggling. Max found himself thinking this would be a fun place to retire to.

He sat down at a table in the corner, out of view of most people. He had a few minutes to kill before the meeting time.

"What'll you have?"

Max looked up to see a skinny waitress holding a pen and paper.

"Hmm." He searched the table for a drink menu. "To be honest, I haven't had a chance to look at—"

"He'll have a mojito. So will I."

A tanned woman stood over him. She wore Ray-Ban sunglasses and a tube top covered with tropical flowers.

"I guess I will," Max told the waitress, who went off to fetch their drinks. He stuck out his hand. "My name's Max."

She shook his hand. "Don't be silly, dear. We know each other." Wide smile as she leaned in and kissed him on the cheek.

She sat down, crossing her legs. Max noticed that her tight black skirt revealed quite a lot of skin. He decided he didn't mind that one bit.

"Of course we do. Remind me of your name?"

"Charlotte Capri." She had an accent. British, he thought. So far so good.

"It's a pleasure to see you again, Miss Capri."

She didn't reply. Just kept giving him that bright smile. He disliked not being able to see her eyes behind the sunglasses. Max found her rather striking. Full lips. Smooth and tanned skin.

The drinks came quick. Tall glasses. Crushed ice and mint. Limes, rum and sugar. Hard to beat. Max took a sip and found it deliciously refreshing.

Max held up his glass and toasted with his guest. "So I take it I don't need to meet you at our location anymore? Where was it again?" He wanted to hear her say it.

She said, "The southernmost point? No. This will be fine."

"So what can I do for you?"

"Actually, I think it is I who might be able to do something for you."

"And what might that be?"

She leaned forward in her seat, pulling down the sunglasses, and Max saw that her eyes were not playful and flirtatious the way her voice sounded.

She leaned in and whispered in his ear. "I know about the cyber intrusion on your father's company—the one that the FBI has been investigating. Someone hacked into the Fend 100 program. *And they're going to do it again.*"

Max put his drink down.

"What do you mean, they're going to do it again?"

"We need to go somewhere more private. Somewhere we can talk. We're too out in the open here."

Max fought the urge to look around. Tourists were everywhere, enjoying the ocean view. The pink-and-orange sky—the perfect sunset of Key West—mesmerized most of the crowd.

"Alright. Let's go." Max stood, took another sip of his mojito and then signaled the waitress to come get the check.

She took his hand. "Come on, follow me."

They walked through the crowded street and then stepped into a dive bar. A man onstage wearing a cowboy hat played guitar and sang into a silver microphone. The woman kept gripping Max's hand as they weaved through the throngs of dancers.

They stopped in the corner of the bar. It was so loud he could barely hear her. But she pressed in close to him, speaking into his ear. "We'll just stay here and pretend we're dancing. The noise will make it impossible for any listening devices to work. I can't be completely sure that one of us wasn't followed. So we need to take precautions."

The crowd around them screamed as the guitar player switched to his next 1980s rock ballad.

Charlotte Capri swayed to the music, playing the part. "I know who you are, Max Fend," she said. "And I know who you've worked for in the past." She brought her head back a bit, locking eyes with him.

"Alright," he said. "So who are you really? And how do you know about the cyberattack on my father's company?"

"You can call me Charlotte, just like I told you. I suspect you already know who I work for." She gazed into his eyes.

"For queen and country?"

"Indeed."

"They have me working for a Russian businessman right now. His name is Pavel Morozov. Have you heard of him?"

"I have. So what are you doing for Morozov? What's your cover?"

"I'm an executive assistant." She smiled.

"Like a secretary?"

"Sort of, yes. He's on a working vacation. Morozov sent his yacht so he could stay on board while he was here. He's going to do a month-long tour of Florida and the Caribbean, meeting with investors and business partners along the way. I'm helping to manage things for him."

"What does he have to do with my father's company?"

"A few months ago, a member of the Russian mafia named Sergei began fishing for a buyer. He was selling access to Fend Aerospace's corporate data center. Word on the street is that you knew Sergei."

"We were professional acquaintances."

"Morozov got word of this plan. But he knew that Sergei had worked with the Americans before, and he didn't trust him as a partner."

"Morozov was right. Sergei would have sold him out if it suited him. So Morozov stole Sergei's idea?"

"More or less. Morozov went and commissioned his own hackers. Their objective was to steal the most valuable technology your father's company owns—the artificial intelligence software for the Fend 100 aircraft."

"I'm told that they failed."

"That's right. They were able to steal some of the aircraft blueprints but couldn't get into the hardened servers located in the Fend 100 control center—the ones that housed the AI program."

"You said that they were going to try again. What's changed? Why would it work the second time around?"

She looked worried. "There's a vulnerability window. When the Fend 100 is flying, it uses an encrypted datalink that sends information back and forth between it and the Fend 100 control center. This sort of opens up the firewalls for the Fend 100. We think that the first cyberattack planted a virus that will allow Morozov's hackers to take advantage of this vulnerability window."

"How?"

"I don't know. We're still trying to find out. But the point is that there will likely be another attempt to steal the Fend 100 AI data—during the big demonstration flight they're having in a few days."

"Why is MI-6 so interested in this?"

She shrugged. "Morozov is wrapped up in a lot of bad things. This is just one of them. It's possible that he intends to do the same thing as Sergei—sell the information or hold it for ransom. That's standard operating procedure for these cybercriminals. But there is a darker scenario— there are many people who are very concerned about what one would be able to do with the technology."

"What does that mean? What could he use it for?"

"Your father's company has big defense contracts for drones. The AI software he's developed doesn't just have commercial implications. Imagine how AI learning machines could improve the effectiveness of combat drones. The AI software could turn them into a robot air force, thinking and learning on their own—dominating the battlespace."

Now Max understood why someone like Morozov might be interested. His expertise in the defense sector, and his connections at the highest levels of the Russian government, would make this a valuable steal.

"You said Morozov was going to hack into my father's plane again. When?"

"In a few days. Fend Aerospace has their final approval test flight with the FAA. It will have people on board this time. Mostly reporters and company executives. The FAA has already declared it safe. Now they want to observe it with passengers aboard. We think he'll try to hack into the network during that flight—during the vulnerability window."

"None of this explains why I was set up. What's all this got to do with me?"

"We think Morozov knows about your background in Europe—you had a lot of connections there to unsavory characters. And he needs someone to divert the FBI's attention—an inside man at Fend Aerospace. If they're off worrying about you, then that's taking eyeballs away from him."

Max had an idea about that. Renee's theory was holding water. "So he just wants to hang this on me because he thinks I make a good scapegoat? That still doesn't explain it."

"There is one more thing. I'm not a hundred percent sure, but I think that Pavel Morozov really does have someone working on the inside at Fend Aerospace."

Max couldn't stop his jaw from momentarily dropping. "Who?"

"I don't know."

"What do you know? Why would you say that?"

"That's what MI-6 thinks. The cyber experts there think it seems logical. They think that someone with inside knowledge and access to the Fend Aerospace network would be needed to pull it all off. That's how they were able to frame you. And that's how they know so much about the Fend network."

"Has Morozov or his team mentioned anything about someone on the inside of Fend Aerospace?"

She shook her head. "No. It's an MI-6 theory that they want me to look into. Morozov runs a very tight unit. They're some of the best-trained operatives in the world. Many of them are former FSB. His security team is all former Spetsnaz."

"I met some of them recently," Max said. "Nice guys."

She swayed to the music like she was just a regular tourist, here to dance. "That was quite an escape," she whispered into his ear. "He was very upset about that." A smile. She really was attractive.

Max could feel her body pressing up against him. He smelled her perfume, too. It smelled good.

"So one minute he's trying to set me up to take the fall for my father's company sabotage. Then he's trying to kill me. Why? Why not just kill me in the first place?"

"We think that at first, he needed you to take the fall. But now that the FBI has taken the bait, he doesn't need you alive anymore."

"Isn't he worried about this all leading back to him?"

"It won't." She seemed very sure of herself.

Max thought about telling her that Renee had already traced it back to one of his subsidiaries, but he didn't want to give her more information than he needed to. Not yet.

"In a few days, he'll be taking his yacht to Jacksonville," Charlotte said.

"Jacksonville? Where Fend Aerospace headquarters is located?"

"Yes."

"Why in God's name would he do that?"

"I think he wants to be there when it happens."

Max shook his head. "I need to warn my father. He needs to cancel the Fend 100 flight."

"Absolutely not."

"What? Why?"

"We went out on a limb and freed you, Max. We gave you a second chance for a reason. We have a plan. Now hear me out."

He folded his arms. "What do you want me to do?"

"They've planted a computer virus in the Fend network. One that will allow them to steal the Fend 100's AI data during the flight next week. But you can stop it, Max."

"How?"

"MI-6 is working on a fix. It would be another software program—one that would serve as a sort of antidote to the virus they put in there. This would make sure that they couldn't hack into the aircraft."

"So why do you need me?" Max said. "Why not just contact the CIA?"

"We've tried working with the CIA on this, but they aren't seeing things our way. They preferred to wait. We wanted to move. They weren't sure what to do about you. We decided that the best option was to break you out of custody in D.C. and get you to help us out."

"Why?"

"You hold your father's confidence, Max. He'll listen to you. You can't let him cancel the flight—this cyber antidote is the best way."

"What will it do?"

"It will allow British intelligence—and the US, when they get on board—to turn the tables on Morozov's hackers. It will make sure that they can't steal the AI data. And it will give us the incriminating evidence we need to bag Morozov."

Max was taken aback. Was she saying that the CIA and MI-6 wanted to let Morozov conduct another cyberattack on his father's company?

"Who are you working with at the CIA?"

"Caleb Wilkes."

"Wilkes?" Max knew the name. Not well, but well enough. Wilkes was CIA counterintelligence. He was a very shadowy figure—even for Langley.

"He's the one who's going after Morozov," Charlotte said. "He intends to take him down or turn him. He's fishing. And trying to let out enough line that Morozov doesn't break the hook."

"Is Wilkes on board with this plan?"

"We're working on it."

"What's the problem?"

"I don't know why Wilkes doesn't see it our way. So far we haven't been able to convince him to take an alternate path. But now we have you involved. I'll give you a thumb drive with the cyber antidote to plug into the Fend 100 control center. Can you do that?"

Max thought about it. "Yes. I think so. Do you have the thumb drive now?"

"I won't be able to give it to you until the night before. They're still working on the software program. You'll have to meet me in Jacksonville."

"Okay."

"I need to go."

"How will I hear from you?"

She reached up and gripped the back of his neck, leaning in like she was going to kiss him on the cheek. Her lips hovered over his ear. "The night before the test flight—I'll call you and tell you where to meet me. Give me your number."

She held out her phone and he typed a number in.

She looked into his eyes. "It will be alright, Max." Then she softly kissed him on the cheek, turned, and disappeared into the crowd.

* * *

Pavel Morozov watched the speedboat approach from the second deck of his yacht, which was anchored several miles north of Key West.

His security man looked at Pavel, and then at the girl. Pavel gripped her ponytail with his strong right hand, pulling back so that her head was arched over the rail of the vessel. The drop was a good forty feet to the warm water below.

The girl had been pretty, before his knuckles and ring had gone to work on her face. Her eye was swollen. Blood dripped down from her nose and lip.

The security man nodded toward her. "Would you like me to finish her?"

Pavel shook his head slowly. "No. Please just send up our new arrival."

The woman who had just arrived on the speedboat came up a minute later. Pavel looked her up and down. "Ah, hello, Miss Capri."

Charlotte regarded him, her eyes glancing at the scared and bloodied woman that Morozov was holding by the ponytail.

"Good evening, Mr. Morozov."

"Did you have a good time tonight?"

"I did."

Pavel looked back at the girl by his side. The position of her body looked painful, but she didn't cry. She didn't beg. Her eyes were afraid, but her voice was silent.

Morozov stared at her. "I intend to drop you into the sea. But before I do that, is there anything else you care to tell us? If it is helpful to me, perhaps I will change my mind about your fate."

Still the woman didn't say a word. She just sniffled quietly.

With his left hand, Morozov removed a small black object from his pocket. He kept holding the girl back with his right hand. With his teeth, he carefully pulled open the folding blade of the knife.

The girl he was holding began struggling to free herself from his grasp, her eyes widening at the sight of the blade.

"Do you want to do it?" Pavel asked Charlotte.

She let out a sound of disgust and walked away.

Morozov smiled. He turned back to the girl and shoved the knife into her back several times, careful that he punctured her lungs. He then flipped her over the rail and off the yacht. Her legs had been tied together, with weights attached to them. That would send her down to the bottom.

Her body made a big splash, but it was dark. Morozov couldn't see her after she sank below the surface. But he felt good, wiping his bloody hands on a towel. It was always satisfying to remove a bad employee from his organization.

15

When Max returned to the cottage, Renee was still out back, sitting by the pool, her computer in her lap. She looked relieved when she saw it was him.

"Worried?" Max said.

"A little."

"Good. That's healthy. You were right about Bear Security Group. Pavel Morozov is involved." Max filled Renee in on who he'd met and what he had learned.

"Do you trust this woman? The MI-6 agent?"

"They freed me from the clutches of the FBI."

"You don't think a good lawyer could have done that?"

"Depends what the FBI has on me."

"But you're innocent."

Max waved off the comment. "If what Charlotte said is right, the CIA is intentionally allowing Morozov's cronies to hack into my father's network. Someone in our government has an agenda."

Renee looked up from her computer. "Do you believe that?"

"I don't know. It sounds reckless. There must be another side to the story."

"I wonder if there's a way we could find out who at Fend Aerospace might be working for Morozov."

Max looked up. "That would be a big help. Do you think you could do that?"

Renee was looking at her computer again. She whistled.

"What is it?"

"I'm taking another look at Morozov's boat. It's really something." She turned the computer so he could see.

"That's Morozov's?"

It wasn't a normal yacht. The ship was a massive gray vessel that looked like a futuristic version of a sailboat. Giant metal masts rose up two hundred feet above the deck. Narrow tinted portholes lined the sleek hull. There was a helipad. Multiple spots for small motorboats to pull up. Wooden sundecks. Indoor and outdoor pools.

"It's incredible."

"It says here that it's one of the most expensive ever built."

"How much?"

"Nearly half a billion dollars."

Max looked up at the sky. "Hmm. I'll think about it."

"About what?"

"Getting one. I'm sure that would help with my playboy reputation."

"Right," Renee said. "It arrived in Key West just two days ago." She looked up. "So they were here at the same time that hackers from this region located us in Georgia."

"You think that they did it from the yacht?"

"I don't know. This yachting website says Morozov is taking it around the Caribbean and Florida for the next month."

"Why?"

Renee typed some more. "Because when you're rich," she said, "you can do whatever the hell you want. You know that." She smiled at him.

"Easy, now."

"It appears as though he's throwing a party on the yacht tomorrow night."

"Oh, really?" Max was interested. "I wonder why I wasn't invited."

"A lot of big investors are showing up. You know, Max, if I can access the computer network on that yacht, that might be an opportunity to—"

"No," Max interrupted, a stern look on his face. "That would be a terrible idea."

"You wouldn't have to go, of course. They would recognize you. But they don't know me."

"That's an even worse idea."

Renee looked hurt. "I may not be an expert at fieldwork like you, but I was a trained member of the CSE."

"What did they train you in, how to avoid paper cuts before you sat down in front of your computer terminal?"

She frowned. "We didn't use paper. Security protocol."

"Renee, dear, now I haven't been to a good yacht party for the ungodly rich in months—and that is a long time for me—but if I walk onto that yacht, I would get shot in about ten seconds. And you..."

She crossed her arms.

"Renee, the truth is, I feel guilty for dragging you into this in the first place. You could have been killed in Georgia. I won't place you in harm's way like that again."

She saw the look on his face and knew she wasn't going to convince him right now. "Well, I'd at least like to get a better look at this thing. Maybe we can just go check out the yacht from a distance?"

"That's a more reasonable idea." Max took off his sandals and placed his bare feet in the cool pool water. "You know, Renee, I think it's time I treated you to a nice trip on the water."

* * *

Two Days Before the Fend 100 Flight

Max and Renee snapped the buckles of their life vests. The sound of seagulls overhead mixed with the clangs of the sailboats floating in their slips. Deep-sea fishing boats motoring out into the Caribbean. The smell of salt in the air. Max loved the sea.

"You guys want to rent one or two?" said the freckle-faced kid working the counter of the Jet Ski rental shop.

"One should be fine," Max said.

Renee said, "Two."

The kid looked back and forth between them.

Renee whispered, "I'm not going to be one of your pretty girls, hugging you and hanging on."

"Don't say that. You look great in your bikini."

She frowned.

Max turned to the boy behind the counter. "Two Jet Skis will be fine, my friend."

A few minutes later, they were headed out of the small harbor, their engines barely above idle. Renee was the first to pass the buoy, which signaled the end of the no-wake zone. She immediately gunned the throttle, and a spray of white seawater shot up from behind her. She looked back at Max, smiling as she left him behind. A second later, he accelerated and felt his body sliding back as he neared fifty miles per hour.

The wind and seas were calm. Uninhibited by a rough ocean, the Jet Skis skimmed above the water at a very high speed. Riding them was pure fun.

Max reminded himself to do this again soon. They zoomed in between Sunset Key and Wisteria Island, turning right, towards Fleming Key. From there, they headed towards a group of tiny islands about two miles to the north, a large sandbar interwoven between them.

They arrived at Cayo Agua. The small island was barely more than a few hundred yards around, carved apart by multiple turquoise seawater streams. Both Renee and Max slowed their Jet Skis and headed into one of the inlets. The water below was crystal clear, and Max saw flashes of color darting underneath him. Tropical fish, not used to being disturbed here. As they slowly motored along the stream, they were surrounded closely on either side by tropical plants and trees. Banana trees. Mahogany trees. Coconut palms. A scattering of bright pink orchids. It was at once quiet and beautiful.

Renee turned her Jet Ski towards a sandy bank. About fifty feet further ahead, the stream opened back up into the ocean on the other side of the island. They didn't want to come out that far.

Max and Renee pushed their Jet Skis up onto the bank, beaching them. They removed their vests, hanging them on the handlebars, and waded the rest of the way through the stream, soft sand under their feet.

Max couldn't help but noticing that he was right about Renee in her bikini. She kept in good shape, and the years had been kind.

"There it is," Renee said.

She had lowered herself into the deep middle section of the stream and peeked out around the corner where it emptied into the ocean. About half a mile to the north, just past the sandbar, Max could see Pavel Morozov's yacht.

"Wow. That is an incredible piece of work."

He took the pair of waterproof binoculars from around his neck and scanned the vessel. It was even more impressive in person. Sleek and aerodynamic, it looked more like a modern warship than a private yacht —although the three tall metallic masts made it more like a work of art than a warship.

On the upper aft deck, he could see private security. Big, thick men wearing black vests over white tee shirts. Each wore wraparound sunglasses. Each looked to have a holstered weapon at his waist. Max counted five of them that he could see. Probably three less than there were a few days ago.

On the two decks below that, there were sets of scantily clad women. Some were rubbing oil on each other's backs, bathing in the sun. Others carried tall glasses of champagne. And there in the middle of it all was the man of the hour.

Pavel Morozov.

He was speaking with someone. A woman. Her back was to Max. She wore a long, flowing skirt and a bathing suit top. Max wished he had a long-range microphone, because he knew who it was.

"That's her," Max said.

"Who? The MI-6 agent?"

"Yes. Wish we knew what they were discussing. Hmm."

"What is it?"

"I see something that wasn't in the picture of the yacht," Max said. "There are antennae on the fore and aft of the ship. They look like big orbs. Do you see them?"

"Yes, I think so."

"Those look very similar to the datalink antennae on a Navy warship."

"How do you know that?"

"DIA, remember?"

"So why is that significant? The antennae."

"Because Charlotte told me that the Fend 100 was vulnerable through its encrypted datalink. I wonder if those antennae are how they'll hack in to the Fend network this time."

"But it's encrypted. They'd need some type of passcode to get in."

"If Morozov has someone working for Fend Aerospace, they could help them with that."

"If we could get aboard that boat, I might be able to answer some of these questions, Max."

"Renee. No. You see the security guards. They missed us in Georgia. It would be stupid to hand ourselves over to them now."

"But they're throwing a party tonight."

"So?"

"So it'll be somewhat public, right?"

"No. A private party. The *opposite* of public."

"You know what I mean. What if I placed myself on the guest list and snuck on? I would only need a half hour. I could go as a maid."

Max shook his head. "This isn't the movies, Renee. Don't put yourself in a position of weakness. If they get their hands on you—"

"I can handle it, Max."

"I saw you *handle* it in Georgia."

She reddened. "I said I was sorry about that."

Max sighed. "I didn't mean that the way it sounded. It's just that I don't want to risk *you*."

"Max, if I can gain access to the computer network on that boat—"

"I said no. It's not worth it. We'll leave tomorrow and fly to Jacksonville. Then I'll get in touch with my father and use Charlotte's thumb drive to disarm Morozov's virus."

Renee scrunched her lips together. She didn't like it.

"Come on. Let's go back to the Jet Skis and head back. I'll give you cash and let you go shopping. Girls like shopping, right? We need food and clothes. I'll give you a grocery list and then I'll cook you up the most delicious French cuisine you've ever had."

"I'm not sure whether to respond to the good or the bad part of that."

"Always look on the bright side of things, Renee."

She rolled her eyes.

* * *

Pavel Morozov had two qualities that had helped him to attain his level of wealth: cunning and ruthlessness. These qualities had served him well prior to the fall of the Berlin Wall. His rise through the ranks of the KGB had been swift. But one could only go so far in the Soviet Union. The idiocy of the Communist bureaucracy meant that natural talent had its limits. Politics and ideology always got in the way.

But not anymore. The fall of the USSR had been a godsend to men like him. Men who didn't have any scruples about getting their hands dirty. Men who projected strength. Once the politicians were no longer in charge, there was a huge power vacuum. Former KGB members were only too happy to fill the void.

Pavel found that he was quite a talented businessman. There were so many similarities to his work in the KGB. You always had to be one step ahead of the competition. Deception and innovation ruled the day. To Pavel, business was just a new way of playing the same old game.

After the collapse of the USSR, the Red Army had an enormous inventory of weaponry, and very little need for it. The Cold War was over. Where there was confusion, there was great opportunity, Pavel knew.

The first time he walked into a former Soviet weapons cache and demanded to see the commanding officer, he expected to get pushback. But Pavel was surprised to find out that the same methods of influence and persuasion he had used in the KGB worked just as effectively in his new field.

Arms dealer. The bottom rung of the long ladder he would climb.

There were national armies around the world that would pay top dollar for Russia's unused weapons. The Russian military men who oversaw the weapons didn't care where they went. Those men just didn't want to get in trouble. Don't rock the boat. That way of thinking had served them well in the Soviet era. But in the post-Soviet world, there were so many possibilities. The Russian military men were happy to accept cash and black market items in exchange for misplacing crates of weapons.

The first man to question Morozov got shot on the spot. The second man suddenly had no questions.

The money started rolling in after that. Pavel Morozov sold Russian weapons to whoever wanted them, all around the world. If you were looking for an AK-47, go somewhere else. But if you were looking for ten thousand of them—Pavel was your man. Need a tank? How about twenty? The first pallet of shells would be free.

But others were in on the game as well. The mid-90s—that was when the Russian and Ukrainian mob had gotten their legs under them. They were also staffed with former KGB, GRU, and Red Army veterans. The imbalance of supply and demand quickly sorted itself out. Competition got stiff.

Pavel Morozov had made his first pile of cash. It was time for him to think bigger. He began investing. Putting money into companies and nation-states that couldn't get loans from anywhere else. Iran. Iraq. North Korea. African militias. Some of his best customers.

As oil money pumped up Russia's economy, it breathed life back into the sleepy bear. Russian leadership wanted to flex its military muscle once again. But some of the objectives would be seen as questionable on the world stage.

Morozov saw an opportunity.

Why arm militaries around the world when you could get paid more by fighting their battles? The Russian soldier was still one of the best in the world. So he founded Bear Security Group. Soon, ex-Spetsnaz commandos were training troops and even doing some fighting in hot spots around the world. Places no one else wanted to go. Places others couldn't go, because the political will wasn't there. When Russia wanted to invade Crimea, they first sent in teams from Bear Security Group. When Russia wanted to help anti-American forces in Syria, Morozov's mercenaries were flown in.

Eventually, Pavel's men would fight right alongside Russian special forces soldiers. It often became hard to distinguish between them. Such was the beauty of the private sector. For the right price, one could get the best quality.

Morozov didn't stop with creating a private military. Anyone could do that, although surely not as well as he. But what very few other firms could do to his level was espionage. A private security contractor was nothing without a good intelligence network.

Private spies. Perhaps his greatest idea.

Morozov supplied critical intelligence field agents and information to the highest bidder, around the world. Often times he had opposing national intelligence organizations bidding against each other to gain access to his information. They *had* to, lest it fall into their competitor's hands. Even the CIA had paid to access some of his dossiers. Although they would never admit to it in a million years.

Now, having conquered the world one bullet at a time, Pavel Morozov sat on his yacht, basking in the glorious sunlight off the coast of a nation that had once considered him an enemy. He was too rich and powerful for that now. As long as he kept himself separated enough from the many private wars his companies fought, he was untouchable. Besides, as a master spy, he knew how to keep clean.

Life was good. Especially when it gave him gifts. Like it had last year, when his men had stumbled onto Max Fend in the South of France.

"Mr. Morozov, we will be lifting anchor and heading back into Key West."

He looked up at Charlotte. "Very well. Thank you, dear."

"Is there anything else I can get you?"

"You still haven't told me about last night. You went out into town—how did it go?"

"It was fine," Charlotte said.

"Any details you need to tell me about?"

"No."

Pavel looked at the topless girls next to him. Oiling each other up so they would tan better. Drunk off expensive champagne.

One of them said, "Mr. Morozov, what happened to that other girl who was always with you? The blonde?"

"Her? I think she went for a swim." He laughed to himself.

They looked at each other and didn't ask any more questions.

He turned back to Charlotte and quietly asked, "Are we all set for next week?"

"We're all set to head up the Florida coast tomorrow morning, sir. We'll be in St. Augustine by Wednesday, just as you requested."

He nodded. "Good."

"Anything else?"

He shook his head and waved her away. She left without saying another word. He looked at one of the girls next to him and snapped his fingers. "Hey. Go get me a champagne. Make sure it is cold."

The girl hurried off, not wanting to take a swim.

* * *

Jake Flynn knew that his investigation was high-priority now. The FBI had sent one of their Gulfstreams down to Brunswick to get him. That was a first. He'd briefed the director and deputy director via conference call on the way back up to D.C. While the Bureau leadership was interested, Flynn still got the impression that there was more to Max Fend than they were letting on.

He had just been dropped off at his car in the Reagan International Airport parking lot when his phone rang.

"Special Agent Flynn."

"Jake, it's Steve Brava. Can you meet for coffee again today?"

"Definitely. Same place?"

"Yeah. Seven p.m. work?"

"See you there, thanks."

Flynn drove his G-car with the blue light on the dash. The light wasn't flashing, but most people driving in the left lane of the highway got out of the way once they saw it. They figured him for an undercover cop. The worst was when people didn't get out of the way. They just slowed down to the speed limit, while everyone else zoomed by. But he didn't get any of those on this trip, thank God.

He arrived at the coffee shop in Springfield a few minutes before seven and ordered a cup of decaf. Damn caffeine would keep him up all night if he had one now. He sighed, realizing he would probably be up all night anyway, working on the Fend case.

After the killings on Jekyll Island, the FBI had thrown a lot more agents his way. But he still hadn't turned up many new leads. The CIA was "helping them out" now that they thought the Russians might be involved.

That was a joke.

The CIA expected to get all the information that Flynn's investigation turned up, but offered little in return. It was just more of the same bullshit that he had dealt with when he had driven out to the Farm.

Steve walked in a few minutes late, apologizing. "Traffic was a mess on 66."

"No sweat, man, have a seat. You want anything?"

"Nah. Thanks, though. I can only stay for a moment."

They sat in the far corner of the coffee shop. It was dark and there were no customers at the adjacent tables.

Flynn said, "What have you got?"

Steve had that same concerned look on his face. Disclaimer time, Flynn figured. Steve said, "Now let me just reiterate how much trouble I could get in if they found out I was sharing this. I'm doing this as a personal favor. Capiche?"

"Of course. I swear to God, Steve. This stays between us. I just need a little help on this. You heard about Jekyll Island, right?"

He nodded. "Yeah."

"Well, the CIA's involved now. And they're still stonewalling me."

"Who from the CIA? Is it that guy Wilkes you talked to?"

"No. Someone else. Why?"

"I got more on Max Fend," Steve said. "I told you the classification level on his personnel file was unusually high. Codeword level. But his personnel file was flagged in a particular way."

"Yeah, you said that."

"I asked my friend at DNI what it meant when a personnel file is flagged like that. He knows about these sorts of things. My friend told me it was something he's only seen a few times."

"When?"

"Once was for a guy who was a member of the Army's Delta Force, and then went into some even more spooky black ops unit. Some task force they use to track down terrorist leaders."

"And the other time?"

"The other time he saw that classification level on a personnel file was for an active CIA field agent. But not just any agent. A very high-profile agent. Someone a lot of people know."

"I don't understand."

Steve looked around the coffee shop. "Okay. We never had this conversation."

"I get it. What do you have?"

"There is a certain *subset* of NOC agents."

"NOC—you mean nonofficial cover."

"Yes. But not just any NOCs. Sometimes...well, this is going to sound silly. But—celebrities or famous businessmen get recruited by the CIA. They get special access and trust that would be very useful to the US intelligence services."

"You're kidding."

"No. I'm serious."

"So what are you saying, the CIA has Oprah working for them?"

"I doubt it. But, yes, that's what I'm saying, essentially."

"Come on. Give me a break."

"Jake, there are plenty of famous celebrity spies in history. Julia Child, Frank Sinatra, Cary Grant..."

"Those people are all dead," Flynn said. "It was a different time back then. Hollywood was more patriotic then."

Steve sighed. "Ever hear the expression that there are no new ideas? Well—supposedly the CIA is still using high-profile public figures as spies."

"Come on."

"Don't believe me? Well, maybe *this* will interest you. My friend gave me one name—the CIA guy in charge of the current program. Do you know what name he gave me?"

"Who?" Flynn asked, and then he answered for himself. "Wilkes?"

Steve nodded.

"That lying bastard."

"You asked me to help you. I'm just trying to tell you what I know."

Flynn said, "Okay. So Max Fend is pretty well known. Well, at least his father is. Let's say it's true. What are you thinking?"

"So, hypothetically—if Max Fend was involved in the Clandestine Operations side of the house, they might have realized that he had the potential to someday inherit his father's company. He would qualify for that program—he's rich and famous. I mean, who doesn't know Charles Fend? He's like Howard Hughes and Richard Branson rolled into one. So if Max Fend is going to inherit the throne someday, maybe they have enrolled him. I can tell you one thing, his DNI personnel file certainly fits the bill."

"Can you tell me what's inside it?"

"Not without going to jail. And I like you, but not that much."

"Got it. Okay. Sounds like I need to pay Wilkes another visit."

* * *

When Jake Flynn called the contact number the CIA had given him and asked to be connected with Caleb Wilkes, he was told that Wilkes was unavailable.

Two minutes later, Flynn's phone rang.

"Special Agent Flynn, I hear that you are trying to reach me."

"Mr. Wilkes, I was hoping that we could sit down and have another chat."

"Concerning?"

"Our mutual friend."

The phone went silent for a moment, and then Wilkes said, "I'm heading to Jacksonville, Florida, right now. Would you be able to meet me there?"

Who did this guy think he was? "I'm in the middle of an investigation. No, I can't go to—" Besides, he had just come from there.

"Mr. Flynn, I know all about your investigation. And I know that you've been getting information from someone at the DNI's office. Looking into our mutual friend."

How the hell did he know that?

"Relax," Wilkes said. "I have no reason to inform your superiors. But I think the best thing you and I can do now is lay all our cards on the table. And my table is located in Jax. So do what you need to do, and catch a flight down here. This isn't a conversation you'll want to miss. Besides, if you're doing your investigation well, it'll lead you there anyway."

* * *

By evening, Morozov's yacht had tied up to the pier just off Mallory Square. Normally reserved for commercial cruise liners, Renee had found out that it cost him an extra $150,000 to dock there.

The party that night was for some of Morozov's wealthiest investors and business associates. Renee had been able to access the guest list and add her name. The security guard didn't know any better. All he knew was that her name was on the list.

As she walked up the gangway, Renee was on edge. Max was going to be furious when she didn't come home from the grocery store.

Renee was struck by the beauty of the vessel's design. Everywhere she looked, the ship was a work of art. Dual circular staircases on both sides of the ship. Titanium tables of modern construction. Light-colored hardwood flooring.

Beautiful women in skimpy outfits served refreshing cocktails and delectable hors d'oeuvres. The guests wore a mix of attire. Some were in suits. Others wore expensive-looking marine-themed clothing. A few Arab men wore traditional white robes.

Renee was worried that she would be overdressed, but she wasn't. She had purchased a long, flowing satin gown, like something you'd see at the Oscars, at one of the high-end Key West shops.

She tried to act natural. Standing out on the deck in the midst of the crowd. Looking around and wondering where she should start. Perhaps she had made a mistake in coming here.

Her pulse began racing as an older man in a suit walked toward her. His skin was flecked with the discolorations of age, his oddly colored hair thrown in a pitiful combover. He looked at her like she was his prey—he must know that she was an impostor. What had she been thinking, coming here like this? She should leave.

"What are you doing here?" he said.

"I'm sorry?"

"A woman as beautiful as you shouldn't be standing without a date or a drink. Allow me to provide either that you choose." Russian accent.

She forced a smile. "I'll take a drink. Thank you." Anything was better than raising suspicion.

"Of course." The older man caught the eye of one of the waitresses. He took two flutes of champagne from her, handing one to Renee.

"My name is Vasily. And you are?"

"Renee."

"It is very nice to meet you, Renee. Come—this area is getting crowded. Let's go up here, away from the noise."

He took her arm and led her up three steps to the elevated aft section of the open-air deck. It was only fifteen feet from where they had been standing, but there were considerably fewer guests up there. And the view of the ocean was better.

A waitress headed toward them with coconut shrimp. Vasily grabbed a few, fitting an impossible quantity all onto his tiny white napkin. The waitress left, and the two of them were alone and out of earshot.

"My God, these are delicious." He examined one of the coconut shrimp before stuffing it in his mouth. He used the back of his hand to wipe off some of the sauce that was dribbling down his chin. "Have you tried these?"

"Not yet."

"Here. Would you like one of mine?"

"I'm not hungry, thank you."

"What do you do, Renee? Why are you here?"

Renee had gone over this in her mind a dozen times on the ride over.

It felt so inadequate now. "I'm an IT security consultant. I hope to work with Mr. Morozov in the future."

"Really?" He stopped eating the shrimp and looked at her with new interest.

She spoke before he could get off another question. "What do you do, Vasily?" All men liked to speak about themselves, if given the opportunity. Keep it about him.

"I work at the Russian Embassy."

"Really? That's very interesting." She managed an impressed look.

A gong went off. A sharp staccato sound, silencing the party.

Each of the heads turned to the entrance on the top deck. Two glass doors slid apart and Pavel Morozov walked out, a nameless blonde bombshell at each arm. The guests clapped. Several raised glasses in admiration. Pavel smiled, scanning the crowd.

His eyes settled on Renee and Vasily, and his smile faded.

* * *

Max chopped three cloves of garlic on his wooden cutting board, sliding them onto the knife and then into the pan of sizzling olive oil. The garlic crackled, its pleasant scent wafting through the room.

Max had decided on Italian instead of French food. He threw a sprinkle of crushed red pepper and minced onion onto the now-browned garlic. Once the onions were soft, he added two cans of crushed tomatoes, some salt and pepper. He dipped in his wooden spoon and gave it a taste. Not bad.

Turning the heat to low, he was almost ready to place the eggplant into the oven. Eggplant parmesan was one of his specialties. The key was to use salt to dry out the eggplant before breading it. This gave it a nice crunch.

But one couldn't enjoy an Italian dinner without red wine. And Renee had forgotten the wine—so she had run back out to get a few bottles.

He checked his watch. She had been gone for over an hour. How long did it take to get wine?

Max breathed through his nose, slowly stirring the sauce. A feeling of dread grew in his chest.

He placed the spoon down on the counter and stormed into her empty room, looking among her things.

Max and she had agreed that she should do the shopping alone that afternoon. Max needed to keep his face out of public view. It was a gift that he wasn't already in the news, and they shouldn't push their luck.

So Renee had gone out on her own after lunch. She'd said she wanted to check out a few of the shops. Then she'd finished up at one of the few grocery stores on Key West—an overpriced market a few blocks from their rental.

Max had seen the clothing store bags when she came in. She had held them up with a look of defiance in her eyes. It had been his money she was spending. Max had figured that the purchases were a playful way of getting back at him for what she considered a sexist remark about women and shopping.

He was wrong.

That wasn't why she had made the purchases. He was looking through the bags. Empty but for a receipt. *What did you buy, Renee?*

A dress. A pair of shoes. Platinum-and-diamond drop earrings and a necklace. Holy shit, those were expensive. But that wasn't what upset him. He looked around the room. In the closet and in the drawers. Then he checked the bathroom, just to be sure.

None of the clothing or jewelry she had purchased was there. And she sure as hell hadn't been wearing it when she'd left.

He closed his eyes, shaking his head. *Renee, Renee, Renee. Why would you do this?*

He knew exactly where she was. He just couldn't believe it. He ran into the kitchen and turned off the stove, then checked that the oven was off as well.

Back in his room, he opened his travel bag, grabbing a pair of binoculars, his pistol, and a silencer and placing them all in a fanny pack. He threw on his sunglasses and ball cap and hurried out the door.

It would take him a good fifteen minutes to reach the yacht, and he had no idea what he would do once there. It was getting dark. He needed to come up with a plan.

* * *

Morozov walked directly over to them. A strongman's walk, confident and showy, with just a touch of what Renee's brothers liked to call ILS—Imaginary Lat Syndrome. The way some guys held out their arms like their lat muscles were bigger than they really were.

Pavel Morozov had walked past his guests and stood uncomfortably close to Vasily. His hand was extended.

"Good evening, Vasily. I hear we have business to discuss."

Vasily shook Morozov's hand, replying in Russian.

"And who is your guest?" Morozov looked at Renee, an eyebrow arched.

After an uncomfortable silence, Renee said, "We only just met. Please excuse me, I'll let you two talk."

Morozov turned back to Vasily and spoke to him in Russian. Renee walked away, trying not to rush. She didn't want to draw any more attention than she already had. Renee could see two of Morozov's security team holding their earpieces across the room. One of them began heading her way. Renee again began to wonder if she had made a mistake in coming here. But then the security man walked past her and she exhaled.

She traveled along the outer walkway of the yacht. It was time to get to work.

* * *

Renee stepped out onto a forward observation deck. She was alone. The first twinkle of stars began to overcome the fading sunlight. She could hear the noise of the boozy party coming from the opposite end of the yacht.

There were seats and couches in various places. It took her a moment to find what she was looking for. A docking station near the armrest of one of the built-in seats. Luxury yacht owners wanted to be able to charge their phones while they lay out in the sun, right?

She looked around to make sure no security guards were near. Seeing no one, she sat down and removed her laptop from her shoulder bag. She didn't know how long she would have. She checked the docking station. It was equipped with a USB Type C port. That would get her speeds of at least 5 Gbps as long as there were no bottlenecks in the network.

Her fingers danced over the keyboard. Each keystroke was a moment closer toward solving the riddle—or being discovered.

There.

She had accessed a part of the ship's network that showed an enormous number of data transfers over the past week. It was a treasure trove of information. More than she could analyze right now. But she didn't need to. She just needed to send it off the ship so that she could look at it later.

While the data was transferring, she decided to dig into any communications between anyone at Fend Aerospace and the ship.

There were two account IDs listed at Fend. She couldn't trace them to a name right now. But if she could get into the Fend database later, she would be able to match them up. She added those files to the transfer.

Her eyes darted up at the sound of two security men walking out onto the observation deck. One of them held a silenced pistol, pointed at Renee.

"If you'll come with us, please."

It occurred to Renee that perhaps her tour of the ship should have stuck to places visible to potential witnesses. She hit a series of keystrokes that locked her computer and wiped her hard drive, then closed the laptop.

Renee said, "I'm a guest of Mr. Morozov—"

"We just received instructions from Mr. Morozov. He wants you *below deck*—now."

* * *

They threw Renee in a small bedroom deep in the bowels of the ship. They had taken her computer, but it was useless now anyway.

The room looked like it was meant for the crew. Bunk beds pressed up against the curved wall. Very little storage. There was a guard outside. At least one, by the sound of it.

She waited in the small room, cursing herself for not listening to Max. She'd just wanted to help. To make up for almost getting them killed in Georgia. And to prove that she was worthy. It was a colossally stupid motivation.

During hour one, Renee convinced herself that Morozov wouldn't kill her. She was an American. And people had seen her.

During hour two, the door opened up and a towering man entered. The look in his eyes told her everything she needed to know.

He watched her for a moment before speaking, his eyes examining every inch of her. "My name is Mikhail. What is yours?"

She didn't respond.

He said, "They want me to find out what you were doing with your computer. They say that you erase everything on it. I say, no problem. You will be good to Mikhail. You will tell me what you were doing, and then maybe we let you go?"

Her lip began to quiver, so she bit into it. Her voice was hushed and hopeful. "I was just sending my husband an email. I forgot to bring my phone and..."

He slapped her hard across the face.

The force of the impact sent her onto the floor. Her left ear rang. She placed her hand against her cheek. She could feel it swelling up. Involuntary tears streamed out of her left eye.

Mikhail spoke in a casual manner. "So we will try this again. You tell me truth this time, yes? Then I don't hit you. Or, you can lie to me again, and I hit you. That is how we do this. Yes?"

Renee began to cry.

Mikhail clicked his tongue. "Oh, my pretty little girl. Do not cry. Mikhail will take good care of you."

The large man knelt down over her. She was still in a crumpled heap on the cold floor. Mikhail's thick fingers stroked her cheek and then wandered downward. Caressing her satin dress. His thumb and fingers cupping her breast as he looked into her eyes. She could smell the stench of his breath.

The movement was so fast. He gripped her by the arms and brought her back to a standing position. Then he tore her dress at the seam, pulling it down so that it began to reveal her body.

Mikhail smiled, nodding his approval. "Yes. You will tell Mikhail everything. Yes?"

She looked away and nodded. Tears streaming down her face. "Okay."

A knock at the door.

Mikhail yelled in Russian, a clear annoyance in his tone. No reply. He frowned and went over to the door, cursing.

He opened the door and found himself staring at Max Fend's silenced pistol. The unconscious body of a guard on the floor behind him.

Max eyed Renee, her cheek red and swollen, her dress torn and half hanging off her. Max turned back toward Mikhail and fired two shots into his chest. The big Russian fell backwards into the lower bunk and then collapsed on the floor, a shocked expression of pain on his face.

Max turned and grabbed the other Russian in the hallway, dragging him into the room.

Renee began sobbing and started hugging Max.

"I'm so sorry, Max."

Max closed the door almost all the way and held a finger over his mouth. "It's okay. It's okay. Calm down. We need to get out of here."

She wiped her tears away with her arm and tried to pull her dress back up over herself. "Any ideas?"

A single, prolonged horn sounded throughout the ship.

Renee said out loud, "What was that?"

"One long horn blast—it means the ship is departing the port. The yacht is leaving."

Renee felt a rumble in her feet, and the sway of the deck as it began motoring away from the pier.

"Let's go. Follow me, and be quick about it. Don't make a sound."

Renee did as instructed, walking down the carpeted hallway. They wound through the ship's passageways, and she began to wonder where he was taking them. Then Max opened a watertight doorway and motioned for them to go in.

The two of them entered into a cave-like room at the aft end of the ship. Renee realized they were in some kind of boat-launching chamber. A pool of dark water took up most of the center of the room. Two small Sea-Doo watercraft were tied up on either side of the pool.

Max smacked his fist against a red button on the wall, and a spinning yellow light came on. The huge aft wall separated, revealing the dark ocean outside. The lights of Key West were in the distance.

As the rear doors opened up, the pool water began whirling and sloshing around, the ocean water now seeping in.

Max spoke quickly as he untied one of the Sea-Doos. "Get in, they'll find those two guards soon."

Max and Renee jumped in. As Max started up the Sea-Doo watercraft, Renee said, "How were you able to—"

"Charlotte."

"She let you on board?"

"She wasn't here. I called her. But she's in Jacksonville—she did, however, tell me the name of the company that was catering here tonight."

"So you snuck on with the caterers?"

Max put the Sea-Doo in reverse and they began drifting backward. "There isn't a lot that five thousand dollars in cash won't solve."

"How did you know where I was?"

"I found one of the guards and persuaded him to tell me."

They backed up into the black ocean, rolling on the wake of the yacht. When the Sea-Doo was about fifty feet behind the yacht, in open water, Max took the throttle out of reverse and put it into neutral. They floated there for a moment, Renee's hand on his shoulder. She stood in back of him, watching the massive vessel sail away.

"They have my computer and purse," she said.

"Was your ID in there?"

"No. And I wiped the hard drive—but they'll still be able to tell what information I was accessing from their own network. If they're any good, they'll probably figure out what we were up to."

"It won't matter. We got what we needed, right?"

"I think so, yes." She placed her body close to him as he ramped up the throttle, speeding over the waves and back toward the shore. She was shivering.

Max and Renee made it to a quiet dock and tied up the Sea-Doo. They walked to the street and hailed a cab back to their rental place. They quickly grabbed their personal items and then had the driver take them to the airport. The cabbie was happy to take a break from ferrying around the drunks who stayed until close.

Max started up the Cirrus while Renee paid for the FBO fees. He kept looking around. It was a dumb idea to leave the Cirrus at the Key West airport. And it might have been dumber to go back to it. Morozov's men had seen them fly away in Georgia, so they knew that they used a small plane. There weren't very many general aviation aircraft at Key West, relatively speaking. Not when compared to cars.

But he wanted to get away quick, and Morozov's goons were all out on that yacht. He hoped.

16

One Day Before the Fend 100 Flight...

The sun rose shortly after they took off from Key West. Max decided they would land in St. Augustine. It had a small airport, and it was close to his father's home in Ponte Vedra.

They flew north along the beach. Lots of heavily trafficked airspace, but a pretty view.

"Are those sharks?" Renee asked through her headset, looking down at the turquoise waters near Miami.

He did an S-turn in the aircraft so they could get a better view. They were only at five hundred feet, and some surfers waved up to them. There was a school of sharks swimming a mere fifty feet away.

Max said, "Yeah. Pretty wild, huh?"

"Oh my God. Should we warn those people?"

"Nah. They'll be fine."

"Are they always that close?"

"A lot of the time, yes. Usually people don't realize it, but sharks are always around." He looked at her.

"I'm sorry that I didn't tell you where I was going. I was only trying to help. I thought that I could..."

He shook his head. "I appreciate what you were trying to do. Just promise me that you won't keep secrets from me anymore."

She pursed her lips and nodded. "You saved me. I don't know what that man would have done."

Max glanced at her and then looked back ahead, flying the plane. "It's done now."

She didn't say anything else about it while they flew. She put her head down on the seat and fell asleep.

Renee slept most of the way. They were passing Daytona when she awoke.

"You okay?"

"Yes. I'm fine."

"So you were able to tap into the yacht's computer network?"

"I was. I transferred a lot of data off the ship. But I'll need time to analyze it."

"How much time?"

"A day at least."

Max said, "We'll find a place to lay low near St. Augustine. You can work there. But the Fend 100 flight is tomorrow. You'll have to work quick."

Renee nodded. "You said you were going to warn your father. What did you intend to do?"

"I'll need to set up a private meeting with him. My guess is that he's being watched closely by law enforcement, in case I show up. I won't be able to contact him through normal means."

"I may be able to help," Renee said.

"How?"

"Think of a way to get him alone. Is there anyone he would meet by himself? Someone he hasn't seen in a while? Someone who, if they called, it would be unusual?"

Max thought about it for a moment. "Yeah. My aunt."

"Now, is there anywhere that this person and your father would go by themselves?"

Max said, "Yeah. Yeah, I think I have an idea. But you'll have to make the call. Do you have a way to make it look like it's from a different number or location?"

"Come on. Challenge me."

He laughed.

They landed at St. Augustine, and Max pulled his hood over his head, waiting out in the parking lot until Renee finished paying and then pulled up with the rental car. They were getting into a routine.

He again waited in the car while she paid for their motel, making sure to get a first-floor exterior entrance. Max was exhausted once again after flying all night. But he couldn't sleep. They flipped on the news, and the coverage was a mix of stories about the upcoming G-7 conference and the Fend 100 flight.

Renee had started the shower. The door to the bathroom was open. Max tried to give her privacy, concentrating on the TV as articles of her clothing began to grace the floor of the hotel room.

"Do you want me to leave the shower on?"

"Sure," Max said, biting his lip as he stole a glance of naked flesh.

She walked out of the bathroom with a white hotel towel wrapped tightly around her, and a look in her eye that he hadn't seen in some time. Renee slowly walked over to where Max sat on the bed.

Renee never said a word. She just reached down, her soft fingers curling around his neck and pulling his head close to hers. She kissed him. A long, wet, deep kiss.

Max could feel his heart beating harder in his chest. She reached for the remote and shut off the TV, her towel loosening around her.

The hot shower continued running, steam filling the room.

* * *

They met at the Seven Bridges restaurant in Jacksonville and sat at a secluded strip of the bar. It was 1 p.m. on a weekday. Not many people were in the restaurant.

Wilkes bought a round of IPAs. That got their tongues loosened up enough that it didn't take long to get into the meat of the discussion.

"You said Max Fend wasn't in the CIA."

Wilkes sipped his beer. "He *wasn't*."

Flynn tilted his head, a skeptical look on his face.

"What? He's not," repeated Wilkes. "He was in the *DIA*."

Flynn frowned. "The Defense Intelligence Agency?"

Wilkes nodded.

"Is that really your excuse for lying to me? You purposefully misled me."

"I didn't."

Flynn thought about getting up and walking out. This guy had some nerve. Instead he took another drink of his beer. "Then what's your interest with Max Fend?"

"The DIA and the CIA often work closely together on things. We actually train our clandestine operatives at many of the same schools. Sometimes we transfer folks between agencies. Sometimes we *recruit* folks from the other agency for a specific program."

"So you were recruiting Max Fend for a program?"

"Maybe. It's not something that I can talk about," Wilkes said.

"What *can* you talk about?"

"I think you're barking up the wrong tree."

"What's that supposed to mean?"

"I don't think Max Fend is working with the Russians. And I don't think he allowed anyone to intrude on the Fend computer network."

"Then why did he run away from us last week?"

"Don't know."

"Did you break him out?"

"No. I'm looking into what's happened as well. It wasn't my people who helped Max escape Washington, D.C. We obviously wouldn't have done that. We would have talked to the FBI about it and resolved it quietly."

"Who was it, then?"

Wilkes shrugged. "I have a few ideas, but I'm not at liberty to discuss them."

"So is Fend still working for the DIA, then?"

Wilkes sighed. "He's out of the DIA now."

"As of when?"

"It's a recent development."

"What was the reason?"

"I can't discuss it."

"Look, you called me. Do I need to speak with someone at the DIA?"

"My guess is that *they* won't discuss it either, unless you get someone very high up to pull some strings."

Flynn tried to stay calm. "Do you know where Max Fend is right now?"

"No. But I think I know where he's headed."

* * *

Charles Fend hated reading the news on smartphones. He liked the feel of a good old-fashioned Sunday newspaper in his hands. Heavy and thick. The smell of the ink. No clickbait articles on the bottom of the page, trying to distract him with some meaningless pursuit.

He sat reading the *Florida Times-Union* on the beachfront patio of his Ponte Vedra beach home. A few palm trees, nestled next to the stucco exterior, provided shade. His gaze occasionally switched between the sand dunes on the beach and the article he was reading.

FEND AEROSPACE SET TO MAKE HISTORY

The article was kind. It painted Charles in the best light possible. It could have been much worse had the controversy with his son made headlines.

Charles was sick with worry about Max.

The FBI was saying that Max was linked to the hacking, and that there were possible ties to a terror-linked group in Syria.

Charles knew that couldn't be true. But he still didn't understand why Max had run from the FBI. Seeing the footage of those motorcycles racing across the bridge out of Washington, D.C., was shocking. He wished he could have talked some sense into his son. Whatever the trouble he was in, there was nothing worth the risk that he was taking. And there was nothing his father wouldn't forgive. Charles just didn't want something awful to happen to Max.

He wondered if this all wasn't his fault somehow. Perhaps he had pampered Max too much. He had shown so much promise as a boy. Max had buried himself in his studies and athletics at his elite prep school. Princeton had introduced him to a great group of friends, and a world of opportunities. But college also introduced young men to a world of temptation. Charles worried about the choices his son had made as an adult. This generation today...

After Max graduated college, he had worked for the Department of Defense for a few years in Washington. Charles hadn't understood why he had chosen that path. His father could have helped Max get into the best business or law school, if that was what he wanted to pursue. He could have helped him get a job at one of the Big Three consulting firms, or something on Wall Street. Charles's network was world-class.

But Max hadn't wanted any of that. He'd wanted to try something on his own. Charles admired that spirit, in a way. He'd given his son the benefit of the doubt. But then Max had abruptly left the Department of Defense and traveled to Europe to work as a freelance consultant. He had taken money from his trust fund and bought a home in the South of France, sparing no expense. Charles should have objected, but hadn't. He still didn't know why.

That's when the stories had started rolling in about Max's wild parties and behavior. He sounded like he was out of control. It got bad enough that board members had mentioned it to Charles. They didn't want to see Max someday inherit the company if he was really as wild as depicted.

So Charles had flown to France, hoping to stage an intervention. The father and son had spent a week together, hiking along the Nietzsche Path near the medieval village of Eze. Walking along the path, seven hundred feet over the Mediterranean Sea, they spoke candidly about their lives.

Charles watched his son easily navigate the steep path, shaded by olive trees and tall oaks. Max looked tan, fit, and in good spirits. Healthy and in control. It didn't match up with the persona that was being portrayed in the media. But he seemed down about something. Bothered.

Later that day, they sat at an outdoor restaurant near the seaside town square, sharing a bowl of steamed mussels and fries. Charles confronted his son about the stories he had heard. He told him that he was worried that Max would end up wasting his life here in France. He didn't want him to succumb to the temptation wealthy children often faced. Max was better than that.

Max had told his father that he had expected the talk, but not to worry. Max assured him that things would change. He was thinking about leaving France and was interested in taking a more stable job in the States.

Charles had been incredibly relieved. He offered his son a job on the spot. Max told him that he thought he needed a business degree first. He didn't want to walk into a company without the requisite knowledge and skill to do the job. While Charles wanted to ask him what the hell he had been doing out here if he wasn't gaining any business skills, he let it go. Charles told his son he could join Fend Aerospace whenever he was ready. And if he wanted to earn another degree to help him prepare, that was absolutely fine.

Now Charles wondered just what it was that had triggered Max to make such a dramatic life change. While the direction was opposite, it was very similar to the way he'd suddenly dropped his DoD job. It was almost like someone else had instructed him to make the move. *Like it was out of Max's control...*

"Mr. Fend, you have a phone call. Your sister, sir."

Dolores? At this hour? Perhaps she was calling about the news article.

His assistant walked over and handed Charles his phone.

"Hello?"

"Hello, Charles. It's Dolores. I would like to visit Mom's grave today. I was wondering if you would join me?"

It wasn't Dolores. It wasn't her voice. He overcame the urge to ask who it was, because he was pretty sure that he knew.

"Of course. What time shall I meet you?"

"How about half past three? Will that work?"

"Sure thing."

"Wonderful. And, Charles, I would really like to spend the time together, just the two of us. Please be a dear and come by yourself."

"Will do."

He hung up the phone and called to his assistant to have his car ready in the driveway.

"Which car, sir?"

"I'll take the Mercedes."

"Very well, sir."

Charles looked at his wristwatch and thought carefully about what to do next. He knew what he *wanted* to do, and what he had *agreed* to do.

Duty won out.

He dialed the number from memory. The voice on the other end answered immediately.

"It's me," Charles said.

"What is it?"

"You were right. He called."

* * *

Max and Renee pulled into the empty parking lot of a small private school. The kids were out for the summer, so no one would see them walk through the property.

Max looked at Renee. "You stay here. If you don't hear from me in twenty minutes, leave and go back to the hotel. I'll call you tonight."

"Be careful," she told him, affection in her voice.

Max smiled. "I'm always careful. That being said, if I don't call..."

"You don't need to tell me what to do in that situation. I'll know."

Max squeezed her shoulder and turned, closing the car door behind him. He walked through the school playground, ducking under a bright blue-and-red jungle gym. Fresh mulch covered the ground.

He hopped the white picket fence to the rear of the playground and walked through a grove of trees until he came to a flat open field.

The graveyard. His mother's graveyard.

Max visited it about once per year, although normally he entered through the main drive. The entire cemetery was the size of four football fields put together. A few trees provided occasional shade, but most of it was wide-open field.

Max's mother had died when he was very young, but he tried to keep her memory a meaningful part of his life. The grave markers were all flush with the ground. Simple granite, mostly. Max walked towards hers. A location he knew well.

The blistering hot Florida sun beat down on him from above. Her grave was just to the east of a large oak tree. He could see a figure standing over the spot. His father's black Mercedes-Benz sedan was parked nearby.

Max didn't see anyone else.

The figure was a man. That much was for sure. But he was facing away from Max. Max reached into his fanny pack and gripped his pistol with both hands. His eyes scanned the Mercedes, and the trees. Still no sign of anyone else.

The man turned to face him when Max was about thirty feet away. Max smiled.

For a moment.

The door of the Mercedes opened, about twenty-five yards away.

"Dad?"

"It's alright, Max."

Max stood his ground, still holding his concealed weapon. He shook his head. "Dad. Who else is here?"

"Trust me, son. It will be alright."

"Dad, I didn't do what they say I did."

"I know, son."

A man got out of the rear of the Mercedes. Max knew the face. Where did he know him from? He searched his memory. At last it came to him.

He had met him down at the Farm once. He was a CIA agent—Caleb Wilkes.

* * *

Charles drove them back to his home in Ponte Vedra. He had called ahead and asked his staff to leave. They needed privacy for the evening.

Wilkes had assured Max that he would be free to go after their meeting. No one knew that the three of them were speaking. When they sat down at the house, Wilkes set a small device on the center of the table. It looked like an old walkie-talkie.

"What's that?"

"It's a device that'll make it near impossible for someone to listen in on our conversation through one of our phones or some other electronics in the house," Wilkes said.

"Does it work?"

"Oh, yes."

Max said, "I assume you've told my father a little bit about my work in Europe?"

"I gave him a rundown, yes. But I think you'll find that you both have a thing or two to learn about each other."

Max looked at his dad inquisitively. Charles nodded. "It's time we let you in on some family history."

Max knew enough to stay quiet.

Charles turned to face him, leaning back in his swivel chair. "In the late 1970s, I met your mother while traveling through the UK. Her father, as you know, was from Poland. Her mother was English." His father's face looked strained.

"That's where you were married," Max said.

"Correct. We married near Cambridge. It was shortly after our wedding that a man named Hoopengardner approached me in London. Hoopengardner knew that Fend Aerospace was about to get contracts with the US government. Military contracts. This was a few years before you were born. Hoopengardner said it would be in my best interests if we could have a cup of tea. Somewhere secluded, where we could speak about a quiet business proposal.

"As it turned out, Hoopengardner's business proposal was nothing short of extortion. He was a KGB agent. You know him by a different name —Pavel Morozov. His proposal was for me to provide him with information on the military aircraft we were developing. If I didn't, he had access to your mother's family in Poland. By that time, your grandmother had passed away, and your grandfather had moved back to Poland to live."

Max looked at Wilkes, who stayed quiet. He thought about what type of man Morozov was. He could see where this was going. "What did you do?" Max asked his father.

"I'm a patriot, Max. And I wasn't about to let some Soviet bastard blackmail me. When we got back to the States, I quietly contacted the FBI. I had thought they might be able to help me get your mother's family out of Poland. I was naive."

Now it was Max's father who looked at Wilkes, anger in his eyes.

Charles said, "The FBI handed me over to the CIA. The CIA did not want me to break off contact with Morozov. To my surprise, they *wanted* me to give the KGB information on Fend Aerospace's military contracts. But they wanted to control exactly *what* information was sent out. They turned me into a double agent."

Max knew how it went. The counterintelligence types rarely wanted to just solve a problem and make it go away. They wanted to turn agents and provide corrupt data. To manipulate the other side's network of spies.

"How long did you do it for?"

Now Wilkes spoke up. "Your father worked for us for over ten years, Max."

Max looked at his father. "Why ten years?"

"Because after ten years of providing secrets to the KGB—secrets that the CIA was providing me—things began to change," Charles said.

"How so?"

"For one, Morozov got suspicious. It was 1987 when it happened. Reagan was president. The Soviets were getting their asses handed to them by the CIA-armed Mujahedeen in Afghanistan. Morozov was growing desperate. Threatening me more and more every time I saw him."

"Why?"

"He had other sources in the US who were providing him information that conflicted with mine. But my information had made Morozov a star in the KGB. When his star began to fall, he blamed me."

"So what happened?"

"He approached your mother."

Max felt a chill run through his body. His mother had died in a car accident when he was a boy. He had only vague memories of her, along with a few cherished home videos and pictures.

"Your mother came to me one night and said that Morozov had told her everything. That I'd been spying for the Russians. And that he wasn't happy with the information I was providing. Morozov wanted her to put pressure on me to step up my contributions. Or else."

"Or else what?"

"He threatened to harm *you*, Max. You were young—six years old at the time. Your mother became a wreck."

"I see." Max shifted his weight, suddenly uncomfortable.

"I went to the CIA. I told them that we needed protection. Your mother was brought in to meet my CIA handlers. She agreed to participate with me in the counterintelligence operation, despite the threat to her family. She said that her father hated the Soviets, and that he would never want to be used as leverage by them. She demanded one thing— protection for you. The CIA agreed and stationed a security detail at our home, around the clock. They were disguised as butlers. But I was to continue to play the game with Morozov for a little longer."

Max shook his head. "Dad, I had no idea about any of this. What happened?"

"The next time I met with him, Morozov told me he wanted the raw data on the new stealth jets that Fend Aerospace was designing for the Air Force out in Nevada."

"I didn't know Fend Aerospace was involved in that type of work back then."

"They weren't," Wilkes said. "It was part of a charade. A disinformation campaign."

"This was all happening right around the time that Mom got into her car accident."

His father had a grave look in his eye. "Yes. *Exactly* that time."

"Dad..."

His father looked out over the water.

"Did my mother die in a car accident?"

Wilkes said nothing, just watching the exchange between father and son.

His father looked down at the table while he spoke. "No."

"So then how did she die?"

"Morozov."

Max clenched his fists. "How?"

His father was having trouble getting the story out. "The Cold War was ending. Everything was coming to a head. Morozov had finally had enough. The information I'd supplied him on the stealth jets was obviously false. He stopped taking my calls. That's when we got scared. As it turned out, our fears were warranted. Your mother left you with the nanny and one of the security men that day. Then she drove to the store with the other security man to pick up some things. She was found dead in the vehicle. They made it look like the car ran off the road, but I knew the truth."

"What do you mean?"

"The autopsy showed that your mother had died from the impact of the car driving off the cliff. But the security guard had been shot. That part was never reported to authorities. The CIA took care of that. Morozov contacted me the day of the funeral and asked how she was, delight in his voice."

Max's mouth was wide. "Why didn't you...?"

"What? Seek revenge? He threatened to kill you if we went after him. And during the Cold War, the CIA and KGB would kill each other's spies all the time. At the end of the Cold War, no one wanted any errant sparks to ignite a fire. Your mother's death was covered up, just like many others. For the good of the nation, and for your safety."

Max sat in silence for a few moments, taking it all in. *Leaving a single family member alive was a sort of calling card.*

"I'm sorry, Max," his father said. "I should have told you that story a long time ago. It isn't something I like to discuss. Not really something that I was allowed to discuss."

Max spoke quietly. "What happened after that? With you and the CIA?"

"I told the CIA I was done." Charles turned to face Wilkes. "But one is never truly done with them. I realize that now. When I told them that I was finished, the CIA was unhappy. But they didn't push it. They gave me protection, and I've helped them from time to time."

Wilkes said, "As far as we know, Morozov never told anyone else that your father was working with us."

"He knew and he never told the Soviets about my father working for the CIA? Why not?"

Wilkes said, "In a word? Pride. And maybe fear. Morozov didn't want to look bad. You have to remember the way the Soviets worked back then. Your father was feeding the KGB false information for years. Military secrets. Their government made major decisions to increase military spending based on the information that we provided. It was all part of a huge misinformation campaign. We wanted the USSR to spend itself into oblivion. We knew their economic engine couldn't sustain it. It couldn't keep up with the United States' manufacturing power. But why stop there? Why have them think they needed to keep up with reality, when we could provide them an alternate reality that was even more grave?"

"What did you tell them?"

"We gave them information about a classified stealth aircraft program —claiming that they were in development out in the Nevada desert."

"Didn't we actually have something like that?" Max asked.

"Yes. Lockheed's Skunkworks program was very similar. They developed the F-117, the B2, etc...."

"So what did they think *you* were doing?"

"They thought Fend Aerospace was developing a set of supersonic stealth fighters. We made it look like we were decades ahead of where we really were. We even created cardboard cutouts and placed them in the desert. We had an entire base filled with fake aircraft. Hundreds of personnel were involved. Only a few knew that it was a deception, however."

"But Morozov found out."

"Yes."

"And he never told anyone."

"It would have ruined him. He might have even been executed, for not catching that it was all fake."

Max was incredulous. "So he just let the Russians think that it was real?"

Charles shrugged. "Why not?"

"By the time he found out, it was 1989. The Soviet Union was in decline. The Red Army was getting slaughtered in Afghanistan. Bread lines in Moscow. He saw the writing on the wall. Why hurt his reputation? It was better for him if he kept the failure quiet. I have to admit, considering his position today, he was right about that."

"Why didn't you tell me any of this before? About my mother..."

"You were too young to understand. And much of it was classified at the highest levels."

"Still is," Wilkes said.

Max frowned. "Who cares, now?"

Charles looked at Wilkes.

"Because as you now know, Pavel Morozov still presents a threat to national security," Wilkes said. "And the CIA wants to bring him down."

* * *

They ordered an early dinner delivered from a local seafood restaurant. Max ate a grilled mahi-mahi sandwich while he filled them in on what he had witnessed over the past few days.

Wilkes had a lot of questions. "So you think it was MI-6 that helped you escape?"

"I do."

"Why do you think it was them?"

"British accents, mainly."

Wilkes said, "That's great detective work."

"Because they were *good*. And I recognized one of them, from an op a few years ago. I *know* that he was MI-6."

"Fine. Tell me about your interactions with them again. MI-6 had you meet with their woman in Morozov's outfit?"

"Yes. Down in Key West. Morozov had his yacht docked there until recently."

"How'd you know Morozov was there?"

"The MI-6 woman told me to meet her there."

Wilkes looked bothered. "Why didn't they go through normal channels to resolve this?"

"They said they *did*," Max said. "They said the CIA didn't want to halt the Fend 100 passenger qualification flight. They said you wanted to let Morozov keep going so that you could catch him red-handed or something like that. Is that true?"

Wilkes clenched his jaw. "Not entirely."

"Now what the hell are you playing at, Caleb? If that Russian lunatic is putting people in danger, then we need to do something about it," Charles said.

Wilkes didn't answer. He was distracted, looking off into the distance. Like he was trying to sort something out in his head.

"You're right about Morozov's being a threat," Max said. "He's planning to steal all of your company's data—he's going to launch another cyberattack. He'll have the technology for the Fend 100 and be able to sell it on the black market."

Wilkes and Max's father looked at each other. "We know," Wilkes said. "I told your father about it last week. After you made your escape from D.C. What we don't know is how he's going to do it."

"Well, I might be able to help with that part."

"How?"

"The MI-6 woman I met—Charlotte Capri. She told me that Morozov's hackers have a way to get access to the secure servers where the Fend 100's data is stored."

Max told them what he'd learned from Charlotte, and what Renee and he had figured out on their own. When he was finished, both Charles and Caleb Wilkes looked impressed.

"You were actually on his yacht?"

"That's right."

"You're lucky to be alive."

"Agreed."

"She's supposed to meet with me again. She says MI-6 is working on software that will be able to defend against Morozov's hackers."

"Where and when is she meeting you?" Wilkes said.

"Somewhere in Jacksonville, tonight. Morozov is sailing his yacht up the Florida coast today. Which continues to bother me. Morozov must know that we're on to him. Especially now that I've gotten away. Why isn't he more frightened of US law enforcement or counterintelligence taking him into custody?"

"He's a pro," Wilkes said.

"So what?"

"He's been at this a long time, and he knows the rules. We can't touch him right now. We don't have evidence that he's done anything wrong, other than your word. Which is tainted, at the moment—thanks to him. Like I said. A pro."

"What about the forensics that the FBI had?"

"It's been tampered with, obviously. It links to you. So if we want to go after Morozov, we'll also be using the same forensic evidence that implicates you. Does that sound like it would hold up?"

"No. But this isn't court..." Max decided it was time to bring up Renee. "I have someone I've been working with. A Canadian woman that I know, Renee. She's former CSE. A real black hat ninja."

"A what?"

"A hacker, Dad. Renee has been able to uncover a lot about Morozov. He has an outfit called Maljab Tactical. They're a group of Uzbek defense consultants, and they operate mostly out of Syria. They specialize in working with Jihadi extremist groups. They also have some pretty good hackers. Our working theory is that this group was involved in the Fend cyber intrusion. They probably linked the network breach to me."

"Why is Morozov interested in Max?" Charles asked.

Max turned to his father. "Whatever he does, Morozov is planning to hang the blame on me. He laid the groundwork with the hacking incident. He'll finish the job by seizing control of the Fend 100 during the passenger qualification flight, and the cyber forensics will point to yours truly." Max paused. "I'm beginning to think you should just postpone the flight. Use whatever excuse you need—including the false evidence that ties me to the Russians. If it's what we need to do..."

"No, Max," Wilkes said. "There's a better way forward. Do you know why we pulled you out of Europe last year?"

"The DIA pulled me out. They said my cover was blown, after the incident with the two Russian arms dealers."

"Not exactly. Max, Charles, it's time that we discussed a long-term relationship between the Fend family and the CIA."

"I've heard this talk before," said Charles.

"Charles, your son was working for the intelligence community, just as I told you. Specifically, he worked under the purview of the Defense Intelligence Agency."

Charles looked at Max as if seeing him for the first time, a mix of fear and pride in his eyes.

Wilkes went on, "The CIA has a network of high-profile agents. Wealthy businessmen. CEOs. Celebrities. Heads of state. People with *access*. They have various levels of training. Some are little more than informants, but the network is one of our most valuable."

"What does this have to do with your reason for not wanting to cancel the Fend 100 test flight? And for pulling me out of Europe?" Max said.

"The Agency doesn't like to shut down potential sources of information. It sort of goes against our mission," Wilkes said. "If there's a way to keep a valuable asset in play, we'll take it. Charles will be retiring from the Fend Aerospace Company soon. We recognize that, and have planned for it. Max, ironically, the best place the US government can place you is in your father's company."

"So what are you saying? That me leaving the DIA was intentional? But I thought my cover was blown."

"A partial truth. *Morozov* knows. But few others, if any. The CIA would like you to continue to serve. When your father retires, your position with the Fend Aerospace Company, as well as your family name and status, will create many opportunities for us."

Max nodded. He didn't completely trust Wilkes, but as much as he hated to admit it, he wanted to get back in the game.

"So the two Russian men in France—that was Morozov?"

"We believe so, yes. We think he set up the deal to test you. He wanted to see for himself whether you were really working as a spy. But he didn't tell anyone else. Just like he never told anyone that your father was working for the CIA."

"So then why did he test me? And if he thinks I work for US intelligence—why did he keep it to himself?"

Wilkes said, "Who knows? Maybe he wanted to finish what he started with your mother. The one thing that keeps KGB agents warm during the cold Russian winters. Revenge."

"Why would he do this now?" Charles asked.

Wilkes continued offering ideas. "Maybe seeing Max in France reminded him of you, Charles. And don't forget Sergei—Max's asset in France. We think he was planning this cyberattack with one of his Eastern European cyber ransom gangs. Morozov must have caught wind of it. He's well connected to the Russian mafia. Hell, it might not even be about revenge as much as it is an opportunity that he stumbled into."

Max rubbed his chin. "Maybe." That seemed like too much of a coincidence for Max, but he didn't say it. "Whatever the reason, it seems as though Morozov plans to launch another cyberattack during the Fend 100 flight."

Charles shook his head. "Wonderful. If I don't proceed with the Fend 100 flight, Morozov may start selling bits of the Fend technology on the open market, which will spook the investors and threaten to cancel our government contract before it's finalized. But if I do proceed with the Fend 100 flight, we risk another, more effective cyberattack. Is that about it?"

"In a nutshell."

Charles said, "We have to go on with the flight. If we don't, the company will be devastated. We'll have to ensure that we protect ourselves from this next cyberattack. That is the only satisfactory answer from my end."

"Good. That's exactly what I want as well." said Wilkes.

"Why?"

"Proof. The forensic evidence we capture will provide us with leverage against Morozov and the Russians. But there's another reason. Something I haven't told you yet."

Both Fends stood in suspense.

"I think Morozov has a man on the inside of Fend Aerospace. And I don't want to change any of our plans until we find out who that is, lest we tip him off."

"Why do you think that?"

"The FBI told me. I've been speaking to the man who's investigating the Fend cyberattack. The FBI forensics team tells him that the only way someone could have penetrated the network the first time—however limited its success—was with inside knowledge."

"You're working with the FBI?"

"Yes."

Charles frowned. "You think there's someone who works for me that is helping Morozov?"

"Possibly. I think we should bring the FBI investigator into the fold here tonight. Special Agent Flynn. I would like him to provide his theories on the matter."

Charles clasped his hands together. "We need a way to protect ourselves against this."

Max said, "Like I said, the British agent I met—Charlotte Capri—said she'd give me a software program designed by MI-6. MI-6 is designing this software program to protect the Fend 100 from being hacked by Morozov's cyberoperators."

Charles said, "Caleb?"

Wilkes nodded. "They mentioned something to me about this. But we weren't ready to commit."

"Why?"

"At the time, we weren't convinced that Morozov was going to be able to break through the Fend network. And we were hoping that his initial attempt would give us enough evidence to connect it to him."

"But?"

"But so far, the cyber trail just leads to a Syrian group. If we allow them one more attempt, the gentlemen at Fort Meade will be ready. We'll be able to prove that Morozov's group is responsible for the cyberattacks. Our government can't move on Morozov until that point. When we're done here, I'll call my counterparts at MI-6 and find out about their progress with the thumb drive option. They need to work through me from now on."

Max watched Wilkes when he said it. He looked anxious, a hint of worry in his voice. *Like something wasn't going according to plan.*

Wilkes said, "I realize that I'm asking a lot of you both here. But I would like to keep pressing on with the Fend 100 flight."

"It's something I want as well. But I want to talk to some of my people about this," Charles said. "If there's a vulnerability in our system, I want them to know."

Wilkes said, "Let's keep this information among a small group. Pick one person that you trust implicitly on your team."

He thought for a moment. "Maria Blount. She's the program manager. But she has an engineering background. She would be able to find out if we have a problem."

"Is there a way that Maria can provide another layer of security, to make sure that the Russians can't hack into the aircraft controls?" Max asked.

Charles said, "We'll meet with her and find out. I won't allow the flight to go on unless she can guarantee it will be safe."

Wilkes held up his hand. "Let's run her name by the FBI first. I want to make sure that they approve. I'm going to call the FBI agent I've been working with. He's already in Jacksonville. We'll fill him in and run this Maria Blount name by him. As long as he approves, we'll bring her into the fold as well."

"Make sure that the FBI knows this rubbish about Max being complicit in the crime is not true."

"Yes. Please do that," Max said, his brow arched.

Wilkes smirked. "Of course. I'll make my call."

* * *

An hour later, Special Agent Jake Flynn showed up at Charles Fend's home in Ponte Vedra. Max had thought about inviting Renee but decided against it. He preferred to keep her behind the curtain for now.

Flynn stood in the doorway, greeted by Wilkes and Max Fend. He didn't look happy.

Max was half-expecting a load of FBI agents to come storming in behind him. Instead, he got a disgruntled nod. "Mr. Fend."

"Hello again."

Max assumed that Wilkes had prepped Flynn and decided not to press it any further for now.

Wilkes summarized the earlier conversations for Flynn.

"So this Pavel Morozov is former KGB, and is responsible for the cyberattacks on Fend Aerospace."

"We think so, yes."

Flynn looked at Wilkes. "How do you want to play this?"

Wilkes filled him in on what they were thinking.

As promised, Wilkes made sure to get his superiors at the CIA involved. Wilkes and Flynn jumped on a secure conference call with the bigwigs at the CIA and FBI for the next fifteen minutes. Wilkes smoothed things over and let them know that Max Fend was working with the CIA and should not be considered a suspect in the Fend cybercrime. From the short duration of the call, Max got the impression that the FBI and CIA leadership had already discussed the matter.

When the two men emerged, Wilkes said, "Special Agent Flynn, would you be able to share with the Fends what you were telling me yesterday? Your suspicions about an insider at Fend Aerospace."

Flynn looked uncomfortable. "We're looking closely at a few employees there."

Wilkes nodded. "Could you say who?"

"I would rather not. No offense."

Charles said, "Agent Flynn, with respect, it appears to be in our collective best interests to proceed with the Fend 100 flight tomorrow. The CIA and FBI both want to collect more cyber evidence on Pavel Morozov during that time. We'll need at least one of my experts at Fend Aerospace to help us reduce the risk of Morozov actually succeeding and stealing all of the Fend 100's artificial intelligence technology. But if you won't share your suspects with us, then I don't know who to trust."

Flynn looked thoughtful. "How about you give me a name, and I help you pick who I think would be best suited for the job?"

Wilkes said, "Charles, who was the person that you mentioned earlier?"

"Maria Blount."

Flynn looked at Wilkes. "She should be fine. She was actually the one who first contacted the FBI about the cyber intrusion on the Fend network."

"Alright, let's get her over here."

Maria came thirty minutes later, and they quickly brought her up to speed.

Maria said, "So let me see if I understand. Max, I think what I hear you saying is that this Russian is planning to remotely tap into the Fend 100, and use the datalink connection between the Fend 100 and the Fend 100 control center to steal our most precious AI technology. Is that right?"

"Exactly."

"Okay...and someone who you all trust is going to give you some sort of software that will act as an antivirus—to neutralize any threat that the Russians could actually do this." They hadn't told her that MI-6 would be providing the thumb drive. She didn't need to know who it was, just what it would do.

"Correct."

Maria paused. She frowned and said, "Well, this means they've already infected the aircraft or our control room software. If that's true, they must have done it the first time they hacked in. I find that highly doubtful. But it's possible that we overlooked something. If...and that's a *big* if...they really have a worm in our system, I don't know if it will be enough to just trust that this magical thumb drive software will inoculate us from another attack. Especially with as much as we have riding on this Fend 100 flight. I mean, this is everything to the company, Charles."

"I know, Maria. I understand the importance."

"Sorry. It's just...I know this means a lot to our bottom line."

Max knew it too. While he tried not to let that influence his decision-making, he realized that if the Fend 100 test flight didn't pass with flying colors, his father's company would take a pummeling on Wall Street. His father still owned a controlling share of the stock, but a failed test flight could ruin his life's work. It could mean massive layoffs, not to mention the effect it might have on the whole aviation sector. If the first autonomous commercial airline flight were hacked, no one would want to fly on them. There was already enough fear about riding in one of these things.

Max said, "Maria, do you see any other way that we could provide a fail-safe? Some way of preventing the flight from getting hacked?"

Her eyes glanced up, twitching back and forth as she thought. She started nodding to herself. "Yes. I think I know what we can do. I can go on the flight."

Charles said, "You want to go on the flight?"

"Yes. I'll rewrite some of the remote override code tonight. It will take a while, but I can do it. If anyone *does* hack into the flight, like last time, I'll be able to override it from inside the aircraft." She smiled, pleased with her solution. "It's the safest way."

"What about the thumb drive with the antivirus software?" Max said.

Wilkes eyed Max. "Let's consider Maria going on the plane as a fail-safe. But we should also continue to plan to get the thumb drive from your contact, Max. And I'll check on that solution with my contacts."

Charles said, "Okay—do we feel like there are enough controls in place that this will be a safe event?"

They all nodded slowly.

"And we'll be watching Morozov's yacht," Wilkes said. "If he tries anything, we'll finally have the evidence we need to prosecute him. Mr. Flynn, would you be able to help with a takedown, if we need it?"

Flynn nodded. "The FBI can handle that. Let me talk to my superiors."

They spoke for a few more minutes, and then Maria left to go get to work. Flynn did as well.

Wilkes said to Max, "You need a ride?"

"Sure. Thanks."

Max asked to be dropped off at a gas station near his father's home. He had texted Renee a few minutes before, asking her to pick him up there.

Wilkes smiled. "What's the matter? You don't want me to know where you're staying?"

"Sorry."

Max's ride pulled up. Renee looked at both Caleb Wilkes and Max through her window.

"Is that your Canadian hacker?"

"It is."

Wilkes nodded his approval. They then traded phone numbers. Before getting out of the car, Max said, "Let me ask you something. Why didn't you tell me you were going to recruit me after I began working for my father's company? I mean, why did the DIA—and you—let me think that I was done?"

"Isn't that obvious? Your father is the owner of Fend Aerospace. We received intelligence that Morozov was planning something big, and it involved Fend. I couldn't be certain that you *weren't* part of it."

"You really thought I might be compromised?"

"No. But I'm not paid to get it right *most* of the time. I'm supposed to get it right *all* of the time. So I quarantined you. I couldn't let you in on my operation until you were cleared."

"Are you sure now?"

"One hundred percent."

Max thought something still didn't fit. Wilkes wasn't giving him everything, and both of them knew it. But a good intelligence operative knew when to stop asking questions.

"Alright, thanks. I'll let you know what I hear from Charlotte."

"Max."

"Yeah?"

"Relax. I'm from the government, and I'm here to help."

Max gave a small smile. "That's what I'm afraid of."

He got in Renee's car and they drove away, careful to check that they weren't being followed.

17

When they got back to their hotel, Max and Renee took a quick walk on the nearby beach to talk and go over their plans. Their hands brushed together a few times as they walked, and Max caught Renee glancing at him when it happened, an unmistakable look of affection on her face.

Neither had said much about the rekindling of their old flame. There hadn't been time. Was it just a byproduct of the fear and adrenaline that was pumping through both of them after nearly being killed twice in one week? When this was over, would they go their separate ways? Or would it grow into something more?

All Max knew was that he loved the feel of her smooth bare skin on his body. And he loved seeing her smile at him in that special way.

But he was glad they hadn't spoken about it. He wasn't exactly the kind of guy that liked to talk about relationships or feelings. And they had plenty of other things to discuss.

"You don't trust Wilkes, do you?" Renee said.

"Not really, no."

"Why?"

"There's just something bothering me about the whole thing."

"About what Wilkes wants you to do?"

"More than that. Why would MI-6 go out on their own within the

United States? Why does Wilkes want Morozov to hack into Fend Aerospace for a second time? It's all highly unusual."

"Didn't Wilkes say—"

"I know what he said, but it just doesn't feel right."

"There will be passengers on the flight?"

"There will be tomorrow. They have a few dozen aviation and tech writers sitting on the aircraft. And some company executives."

Max stopped and picked up a stone, throwing it out towards the water. It skipped a few times before it plunged beneath the surface.

He said, "I'm letting things influence me that I shouldn't, in this situation. The well-being of my father and his company. And my desire to hurt Morozov. I'm still wrapping my mind around everything that they told me yesterday."

She placed her hand on his shoulder. "You mean about your mother?"

He nodded. Her hand dropped and they continued walking. The sun reflected off the water. A light breeze kicked up a whitish haze of fine sand.

"What if Wilkes has another motive?" Renee said.

"Like what?"

"You said MI-6 disagreed with him, right?"

"Yes."

"Think about it from his position. What actions has he taken? Ignore what he's *said* his objectives are. What has he actually *done*?"

"He has been working with the FBI. He contacted my father and convinced him to help bring me in to him. And he had a disagreement with MI-6."

"What did he say about Georgia, when you told him we were attacked there? Did he seem surprised?"

"No. But I wouldn't expect him to be. Our fingerprints were all over that place. The FBI knew about us being there, so he must have."

Renee looked troubled. "I'm worried that Wilkes is playing you."

"To what end?"

"What if he *wants* Morozov to succeed in stealing the Fend 100 data tomorrow?"

Max stopped walking and turned to face her. "Why would Wilkes want that?"

"What if Wilkes wants you to take the fall for it? Maybe both you and your father?"

"I don't see what he has to gain."

"He's saying he's working to entrap Morozov. But what if he's not? What if he's working *with* Morozov?"

* * *

The call came at eight p.m. sharp.

Renee and Max were both in the hotel room. Renee analyzed the data she had stolen from Morozov's yacht, while Max worked out on the floor beside the bed.

Max picked up the phone with a sweaty hand.

"Hello, Max."

"Hello, Charlotte. Are we still on?"

"Can you join me for a drink?"

"Where?"

"The Lemon Bar. Do you know it?"

"Yes. When?"

"One hour."

"I'll see you then."

The Lemon Bar was situated right on the shore of Atlantic Beach— one of the great bars in a great bar district of Jacksonville Beach.

A group of tall blue tables on an outdoor patio, umbrellas over some of them. The smell of the ocean to the east. A long outdoor bar to one side. The nearby street was lined with palm trees, and the shallow dunes to the east didn't quite hide the magnificent ocean view.

The bar was packed with people. A mix of local twenty-somethings and off-duty Naval personnel from the nearby base at Mayport. The atmosphere was lively. Mixed drinks garnished with slices of fruit. Live music. Everyone smiling.

Max saw her standing alone as he walked towards the bar from the beach.

She looked stunning in a tight black dress that hugged every curve on her body. Not much left to the imagination. But Max had a lazy imagination anyway.

"Hello, Max." She smiled and kissed him on the cheek, then sipped a pink concoction through a straw.

He smiled. "Drinking on the job again? You seem much happier than when I last saw you."

"Well, you aren't disobeying me this time. That was some stunt you pulled on the yacht."

"I don't know what you're talking about."

"There is video, Max."

He raised his hands, palms up. "Sometimes you need to break the rules."

"Well, Morozov was furious. But if you can pull this off tonight, we'll have him—and my job will be over, thank God."

"Where is it?" Max asked.

"Up in my room."

She thumbed behind her. Max followed her gaze over to a tall resort hotel. She finished her drink. "Come on. I'll take you up."

The playful look in her eye was not something Max expected. But it was familiar. There were competing voices in his head. The quiet and reasonable voice of a professional intelligence agent, and the loud shout of her dress, clinging to her derrière.

Max felt his phone vibrating in his pocket. He silenced it. "Okay, I'll follow you."

Charlotte held his arm as they walked out the same way Max had come in. Once on the beach, she removed her shoes and strode barefoot on the sand.

"I'm ready to be done with this dreadful assignment. Things were a little rough after your shenanigans in Key West."

"I was wondering if you would suffer any repercussions."

"It wasn't bad. I know how to cover my tracks."

Max felt the phone going off in his pocket again. They stopped outside her hotel. She was wiping off her sandy feet and putting her flats on again before they walked inside.

"I'm sorry," Max said. "I need to make a phone call. Can I meet you up there?"

"I can wait."

"No, really. It's okay. Just tell me the room number."

She gave him the room number, and he held his phone until she was through the door and into the lobby of the hotel. He looked down at his missed calls.

Wilkes.

He turned to make sure no one was around him and called him back. Charlotte was out of sight now.

The phone rang as Max opened the door to the hotel stairway. She was on the fourth floor, but the stairway would give him both privacy and time. He was making his way past the second floor when he finally got an answer.

"Max."

"Wilkes."

"Why haven't you been answering my damn calls?"

"I'm busy. Did you hear from MI-6 and confirm their thumb drive approach?"

He was up onto the third floor now, trying not to sound strained as he took several steps at a time.

"Now listen up, Max. I've got something urgent to tell you. There's a problem."

Fourth floor. He pushed open the door and began walking down the hotel hallway, reading the room numbers as he went.

"What is it?"

Max found her room. Two more doors down. He walked slower, wanting to hear what Wilkes had to say.

"*I just spoke with MI-6. I replayed everything you told me about Char-lotte Capri. It wasn't her, Max.*"

The door opened.

"What do you mean?"

Charlotte stood there. She smiled, holding a drink in her hand. That same flirtatious look in her eyes. Max could feel his blood pressure rising.

Max had his phone pressed up against his ear.

"*Charlotte Capri was found dead in Key West several days ago.*" Wilkes's voice was frantic.

"Get off the phone and come in." Charlotte smiled.

Max held up his finger. He mouthed to Charlotte, "One minute."

"*Did you hear what I just said?*"

"I'm sorry. Could you say that one more time?" Max said into the phone.

"Charlotte Capri. The MI-6 agent. *Is. Dead*," Wilkes said. "Her body was found by some snorkelers in Key West. MI-6 thinks Morozov found out about her and had her killed. The estimated time of death was several days ago. Right when you were down there."

How was that possible? Max was looking at Charlotte in the flesh.

Max's voice was quiet. "Any thoughts about that?"

Charlotte twirled her hair, her head tilted. Her eyes staring at Max's own. Studying him.

Wilkes's voice whispered through the phone receiver. "Whoever you've been talking to, it *isn't* Charlotte Capri."

18

"Got time for one quick drink before you leave me?" Charlotte said.

Max pressed the end call button on his phone and slid it into his pocket. He smiled. "Sounds lovely."

She closed the door behind him. "Hope you don't mind coming up here?"

She walked across the room. Max's eyes followed her closely.

"Before I forget, here's the thumb drive. The flight is tomorrow, so you'll need to do this tonight."

"Sure thing," Max said, taking it from her hand and placing it in his other pocket.

She approached him, looking into his eyes, and kissed him. Her chest pressed up against his polo shirt. Then she pulled away and said, "I'm excited. I hope you will forgive me being forward. I always get this way near the end of an assignment."

Max didn't react. He hadn't kissed her back. He just stood there like a stone, his heart pounding in his chest. Thinking about what to do next.

Charlotte gripped his arm, her bright red fingernails digging in ever so slightly. "How rude of me. Let me get you a drink."

She walked over to the minibar.

"What's your poison?"

Did she have to use that choice of words?

"Scotch if you've got it."

He cursed himself for not bringing his gun. He hadn't expected to be up here with her, alone.

"So where did you tell our friend you were today?" Max asked.

"Morozov? He lets me do my own thing when we're ashore. For the most part. Do you want ice?"

"Neat, please."

She ducked down into the minibar and brought up a few tiny bottles of scotch whiskey, pouring them into a hotel glass, which she handed to him. "To finishing the job."

They clinked glasses and she took a sip. He refrained. She placed her glass on the table.

"Anything wrong?" she asked.

"Yes, actually. Hopefully you can help me understand something. Morozov tried to kill me in Georgia. But in Key West, he decided to let me live."

"He did?" A change of tone. The first crack in her mask.

"I know that you're not MI-6. So you must be working for him, right? Which means that he had me located in Key West. You could have easily killed me that night when we first met, but you didn't. Why?"

She kept staring into his eyes. Her face lacked expression, even as she pulled a small pistol from the purse next to her and aimed it at Max.

"Who was that on the phone?"

"Are you going to answer my question? Why did Morozov let me live? You work for him. You must have killed the real Charlotte at some point when I was in Key West."

"I didn't kill her. That was all Pavel. He stabbed her and threw her off the yacht."

Max saw a flicker of distaste as she said it. Maybe he had an opening.

"Why work for a man that would do that?"

She smiled. "Max. Come now. Don't bother trying to drive a wedge between Pavel and me. The bitch deserved it. Pretending to be one of his whores was a stupid idea. Sunbathing with the others all day. Did MI-6 really think that was the best cover? My issue with it was the matter of the location of the body. If I had known he was going to throw her over there, I wouldn't have let him do it. That area was much too close to all the touristy spots. But the girl had to be killed."

The door behind her opened. Two large men, whom Max assumed were part of Morozov's team, entered the hotel room. One of them made a comment to Charlotte in Russian. She said something back in Russian and the man grunted.

The two security men both pointed silenced pistols at Max.

"Max, if you would please come with us," she said. "Mr. Morozov would like a word."

* * *

They took the freight elevator down to the ground floor and then walked in an unusually tight grouping out to the parking lot. Max was shoved into the back of the SUV, sandwiched between Charlotte and one of the thugs.

Max had flashbacks to the similar situation he'd been in with the FBI, only a few days ago. Ah, to be in the custody of the FBI again. The good old days.

"Charlotte—I've got to ask you, just to be clear—I take it that you really weren't interested in me?"

She rubbed his stubbled cheek with her soft hand. "Oh, Max. Maybe in another life, darling."

The thug in the driver's seat eyed him in the rearview mirror.

Max winked back. The man gave him the finger.

"So what's Pavel want to discuss?"

"You'll see when you get there," Charlotte said.

Max watched as the vehicle turned right on Mayport Road, and then veered left onto A1A. He knew the area well, having spent many summers down here in his youth. He used to go surfing near the Naval Station at Mayport. The waves fell just right, and there was a nice point break.

To his right he could see Navy helicopters taking off and landing at the runway on the base. Their car drove past the area where they could view the runway and turned left into a short line of cars. They waited in line for a moment and then drove right up onto the ferry.

"You stay here."

Thug One got out and headed to pay for the ferry across the St. John's River.

Max turned back to Charlotte. "So why the ruse about the thumb drive? And why let me live?"

Charlotte turned to him. "The thumb drive idea wasn't a ruse. It was real. MI-6's idea."

Max frowned. "But why...?"

She petted his knee. "Just be patient, my dear. If Pavel wants to tell you, he will."

Max searched the vehicle for a way out but didn't see one. He could try to overpower Charlotte and the Russian security man right here. It might be his best chance. Before the other goon returned. But truth be told, Max wasn't sure he could take him. The man was a monster. And an alert one. He was staring right at Max, the veins in his neck bulging. No expression. Maybe no brains. Just thick shoulders and arms. This guy was on steroids, no question. If Max tried to fight him in close combat, it would end badly.

There was another reason Max didn't want to try and escape just yet. He wanted to hear what Pavel Morozov might have to say. Max needed to find out what he was up to. But as the ferry began to rumble ahead, Max realized that the Russians likely did not plan to release him.

* * *

Renee looked at Max and cursed. Men could be such *idiots*. That slut shows up wearing a tight dress and he just follows her up to her room? Didn't he realize people were trying to kill him? Why was he so trusting? Max Fend had to be the worst spy in the world.

She took a deep breath. "*Merde.*"

Renee had been in her car in the parking lot outside the Lemon Bar and watched Max and Charlotte leave via the beach exit.

She had wanted to run up into the hotel and start beating the hell out of both of them. Max was hers. Maybe he didn't realize that yet, but she would tell him. Hell hath no fury like a French Canadian whose man was being seduced away by another woman.

A few minutes later, when Renee saw the two large men accompanying Max and Charlotte back out to the lit parking lot, she was glad she had remained in the car. It was no seduction. She realized that something was terribly wrong.

Now the SUV was several vehicles ahead, driving onto the ferry. Renee needed to decide whether she should risk getting on the same ferry. If she did, they might spot her. The question was whether the men who had apprehended Max would know who she was. Were they the same men who'd manhandled her on Morozov's yacht?

It wasn't a choice. If she didn't drive onto the ferry, she would lose them.

Renee pulled her hoodie over her head. It was dark out. Hopefully they wouldn't be able to see her. One of the Russians got out of the driver's seat of their SUV to pay for the ferry passage. Renee didn't get out of her car to pay. She waited for the man collecting the fees to come to her, and she rolled down her window.

It took about ten minutes before all the cars were on board and the ramp was raised, and another five minutes for the ferry to cross the St. John's River. Renee kept her head down the entire time, pretending to be lost in her phone. Praying for a solution.

* * *

Pavel Morozov was finishing up his round of golf with the counselor to the Russian ambassador to the United States. That was his official title. Unofficially, he was the head of the FSB in Washington. The Federal Security Service was the successor to the KGB.

They were playing at the Amelia Island Golf Club. Pavel noted that while his partner was old and out of shape, he still swung a mean iron.

"Vasily, I think your golf game has improved over the years."

"The Americans love to play this game. Who am I to disagree? I find that playing with them helps with the job." He walked over to the golf cart and removed his putter. Morozov was already on the green, taking a practice swing with his own putter.

One of Morozov's security guards approached and whispered something to him. He nodded and waved the man off. Then he sunk his putt. A five-footer, which drifted from right to left. Morozov watched Vasily take three putts on the green before he was able to get his ball in the cup.

"Well done, Vasily."

"Ah. I may not be the young man I once was, but at least we can enjoy the fresh air."

Fresh wouldn't be the way Morozov would describe it. The air was thick and humid. Much warmer than he preferred.

"Let us go enjoy a few drinks. Have you stayed at this Ritz-Carlton before? I've had them send up a bar directly to the suite. They do a nice job," Morozov said. "I hear that all the Americans are drinking Moscow mules these days. It seems that our country has finally succeeded in influencing the West."

Vasily laughed heartily. The two men rode their golf carts to the exit. One of Morozov's assistants took care of returning everything. Another assistant showed the two Russian men to their car. In a few moments, they were sitting at an outdoor patio table, situated on a private balcony.

The hotel had laid out the finest spread of appetizers. A private bartender prepared cocktails for both men. Morozov's regular harem of imported women were already enjoying their drinks. Two of them began making their way over to Morozov and the FSB man, but Morozov waved them off.

"In a few moments, ladies. We need to speak alone."

Vasily looked at the women and said, "Now that is something the Americans I do business with don't often provide. Are they Russian?"

"I source my talent from all over the globe," Morozov replied. "But to be honest, I can't remember where these two are from."

The two Russian men sipped their drinks. Vasily was admiring the ocean view. The sky was getting dark, but it was still peaceful. Morozov didn't pay the view any attention. He was focused on Vasily.

"When will they arrive?" Morozov asked.

"Tomorrow. Midmorning, Eastern time."

"Flying into Washington, D.C?"

"Yes." Vasily paused. "How will you—"

Morozov clicked his tongue, shaking his head. "This we cannot discuss. But suffice it to say that we have very good targeting information on his plane."

Vasily flushed.

Morozov took a deep breath. "I can see that you are uncomfortable with this."

"If it goes wrong, Pavel..."

"I know."

"*He* is not a man to be trifled with," Vasily whispered.

Morozov's face darkened. "Neither am I."

"And what of the Fend boy? Is he still out on the loose? I told you that I wouldn't give my approval unless he was taken care of."

"He's on his way."

"What? You're bringing him here? Is that wise?"

"You wanted confirmation. I'm giving it to you."

* * *

Max was escorted into a luxury hotel on the coast. He was guessing it was Amelia Island, based on the time it had taken them to get here.

The Russian henchmen led Max to a small hotel room and sat him on a couch. The Ritz-Carlton. Max saw the words on one of the cupholders. The two Russian guards sat on the beds, watching bad TV. Every few seconds, they would look at him. Charlotte—or whatever her name was—had left them when they came in.

They remained in the room for several hours. Max attempted small talk a few times. If the Russians understood English, they feigned a lack of understanding quite well.

Charlotte came in after midnight. "He's ready for him." The guards shoved Max out the door and down the hallway.

Pavel Morozov was waiting for him with another man. Two women in cocktail dresses were draped over them. Seeing Max, Morozov sent the two women away.

Morozov looked at Max Fend. "It's good to finally meet you, Max. I hope your father is well. Did he tell you about our special relationship? About how he worked for me?"

"He didn't work for you."

Morozov smiled. "Is that what he told you? Let me guess. He told you that the CIA was controlling him. That it was all part of a ploy to feed me false information. The almighty American intelligence agency—the saviors of the Cold War. Are those the lies that he told you?"

Max didn't say anything. Charlotte stood in back of them over a rolling bar. She plucked an olive with a toothpick and began chewing it, watching Max. The older man next to Morozov sat quietly in his chair.

"Your father was a traitor to his country," Morozov said. "The only reason he switched sides was because he wanted to save his own skin. He got caught. He was bad at it. He didn't follow the proper precautions like I had taught him. Once the CIA and FBI knew that they could use him, your father cut a deal with them. Before that, I had been giving him everything. His aerospace company would not have been nearly as successful without the documents that I provided him."

"Come on, Pavel. We both know that the Russians stole everything from the US military back then. Not the other way around."

Morozov smiled. "Tsk-tsk. Revisionist history. Of course that is what the American textbooks say. But the truth is malleable. And the CIA, along with your own press, has changed the story of what really happened at the end of the Cold War. Your father wasn't a hero, Max. He was a traitor. And he was responsible for your mother's death."

Max's face reddened.

"He probably told you that it was me, right? *Of course.* Then why didn't he ever come after me? Hmm? Why didn't he go to the authorities? That is what any reasonable person would have done. What any *real* man would have done. But your father? He kept quiet. He covered it up, along with the CIA. Ask yourself—why?"

Max clenched his fists but stayed silent.

Pavel smirked. "The real reason your mother died? Because your father betrayed me. He knew the penalty for crossing me. And he didn't care. Your father only wanted to protect his baby. Not you, Max. His precious Fend Aerospace. That was what he really cared about. He was willing to sacrifice anything to grow that business. Even your mother."

He spoke with conviction. Like he'd had years of practice manipulating others. He had, Max reminded himself. As a KGB operative during the Cold War, Morozov's two main jobs had been to squeeze information out of people, and to insert false information.

Max couldn't play the game anymore. He couldn't stomach it. "You're a sad little man," he said.

"Nothing hurts like the truth. I don't need you to believe me. I have gotten you and your father to do exactly what I want. Now it's just a matter of executing."

"So you're still planning on stealing the Fend 100 technology? Are you an imbecile, Pavel? Everyone knows what you're planning. It's not going to happen. There are probably US law enforcement officers listening to us right now."

"I doubt it. They think I'm on my yacht, which is docked south of St. Augustine, quite a ways from here."

"How do you know what law enforcement believes?"

"The information is all out there, if you know the right people." Pavel turned to the older man sitting next to him. "Enough of this. Vasily, are you satisfied? You heard him, correct? He said *steal* the technology. That is what they think I am going to do. May I dispose of him now?"

The old man studied Max and nodded. "*Da.*"

Pavel made a whistling noise and gestured to his security guards.

"*Wait,*" Max said. His mind was racing. Pavel and this other Russian were planning something else. They didn't intend to steal the Fend 100 technology. "You let me live because you wanted to mislead MI-6? The CIA?"

Morozov smirked. "And you just confirmed that we were successful."

The guards stood over him now. "But you must have intended for me to upload your software into the Fend 100 with the thumb drive. If you're going to kill me, then how are you planning to access the Fend data?"

Pavel Morozov's expression darkened. "Now, Max, there's no reason for you to know that."

"You're pathetic. My father beat you at your own game back during the Cold War. He humiliated you. He let you provide false information to the USSR on his defense projects. And you believed him, you Commie bastard. Now you're trying to get revenge on him by sabotaging his company. They know what you're doing, Pavel. No wonder the Soviet Union collapsed. It was filled with morons like you."

Pavel looked at Charlotte. "Miss Capri?"

"Yes?"

"I am ready for you to take our guest away."

"Very well."

Pavel breathed in deeply and exhaled. "Max, I bid you farewell. Rest assured that your death and subsequent blame for what happens tomorrow will allow you to live on in infamy."

Morozov nodded to his security men, and they grabbed his arms.

Max struggled against the guard's grip. He needed to create options. He kept trying to dig. He wanted Morozov to get emotional and slip up. To give him some tidbit of information that he might find useful.

"You're walking into a trap, Morozov."

Pavel smiled, but didn't say anything.

"This is reckless, even for you. Revenge on my father isn't worth spending your life in an American prison. Think about that. They'll know what you did. They'll know you killed me." Max didn't see any reaction from Morozov.

The men began dragging him away. "You think this will make you feel better about losing the Cold War for your country? This won't change anything for you. You'll still be just another stooge for your president."

At that, Morozov's face went red, and he held up his hand. "Wait."

Morozov walked over to Max. The guards held him tight. Pavel shot a leathery hand out and seized Max by the jaw.

"Say that again."

Max tried to seem as insolent as possible as he choked out his words, staring down Morozov. "That's right, Pavel. There's only one leader in Russia, and it ain't you."

Morozov nodded slowly. "Okay."

He let out a weird snort. Then he unleashed a furious blow into Max's stomach. His eyes nearly burst out of their sockets, and all the air shot from his lungs. The pain was excruciating. Max couldn't breathe.

Pavel whispered in his ear as Max's mouth remained open, empty gasps trying to suck in air.

"I know that I may be vain, young man. But I am not stupid. And you don't have enough respect for me, or where I came from. Yes, the Soviet Union collapsed. But *I didn't*. My people are everywhere. My plans are often years in the making. For this operation, you were just my personal cherry on top, as they say. But I'm happy to exclude you if it means that everything else will flow smoothly. Tomorrow your father's life's work will be destroyed, and you'll take the fall. But a man like me wouldn't go through all this trouble *just* to exact revenge upon your father. I have a much grander vision than that."

Destroyed?

Max's thoughts were a swirl of activity. The way Morozov was talking —it didn't fit with what they knew. Something was wrong, and it was staring him in the face.

They started to drag Max away, and then it clicked. Max's eyes widened. He finally knew what they were really up to. Holy shit. *Of course...*

"You aren't trying to steal the data at all, are you, Pavel? That was just a ploy..."

Vasily looked uncomfortable. "*Pavel.*"

Morozov waved him off. "Relax. He'll be dead soon."

"It won't work. We know who your insider is."

Morozov scoffed. "Who, then?"

Max thought about guessing, but in truth, he hadn't a clue.

A wide smile formed on Morozov's face. "The desperate words of a condemned man, I think."

Then he said something in Russian to his men, and they took Max away.

19

Renee had seen the Russians' SUV pull into the parking lot of the Amelia Island Ritz-Carlton. Renee had parked about one hundred yards away, near the resort's tennis courts. There were lots of cars. She was pretty sure she wasn't noticed.

Renee had seen the Russians leave their SUV in the parking lot and walk with Max into the hotel. She'd thought about calling the police. But Max had specifically forbidden that. He couldn't have foreseen this circumstance, however. She had to get help somehow. Why hadn't she gotten Wilkes's number from Max?

Calm down. Give Max some time. Maybe he had gone here on purpose. Maybe this was part of some plan. He would be okay. He did this for a living. Right?

She needed a weapon. If she went fast and came back here, she could be ready for when Max reappeared.

Five minutes later, Renee walked into a local sporting goods store and scanned the rows for what she needed. Football. Golf. Pool equipment. *There.*

Hunting and fishing.

The department was back of the store. Renee practically ran there. An overweight man in his early twenties stood behind the counter. He wore a red shirt with the words "Go Dawgs" on the front, a toothpick in his mouth.

"Can I help you, ma'am?"

She tried to act normal. Behind him, rifles and bows lined the wall. Under the glass counter he was leaning on were dozens of models of handguns.

"I need a weapon."

The man stared back at her. "Mmm. Okay. Well, it appears that you've come to the right place."

"It's for self-defense. But I prefer not to use a gun."

The man eyed her. "Right. We've got this little sucker over here. Ain't had nobody interested in it before. But there's always a first, I guess."

"What is it?"

"It's kind of like a paintball gun. But these little plastic balls are made special. They're filled with some sort of pepper spray mix that stings the eyes something awful. Blinds you for a few seconds and then you just go down until you can wash it out. Never tried it myself, but—"

"I'll take it."

The store clerk looked at her. "You alright, miss? You sound like you're in some trouble."

"I'm fine. Just in a hurry. Can I pay here?"

"Sure."

"Do you have flashlights?"

"Yes, ma'am. Right over there."

"Good. And one more thing...do you have any field hockey sticks?"

She paid and hustled to her car, then drove back to where she had seen the Russians park their SUV. She waited in the parking lot of the Amelia Island Ritz-Carlton for several hours. As the night went on, she drove herself insane wondering if she hadn't made a mistake. What if he was already gone? What if they had killed him?

All she had to hold on to was the car they had arrived in. She watched it to see if Max would reappear.

* * *

Max was once again in the backseat of the Russians' SUV. They drove south along A1A, back the way they came. It was dark now, and no one spoke. Max could hear the rhythmic thumping of the tires against the slabs of highway.

They turned left off the highway and onto a single-lane road, driving deeper into the darkness. The headlights briefly illuminated a sign for Little Talbot Island State Park. Palms and swampy trees hugged both sides of the road.

Max tried to remain calm, but his mind was racing with what he had just learned. Morozov wasn't trying to just steal the Fend 100 technology. He was trying to do something far worse. And he was going to blame it on Max somehow. Maybe that's why he had decided to let him live, when they could have killed him in Key West.

No. It was more than that.

They had misled Max and used him to feed bad information to...who? To Wilkes? To his father? What was the bad information he had given them?

The thumb drive solution? Max had told them of MI-6's plan to defend against another one of Morozov's cyberattacks.

But Wilkes and the people at Fend Aerospace weren't even going to use that now. They had a backup plan in Maria. None of this made any sense...

Max needed to get out of here and warn them. They couldn't let the Fend 100 get airborne.

He examined his driving companions. Two large Russian men. Ex-special forces, likely. Both armed and deadly. Driving along a deserted street at night. Max would only have one chance. He would have to make it count.

The car came to a halt in a large open parking lot. Max thought he could make out a few other cars there, on the other side of the lot. But it was hard to tell in the darkness.

The Russians were talking to each other, but they were speaking in their native tongue. Max couldn't understand a word. The one in the backseat kept his weapon out, pointing it at Max. The one in the driver's seat got out and walked around to Max's door, opening it. The man sitting next to Max in the backseat started pushing him forward, weapon trained on Max's back.

Max had been hoping to have an opportunity to take on just one of them at a time during the transition out of the vehicle. But they had obviously done this before. He would wait. Maybe try falling in the sand and...

"This way," Thug One said, pointing with his silenced pistol.

They marched him along the dunes, parallel to the beach. It was slow going, their feet sinking into the sand. Lots of brush. Crabs scattering as they trudged through.

Waves crashed on his left side. Slow rhythmic bursts of white noise. Max made calculations in his head. They were getting farther from the parking lot. It was now or never. He gave himself about a ten percent chance.

Someone called out from behind them.

"Hey! Excuse me?" came the female voice. "Can you help me out?" A flashlight cut through the night behind them, shining on the sand and illuminating the ground between the Russians and a woman walking towards them.

The men said something to each other in Russian. Max imagined that they were wondering whether Morozov would get mad if they killed her too.

The flashlight changed direction and reflected the body of the woman approaching them. Her white shirt was unbuttoned and wide open, revealing a bright-pink-and-white bikini top and tight jean shorts. Seeing that, one of the Russians whispered something to the other, which was followed by snickering.

The way the light was pointed, her face wasn't visible. One of the Russians grumbled to Max, "You stay quiet or we shoot you both right here."

He didn't reply.

The flashlight moved erratically, shining towards them and then back towards the woman. Both Russians clumsily hid their weapons from the woman behind their legs. If she was looking carefully, she would probably notice.

"I'm so sorry," the woman said, "I'm lost. Would you gentlemen be able to help me find…" Max recognized the voice.

The light flashed back in their eyes. Max and the two Russians instinctively winced. What they didn't realize was that the flashlight was connected just under the barrel of Renee's pepper spray gun.

It had the look and feel of a large plastic 9mm Beretta, but it fired paintball-type rounds, filled with a combination of tear gas and pepper spray.

Renee fired multiple times into both of the Russians' chests and faces. Quick clicks and pops, and the sound of high-speed plastic pellets bursting into the muscle-bound men.

Renee then turned out the light and ran towards them. She dropped the pepper spray gun and gripped the field hockey stick, which she had been holding under her left armpit.

She headed towards the sound of Russian cries and cursing. Renee had made the field hockey team at Princeton University many years ago for her athleticism and speed. But once there, she had been known for the power of her shot.

Renee's vision was barely adjusted to the low light level, but it was enough. She bent her knees as she approached, twisted her hips for maximum velocity, and drove the heavy wooden stick forward and up into the head of the first Russian.

The crack she heard was at once frightening and satisfying. The man collapsed into the sand. Renee tried not to think about whether she might have killed him. She just moved on.

But during the swing, she had become disoriented. When she looked up, she was no longer sure which of the dark figures before her was the other Russian.

All three of them had been pelted by the pepper spray bullets, she realized. Unsure of what to do, she looked back to where she had dropped the pepper spray gun. There. She snatched it up from the ground and listened, trying to discern who was who.

* * *

Max, blinded and in pain from just being near the pepper spray bursts, ran away toward the beach. He tripped several times, falling into the sand and beach grass.

"Max!" Renee shouted as loudly as she dared.

Max felt his feet enter the surf. He knelt down and splashed saltwater up into his face. It helped. The pain subsided as he kept washing the saltwater in and around his eyes.

"Max." He could feel her holding on to his shoulder. "Are you alright?"

"What the hell was that stuff?"

"It's a self-defense gun. Pepper spray and mace."

"God, it stings. Why didn't you bring a real gun?"

"I don't like guns. I told you."

"Holy shit, Renee. This hurts. Next time just shoot me with a real gun."

"Men are so ungrateful."

Max squinted up at the dunes. Between his blurred vision and how dark it was outside, he could barely see a thing. "Where are they?"

"They're still up there, but I hit one pretty hard with this field hockey stick," Renee said. "Here. Hold the stick and come on. We should get to my car before they make it back to the parking lot."

"I'm not sure that's such a good idea. Look."

A set of headlights was visible in the parking lot. Renee cursed.

"You think it's more of them?" Over the sound of the waves, they could hear car doors opening and closing. Anxious shouting in Russian.

"Come on. We're not going to be able to go back to your car. Let's jog. This way."

They ran away from the parking lot, south along the beach. It took about five minutes for the Russians to get smart and start driving along the beach in their SUVs. With the headlights on, it was easy for Max and Renee to see them coming. But that also meant that there weren't many good hiding places.

"It's into the brush or into the water, which one?"

Renee said, "I..."

"Water, then." Max pulled her arm. They waded into the ocean. The waves were only a foot or two. When they got neck-deep, Max began to second-guess his choice of hiding in the water. He wondered if they would have night vision. Or infrared. Dammit.

They were pretty far out. "Alright, let's hold our breath and try to stay under for a bit, until they drive by."

Both Max and Renee took a deep breath and went under. Thank God the sea was warm. Max hated cold water. He went up for air about thirty seconds later, and then went back down underneath. He had gotten a glimpse of the SUV, motoring along the beach at five miles per hour.

Max tried to think about their options. A1A was the main highway that ran north-south, parallel to the beach. Anyone with common sense would have headed for the road. But the Russians would know that. So they would keep one team at the beach, searching for him, the other team patrolling the road, waiting for Max and Renee to pop up.

When they came up for air again, he said to Renee, "I say we keep heading south along the beach. It'll be a few miles, but we'll get to the end of Talbot Island. Then we can swim across the inlet. We'll end up at Huguenot Park, right across from Mayport."

"Then what?"

"Then we'll be far enough away from them that we can go try and find a ride," Max said.

"How far is that?"

"A few miles."

"It sounds like it's going to take us all night. It's already three a.m. The Fend 100 flight launches at seven. Do you have a phone?"

"Of course not. Don't you?"

"I'm sorry—I needed to carry a few things to *rescue you.*"

They waded back towards the beach and walked along the shore. She was right. This was going to take all night. But he didn't see what choice he had.

* * *

Flynn was in his hotel room, fielding calls from Washington and scanning the news about the Fend 100. Many aviation news sources were calling it the dawn of a new era in automated flight.

But the big story that most people cared about was the human element. The *Washington Post* was the first to the punch. They had a source saying that Max Fend was under investigation for a cyberattack on Fend Aerospace. The news channels had fallen all over themselves when they'd heard about it. Even Flynn had to admit that it was a great story. On the eve of one of the biggest moments in aviation history, Max Fend attempts to sabotage his own father's achievement.

The FBI sent out a press release shortly after. Now, they were talking just as much about him, but proclaiming his newfound innocence.

BILLIONAIRE PLAYBOY NOT A SUSPECT, SAYS FEDS

Wonderful. Flynn was reading one such article when he heard the knock at his door.

He looked through the peephole and saw Wilkes staring back at him, still wearing a suit and tie. Flynn checked his watch. It was close to midnight.

Flynn removed the chain. "Come on in."

"Sorry to disturb you, but I thought you'd want me to fill you in."

"Of course. Excuse the clutter." Flynn tried to clean up the remnants of his room service. A twenty-three-dollar burger and fries. Pretty good, but you could get a lot better at Five Guys for a lot less.

The two men sat down. "What's up?" said Flynn.

"We have a problem. Max Fend has gone missing."

"Missing?"

"I told you he might be in contact with a foreign agent," Wilkes said.

"Yes."

"Well, he made contact earlier this evening, and now he's off the grid. I'm worried. I may need your help."

"What did you have in mind?"

"I need backup plans in case this thing goes sideways," Wilkes said. "I think the FBI might be best equipped to respond."

"Caleb, just say what you need."

"How soon could you get HRT down here?"

* * *

The FBI's Hostage Rescue Team is one of the premier counterterrorism units in the world. Made up mostly of ex-special operations personnel, they function as the elite national tactical response unit for the FBI. Based in Quantico, Virginia, HRT has over one hundred operators assigned to its team.

HRT operators conduct training with many of the other Tier One special forces units in the United States military, including the Army's Delta Force and the Navy's DEVGRU—commonly known as SEAL Team Six.

HRT trains in maritime and airborne assault techniques, and also has its own sniper teams and regularly responds to the most dangerous incidents around the world.

Because they need to be ready to go at a moment's notice, HRT always rotates its members on a deployable watch bill. They are required to be on base and ready to deploy within thirty minutes of being called.

Twenty of them got the call tonight.

Within an hour, all twenty men were on a plane to Florida. An hour after that, two US Air Force transport aircraft flew to the same destination. Those aircraft contained members and equipment of the Tactical Helicopter Unit. These were the HRT's elite aviators. Helicopter pilots and aircrew who trained and operated with the HRT and were ready for anything.

Before takeoff, the group's leader made the call to Jake Flynn. "We're headed to Naval Air Station Jacksonville. Where do you want us after that?"

"Have your aircrews set up shop there. The Jacksonville SAC will send vehicles for your team as soon as you arrive. We'll bring you to where we need you."

"Roger. We'll be there in a few hours. I'll call you back in a few minutes. We'll need you to brief us on the plane so that we can mission-plan on the way down."

* * *

Max and Renee had switched from wading along in the water to trudging along through the beach grass, up on the small dunes.

"I should probably say thanks for coming to rescue me," Max said.

"Hmm. Now you say it." She punched his arm.

"How were you able to find me?"

"I followed you after you left the Lemon Bar. With Charlotte Capri."

"That's not her real name, you know. The woman I met with was an impostor. Working for Morozov. Wilkes called me and warned me about it."

"You're kidding." Renee was shaking her head. "But I don't under-stand. They tried to kill you in Georgia, then this impostor meets with you in Key West and lets you go. Now they're trying to kill you again? Why do they keep changing their minds?"

"I'm their scapegoat. They aren't just trying to hack into the Fend system to steal the technology."

"*What?*"

Max told her about what he had learned, and what he thought Morozov was planning.

"If I'm dead or in captivity, I can't screw up their plans."

"But why leave you alive in Key West?"

"That must have been when they found out about MI-6's agent. The real Charlotte. By leaving me alive, thinking I had met Charlotte, I helped Morozov deceive someone."

"Who?"

"I don't know exactly. MI-6. The CIA. Both? But whoever it was, it worked."

"How do you know?"

"Morozov told me as much. And now he's decided to kill me again. So I've served my purpose."

"But why bring you up to Amelia Island to see Morozov? They could have just shot you in the hotel in Jacksonville, right?"

Max shook his head. "That's one thing I'm still trying to figure out. There was another man there with Morozov. What name did he use...? Vasily, I believe."

"Vasily? I met a Vasily. An older Russian man?"

"Yes."

"When I was on the yacht, I spoke to him. Morozov came over and interrupted, and they began talking."

"What did they say?"

"I don't know. They were speaking in Russian, and I left."

Max frowned. "Morozov wanted him to see me. He said something like 'Now are you satisfied?' to Vasily. But why? Why would seeing me alive mean anything to Vasily?"

"Maybe it wasn't seeing you alive. Maybe it was knowing that you would be dead..."

Their eyes met, and they kept walking.

A bright white moon began to rise over the ocean horizon. Max thought how pretty it was, and how much he would enjoy this night, were he not also watching the headlights about two miles down the beach. Headlights that were searching for him so they could put a bullet in his head.

Renee shook her head. "Why does he want you dead so bad?"

"I told you, I'm his scapegoat for what he's planning."

"No, I mean, why you? Why couldn't he make someone else the scapegoat? It would be more believable."

"He hates my father, and he's responsible for my mother's death."

Renee gasped. "So it's all about revenge, then?"

"I think that's why I'm involved. But now I'm not so sure revenge is his only objective."

"What do you mean?"

"I was trying to dig at him. To get him emotional and see what he would say. He made one comment that stuck with me. I said something about revenge, and he responded that his plans are much grander than that. Something to that effect."

"What if he's trying to mislead you again?"

"That's possible. Never trust an ex-KGB agent. That's always been my motto. Well, that and never fall off a barstool."

"Both good pieces of advice."

"Here comes the truck again. Better get down." They lay flat against the sand, hiding behind a large clump of grass.

While they were waiting, Max whispered, "I'll tell you another thing that bothers me. He's too confident. Like he knows he won't be caught."

"You told me the FBI thinks he has someone on the inside."

"Yes, but wouldn't you still be worried if you were him? It's pretty ballsy of him to be here in America."

Max thought about the cryptic way Morozov had said it. *My people are everywhere. My plans are often years in the making.*

The SUV rumbled slowly past them. Only fifty feet away.

Then it stopped. Brakes squealing.

The lights went out, and the doors opened. Two men got out from either side. The doors slammed shut.

Max could make out a faint green glow near their heads. Night vision goggles.

* * *

Flynn hung up the phone and looked at Wilkes. It was almost 3 a.m. now, and he was still in his room. They had ordered coffee and set up shop. There would be little sleep tonight.

"HRT is on the way to Jacksonville now. I've finished briefing them, and they'll be doing scenario planning the whole way down. The Jacksonville SAC will meet us at the Fend Aerospace headquarters tomorrow. Are you sure we shouldn't just call this thing off?"

Wilkes shook his head. "We can't. I need Morozov to make his move tomorrow. It'll allow us to snare him and his agent working for Fend."

"Okay. We'll get the HRT team ready to go in with an air assault on his yacht when ready."

"Let's walk through what we think will happen tomorrow," Wilkes said. "The Fend 100 will take off at seven a.m. It's roughly a three-hour flight. They do a bunch of circles over Florida and then land back at the Fend Aerospace headquarters near Jacksonville."

"I'm with you so far."

"Morozov will, at some point, initiate a cyberattack on the Fend 100. That electronic signal is expected to come from the yacht. I have a team of experts at the NSA who are ready and waiting for that electronic signal. Once it occurs, we'll have what we need. The HRT team can then move in and take control of the ship. We have surveillance teams that will be monitoring communications from our suspects within Fend Aerospace."

"You still think its Karpinsky or Hutson?"

"Honestly? I don't know. But we'll be watching them both closely."

"We'll need a cyber expert on the yacht."

"I got a guy who'll be here," Flynn said. "HRT can take him when they go assault the yacht. If there are any problems with the aircraft link, he'll solve them."

"What about Charles Fend's employee that he's got on the plane—what's her name?"

Flynn said, "Maria Blount. She's plan A now. Once we get the signal that Morozov's hackers are trying to steal the Fend 100 data, she'll be able to shut them down."

"Good. Without Max Fend, we'll need to rely on her."

"Is Max going to show back up before the Fend 100 gets airborne?"

"I hope so."

* * *

Max watched one of the Russians head their way, scanning the beach with his night vision goggles in a side-to-side sweeping motion. The other Russian was doing the same thing, but walking along the beach in the opposite direction. The moonlight would make his night vision much more effective. And the moon was rising.

Max touched Renee's hand. Then he made his fingers into a gun. She gave a barely perceptible nod. She carefully raised the pepper spray gun. Max still held her field hockey stick. What he wouldn't give for his Sig right now.

The Russian security man was only a few steps away now. Renee raised her plastic pepper spray gun and fired. Three pops in the night air.

The plastic pellets filled with caustic gas burst after impacting his chest. The Russian screamed in pain as the gas hit his eyes, then swore loudly. Max was already sprinting forward. He tackled the big Russian by jamming his shoulder into his chest, knocking him off of his feet and into the sand. The Russian crouched on the ground, trying to regain his balance while holding on to his weapon. Max chopped down with the field hockey stick, knocking the gun out of the man's hands. He then wound up and slammed the stick into the Russian's face as hard as he could. Lights out. The night vision goggles shattered, and his neck snapped back. He fell limp to the ground, unconscious.

Max heard the other Russian security man calling out from fifty feet away. Renee was now standing next to Max.

Max frantically searched around in the sand for the Russian's fallen pistol. It was so dark he could barely see. He felt among the clumps of sand and grass, desperate to find the weapon.

There.

He clutched it in his hands. Cold metal, his fingers fitting neatly around the grip and trigger. He kneeled down and aimed at the Russian, who was running towards them.

Max fired three times.

At least one of the rounds must have found its mark, because the man spun around and fell to the ground.

"Come on!" Max called back to Renee as he headed for the empty SUV. He pressed the keyless start button, but nothing happened. He cursed and turned back to Renee.

"Check their pockets for a key fob," Max said to Renee.

She ran to the unconscious man, found the keyless remote, and headed back towards the SUV.

Headlights lit up the dunes in the distance.

"That's the other set of Morozov's security men. It's got to be. These guys must have radioed them."

"Hurry, then."

Max pressed the ignition button and the engine rumbled to life. He cursed as the headlights came on automatically, alerting the incoming vehicle to their presence. The headlights also illuminated the second Russian, the one who'd been spun around when Max had shot him. He was still on the ground, but now he was sitting up, aiming his weapon at Max and Renee from thirty feet away.

The windshield of their vehicle filled with holes as a barrage of bullets whizzed through the glass.

Max instinctively crouched down, put the SUV in drive, and slammed on the gas, turning the wheel hard left. The vehicle accelerated to near fifty miles per hour, moving through the beach sand.

Glancing up in the rearview mirror, Max saw that the other vehicle had stopped to pick up the wounded Russians.

"Where are you going?"

"If we keep following the beach, I think it connects with the road again."

"I thought this was an island."

He glanced at her. "Why do women have to question everything?"

She muttered something in French.

"You know I spent several years in France, right? I know the word for stupid."

Renee began playing with the car's center display.

"What are you doing?"

"Checking the GPS. I want to see if I can find out where they've been."

Smart, Max thought.

In the rearview mirror, Max could see the other SUV catching up now, its headlights springing up and down as it raced over the mounds of sand. The beach ended just ahead. But as he suspected, the road met with the beach at that point.

"I'm going to turn over the dunes and try to make it to the road. Once we get there, we can try to outrun them or get to a police station. They wouldn't risk making a scene there...I don't think."

Their SUV launched itself over the dunes, bouncing hard against the suspension. Renee yelped as they went.

"They're gaining on us," she said.

As they reached the road, Max accelerated and turned hard left onto the pavement.

Loud metallic bangs emanated from the rear of the vehicle, and both Max and Renee ducked. *Gunshots.*

They heard a huge pop as one of the tires burst. Streetlights lit up the road as Max held his foot down on the accelerator and they began crossing the bridge. Bright white light revealed dozens of bullet holes throughout the vehicle. Their vehicle was slumping to one side, and the flat tire was making rhythmic slapping noises as they drove.

"What's that? Someone's at the other end of the bridge—*who is that?*"

Max saw it too. There was a sedan parked across both lanes of traffic near the end of the bridge they were trying to cross.

In front of the sedan stood a woman. She was aiming a large semiautomatic rifle at them.

"I think that's *Charlotte.*"

Max looked in his rearview mirror at the SUV behind them, which was just coming onto the bridge.

"You need to ram her or go around her," Renee said.

"There doesn't look to be enough room to get around her," Max said. "And if we ram her, they'll catch up." He glanced outside, trying to see where they were. Darkness lay on either side of the bridge. Nothing but a small bay.

"You're a good swimmer, right?"

"I'm sorry?" She sounded afraid.

"Okay, lower your window and hold on. This is probably going to hurt."

He swerved hard left and the tires slammed into the short concrete barrier. At the speed they were traveling, the barrier served as a ramp. The SUV left the ground and launched over the metal bridge rail. Max and Renee went weightless as they fell, the engine's RPMs spooling up without the resistance of the road.

The front of the vehicle impacted the water, and both of them were jolted forward, their seat belts restraining them. The airbags burst open on impact, pounding them both in the face, but minimizing the whiplash.

The vehicle began sinking into the shallow inlet. Max and Renee had lowered their windows several inches before he'd made the jump. The SUV began to fill with rushing water.

The water rose above their heads and they sank, fast and quiet. The vehicle hit the seafloor seconds later, at a depth of about fifteen feet.

Max and Renee both unstrapped and swam out and away from the bridge. They were disoriented, but still aware enough to stay underwater as long as possible. After about fifty feet of swimming, Renee tapped Max on the back and signaled that she needed to come up for air.

They broke the surface, for just a moment, gasping for air as quietly as they could, and then went back under, continuing to swim away from the crash scene. Max had taken a snapshot of the bridge in his mind.

Charlotte had been standing near the edge of the bridge, where they had broken through the barrier. She was looking down at the wreckage. The Russian security team was in their SUV behind her.

His instincts told him that Charlotte hadn't seen them. The streetlights shined bright white light onto the bridge, and the water was quite dark.

Max and Renee continued to swim underwater, both doing a sort of submarine breaststroke. Max's shoes and clothes were slowing him down, but he didn't want to take the time to remove them. Renee was indeed a good swimmer. She was keeping up with him no problem. She tapped him on the back again, and they came up for air.

Now they were substantially closer to an uninhabited section of shoreline. In the darkness, it looked like nothing more than a large sandbar with a swath of beach grass on top. They were far enough away from the Russians that they were treading water now, slowly sidestroking their way towards the shore.

"Do you think they saw us?" Renee panted.

"They would have fired at us if they did. It looks like they're leaving now. They probably don't want to be around when the police come to investigate the crash."

He felt his toes scrape the slimy bottom of the bay. "We can stand."

They swam a little further and soon enough both of them were wading, then walking along the beach, their clothes heavy and drenched with seawater.

"Where are we?"

"I'm not sure. I think we're on the opposite side of Mayport."

Max checked his watch. It was almost 6 a.m. The eastern horizon was starting to lighten up. The Fend 100 was scheduled to take off in less than an hour.

"We need to hurry."

20

The morning had not yet risen over the Atlantic horizon, but the sky was already a fiery red over the shore. The day had arrived. Charles Fend had not slept much. Partly due to his age—sleep was getting harder to come by—and partly due to his anxiety over the day's events.

His personal assistant and chef were waiting in the kitchen. The news played on a small TV in the corner.

"Sir, can we get you anything?"

"Earl Grey tea, please. And perhaps a grapefruit."

"Right away, Mr. Fend," the chef said.

His assistant had laid out the usual clippings and daily schedule on Charles's outdoor table, where he liked to eat during the nicer weather. Small metal weights in the shape of Fend airplanes rested on top of the paper stacks so that an errant sea breeze wouldn't blow them away.

His assistant had tried to convince Charles to switch to an iPad or some other electronic device to get his morning briefing, but Charles couldn't do it. He liked the feel of paper. It was real. And it wasn't trying to sell him something half the bloody time. Well...it wasn't trying to sell him *products*, anyway. Just ideas.

He ate his grapefruit and sipped his tea, reading over the news clippings that mentioned him and his company. There were quite a lot of them today. The kinder headlines hailed him as a champion in technology and aviation progress. The less friendly news stories were all gossip about his son. One of them showed a picture of Max with women in lingerie, dancing at his French villa.

Charles wondered how much of that was real and how much of it had been for show. Now that he knew Max had been working undercover for the DIA in France, things made much more sense. These wild parties didn't fit with the son he knew. Max was too driven to get caught up in that nonsense.

"Have I any messages?"

"Dozens, sir."

"Any from a Caleb Wilkes? Or from Max?"

Charles knew that his assistant wouldn't have simply taken a message if Max had called, but he asked anyway. The assistant was a loyal man, but Charles had yet to tell him everything about Max. And he had no doubt seen all the headlines. He would naturally be curious. It was even possible that reporters had called to try and fish out details. Charles laughed at the thought. They would have more success breaking into a bank vault.

"Just Mr. Wilkes, sir. He asked to speak with you when you woke."

"Please dial him for me."

A moment later, the assistant handed Charles the phone, already ringing. Charles looked at his watch. He needed to be on the road. The Fend 100 team had already been working for hours today, and Charles would be in high demand the moment he walked in to the building.

"Good morning, Mr. Fend."

"Morning, Caleb. What's the good word today?"

"I'm afraid we've had a few setbacks."

"Oh? Is Max alright? Anything I need to do?"

There was no answer.

"Caleb?"

Charles checked the phone, but the call had gone dead. After trying to call him back for a minute, he gave up. He tried calling in to work, but his phone wasn't connecting to the network.

Charles pointed it out to his assistant, who offered his own phone. But

Charles suggested that they just go in to the office. Everyone he needed to see would be there.

His assistant briefed him as they drove.

"You'll be speaking with the *Today Show* again—live at eight oh five a.m.—followed by two other morning shows later in the morning. Reporters for the *Times* and the *Post* both wanted to speak with you, if you could give them a few minutes. And *60 Minutes* will be doing a profile on you."

"Again?"

His assistant was diplomatic. "I think they feel that they have more material."

Charles grunted. "They're probably right."

The drive from Ponte Vedra to Cecil Field took slightly under an hour. Their car entered the private drive to his headquarters and saw several large dark vehicles parked in a column along the curb. Government vehicles.

Wilkes and another man stood next to the lead SUV.

"We were disconnected."

Wilkes said, "Good morning Mr. Fend. I'm sorry about that. Several of us have been having phone trouble this morning." He gestured to Flynn, who was standing beside him. "You know Special Agent Flynn."

Charles eyed the man. "Hello again. What are all these vehicles for?"

Flynn cleared his throat, looking between Wilkes and Charles. "Mr. Fend, we want to make sure we're ready for anything. So we have a special team of FBI agents ready to step in if anything should go wrong today."

"Well, they can't be seen by the press. That would look suspicious. It'll ruin the whole event. I know that we need security, but I have a business objective here as well."

"I understand, sir. We'll keep them out here, in your private parking area. Only some of your employees will see them."

Charles raised an eyebrow, looking back and forth between the CIA and FBI men. He wondered how much the FBI knew. Did Flynn know everything about Morozov? About Charles's own history with him? Unlikely. Wilkes played things too close to the vest. Just like all the other handlers Charles had worked with over the years. The CIA was filled with boys who had never learned to share.

Charles looked at his watch. "Takeoff is coming up. I need to head inside, but I've asked my team to set up an office space for you to work out of—have they shown it to you?"

"Yes. Thank you."

"Of course. It will be right next to the Fend 100 mission control center, so you'll be able to monitor the flight"—he shot them a knowing look —"and the personnel involved."

"Thank you, Charles. We'll try to stay out of your way. Have you heard from Max?"

"No. You were telling me something before we got disconnected— something about setbacks?"

Wilkes's face darkened. "I'm concerned that Max might be in trouble."

"What kind of trouble?"

"Morozov. Max never came back from his meeting yesterday afternoon. Listen, we'll do everything we can to find out where Max is. You just focus on the Fend 100 this morning. I promise you that we'll let you know the moment we hear anything on Max. I'm sure it will turn out okay." He didn't sound convincing.

Charles stood on the steps of his building entrance, looking into Caleb Wilkes's eyes. Through gritted teeth, he said, "Please do let me know when you have more."

With that, the CEO of Fend Aerospace turned and walked up the steps and through the large revolving door of his building. Several employees were waiting for him inside.

"Congratulations, Mr. Fend. You're about to make aviation history. Do you have a minute?"

Charles looked up at his chief marketing officer. "Yes. Thanks. I'll be there momentarily." The other employees took the hint and sauntered off.

He strode into the open atrium, surrounded by the excited crowd noise and flashes of professional cameras.

This section of the Fend Aerospace building was of modern architecture. Open floor plans. Lots of high ceilings, stone, and clear glass walls. An upper-deck observation level with a glass barrier.

Hundreds of aviation reporters and industry analysts were gathered around the Fend mission control center—observing through thirty-foot glass walls. Those walls encapsulated the Fend engineers and scientists, clicking and typing as they monitored today's flight from their rows of computers.

The Fend mission control center reminded most onlookers of the NASA space shuttle mission control. That was intentional. But there was a major difference—this space was specifically designed to be observed by an audience.

Ever the marketer, Charles had made sure that his team of industrial designers and advertising gurus had taken part in the creation of the facility. He wanted the building to provide a home court advantage at these sorts of press and media gatherings. Events like these would help feed the frenzy in the technology blogosphere. These test flights were a show. He was the Steve Jobs of flight. And this was his iPhone presentation. Charles would need the positive buzz if he was to succeed in having people begin using his new product.

As the CEO of Fend Aerospace, he wasn't just asking people to try a new way of communicating. He was asking them to put their lives in the hands of a robot.

Fend Aerospace was about to become a pioneer in commercial aviation. The crowd had gathered to witness the first passenger flight of their brand-new aircraft, the Fend 100. The FAA had certified the aircraft type a few months before. A seismic government contract for the technology was in the works. But human acceptance of the technology remained an issue. The FAA and other key stakeholders were watching closely.

The Fend 100 was the first fully automated airliner. No pilots required. The pilots were there, of course. Three of them, in fact. All test pilots. They would oversee the flight from the cockpit and be ready to take the controls if anything went wrong.

While the FAA had approved the flight after seeing dozens of demonstrations, most people still weren't comfortable flying without a human being behind the controls. Charles figured it would take five to ten more years, and many millions of lobbying dollars, before the airlines were allowed to take full advantage of the technology.

Baby steps.

Charles's vision was that, over time, the FAA would allow commercial airliners to become single-piloted, with one Fend 100 AI machine taking the place of the copilot. Eventually, the AI machine would operate all of the controls and execute all communications. At that point, the pilot would be nothing more than a safety observer. It wouldn't take long until the pilot stayed on the ground, overseeing multiple automated commercial airliners, similar to the way an air traffic controller was able to guide multiple aircraft simultaneously. This would provide cost savings and improve efficiency. It really would be the dawn of a new era.

That was, as long as nothing went wrong.

Charles looked at the office adjacent to the Fend 100 mission control room. Through the open door, he could see the government men in there, trying to look inconspicuous as they observed his team doing their jobs. Wilkes and Flynn looked worried. And they had good reason to be.

Charles had already been nervous about today's flight going smoothly. But now—with Max in possible danger, and a counterespionage operation underway, today's flight had taken on a whole new importance.

As Charles walked the floor, he could overhear the CMO giving a TV interview with the local news channel.

The reporter said, "So they'll be flying up and down the coast of Florida..."

"That's right, they'll be flying up the east coast of Florida—and returning to land here at our headquarters near Jacksonville."

"And how many on board?"

The man smiled. "We've got a full flight. As you can imagine, a lot of folks wanted to join. Many are reporters and aviation writers. A few are employees of Fend Aerospace that we wanted to recognize for their hard work on the project."

And our lead program manager, who has been placed on board to help protect against a former KGB operative, Charles thought to himself.

The reporter said, "Well, I'm a little sad that I didn't get an invite."

The CMO laughed. "I'm sorry—but hopefully you'll get to fly with the technology soon! We want to begin putting this on all airliners in the US within the next few years."

"Now what makes this different than autopilot?"

"We get that question a lot. Our Fend 100 Artificial Intelligence Pilot System is *way* more advanced than a simple autopilot function that you see today. The Fend 100 aircraft can communicate with air traffic controllers, set up on the approach, complete the landing, and even taxi into the terminal without anyone on board. It's going to revolutionize the way we travel."

Charles hoped so. While drone flight was becoming more and more prevalent in military and commercial use, it had yet to be approved by any major global aviation agency. If things went well today, that could all change.

He entered the mission control room. The Fend 100 mission control team had twenty workers, all sitting at neatly spaced-out computer monitors. Forty-foot ceilings. Giant screens at the front of the room showed the aircraft's location and status. The floor was a glossy stone.

Even within the glass walls, Charles could hear the crowd noise outside. Some were posing for pictures. Many wore press or other VIP badges around their necks. The aviation media had been plastering this story on the front pages of their websites and magazines for the past few years. This was their first real taste of the Fend 100 aircraft.

"How's it coming, Bradley?"

Bradley Karpinsky said, "She's taxiing for takeoff now, sir. Just another minute or so."

Claps and cheers outside as the Fend 100 taxied by.

Wilkes walked through the door and gestured for Charles to follow him. Wilkes said, "Can you join us outside for a moment?" Flynn stood next to him, dread in his eyes.

"Takeoff is in two minutes. Can't this wait?"

"Afraid not. Flynn just got a message from the FBI—a man claiming to be Max Fend contacted the Jacksonville field office. They weren't sure if it was a hoax or not. They said the guy wants us to halt the flight. He said not to let the Fend 100 take off."

Charles looked incredulous. "What? Why? And why wouldn't Max contact me or you?"

Wilkes shook his head. "I don't know, Charles. But the FBI said that

Max was on his way here now. If the timing is right, he should be in the parking lot any minute. We're going to check."

"Should we still have them take off?"

The two government men looked at each other.

Flynn lowered his voice so that only the two others would hear him. "We have Maria on board. We have a backup plan—nothing that we have seen suggests that Morozov will be successful in hacking into the network, let alone getting past Maria's new security measures."

Wilkes said, "I would hate to ruin all of our plans unless we know for sure that this is Max."

Charles nodded. "I'll come out with you." He looked back at his chief engineer. "No need to wait for me, Bradley. Stick to the schedule." They walked outside.

* * *

As the three of them walked down the concrete stairs and into the parking lot, the quiet morning air filled with the loud noise of a commercial jetliner throttling up its engines. The men looked through the chain-link fence and witnessed the Fend 100 starting down the runway.

Charles looked at his watch. "Seven a.m. Right on time."

The giant white aircraft pitched up and began climbing, its landing gear folding up into its belly. The airliner became a slow-moving silhouette against sunlit clouds. As it rose over the Jacksonville skyline, the jet noise gave way to a honking horn.

All three men turned around to see a taxi racing towards them and skidding to a halt.

Max sprang out of the door, panicked. He and the woman with him looked like hell – clothes damp and sandy.

"It took off? Shit. Come on, we need to get to the control room and contact the pilots. You have to recall them."

"Don't be absurd. Why?" Charles asked.

"Hold on now, Max," Wilkes said.

Max pointed up at the departing aircraft. "Listen to me. Morozov isn't planning to steal the Fend 100 technology."

"What are you talking about? What is he trying to do, then?"

The group stared at Max as he spoke.

"Morozov is going to crash it."

* * *

A drink cart made its way down the aisle of the Fend 100. The passengers were a mix of company employees being rewarded for their hard work, aviation enthusiasts who had won contests to go on the first flight, and members of the media.

In seat B13, Betsy Sivers ordered a mimosa and looked out in awe at the beach below. She had worked for Fend Aerospace for almost thirty years. She'd started off in manufacturing at the original plant in Texas, then made her way to Florida when they'd expanded in the early 2000s. This flight was a great reward for her hard work.

Rick Powell sat in G23. He wrote for *Plane and Pilot* magazine and was eagerly typing up everything he experienced so that he could publish it on his blog when they landed. His wife and twelve-year-old son had made the trip up from Daytona and were waiting back at the airport. He couldn't wait to tell his son about the ride.

In seat F57, Bobby Turell thanked the flight attendant for his apple juice and smiled to himself. He had turned thirty-two last week. He was one of the ten contest winners. A self-proclaimed aviation nut, Bobby had been to every SUN 'n FUN air show since he was a boy. Getting to ride in the first passenger flight of the Fend 100 was the thrill of a lifetime for him. Right up there with riding in a Ford Tri-motor at Oshkosh. He couldn't wait to tell his girlfriend about it. In a moment of pure euphoria, he decided right then and there that it was time to go ring shopping. Life couldn't get any better than this.

As the aircraft banked right to head south over the Florida shoreline, beams of electromagnetic energy began to illuminate the Fend 100's data link antenna. The energy beams originated from a large yacht just south of St. Augustine and rapidly intensified in magnitude.

The Fend 100 was being hijacked.

21

While the group marched into the Fend 100 headquarters building, Max did his best to fill them in on what he knew. Renee followed him in, listening.

"Come on," Charles said. "I've had them set up a special office space for you. You'll be able to monitor the flight from there."

"We need to recall the flight, Dad. *Now.*"

Charles said, "We can talk inside."

They walked through the revolving doors and past a throng of reporters who were setting up for their morning interviews. The group watched as Max and his father led the others into an office right next to the Fend 100 control room.

One of the reporters said, "Is that...?"

"No, he's taller," another one said.

A few flashes erupted as cameramen snapped pictures.

Once in the office space, they closed the door. Flynn said, "Okay, spill it, Max. What's going on?"

"Morozov tried to have me killed last night. We barely escaped. You were right, Caleb. Charlotte Capri was working for him. By the time we escaped, it was almost dawn—it took us longer to get a phone and a vehicle. We kept trying to call, but the Fend Aerospace phone network and my father's phone weren't connecting. Neither were the local police. We finally tried the FBI."

"Could be Morozov's hackers trying to prevent you from reaching us."

"Well, it appears to have worked. Can we recall the Fend 100?"

Max was scanning the room, looking to see who was in there.

Wilkes said, "We have fail-safes in place. You know what we need here, Max. I need the Russians to make their move so that we have verifiable electronic data. Leverage to use against Morozov."

"That was back when the risk was a simple cyberattack—stealing a few terabytes of data from my father's company. Now we're talking about people's lives, Caleb."

Agent Flynn grimaced. "Dammit. We shouldn't have let them take off. I agree with Max."

Charles said, "So do I. I'm going to see what I can do." Charles marched back into the Fend 100 control room.

Max looked at Flynn. "Are you armed?"

"Of course."

Max looked through the window of the office and into the adjacent Fend 100 mission control room. "If Morozov was going to kill me last night, that means that he didn't need me to upload any software. But he's still planning to hijack the Fend 100. I think you were right about him having someone on the inside."

Each of their heads turned to look through the window. They scanned the faces in the Fend 100 control room. The engineers and project team working diligently as the Fend 100 had its big show. Now that Max was silent, they could hear the project engineers and radio controllers speaking to the aircraft through the overhead speakers.

"Fend 100, Control, we have good uplink and downlink. What's your status?"

"Control, Fend 100, everything looks good here. We're along for the ride."

The group could hear the voice of the pilot and the project engineer, Bradley Karpinsky, on the overhead speaker system.

The pilot said, "Cecil Control, Fend 100, things are looking good. We're in fully automated mode and everything is proceeding normally."

"Fend 100, Cecil Control, roger. Nice job, boys. We'll see you in a few."

"I am going to head next door for a moment," Special Agent Flynn said. Wilkes followed him.

Renee sat at one of the computer terminals in their office, looking at all of the displayed information. "What are we looking at?"

"So this map here shows the aircraft track, altitude, airspeed, and heading," Max said.

Renee said, "Where are they now?"

"East of Cape Canaveral. Headed South."

"So nothing unusual yet?"

Max shook his head. "Not yet. Perhaps Maria's security fix is working."

Max could see his father standing over the shoulder of Bradley Karpinsky, a grave expression on both of their faces.

Karpinsky's voice came on the radio again. "Fend 100, Cecil Control, there has been a change of plans. We're being asked to cut the flight short due to unforeseen circumstances here on the ground."

"Say again, Control?"

"We're bringing you back, Fend 100. Sending the aircraft new directions now."

Max could see the engineers in the other room becoming agitated, pointing at their own displays and yelling back to Karpinsky.

Renee said, "What's wrong?"

The overhead speaker relayed Karpinsky's voice. "Fend 100, Control, I just input a return to base command, but I'm not showing the aircraft turning."

"Affirm, we're seeing the same thing here, Control."

"Fend 100, Control, I now show you in a descent of one thousand feet per minute," they heard over the overhead speaker. "Please verify. The flight profile has you maintaining altitude at twenty thousand feet for the next fifteen minutes."

"Roger, Control, we see that. We're in fully automated mode. Not sure why it's descending on us. We're troubleshooting now."

Max could see his father speaking to Wilkes and Flynn. They all looked worried. "I think it's happening."

Renee typed at her desktop computer. "I'm going to see if I can get us some more information."

"Fend 100, we now have you descending at a rate of two thousand feet per minute. Airspeed still three hundred and eighty knots indicated."

"Control, Fend 100, roger. Troubleshooting."

"Fend 100, please have Miss Blount get on the radios."

"Control, Fend 100, say again?"

"Control, Fend 100, no joy on troubleshooting. Sorry, folks, but we're going to conduct a manual override."

A few tense moments went by before they heard from the pilots.

"Cecil Control, Fend 100, we seem to have a problem." The pilot's voice sounded agitated.

Karpinsky said, "Go ahead, Fend 100."

"Control...the manual override doesn't appear to be *working*. The electronic flight controls aren't responding the way they should. They...they aren't responding at all. We can't stop the descent."

"Fend 100, Cecil Control, did you try the backup?"

"Control, Fend 100, that's affirm."

"Did you try pulling the circuit breaker?"

"Control, Fend 100, we've tried everything and are retrying all the steps again. So far we've tried the primary system override, the backup override, and pulling both circuit breakers. We're ready to pull all the AC power in the cockpit and try a full restart."

Max looked at the airplane's statistical readouts. They had just passed below ten thousand feet. The hair on the back of his neck stood up. The altitude kept ticking down.

Renee said, "Where are they now?"

"They're still headed south. Heading towards the Bahamas."

Flynn and Wilkes came in. "Have you guys tried to reach Maria on your radio? They aren't putting her on our radio."

"I'll try," Max said.

They had set up a special communications section on the aircraft for Maria to talk on.

"Maria, this is Max, come in."

"This is the Fend 100 flight engineer, who's this?"

Max spoke into the microphone. "This is Fend Control—we have a separate comms channel set up. Please put Miss Blount on immediately."

"Fend 100, Control, we are initiating the override procedures now. You should be able to take control of the aircraft now."

Max could see flashing green text on the bottom of the aircraft statistics screen. *Remote Aircraft Control Datalink connecting.*

"Control, Fend 100, what's the status? We need you to take control now. Our troubleshooting is nonresponsive."

Karpinsky said, "Roger, Fend 100. Stand by."

"Fend 100, Control, I show you passing through four thousand feet."

Then the radio call came that made everyone turn white.

"Mayday, mayday, mayday, this is Fend 100, forty miles northeast of Bimini Island. Flight controls nonresponsive, in an uncommanded descent...we will be ditching in the water."

In the chamber where the press and aviation enthusiasts were watching, some people started to yell in worry. Max could hear the commotion from their office room.

Max said in a firm voice, "Fend 100, *please place Maria Blount on right now.* She will be able to override the remote control."

"Control, 100, say again?"

"Fend 100, Control, get Maria on the horn. She should be able to help."

"Control, Fend 100, Maria is with you on the ground."

The people in the office shook their heads, annoyed at the confusion of the moment.

Max was almost yelling now. "Negative, Fend 100. Maria Blount is on board with you. Go tell someone to find her and get her on the radio —now!"

"Control, Fend 100." Another pilot speaking, now. "I'm positive she is not on this flight. She told us that there was a change of plans this morning. She was there for preflight, but not for takeoff. She said she would be with you."

Renee said, "They just went below one thousand feet of altitude." People were screaming outside the room now. Some were family members of the passengers on board.

They have someone on the inside.

Max closed his eyes.

"It's Maria. Maria Blount is Morozov's person on the inside."

The altitude now read zero.

The door to the mission control room was being held open by one of the FBI agents. Max could hear his father telling Karpinsky to contact the Coast Guard and start a search and rescue. Outside the room, people were sobbing.

*   *   *

Maria typed on her computer inside Morozov's yacht. The vessel was sailing fifteen miles off the coast of St. Augustine.

"Sync complete. We now have control." She spoke to Morozov, who was piped in through the speakerphone in the center of the room. Morozov had left the Ritz-Carlton at Amelia Island and gone to their safe house. It would be too risky to bring him back to the yacht. The yacht had served two purposes: to gain initial control over the Fend 100, and to divert any American response.

Morozov sounded in good spirits on the speakerphone. "Excellent work, Maria. Are the men ready?"

The ex-Spetsnaz man standing next to her nodded. "Yes, Mr. Morozov. As soon as you give us the signal, we'll move."

"Maria, you know what to do at this point. I have received the transponder code that we will need. I am sending that to you now."

Maria turned to a dark-haired young man who sat in front of a computer terminal to her left—a very talented hacker, with a very capable mind. Chechen by birth, he worked for one of Morozov's companies—Maljab Tactical. He served as a consultant for many of the extreme militias in the Middle East. Until recently, much of the work he did was in Syria, helping the Islamic State to maintain a solid social networking presence without getting caught by the NSA or other Western cyber agents.

Maria said, "You get it?"

"Yes," the Chechen responded.

"We have what we need, Mr. Morozov."

"Good. Send out our headline news updates. And get moving."

"We will. Goodbye."

Maria ended the call and turned to the Chechen. "Send it."

The boy made several keystrokes in rapid succession and then hit the return key.

"It is done."

"Ms. Blount." It was one of the security men.

"Yes?"

"The helicopter is ready, ma'am."

"Good. Let's be quick."

Maria and the Chechen entered the cabin of the helicopter, which was spinning on the small flight deck of the yacht. As soon as they were on board, it took off and headed north along the coast, remaining far enough out to sea that it wouldn't be visible from the shore.

* * *

The men and women at the Fend headquarters stood in shocked silence. Some of the engineers were crying. Some were still trying to do their jobs.

The reporters outside the mission control room all wanted to get Charles Fend in front of a microphone.

Max cursed himself for not thinking that Maria could be a part of it. Maria had only been with the company for a few years, but she was one of Charles's most trusted employees. And she had been one of the first to report the cyber intrusion to the authorities. Why would she do that?

But being trusted and being in charge of the Fend 100 program also meant that Maria had access to everything. What would make her do this?

Max turned to Wilkes, who was talking to the FBI agent. "We need to get onto Morozov's boat as fast as possible."

"Already on it. Flynn has the FBI Hostage Rescue Team ready to go outside. They flew in last night."

"Good. We'll need to..." Max stopped talking as he saw a TV outside the glass walls of the control room.

The headline on the news channel read:

ISLAMIC STATE TERRORISTS CLAIM RESPONSIBILITY FOR Fend 100 HIJACKING

The Fend chief marketing officer stormed into the room. "Charles, you've got to see this."

* * *

"Is it true that someone from ISIS has hacked into the Fend 100 aircraft?" A reporter shoved a microphone in front of Charles Fend.

Another said, "Can you confirm that the Fend 100 has actually crashed? Are terrorists responsible?"

Charles held up his hands. "We're just finding things out in real time, as are you. We're working with our team to establish what—"

"The terrorist organization sent a message saying that there's a Fend defense program that's responsible for the deaths of innocent civilians in the Middle East, and that this is retaliation for that."

The chief marketing officer glared at the reporter. "Was there a question there?"

"Can you comment on whether there's a secret Fend drone program?"

Charles shook his head. "No, I can't comment on that. Ladies and gentlemen, obviously we've just suffered a catastrophic event today. If you'll please depart the building. We need to work with the United States Coast Guard to rescue any survivors. If you will excuse me."

He walked away, ignoring the shouted questions behind him.

Max walked out of the building with Wilkes and Flynn. The column of dark FBI vehicles was in a frenzy of activity. Rough-looking men in tactical gear and sunglasses were gathered around the back of each vehicle, checking weapons and equipment.

One of the HRT men walked up to Special Agent Flynn. "This them?" the HRT man asked.

"Gentlemen, allow me to introduce Special Agent O'Malley." Brief introductions were made.

O'Malley said, "Is everything that you briefed us on last night still relevant?"

"Yes," Wilkes said. "How soon will you be able to take off?"

As if on cue, four MD 530 helicopters flew overhead and landed on the taxiway over the fence. The helicopters were similar to the tiny MH-6 Little Birds that the Army special forces used. In fact, several of the FBI's helicopter pilots were former Army helicopter pilots and had flown for the Army's 160th Special Operations Aviation Regiment.

O'Malley said, "We're ready."

"I need to go," Max said. "Do you have extra gear?"

The HRT man looked skeptically at the three others.

Wilkes said, "Max, why don't you just stay here for now?"

Max was stewing, but he could tell it would be a waste of breath to push further.

A few moments later, sixteen of the HRT men filed into their helicopters, which then buzzed off to the east.

22

The flight of four small black HRT helicopters skimmed the water, two sets of legs hanging out each side, weapons at the ready.

The team leader could see the massive yacht now.

"What the hell *is* that thing?" said the FBI agent next to him.

"That, my friends, is what you buy when you have absolutely more money than you know what to do with. Okay, gents, lock and load. Expect civilians on board. Rules of engagement as briefed."

As the helicopters flew closer, fast ropes slung down from each side. The team leader kept scanning the deck of the yacht. So far, there was almost no movement...

There.

"One o'clock. I have two men, armed, one with a set of binoculars, just aft of the bridge."

Yellow flashes came from several different locations on the yacht.

"Taking fire!" came the call from one of the pilots. The four-ship formation broke off into two sets of two aircraft, flying away from each other. They began evasive maneuvers to reduce the chances of taking on enemy fire. Two of the helicopters did an arc around the ship at high speed, angling their aircraft so that the HRT men could return fire.

A burst of controlled gunfire erupted from the cabin of the helicopters.

"One down. *Two* down. Looks like there's some movement on the aft deck."

When the two helicopters finished their arc around the boat, they peeled off and climbed. The other two helicopters were already on their approach to the flight deck of the ship.

Those HRT team members began sliding down the fast ropes. They landed gracefully on the helipad as the next pair of commandos followed suit. The first helicopter finished dropping off its four men, and the next one did the same.

The HRT men worked with fluid precision. Their movements carefully choreographed through hundreds of hours of repetitive practice. Weapons always trained outward—followed by expert eyes, scanning the ship, quickly entering and clearing the compartments.

A moment later, the other set of helicopters dropped off eight more HRT members. They joined the team already on board, systematically searching every compartment of the ship.

Bursts of machine gun fire could be heard at times, the HRT men communicating on their headsets as they neutralized all threats and secured the vessel.

Within ten minutes, five Russian security personnel were dead, and three were taken prisoner. Another seven civilians were on board, and the FBI agents had placed them in confinement near the flight deck. Two of the agents were working with the ship captain to turn the vessel towards Coast Guard sector Jacksonville.

"This door is locked," said one of the men.

The HRT team leader said, "We need to get in there."

One of the men was an explosives expert.

"Fire in the hole!"

A loud bang, and the door lock was blown. One HRT commando threw in a concussion grenade, and it burst as they waited outside the door. Then four of the HRT team members moved in fast.

The team leader knew this was the room they were looking for. "Get the CIA guy in here!"

Wilkes's man—a computer expert—was escorted down to the room. It was empty, filled with rows of computers and electronics—all unmanned. After a quick evaluation, the CIA man concluded that all of the computers had been zeroed out. None of it was usable, let alone active. He radioed as much back to Wilkes, who was standing by at the Fend headquarters.

* * *

Wilkes and Flynn had just finished telling the group what the HRT team had found—or rather, what they hadn't found. Max, Charles, and Renee listened.

Max said, "So where is Morozov?"

"We're working on it," said Wilkes. Flynn nodded.

The group disbanded, each of them needing to speak with someone on the phone to take next steps.

Renee called Max over. "Something isn't right."

He was only half-paying attention. His father was leaning against a wall, his face in his hands. Max needed to speak with him.

"Max. Listen."

"Renee, it's over."

"I don't think so. Look at this."

She pointed to one of the computer monitors. It showed the aircraft status. Airspeed zero. Altitude zero. The latitude and longitude were static.

Max sighed. "What am I supposed to be looking at?"

Her voice was emphatic. "The plane's pilots made their mayday call and said they were forty-five miles north of Bimini. I just looked up these coordinates that are on the screen here. They don't match up."

"What are you saying?"

"I don't know yet. But when I did research on how one would hack into a drone aircraft, I learned that one of the main ways it could be done is through something called GPS spoofing. Basically, they trick the system into thinking it's somewhere else. If Morozov's hackers made the Fend 100 think it was somewhere it wasn't, who's to say that they couldn't trick us into thinking the same thing?"

Max blinked. "What are you saying?"

"I'm saying, what if we're looking at bad data." She pointed to the aircraft status, which showed that it had impacted the water.

Max turned and yelled, keeping his eyes on Renee. "Bradley! Come here. Now."

Karpinsky walked over, a somber look on his face. "What is it, Max?"

"What GPS coordinates should be on the screen here?"

"The last known location of the aircraft. It should be right where it hit the water. Listen, Max, I have to get ready for the NTSB team to—"

Max and Renee looked at each other. Renee said, "The coordinates on the screen here—the aircraft status screen—they don't match up with the coordinates the pilots called out when they made their mayday call."

Karpinsky shrugged. "So what? They probably glided a little farther—"

Renee shook her head. "No. They're one hundred miles off."

Karpinsky's eyes narrowed. "Huh. Well, that is a little weird, but..."

Max looked at Wilkes. He stood in the corner, talking on the phone with an intense look in his eyes.

Like he was still in the middle of an operation.

* * *

Max gathered Wilkes, Flynn, Renee, Karpinsky, and his father into an office.

"What if the plane didn't go down?"

Charles shook his head. "Max, what are you saying?"

Flynn said, "That's silly. Look, we need to look into this Islamic State thing. I'm getting calls from D.C. about—"

"Hear me out, Agent Flynn. Please."

Flynn sighed. "Okay. Where would it have gone?"

"You tell me," Max said. "Bradley, Renee, and I just looked at the in-flight statistics—Bradley told us they're programmed to stay on the last known GPS location of the aircraft. That helps them set up for a search and rescue. Right, Bradley?"

"That's right."

"But those coordinates were one hundred miles away from where the pilots claimed to be when they went down."

"What are you saying?" Charles asked.

"What if Maria reprogrammed the system to make it look like they crashed, when they really didn't?"

Flynn said, "Why would they do that?"

Max said, "Think about it."

The blood drained from Flynn's face. "How far could it have flown?"

"It had enough fuel for another fifteen hundred miles at least," Karpinsky said,

"But people would have noticed it, right?" Flynn shook his head, his voice a pitch higher. "I mean, you can't just fly a commercial airliner around without getting noticed. Right?"

Karpinsky shrugged. "It depends."

Flynn said, "On what?"

"It would attract a lot of attention if they tried to land it at just about any airport. And I'm pretty sure some radar controller would notice if it was flying over the continental United States without its transponder on."

Max said, "I would think so. They at least would have noticed it when it first entered US airspace, right?"

Karpinsky nodded. "Yes."

Renee said, "So we're saying it's possible that the Fend 100 is still airborne right now? How would we know that?"

No one immediately responded. Just sideways glances at each other—faces mixed with hope and fear.

Bradley Karpinsky cleared his throat. "According to our aircraft in-flight stats, it has crashed. We aren't getting any signals sent out from the aircraft. The only way we would know is if someone had it on radar."

Max said, "Who can check that?"

"We can look into it here," Karpinsky said. "The Fend 100 mission control center has several people who are trained as radar controllers. And we've got a good relationship with air traffic control in the area. I'll go talk to them and tell them to start searching for anything suspicious. But at this point, I suggest the government get involved."

Renee said, "Aren't they already?"

Flynn shook his head. "He means NORAD. We need the professionals looking for this aircraft."

* * *

Bradley left to go speak with the radar controllers, and the group kept talking. Wilkes excused himself to go make another phone call. Flynn went to call FBI headquarters and make sure that NORAD was updated on the situation.

Charles said, "I can't believe this is happening."

"Relax, Dad. It's not your fault."

"I was a fool to think we could take a risk like that. I just wanted them to get Morozov. It was all I could think about—I wanted to get back at him for what he did to your mother. But now...all those people. I feel responsible. We should have insisted on stopping the flight. We shouldn't have relied upon—"

Max placed his hand on his father's shoulder. "Dad, let's worry about that later. I have a feeling this isn't over yet."

Max glanced at his father's newspaper, which was lying on the office desk. Below the article about him was a feature on the G-7 summit. It was to be held tomorrow at Camp David, but the world leaders were due to arrive today.

Max picked up the paper and scanned the article quickly. After much political posturing, the Russian Federation was reportedly rejoining the group, and it would be renamed the G-8. Several of the member nations were making a big fuss about it.

Wilkes and Flynn walked back in.

Max placed his finger on the article. "Have you guys seen this about the G-7?"

Wilkes watched Max from across the room. "What about it?"

Max stared back at him. "It would make one hell of a target. The news is reporting that the Islamic State has claimed responsibility for the hijacking."

"I know," Flynn said, "but that's impossible. They aren't equipped—"

"Pavel Morozov has a subsidiary that works closely with the Islamic State," Max said. "They actually do defense contracting for them in Syria."

Flynn said, "You're kidding."

"So Morozov is trying to attack the G-7 conference? And blame it on the Islamic State?" Renee said.

"Oh, Jesus. You think that—"

Renee nodded. "If the Fend 100 is really still airborne, and Morozov's got control of it..."

Flynn's phone buzzed, and he quickly answered it. "Special Agent Flynn. Yes. Understood. Use this number." He hung up and looked up at the group. "NORAD and the NSA are both working to locate the aircraft now. If it's airborne, they'll find it."

23

Eastern Air Defense Sector
Rome, NY

Air Force Master Sergeant Krites sipped his coffee out of a paper cup. He liked his coffee plain black. Cream messed with his digestion, and sugar rotted his teeth. But a good cup of black joe was heaven. He always brought his own coffee in. None of this rotten stuff that the kids around here drank. They liked all the big fancy brands. He knew better. If you wanted good coffee, you had to grind the beans yourself, the same day. So he did, every morning. His wife certainly liked it. She was looking forward to him doing a lot more cooking after he retired. And that day was coming up faster than he could believe.

He had been in the US Air Force for twenty-three years. He'd become an expert in modern air defense and air traffic control. For the past ten years, they'd lived in New York state, and Krites liked it just fine. His job with the Eastern Air Defense Sector was meaningful. Especially after September eleventh.

EADS was the US Air Force command that was permanently assigned to detect and defeat an air attack on the United States. It was his job to identify unknown aircraft and vector in fighter jets to intercept them when needed.

In his eight years working at EADS, he was used to two types of these intercepts: knucklehead private pilots who accidentally flew into restricted airspace, and drills.

After September eleventh, his outfit had drilled a lot. And Master Sergeant Krites took it very seriously.

"How'd your shift go?"

"Did you see the news?"

"Down in Jacksonville?"

"Yeah. Airliner went down in the water. ISIS is claiming responsibility."

The two men were silent for a moment. Then Krites said, "It was supposed to be some new type of plane, right?"

"Yeah, like a drone airliner or something."

"Hell, man. I would never let some drone fly me around. How many died?"

"A couple hundred, I heard."

Krites shook his head. "That's just awful."

The two men finished their watch turnover and Krites sat down at his desk, headset on, looking at the information on the screens in front of him. With the news of the Jacksonville terrorist incident, backup duty sections had been called in to the watch floor. Everyone on the floor was on edge, their eyes and ears alert for anything that might be out of the ordinary.

"Krites!" the watch officer called from the platform behind him.

"Yes, sir?"

"You got a call on line three. FASVAC Jacksonville wants to talk to you."

"Got it."

"This is Master Sergeant Krites, Eastern Air Defense Sector."

"Master Sergeant, this is Chief Slade at FASVAC Jacksonville. We just got contacted by Fend Aerospace with an emergency. Have you heard about the accident that just happened down here?"

"Yes, Chief. Very sorry to hear it."

"Yeah, well, I'm a little confused. First, we get word that they had a crash. That was about an hour ago. Now they're contacting us saying that it might not have crashed. They think that the aircraft might be hijacked, and still airborne."

Hijacked. The H-word.

Krites shot a look over to his watch supervisor and waved, eyes wide. The supervisor came running over, and a few other heads turned. Krites switched the audio to the speaker so they could both hear.

Krites said, "Say that again, Chief?"

"The Fend company thinks their drone passenger plane might not have gone down in the ocean after all. They think it might have been hijacked."

"Someone hijacked a drone airliner?"

"That's what they're saying. A remote-control hijacking."

"And where is it now?"

"We aren't sure. We're looking at the tapes, and we had a radar contact about fifty miles east of Jacksonville with no transponder. It was traveling south to north at twenty-five thousand feet. But that was forty minutes ago —and it's not on my scope anymore."

"Understood. Just to be clear, this is not, I repeat, not a drill. Please confirm."

"That's affirmative. This is real-world. The flight profile matched what the Fend guys said their aircraft would probably be doing." A muffled conversation that the Master Sergeant couldn't hear. "Yup. It was almost the exact same speed and altitude that the Fend 100 was doing earlier, before the crash report."

"Where's it heading?"

"Hell if I know. I don't even have it on my radar anymore."

Shit.

"Thanks, Chief."

Krites looked up at his supervisor. "You catch all that?"

A young airman yelled from across the room, a landline phone in his hand. But not just any phone. The red phone.

"Sir, NORAD is on the line—asking for the duty officer."

Krites's boss got on the phone and began a rapid flurry of *yes sirs* to whoever was on the other line. When he came back, he said, "Okay— we've got NORAD feeding us information now—scan in on Warning Area W-122, off the Carolinas. They're tracking something going northeast at over five hundred knots."

"I see it. They tagged it. Okay, I got it now. It's got no IFF. No transponder at all. It's just flying parallel to the coast, staying out of the ADIZ. Boss, I don't like this at all."

"Neither do I."

Krites said, "I recommend we scramble the interceptors."

His supervisor nodded. "Aligned."

24

Captain Jason Easteadt, United States Air Force, would soon be ordered to shoot down a commercial airliner. He realized this while watching the news and eating his dinner from the on-base sub shop.

BREAKING NEWS

Those two words consumed the entire TV screen. Big white lettering over a red background, ensuring that the audience was held captive for whatever came next.

He took a sip of sweet tea from a plastic straw, curious about what they might announce. He munched on baked chips and wiped away a smudge of mayo on the corner of his mouth.

Bzzz. Bzzz.

His phone vibrated in the breast pocket of his flight suit. He clicked the button to silence the phone, not taking his eyes off the TV.

. . .

"We interrupt this broadcast to bring you this breaking news alert. NBC News has just learned that a commercial jetliner flying near Jacksonville, Florida, may have been hijacked by Islamic State terrorists. We now bring you live to our expert in Washington..."

Whoa. He stopped chewing as he listened to the newscast.

"Easteadt, you catching this?" asked the other pilot on duty with him. The major was yelling from his office one door down the hallway.

Bzzz. Bzzz.

His phone again. He looked down at the messages. It was from the squadron. An emergency notification, telling him to contact the duty officer for instructions. That message had been sent two minutes ago.

He was going to get launched to intercept this hijacked plane.

Jason couldn't take his eyes off the news. The aircraft was the Fend 100. The newscaster said that it had somehow been hijacked. He tried to think how that would be possible. Jason had just read a magazine article on it the other day—the Fend 100 was fully automated. How would it have been hijacked?

His pulse was racing. He thought about what this meant. About all the people on board. And about what he might have to do.

A circular emergency light protruded from the wall. It was flashing and rotating, covering his shocked face with yellow every few seconds. A bell rang in the hallway. It sounded like a school bell. It was joined by other sounds. Men running, yelling orders, their boots beating against the linoleum flooring.

This was not going to be like the other intercepts Jason had done. This wasn't some off-course Cessna pilot.

A banner scrolled along the bottom of the TV screen.

Fend 100 AIRCRAFT, FIRST AUTONOMOUS COMMERCIAL AIRLINER, REPORTEDLY HIJACKED. ISLAMIC STATE CLAIMS RESPONSIBILITY. CONFLICTING REPORTS AS TO WHETHER AIRCRAFT HAS CRASHED OR IS STILL AIRBORNE.

. . .

"Easteadt!"

Jason looked up, beads of sweat forming on his forehead. The major stood in the doorway.

"What the hell are you doing just sitting there? Come on! We have ten minutes to be airborne."

Jason nodded and rose from his seat. His knees wobbled a bit, and his head felt dizzy.

The Air Force major yelling at him to hurry was the flight lead for the two-aircraft interception unit. Easteadt grabbed his gear from his locker and jogged out to the flight line. A golf cart took him and the major out to their aircraft.

The major, noticing his unusual silence, said, "Are you good to fly?"

He hesitated. "Yes." No more conversation. At this point, their training took over.

The major hopped off the golf cart and walked up to their separate aircraft. Their jets were being prepared for launch. Jason climbed up and strapped into his F-16. His hands were shaking as he raced through his checklist.

"Good luck, sir," the plane captain outside said as he removed the ladder, a proud and serious look in his eyes.

Jason waved back, not trusting his voice. The glass canopy descended and enclosed him. He returned a crisp salute from the plane captain.

The engine of the major's F-16 Fighting Falcon started up next to him. His aircraft fired up next.

The major said over the radios, "Angry 509, Angry 515, radio check."

"Lima Charlie, how me?" *Loud and clear.*

The major responded, "Read you the same, 509. You all set?"

Jason said, "Roger."

"Ground, Angry 515 flight of 2, taxi to runway 19 Right."

The ground controller responded, "Angry 515 and flight, clear to taxi to runway 19 Right."

Jason began taxiing his F-16 behind the major's aircraft. The march towards the start of the runway was painfully slow. The sky above was a deep blue, with a few thick puffs of gray, the seeds of summer thunder-clouds beginning to form. He could see commercial airliners on final at Reagan International Airport. He noticed that none were taking off. Had they been grounded?

The major's aircraft jerked, and Jason pumped his brakes.

The F-16 in front of Jason's slowed, then unexpectedly came to a full stop about halfway down the taxiway.

Something was wrong.

* * *

Morozov had sent only one man to do the job. Like many of the men working in Bear Security Group, he was ex-Spetsnaz. But unlike the others, this man's expertise was in long-range marksmanship.

The shots would be challenging. The range was almost one thousand meters. The target would be moving at about thirty kilometers per hour, and the sniper must hit it at precisely the right moment. From a suburban rooftop, adjacent to one of the world's most well-protected military bases.

The sniper had scouted out several locations to take the shot. The woods around Joint Base Andrews were out of the question. He was sure that the Secret Service and base security would have cameras and motion sensors. Even just snooping around there to evaluate the area would likely get him unwanted attention from the US government.

He thought about getting access to the military base. Forging a fake identity or stealing one—and gaining entry for any number of reasons. He could pretend to be a soldier stationed there, or a janitor working at one of the buildings. But there were too many unknowns. What if the base security guard was familiar with the unit the sniper claimed to be from? Taking the shot from the base would also make his escape that much more difficult.

So the sniper had decided on a neighborhood just next to the base. Many of the families who lived on the street were away on vacation for the summer. That was something he had noticed after canvassing the street. He picked the home that was closest to the base. The last home in a circular court. Thankfully there were no nosey neighbors nearby and no home alarm system.

He broke in, quick and silent, climbing through a second-story window in back and onto the rooftop. A small private perch.

He checked his watch. The sniper had been told to expect two pilots to access their fighters. One was a major, the other a captain. He recognized the rank insignia on their flight suits. Through his scope, he watched them enter their aircraft and then waited for the right moment to shoot.

The sniper had been told to fire when they were on the runway, but he thought that to be a stupid idea. What if he missed? Two shots at that range was a tall order. He would fire while they taxied. It was a shorter range to target. And if he missed, he would have several more moments to retry. Great snipers were not just great marksmen. They were smart in their preparation.

He was lucky he'd planned it that way.

Crack.

His first shot missed the front tire of the first F-16. His rifle was bolt-action, and he had another round ready a second later. Sweaty palms. Heart beating fast, but controlled breathing. Trying not to think about neighbors opening their screen doors and looking outside, or dialing the local police department.

Crack.

A hit. The tire of the lead fighter jet burst open, and he saw sparks as the metal of the landing gear drove into the ground. A few seconds later, the jet stopped completely.

He took aim at the second jet, but it was already taxiing around the first. He took aim again and then heard the sound of a siren. He lifted his head up to look but didn't see where it was coming from. When he looked back, the other F-16 was already making its way down the runway. He had missed his chance.

To hell with it. Morozov would still have one less fighter to deal with. And this part of the mission wasn't worth spending the rest of his life in an American jail. He packed up his rifle and began his escape.

* * *

"509, 515."

"Go."

"You aren't gonna believe this, but I think I just had a tire pop. My front wheel. Can you taxi around me?"

"Affirm."

"Alright, 509, you're gonna have to handle this one on your own for now. I'll radio base and have them get a backup bird ready ASAP. You'll be fine, just go by the book."

"Roger."

Jason taxied his aircraft around the F-16 in front of him and called up the ground controller to change his flight plan from a formation flight to a single aircraft.

He switched up to the tower frequency. "Tower, Angry 509 holding short 19 Right for takeoff."

"Angry 509, Andrews Tower, you are clear for takeoff on runway one-niner right."

"Tower, 509, clear for takeoff one-niner right."

Jason felt the same thrilling rush of adrenaline every time he pointed the nose of an aircraft down the runway, and it was especially exciting when it was an F-16 at Joint Base Andrews.

The thrill wasn't there today, however. Today it was dread. Dread at the thought of what he might be asked to do. He hoped to God he wouldn't have to shoot down a plane full of civilians.

"Angry 509, Tower, please execute your takeoff without further delay. We have inbound aircraft, sir."

"Tower, 509, roger."

Jason pushed the throttle forward. Twenty-five thousand pounds of thrust propelled the aircraft down the runway. As the airspeed reached 120 knots, he pulled back on the stick and lifted up into the air, the ground rapidly falling below him.

25

"Renee." Max touched her shoulder, whispering her name.

She was sitting down in front of her computer. They were in the corner of the room, out of earshot.

"If the Fend 100 is still airborne," Max said, "wouldn't that mean that Morozov's team is still remote-controlling it?"

"Honestly, I don't know enough about it. But it makes sense."

"Would there be a way for you to tell if there's a signal, and where the signal's coming from?"

Renee's eyes grew bright. Sensing that Max didn't want everyone to hear their conversation, she whispered back, "Yes. I think so. Give me a few minutes."

"Hey—keep it just between you and me."

"Why? What's wrong?"

He looked over his shoulder, in the direction of Wilkes and Flynn. "I'm not sure yet."

"Okay." She paused. "I'm surprised Wilkes isn't already working on this."

"*Maybe he is.*"

Renee nodded. She began typing—chatting with someone on her computer.

"Okay. I'll be right back. I'm looking for the best location you can find. Try and get me GPS coordinates."

She didn't look up, still typing. "That may be tricky."

"Just do the best you can."

Max walked through the exit and into the parking lot. A few HRT men were gathered there. These were the backups—the ones who were left behind when the helicopters flew to Morozov's yacht.

Max went up to them and introduced himself as DIA.

"We know who you are," one of them said in a southern drawl.

"Right. I keep forgetting that my mug got sent to every FBI agent."

"That really you, running from the police in D.C.?"

"I'm afraid so."

"If you don't mind my saying so, that was a pretty dumb thing to do."

"Yeah, well. Live and learn, right? Listen, I think I have a lead—but I might need help. You guys interested?"

The HRT members kept their arms crossed and stayed silent.

Max nodded. "Okay—tough crowd. So the man who's responsible for all this goes by the name of Pavel Morozov. Are you familiar with him?"

Nods. "We got a brief, yes."

"And you guys just heard from your team that Morozov wasn't on the boat, right?"

"That's right," one of them answered, sounding curious.

Max said, "What if I told you I might know where he is?"

While they might not have entirely trusted Max yet, he was familiar with the breed. The type of men in HRT were like golden retrievers. Brought down here to play fetch and then asked to sit and wait instead. To them, nothing was worse. Now they sensed that they might get in the game after all. A glimmer of hope flashed in their eyes.

"That would be mighty interesting," the FBI man said.

Max said, "When will your helicopters be back?"

"Not for a while. The yacht was pretty far south. They just called in. They got fuel at St. Augustine and are about to start bringing people back and forth between the yacht and the airport down there. The local FBI SAC has his men headed down to St. Augustine."

Max nodded. "Okay. Let's say, hypothetically, that I get Morozov's location. How many of you would be able to come with me to nail him?"

The men looked at each other. "Look, man, we'd love nothing more. But we'd have to run that up the chain, you know? Someone in the FBI would have to direct us..."

Max looked back at the Fend Aerospace building. He wasn't sure whom he could trust in there, but he needed the muscle. "Okay. I'll be right back."

Max walked inside and asked Special Agent Jake Flynn to step into the parking lot with him. He explained what he was trying to do.

Flynn peered down at Max over the rims of his sunglasses. "Come on, Max. What are you trying to pull? You should be just sitting back and thanking your lucky stars I don't have you in handcuffs right now."

"Don't you find it odd that Wilkes isn't working on this?" Max asked him.

"On what?"

"On finding out where Morozov is, after you didn't find anyone on the yacht."

Flynn's eyes narrowed. "Well, we just found out about that, so...maybe he just hasn't gotten around to it yet."

Both of them looked inside, through the glass door. Wilkes was in a glass-walled office. They could see him in there, walking around, headphones in his ears, talking to someone on the phone.

"Mr. Flynn, I've been doing this kind of stuff for a while," Max said. "It sure as hell looks to me like Wilkes is right hot in the middle of something. And he isn't involving either of us."

Renee opened the door and came outside, looking at Max with an eager expression. She stayed quiet, eyeing the FBI man.

"It's okay, Renee. Let us both know what you found."

"I pulled some strings with an old friend. Canadian CSE has triangulated the position of a signal that might be what we're looking for. It has all the right electronic characteristics for the Fend 100 remote-control data transfer. And it's been broadcasting for the last hour and a half. I think we've found it."

"Where?"

"I just did a quick check, but it looks like it's near Amelia Island. A mansion up there. Max, do you remember when I looked through the GPS history of Morozov's SUV?"

"Yes."

"I think this is a house that was in that GPS history. I can't be one hundred percent sure. I didn't write it down, but I saw it on the map..."

"Slow down," Flynn said. "Tell me what you think, Max."

"Morozov put his yacht off the coast of St. Augustine. The HRT had a shootout with them. But no one was there, right?"

"Right."

"The yacht is an obvious base of operations. But it would leave Morozov exposed. I think he kept his yacht as a diversion, close enough for him to get somewhere else he needed to be, but far enough for us not to stumble onto him. I think Morozov and Maria Blount are up at this house Renee just uncovered. Near Amelia Island. That's where they're controlling the Fend 100 from."

"What are their intentions?"

"I'm worried it has something to do with the G-7 meeting. Some of the world leaders have already begun to arrive. The conference is supposed to start tomorrow. I think he's planning something devastating there."

Karpinsky came running out. "Special Agent Flynn, I think you need to see this."

The group ran inside.

"This is our radar controller. He's been monitoring everything that's going on," Karpinsky said.

Wilkes walked in. Renee and Max looked at each other.

Wilkes said, "Fill me in, please."

"The EADS folks have scrambled an interceptor," Karpinsky said. "An F-16. And they've diverted and grounded all flights on the Eastern Seaboard. Nothing should be airborne except the Fend 100."

Max could see a TV in the next room. The media was just as far along as they were, it seemed. The headline read:

. . .

ALL US-BOUND FLIGHTS DIVERTED. OUTBOUND FLIGHTS GROUNDED. IMMINENT TERRORIST AIR ATTACK POSSIBLE, DEPARTMENT OF HOMELAND SECURITY SAYS.

Max could see the Fend 100 radar track on the screen. It was headed northeast, positioned a few dozen miles east of the Outer Banks.

"Where are they going?"

Flynn said, "I think we should consider the G-7 summit at Camp David a possible target. How long until they get there?"

"Maybe an hour?"

Flynn frowned. "Alright, Max, what are you thinking? Tell me what you want to do."

Max looked at Wilkes, who was listening now. "We may have a location on Morozov," Max said. "Up near Amelia Island. I originally thought we could use the helicopters. But they're going back and forth around St. Augustine...and, frankly I'm not sure we have enough time."

"So what, then?"

Max looked outside, on the flight line. There was a Cirrus SR22T parked out there—just like the one he owned.

"I have an idea. But I need you to lend me some of those HRT guys."

26

"Huntress Control, Angry 509, one hundred miles southeast of Andrews at angels twenty."

"Angry 509, Huntress Control, radar contact, turn right heading 180, maintain altitude and make best speed. We will have a tanker for you up shortly."

"Roger."

"509, your contact of interest is due south at approximately two hundred nautical miles."

"Roger, Huntress Control."

Captain Easteadt had just checked in with the Eastern Air Defense Sector controller, callsign Huntress. They would vector him towards the Fend 100 aircraft.

He tried to compartmentalize his emotions. To block out any fear or apprehension. But he kept thinking about the people and families that might be on board the Fend 100 flight. What if there were children?

He began to go through his air intercept checklist.

* * *

Max, Renee, and two of the FBI HRT men were taxiing for takeoff in the commandeered Cirrus. Max wondered who the owner was. Oh well.

Max thought about what they might face. He wasn't sure how many men would be at Morozov's mansion on Amelia Island. He would have preferred to bring twenty agents instead of two, but they didn't have time.

By his math, they had about forty-five minutes until the Fend 100 reached Camp David. Wilkes had wanted to use the FBI's HRT team and their helicopters, but Max had convinced Agent Flynn that there simply wasn't time. It would take HRT almost the full forty-five minutes for them to get ready and fly from St. Augustine to Morozov's location on Amelia Island.

Max had argued that if he flew the Cirrus parked right outside the Fend Headquarters at Cecil Field, his small team would be able to arrive in less than half the time.

There was only one *minor* problem with Max's plan.

"But it's a fixed-wing aircraft," Flynn had argued.

Max said, "Meaning?"

"With the FBI helicopters, we'll be able to land right outside Morozov's house. With that little plane, you'll have to land at the nearest airport."

Max shook his head. "Not with *that* plane." Then he had explained his plan. "It's the only way to get us there in time to fix this. If there's a way to reprogram the Fend 100, Renee can do it. We just need to get her in there, and stop Morozov and his men from interfering."

Wilkes objected. "That's crazy, Max. I think you should wait for HRT to get there."

Max turned to Flynn. "Special Agent Flynn, it's up to you. But you know the math. With the Cirrus, we'll be there in ten minutes. Those helicopters won't get there for forty-five. That'll be too late. And I need a decision now."

Flynn looked between Max and Wilkes. "I agree with Max. Go. Take two of the HRT men. I take responsibility."

It had taken Max about five minutes to locate the set of keys at the airport's FBO, and another five seconds for the HRT men to persuade the person behind the counter to hand the keys over. FBI commandos in full tactical gear could be quite persuasive when they wanted to be.

Now they were about to take off.

"Everyone ready?"

"Yes."

Max pushed the throttle forward and sped down the runway. The Cirrus was heavy. The FBI men weighed at least two hundred pounds each with their gear. As the end of the runway approached and the airspeed indicator slowly crept up, Max began to feel the cold fingers of fear creeping over his body. He hadn't bothered to do a gross weight calculation. It was a hot summer day, and that could be a fatal mistake. He kept the aircraft nose level for a bit longer than normal, gaining more speed, and slowly pulled back on the stick for the climb out.

He exhaled. A safe takeoff. Once they were up, he banked right and headed northeast.

"Renee, see this screen here?"

"Yes."

"Plug in the GPS coordinates you got for Morozov's mansion. Then press this button." She did as he said. A moment later, the needle on his heading indicator swung a few degrees to the right. Max adjusted his heading to fly directly towards Morozov's location. There was a distance indicator that was ticking down.

Twenty more miles.

At over two hundred miles per hour, they would be there in no time.

Max reached up and ripped off the warning panel on the ceiling of the aircraft, handing it to Renee. Everyone was nervous.

A moment later, he rechecked the distance. Only fifteen miles to go.

"Okay, team, I have to tell you, I'm really not sure what to expect here. The landing might be pretty rough. Renee, can you read the instructions?"

Renee's face was white. "Activation Handle Cover—Remove."

"Done."

"Activation Handle…Both hands…Pull straight down."

Max nearly yelled. "*Don't do that.* Just *read* it for now."

"Okay." She continued, "Approximately forty-five pounds of force is required to activate the Cirrus Airframe Parachute System. Pull the handle with both hands in a chin-up style pull until the handle is fully extended. After deployment, mixture...cut off. Fuel selector...off. Fuel pump...off. Bat-alt master switches...off." She continued reading the checklist, including the part that told them the proper way to position their bodies for impact.

Max said, "Everyone get that?"

One of the FBI agents said, "I was in a helicopter crash in Iraq once. This sounds like it'll be easier."

"Good attitude," said Max.

"Max, this is Fend Control, come in, please." It was Special Agent Flynn's voice.

"Go ahead."

"I need to put you on a conference call. Just keep monitoring this radio frequency. We're going to be talking to NORAD."

* * *

"Huntress Control, Angry 509, I have visual of the Fend 100 aircraft."

"Roger, Angry 509. Attempt to establish comms."

Jason expertly maneuvered his F-16 to the left wing of the Fend 100 aircraft. He could see passengers through the windows. Some were waving frantically.

He switched his radio to the guard frequency. Every aircraft and ship would be monitoring that.

"Fend 100, this is United States Air Force armed F-16, you are approaching restricted airspace, do you require assistance?"

For a moment, he heard nothing. Then a woman's voice came on the radio.

"Air Force F-16, this is Fend 100. We do not require assistance. We are having autopilot problems. We are troubleshooting now."

Jason gripped his yoke tightly. Thank God. Maybe this was all just some misunderstanding. He looked in the cockpit window of the massive airliner, but it was hard to see anything.

Then one of the people in the cockpit held up a sheet of paper to the window. But from this distance, he couldn't read what it said.

"Fend 100, Air Force armed F-16, I understand you are having a flight control emergency. Are you able to regain control?"

The woman responded on the radio. "We're working on it, Air Force F-16. We expect to have it fixed momentarily."

Jason put in a little right stick and tried to get closer to the Fend 100. He could almost make out what the pilots had written on the white paper they were holding up.

Then he heard the voice of the EADS controller. Only Jason could hear that radio call as it was on a discreet frequency. "Angry 509, Huntress Control, the Fend aircraft is approaching a National Defense High Security Zone. They will not be allowed entry into that airspace. Are you able to establish communication?"

They will not be allowed entry into that airspace. He mulled over the phrase. It sounded innocent enough, but what the controller was really saying was that Jason would be ordered to shoot the aircraft down if it tried to enter.

"Huntress Control, affirmative. I now have comms with the Fend 100. They tell me that they have almost fixed the problem."

He looked out the window. He could now read what was written on the white piece of paper.

NO COMMS. NO CONTROLS.

He frowned. That didn't make any sense. He was talking to them right now. Of course they had comms.

What was going on?

* * *

Flynn stood with his hands on the desk. "General, I have you on speakerphone. In the room I have a CIA rep, and via radio we have a DIA agent. Please tell them what you told me."

Wilkes and Flynn had taken control of the office and were speaking with a general at NORAD who was managing the F-16 intercept flight and the air defense for the Eastern Seaboard of the United States.

"As you can see," the general said, "the Fend 100 is headed towards the Air Defense Identification Zone. It looks like it'll enter the restricted airspace soon. We can't let that happen. Is there any way to manage this on your end—this thing is supposed to be remote control, right?"

"General, I'm afraid we've spoken with the personnel at Fend Aerospace, and they insist that they are unable to regain control of the aircraft."

Via his aircraft radio, Max said, "I'm still about ten minutes out from our location of interest. I'll be able to tell you more once I get there."

Flynn looked at the radar picture. "General, a question. You said they diverted and grounded all the other flights."

"That's correct."

"Sir, we're looking at the air traffic screen here at Fend Aerospace. We can see most of the Eastern United States. It looks like there is still one aircraft headed towards the Maryland-Virginia area."

A few hundred miles to the northeast of the Fend 100, there was another aircraft track. It was still several hundred miles away, but the Fend 100 was closing fast.

"Hold on," the general said, "I'm trying to find out which aircraft that is. Everyone should have diverted away from the Baltimore-Washington area."

After a momentary silence, the general said, "They said it's a head of state plane."

"Which country?"

"The Russian Federation."

* * *

Max tried to listen carefully to the conversation over his headset as he flew his plane towards Amelia Island. Had he heard that correctly?

The Russian president's plane?

What was it Morozov had said to Max? *A man like me wouldn't go through all this trouble just to exact revenge upon your father. I have a much grander vision than that.*

And all at once, Morozov's plans snapped together.

Max said, "The Fend 100 isn't headed to Camp David. Tell the interceptor not to shoot it down."

Flynn sounded irritated. "But you said...what the hell, Max? What are you saying?"

"Gentlemen, I think Pavel Morozov is trying to assassinate the Russian president. I think we're witnessing a coup."

Max excused himself from Flynn's relayed phone call—he needed to give this his complete attention now. He checked his altitude. One thousand feet. That was as low as he felt he could comfortably go, considering what he was about to do.

He glanced back at his passengers. "Okay, folks. We're two miles out. I'm slowing down. Once I get on airspeed and set up for wind drift, I'm going to pull the chute."

He brought back the throttle, and the engine lowered in pitch and intensity.

"I'm going to try and get us as close to the house as possible. But frankly, I have no idea how this is going to go."

Renee's voice was shaky. "Are you sure this is a good idea? Couldn't we just land at the airport?"

"No time. Now remember the body positions for impact. And while I doubt they'll be expecting anything like this, my guess is they'll probably notice the plane parachuting from the sky. So be ready to fight as soon as we touch down."

One of the FBI men said, "Once we're down, you two follow us. We'll get you in safely and let you take it from there."

Max began sharp S-turns, bleeding off speed until the plane got to below one hundred and forty knots. He moved the stick so that the aircraft was straight and level.

"That's the house, straight ahead, right?"

"I think so, yes," Renee said. The mansion was right next to a beach, and adjacent to a golf course.

"Okay, here goes nothing."

He reached up and pulled down hard on the red metal grip. They heard a loud pop from the rear of the aircraft, and then everyone was jolted forward in their seats. Renee let out a yelp. The two FBI men were grunting and swearing as the aircraft decelerated.

The aircraft pitched down violently, and Max's stomach fluttered as he felt them falling. It took about eight seconds for the plane to slow from one hundred and thirty knots to almost zero.

Max's face was turning red, the blood collecting in his head due to the downward-facing angle. Then the parachute swung them like a pendulum, and the aircraft was once again level with the ground. They were falling, but at a manageable speed. Each of them looked outside.

"Where are we going to land?" Renee said.

"It looks like we'll end up on the golf course. Pretty damn close to the house. Do I get points for that? We'll need to be ready for his security men as soon as we get out." Each of them was armed and wore Kevlar vests.

Max watched the altitude wind down. Five hundred feet. Four hundred. The ground began rushing up to meet them. Three hundred. The descent didn't feel slow anymore. He remembered reading that the impact would feel like they had dropped from four meters in the air.

That sounded a lot higher now that he had pulled the chute.

"The seats are supposed to take the brunt of the impact," he said aloud, trying to convince himself as much as anything. That was the last thing he said before the big crunch.

They slammed into one of the greens on the golf course. When the plane finally came to a rest, the hole flag stood right in front of them.

"Oh, damn, that was hard. My back..."

"Come on, we need to get out." Max's back was aching too, but he forced himself to open his door and tumble out onto the low-cut grass. The others were doing the same, weapons drawn. Each of them was in pain, but they looked to be okay.

Max looked up at the house. "I don't see any security. Are we sure this was it?"

"As sure as we can be," Renee said.

"Oh my God, are you guys alright?" came the surprised voice of someone in a golf cart several yards away.

None of them answered. The two HRT men began running towards the mansion, their HK416s pointed ahead. Renee and Max were close behind, their pistols aimed at the ground as they ran.

* * *

Flynn looked at Wilkes, exasperated by their continuing conversation with the NORAD general.

The general's voice, coming out of the speakerphone, was also noticeably agitated. "Gentlemen, that is unacceptable. I've got maybe five minutes before I need to give the order to shoot that plane down. Tell those engineers at Fend that they need to turn that plane around now!"

"We're doing the best we can, General. We have multiple potential fixes at work."

"I understand, but I can't be sure that your theory is correct. How am I supposed to know if the target is the Russian president's plane or other VIPs on the ground at Camp David? Hell, it'll fly right over D.C. to get there. Maybe it's headed for the Capitol Building. I have to call SECDEF in one minute. He wants an answer. I'm sorry, gentlemen, but we have that temporary flight restriction up for a reason. It's time to enforce it."

* * *

The FBI men were fast. Even Max, who considered himself to be in excellent shape, had trouble keeping up. They flew along the lawn of the mansion. Max noted several large antennae protruding from the roof. A custom job.

The first Russian security man they saw looked shocked to see them. He poked his head out of the double doors of the basement. He was holding a gun, and it got about halfway up before he took two bullets in the chest from one of the HRT men.

The FBI men didn't break stride. One opened the door and entered, scanning the finished basement with his carbine. The second HRT man followed closely behind. Max and Renee took up the rear. The room was very large. A pool table, rows of couches and a full bar. Two big-screen TVs on the wall.

No one spoke. But the other Russians must have heard the gunshots, because two men came running down the basement stairs. They fired a burst from a small automatic weapon, and the assault team took cover.

Max had one of them in his sights when the Russian spun around, hit by a burst of gunfire. The other Russian security man met the same fate. Two more down courtesy of the FBI's Hostage Rescue Team. They were *good*.

Max looked to his side. Renee was hunkered behind a couch. "We need to find the room they're controlling the aircraft from," Renee said. She winced as another round of gunfire erupted from the stairway.

Max took Renee by the shoulder. "Listen. You go back outside the door. Get under the back deck and hide under the stairs. I don't want to risk them hitting you. Once we're clear, I'll come right back down and bring you up. Okay?"

She nodded. "Okay." She looked scared. Max didn't want to risk her getting hurt, both for personal and professional reasons. Renee hurried outside the door through which they had entered, then hid off to the right, under the back deck staircase.

Max turned around and scanned the room. The FBI agents had cleared the basement and were now advancing up the staircase.

His pulse racing, Max followed. He looked up the staircase at a closed door, wondering what was on the other side.

The HRT men were fearless. The first man opened the door and fired several rounds, then recoiled as a barrage of bullets ripped through the wall next to him.

The second HRT man grabbed a concussion grenade from his belt, pulled the pin, and tossed it through the open stairway door.

The sound was deafening.

Max felt it in his chest, and his ears rang.

The two HRT operatives disappeared beyond the top of the stairs. The sound of automatic weapons screamed through the stairway.

Max bolted up the stairs, aiming his pistol forward and scanning the room.

There were three bodies on the floor. The first HRT member was on the ground, gasping for air. He'd been hit in the Kevlar vest. The second HRT operative was spread eagle—Max couldn't see where he was hit, but blood was seeping out from under his uniform and onto the tile flooring.

They were in a large open kitchen, but the center table was covered with computers, wires taped down along the floor and running up the wall.

The third body was a dark-haired young man of about twenty. He was slumped over in front of one of the computers, dead.

Maria sat in front of the other computer, looking dazed.

Max pointed his weapon at her. "Fix it, Maria. Give control over to the Fend 100 pilots right now."

She looked like she was trying to focus on his face. Trying to read his lips. He realized she was probably deaf. Wisps of smoke flowed through the air—remnants of the concussion grenade.

Max was about to go downstairs and get Renee when he caught Maria glancing behind him. He turned, weapon raised toward a dark figure in the next room.

The figure moved awkwardly from the second-floor deck through an open screen door. Flowing white curtains partially masked him and his prisoner.

Pavel Morozov stood behind Renee, a gun to her temple.

"Stay there, Mr. Fend."

Max wrinkled his brow, making calculations in his head. His gun was aimed at Morozov's forehead, about a fifteen-foot shot. Doable on the gun range. But not with a hostage...especially one that he cared about.

Max sidestepped behind Maria, keeping his pistol trained on Morozov.

Seeing this, Morozov nodded at Maria. "You think I won't shoot her too?"

"She's been working for you."

"Is that what you think?"

Max frowned, confused.

Morozov shrugged. "Fine. More fake CIA propaganda, I think. But whatever you may think of her, she is the only one who will be able to turn the plane around for you."

Maria was looking up at Max. A tear ran down her cheek.

A voice from a radio in front of her said, "Fend 100, Air Force armed F-16. Can you do me a favor? I can't read the sign that the pilots are holding up. Can you tell me what it says?"

Maria glanced at Morozov and then began to reach for the radio transmit button.

"Wait," said Max. Her hand froze. "He thinks you're on the plane. Why?"

* * *

Captain Easteadt couldn't understand it. The woman hadn't answered his radio call. What if she wasn't on the plane?

"Angry 509, Huntress Control, has the aircraft altered course, or does it still appear to be entering into restricted airspace?"

"Huntress Control, Angry 509, no change in the aircraft's course or speed."

"Roger, 509. Have you been able to establish communications?"

Jason thought about that. He wasn't sure what was going on. "Negative, Control. No joy with the pilots aboard the Fend aircraft."

He looked at the cockpit window of the airliner. The pilots were still waving frantically, holding up their sign. Jason decided to try to raise them one more time.

* * *

"Fend 100, Air Force F-16, come in, please."

Max kept his pistol trained on Morozov's head.

"That's the Air Force intercept aircraft?" He was looking at Maria.

Max looked at one of the flat-screens on the wall. It showed the Fend 100 heading towards a lone air contact.

Max began stepping forward.

"What are you doing? Stay where you are," said Morozov.

Max continued to creep forward, slowly heading towards the table of electronics. He knew what he was after. And it was only another step.

"I said *stop*."

Max said, "Fine. I'll stop. I'll even place my gun down on the table." But he didn't. He just lowered the gun and used the barrel to depress the transmit button on the radio.

* * *

Jason listened in disbelief. It had taken him a moment to recognize what he was hearing, but once he did, everything fell into place.

Over the radio, Jason heard a man say, "Tell me, Pavel, why did you take over the Fend 100? And why have you had Maria here pretending to be on the Fend 100 while she talks to the Air Force fighter? At first, I thought you two were planning to remotely take control of the Fend 100 to attack the G-7 summit. But now I know that isn't true. Pavel, the one thing that really pissed you off was being subservient to the Russian president. You must really envy him. Similar background and all—yet he's in charge, and you're just his little assistant. Must be hard for a man like you."

"There is nothing you can do at this point, Mr. Fend. You should cut your losses and allow me to leave. Put your gun down." A second man's voice. Jason didn't recognize it. Low in tone, with a Russian accent.

"So you don't deny it?"

"I deny nothing."

"What will happen to you after the Russian president's plane goes down? We know it was you. How did you think you were going to escape?"

"You know only what your news media and intelligence agencies agree on. And it seems as though the Islamic State has already claimed responsibility for this hijacking."

The first man's voice. "Courtesy of Maljab Tactical, no doubt. One of your own companies. Your fingerprints will be all over this."

"You are wrong. I have friends *everywhere*. When those planes go down, I will take the reins in Russia."

"So you're going to fly the Fend 100 into the Russian president's plane right now? And then you think America will recognize you as the new Russian president? Come on, Pavel. Even you aren't that dumb. Why would the US ever recognize your legitimacy?"

"When I am in charge, Russia will forge a new partnership with the United States. It will be better for all."

"Morozov, you're assuming that the Fend 100 continues on its current flight plan and flies into the Russian presidential aircraft. But won't Maria be able to fix that for me?"

Jason couldn't make out the rest of what was said over the radio, except that it sounded like an answer in the negative. He tried to process what that all meant. He looked at the aircraft that was flying next to him. An enormous white airliner, filled with people and fuel. Controlled by computers.

And supposedly heading towards the Russian president's plane...

He had to act. But what could he do?

Jason looked at his air search radar. Sure enough, there was one contact about one hundred miles ahead. At the rate they were closing, they would be there in mere minutes.

Jason pushed forward his thrust lever and hit his afterburner. His F-16 accelerated forward at close to twice the speed of sound. He would be almost out of fuel when he reached it, but he had to try and warn them.

The Russian presidential aircraft was a four-engined beast. A wide-bodied IL-96. Jason buzzed it from the front, passing only two hundred feet away.

That *must* have grabbed their attention. He then pulled and banked hard, arcing his nimble fighter to a position just off the right wing.

Jason flipped a few switches and then fired a burst of machine gun fire well ahead of the Russian aircraft. The tracers were clearly visible against the blue water below.

Now they knew he meant business. He wasn't sure what kind of homing system the other aircraft was using, but he knew enough about dogfighting theory to know that if the Fend aircraft missed the Russian presidential plane on the first pass, that was it. Game over. There wasn't enough of a speed advantage for the Fend aircraft to get a second chance.

Jason was already on the guard radio frequency. Time to make his call.

* * *

Max heard the voice over the radio and smiled.

"Russian aircraft approaching the United States, this is US Air Force armed F-16. You are about to be attacked by an incoming commercial drone aircraft. Begin evasive maneuvers *immediately* to avoid collision."

Maria and Morozov both looked shocked. Then Morozov's face turned to rage as he looked at the radio transmit button, which was depressed into the full detent. He realized that their entire conversation had been played to the American fighter jet. Morozov's wrist muscles flexed as he gripped Renee tighter. She let out a cry.

All of their eyes turned to the radar screen on the wall. The two air tracks were so close, heading right for each other...about to converge.

But they didn't.

The Fend 100 continued on in the opposite direction. The Russian Federation presidential aircraft turned sharply and changed altitude.

Maria could see the aviation stats of each aircraft being displayed on the board. "It didn't hit. The Fend 100 missed it."

"Put down your weapon, Pavel," Max said.

Morozov's eyes were on fire now, his nostrils flaring. "It seems that you have changed my plans. But your aircraft is still at risk. All those people will die if you don't regain control of the Fend 100. So let us bargain, Max Fend."

"Let's."

Morozov pulled Renee up close. "Maria is the only one who can save the people on that aircraft now. If you don't have her, they'll run out of fuel and crash into the ocean."

Max wondered if Renee would be able to analyze and interpret the data on this computer system in time. Unknown. He needed Maria alive.

Morozov began backing away toward a doorway in the corner of the room, holding Renee in front of him. He was heading to the garage.

Max could hear the FBI men on the floor and behind him, a groan from the stairway.

"Leave Renee," Max said, "and I'll let you go."

Pavel Morozov's eyes narrowed. "Done." He pushed Renee towards Max, raised his gun and fired three times.

Max caught Renee and covered her with his body as he returned fire through the closed doorway.

Max ran towards the door, but it was locked. He fired his weapon into the door handle. Wide holes formed and wood splintered. Max kicked the door open and burst through into the garage.

He fired into the fleeing SUV, hearing the sound of an engine revving up and the squeal of tires as Morozov peeled out of view, making his getaway.

But Max didn't have time to worry about him. He ran back towards the computers laid out in the kitchen, glaring at Maria.

She had been shot in the arm.

"Fix this," Max said to her, his weapon trained on her head. Sympathy for her gunshot wound wasn't something he had in him.

Maria nodded and began typing with her good hand, wincing in pain.

He glanced back at Renee. "Are you okay?"

Renee nodded. "Yes, I'm alright."

"I need you to watch her, Renee. Make sure she's really doing what we want her to do."

Renee stood behind Maria, who was typing slowly into one of the terminals.

Max said, "Turn it around now, and give control to the pilots on board."

Maria nodded, flustered and upset. She typed in a command, dragged her mouse, and began clicking a few times. "There. They should be able to control it now."

"Call them on the radio and tell them."

Maria did as requested. "Fend 100, this is..." She paused, not sure what to say. Max grabbed the radio. "Fend 100 on guard, you should have control of your aircraft now. Please respond."

After a moment, the radio came back with, "This is Fend 100 on guard. Flight controls are now responsive. Declaring an emergency and heading to the nearest suitable runway."

* * *

The ambulances and police cars arrived moments later. The EMS crews provided treatment for the FBI men. Both ended up okay.

The one who was hit in the Kevlar vest had two broken ribs. The one who was facedown and bleeding from a gunshot in the kitchen had lost a lot of blood, but was stable.

Max walked up to Maria as she was receiving treatment under police supervision. "What made you do it?"

She didn't answer. Just kept her head down, looking at the ground. A few minutes later, the FBI arrived and took custody of her.

Special Agent Flynn flew to the scene, courtesy of the FBI HRT helicopters.

Max said, "Have you found Morozov?"

"Not yet. But we have agents and local police scanning the area. Roadblocks are set up all over for fifty miles around. And flights are still grounded. He'll turn up."

The FBI drove Renee and Max back down to Jacksonville. They had a prolonged after-action report to complete with the local FBI office. Then they were cut loose in time for dinner. Max invited Renee to his father's house in Ponte Vedra.

"You think you're ready to take me home to your father?" she said with a wink.

"I'm ready for more than that."

"How about a beach vacation? I know a nice quiet spot in Georgia—near Jekyll Island."

Max grinned. "In all seriousness, you did great. Thanks for all the help." He leaned in and kissed her.

"Thanks. You too." She was blushing.

Dinner that night was a busy affair. Charles Fend, understandably, had to work much of the evening. He had invited many of his company executives to his home. They could manage the public affairs nightmare from there. Max and Renee sat by the pool, sipping on cool drinks and watching the sunset.

When the night finally wrapped up, and the majority of his employees had left, Charles came and sat down with them. He sipped on a glass of scotch and looked at his son.

"Your mother would have been proud."

"Thanks, Dad."

"And you, dear. If there is ever anything I can do to repay you for saving the lives of all those men and women on my aircraft, you just say the word."

Renee said, "Your son has already promised me a job."

Charles looked at Max. "An excellent hire."

Max said, "What will happen to the automated flight program?"

His father sighed. "I'm sure it will be some time before people feel comfortable enough with the technology. But I think it's safe to say that we won't be moving forward with the contract as soon as we thought we would. It's too early to say what the fallout will be."

"Well, perhaps we can start making parachutes for commercial airliners?"

His father laughed. "Perhaps."

27

Wilkes met Max at the Conch House restaurant in St. Augustine three days later. They sat in one of the secluded grass huts that overlooked the marina. A waitress brought them waters and appetizers.

Wilkes said, "We'd like to retain your services for the future, Max."

"And what will that entail?"

Wilkes took off his glasses, rubbing them with a napkin. "You liked working for the DIA, right?"

"I did."

"Well, we would like to have you serve your country in other ways. Your position in your father's company, and your fame...or infamy, depending on who you ask...will grant you access that few enjoy. You're a patriot, and a skilled operative. Your talent and loyalty were never in question."

"Funny how Special Agent Flynn wasn't made aware of my loyalty when he took me in last week..."

Wilkes sipped his water. "Look, I agree that the entire situation should have been handled differently. But things turned out rather well for us."

"Did they?" Max looked out over the water and said, "There's something I want to know."

Wilkes said, "Go ahead."

"I spoke with Flynn yesterday. Our final chat, I hope. He suggested that Maria Blount might no longer be in the custody of the FBI. He implied that *another* agency had taken her from them. Perhaps for interrogations? Or perhaps not."

Wilkes didn't say anything.

"I seem to recall a few operations from my days in Europe where our assets were retired by similar means. Sent off to rural lands to live out their days on a government pension, their covers ruined, but their mission accomplished."

Wilkes's face remained a blank canvas. Seeing that he wasn't getting a bite, Max said, "Maria wasn't *just* working for Morozov, was she?"

Wilkes stared back at him. "Who else do you think she was working for?"

"You."

"*Me?*"

"I think you knew that Pavel Morozov was going to try and kill the Russian president. And I think you thought that my father's plane, and the lives of everyone aboard, were an acceptable risk to take for a chance at changing the Russian leadership."

"An interesting theory. But very cynical, Max."

Max said, "If I were a man of low moral character, and the only thing that mattered to me was winning or losing the great game of espionage between the Russians and the Americans, I might see this Pavel Morozov situation as an opportunity."

Wilkes grinned. "I hope you aren't referring to me there. But pray tell, how so?"

Max said, "Let's say that I found out Morozov was able to crash the Fend 100 into the Russian president's plane. What would happen then? The Islamic State had already claimed responsibility for it. From my conversation with him, this was part of Morozov's masquerade. *You* might have been tempted to encourage the public belief that terrorists were responsible for the whole thing. The Islamic State is responsible for so many atrocities. Why not this? It takes out a Russian leader who has been a thorn in our side and increases the American desire to pour more resources into fighting terrorism."

"I hope you have more faith in me than that."

Max said, "I do, actually. And I have more faith in the CIA. I can't see them signing off on that."

"Good."

"But I think it was a worst-case scenario for you. A high-magnitude, low-probability risk that you were willing to take. And instead, I think you ended up getting exactly what you wanted."

"Which is?"

"Either way it was a win-win for the CIA. But now, you got rid of Pavel Morozov and have the Russian president in our debt."

Wilkes raised his eyebrow at that. "I hadn't thought of that. I guess he is, isn't he?"

"I noticed on the news yesterday that the Russians have announced they're pulling a large number of their troops out of Syria. Interesting timing."

"Well, I suppose it is, isn't it?" Wilkes sipped his ice water.

"The enemy of my enemy is my friend. If you took out Pavel Morozov and saved the Russian president's life, I could see how something like that might present you in a very favorable light. Stopping a coup d'état? Maybe that appearance of savior-ship would help influence a deal. Maybe it could start a more peaceful relationship."

Wilkes shrugged. "Maybe."

"I remembered something about one of my Russian mafia contacts in France. Sergei. He was introduced to me by his former handler. But his former handler wasn't DIA—he was CIA. It happened so long ago, and it didn't seem important at the time. Just one agency sharing with another. Now, though—I'm not so sure that wasn't orchestrated more carefully."

Wilkes was chewing his ice cubes. "Alright, Max. I can see that you aren't happy with me."

"You used my father and me as bait, didn't you? You knew that Morozov was working with some of his contacts in Russia to orchestrate a coup. But you wanted to manipulate how it happened. So you dangled a carrot that you knew he couldn't resist. A chance to twist the knife in my father's back, by hurting his company—and by blaming me. That got

Morozov's mouth watering. Just like you said...revenge keeps KGB agents warm at night."

Wilkes said, "You have no idea how big this operation was, Max. We didn't just dangle one carrot. We put out hundreds. You and your father weren't the only bait. You just happened to be the bait that Morozov went for. And once he did, we had to keep up appearances."

"That's why MI-6 was used to break me out. There couldn't be any connection to your operation."

Wilkes nodded.

Max continued. "You didn't want any chance of Morozov finding out the CIA was involved in all this. So you called in a favor to your friends at Legoland. But why did you care whether I was in FBI custody or not?"

"Because MI-6 got word that Morozov had ordered a hit on you, so that you couldn't prove your innocence. We preferred that not to occur."

"Why, thank you."

"See? And you say I wasn't looking out for you."

"My guess is that very few people knew the risk you took with the Fend 100 aircraft. That was dangerous. Did the Russian president know what was happening as he flew towards the Atlantic coast of the US? Was it used as leverage while he was in flight?"

Wilkes looked like he was thinking of something to say.

"Don't bother answering. I don't need to know. There's only one more thing I want you to tell me. What happened to Morozov?"

"I'm afraid that isn't something I'm at liberty to discuss, Max."

Max snorted, disappointed.

Then Wilkes said, "But if, hypothetically speaking, of course, I knew where he was, just know that you would probably be quite satisfied with his present condition."

Max's eyes were hard. "Good."

* * *

The unmarked jet touched down at the airstrip near Sevastopol, on the Crimean Peninsula. After the annexation of Crimea, the airport was predominantly used by the Russian military.

It had been a long flight. The aircraft taxied to a stop near the end of the runway. Three black cars waited on the flight line. Security men opened up the door for one of the cars, and the Russian president stepped out.

As the door opened and the CIA men began taking their prisoner down the steps of the aircraft, a broad smile formed on the Russian president's lips.

Wilkes walked up to the Russian president and shook his hand.

"I trust that you finished getting everything you could out of him?" he asked, a smirk on his face.

Wilkes shrugged but didn't say anything. *No more than you must have done working in Berlin many years ago, old man.*

Wilkes's men had to put Morozov through an accelerated interrogation regimen. He would have preferred to take more time, but they had still obtained a great deal of valuable intelligence.

The Russian president looked at the prisoner like he was a precious gift. "Mr. Wilkes, my thanks for this. Even if he is a week overdue."

Pavel Morozov was gagged, bound, and blindfolded. The Russian president walked up and removed the blindfold. Red, bloodshot eyes looked back at him, filled with fear. The president patted Morozov's cheek a little too hard, then gestured for his men to take him away. Then he got in his car, and the motorcade departed.

Wilkes began walking back towards the jet. He shuddered to think what might be in store for Morozov. But the man deserved his fate. Wilkes looked back from the top of the stairs once more, watching the motorcade speed off down the road. He pulled his jacket tight to fight the cold. The winds coming off the Black Sea lent a chilly bite to the air.

THE OSHKOSH CONNECTION

A MAX FEND THRILLER

If you can walk away from a landing, it's a good landing. If you use the airplane the next day, it's an outstanding landing.

— Chuck Yeager

1

Hugo the assassin arrived at Baltimore-Washington International Airport on the 4:35 p.m. flight from London. He grabbed his Samsonite carry-on bag from the overhead compartment and walked confidently through the airport.

The stop at immigration was quick. He had nothing to declare. On a personal visit. Staying about a week. Thank you. You have a nice day as well.

Hugo left out the part about being paid to kill people while he was here.

The muggy July air hit him like a wall as he stepped outside to fetch a cab. The drive to Dupont Circle took just over thirty minutes. Hugo had rented a flat online the night before. Just a five-minute walk from James Hoban's Irish Restaurant, where he ate a BBQ burger with bacon and grilled onions at an outdoor table, sweating while watching the streets and waiting for his assignment. He licked BBQ sauce off his fingers. He had to admit, Americans knew how to cook good burgers.

The courier arrived by bicycle. A know-nothing. Just a shaggy-looking man wearing spandex, eyeliner, and a nose ring who delivered envelopes for a living. Sometimes there were special instructions. This was one of those times. The courier placed a manila envelope on the table with the bright red scarf, then departed without saying a word. A block down the street, a man watching from behind a half-closed set of blinds texted confirmation that Hugo had received the envelope. Within seconds, that confirmation message was relayed to the second-highest-ranking intelligence officer stationed in the Pakistani embassy.

Inside the envelope was a hand-written note. A coded meeting location. Hugo took the strip of paper with the writing on it, ripped it up, and dunked it into his ice water. It dissolved instantly. The assassin left the rest of his meal uneaten and hailed a second cab.

"The Smithsonian."

"Which one?" asked the cab driver.

"The Castle."

The driver nodded, and the car began moving. Hugo caught the driver's curious glance at him through the rearview mirror.

"Where are you from?"

Hugo didn't answer, and the cab driver didn't ask a second time, not wanting to affect his tip. The car dropped him off a few minutes later and Hugo paid in cash. He then made his way along a brick walkway that wound between several Smithsonian museums. The Smithsonian Institution Building—"castle" was probably too generous—stood to his right. The red sandstone, faux-Norman architecture, and four-story towers seemed out of place in this city. But it made a good meeting spot.

A wide-open courtyard before him. Pedestrian tourists strolled and sat along a peaceful garden filled with lavender and goldfish ponds. The smell of honeysuckle hung in the air.

The assassin's eyes darted from person to person, scanning each face, each set of belongings, each person's wardrobe. Checking for inconsistencies—red flags that might give away someone in the American government. It was a crowded summer night, and most of the people he saw were tourists, walking to and from some festival being held on the National Mall one hundred meters away.

A Pakistani man sat on a bench fifty feet ahead of the assassin.

The assassin's client.

* * *

Abdul Syed wiped sweaty palms on the front of his khaki pants. He had taken all the proper precautions. His team of ISI countersurveillance experts had been watching the assassin since he had departed the airport. Still, now was when things got tricky.

If Hugo had a tail, the Pakistani operatives performing countersurveillance would let Syed know, and the meet would be aborted, along with tonight's mission. But this close to the rendezvous, even an aborted mission presented the risk of his man being detained and questioned.

Syed had participated in many operations like this before, but never on US soil. The Pakistani intelligence officer's blood pressure was abnormally high, triggered by the persistent worry that one of the FBI's counterintelligence teams might be watching.

While Syed's official posting at the Pakistani embassy was that of an agricultural counselor, the Americans knew better, and they regularly followed him. Syed had spent every night for the last few weeks in the same fashion. Riding the Metro around D.C., visiting different museums and restaurants, meeting acquaintances in locations far from one another. Innocuous locations using hard-to-follow routes. It took considerable time and effort, but Syed was sure that he had lost his surveillance each and every night for the past week.

Every one of those surveillance detection routes had been in preparation for this meeting. The assassin could have no connection to Pakistani intelligence. The Inter-Services Intelligence agency, or ISI, had been accused by Western governments of holding double standards in the fight against terrorism. Syed must not give them any more reasons to support that belief. Even more important, he must not allow them to discover his current operational plans.

Despite what both nations proclaimed, the United States was not a friend of Pakistan. And it was up to the ISI and its officers, brave men like Syed, to ensure that American imperialism would falter. American minds were brainwashed with propaganda. In Pakistan, everyone knew that Al Qaeda was not responsible for the attacks of September 11, 2001. Several ISI and Pakistani military officers had known of Osama bin Laden's whereabouts, less than a mile from the prestigious Kakul Military Academy in Abbottabad. Syed himself had known. He had been infuriated on that day when US Special Forces soldiers had illegally flown their stealth helicopters into his country, killing innocents and taking bin Laden. The CIA had not shared that operation with the ISI ahead of time, because they had known what Syed had known.

The US and Pakistan were enemies, playing at a dangerous game. The ISI and American intelligence agencies put on the charade of friendship, as the politicians demanded. But each agency did its best to sabotage the operations of the other. The Americans would love nothing more than to catch him tonight, planning the assassination of American citizens on American soil.

A man sat down next to him on the park bench.

Syed did not make eye contact with the man. Instead he continued to scan the courtyard for American agents who might be posing as casual observers as he removed an envelope from his pocket and placed it between them on the bench. An encrypted thumb drive was inside. One that, unless the correct procedure was used, would delete its contents upon insertion into a device.

The man took the envelope, stuffed it into his pocket, and walked away without saying a word.

Syed couldn't help but cast a sideways glance in his direction as he departed. He snorted air out his nose, shaking his head. The assassin was quite unremarkable. It was hard to believe that he was responsible for so many deaths...and would soon be responsible for so many more.

2

Blue Ridge Mountains
4000 Feet Above Ground Level

"We're going to crash."

The plane's nose was angled down, the green Appalachian Mountains now filling most of the cockpit windscreen.

Max Fend said, "You're overstating the problem, Renee. You really need to learn to relax. It's so peaceful up here. Away from the world, away from all of your troubles. Nothing but blue sky...well, as long as you look up. Maybe not straight ahead. Those are mountains."

Renee's voice was an octave higher than normal. "I'm not kidding, Max. Please, just..." She gripped the yoke of Max's Cirrus SR-22 tight enough that her knuckles went white, and she was unable to finish her thought.

Max grinned, scanning the various digital readouts on the instrument panel. "Hmm. Actually, you *are* losing quite a bit of altitude, now that you mention it."

"Max, *please*. Take the aircraft. This is not funny."

He looked over at Renee, who was sweating through her tank top. They sat side by side in the small single-engine aircraft. Renee sat in the left seat, holding the side-mounted yoke with her left hand and the throttle with her right. Ray-Ban aviator-style sunglasses—a gift from Max —hid what was likely the look of genuine fear in her eyes.

Max's voice remained steady, and only slightly condescending, as he spoke through his headset. "Look, this is how you learn. Finding your way out of a sticky situation on your own will make you a better pilot—"

"Take the aircraft right now."

He folded his arms across his chest. "No." He was a teacher, and she his pupil. Sometimes the teacher needed to be stern.

"*Fine.*"

Max began second-guessing his teaching approach as Renee pulled back much too hard on the yoke and the nose pitched way up, filling the windscreen with a hazy white sky and bright yellow sun. Compounding the rather excessive control input was the unfortunate fact that she had forgotten to add power.

"Well, *this* is going to be interesting," Max said as the nose continued to pitch up. Max watched their airspeed bleed off precipitously. And, like a heavy truck trying to get up a hill without adding any gas, their climb slowed, the airspeed continued to decelerate, and the sinking feeling in Max's stomach grew as he knew it would only be a moment until...

A high-pitched warning tone sounded.

"What is that?" asked Renee. Her voice panicked. "Max. I'm not joking..."

The nose of the aircraft plunged downward like the lead car of a roller coaster as it dropped past the peak of a towering hill.

Renee screamed profanity all the way down.

Max grinned as the aircraft dove, his stomach left somewhere five hundred feet above. "You are using your French-Canadian churchy curses again. I must tell you, I really love it when you do that."

The aircraft's dive caused their airspeed to rocket back up. Max laughed to himself. Renee still had too much back stick. The increase in speed would cause the aircraft to nose back up, and the roller coaster would soon begin again. Yes, they were getting lower—closer to the Appalachian Mountains—but Max was paying close attention to their altitude and would make sure they didn't really get into trouble. This was fun. He was glad that Renee had finally agreed to take lessons.

Max said, "There's nothing you can say that will make me take the aircraft. It's important that you understand aerodynamic principles if you ever want to—"

She looked at him over the top of her sunglasses, her dark eyes menacing. "Take the controls *right now* or I will *never* sleep with you again."

Max immediately placed his grip on his yoke and throttle. He cleared his throat. "*My aircraft.*"

Renee let out a long steady breath, collapsing backward into her seat and letting go of the stick. She closed her eyes for a moment, her chest heaving. Then she opened her eyes, turned, and punched Max in the shoulder. "*Don't* do that again."

Max added more power and climbed back up to altitude. He watched as the altimeter ticked up, saying, "I think you're really getting the hang of it. You showed a lot of grit today."

Renee glared at him.

"Okay, enough fun for now. We'll have to head back if we're going to make the surprise I have in store."

"Which is what, exactly?"

"It's not a surprise if I tell you."

Max banked the aircraft into a wide right arc. Beneath them, a shimmering Shenandoah River wound through the Blue Ridge Mountains like a snake. Renee was looking out the window, admiring the view. Hopefully the scenery would improve her mood by the time they returned.

Max made his approach from the west into Leesburg Executive Airport. Another single-engine aircraft, a Cessna 172, was in the downwind ahead of him. He made all of his traffic calls over the radio, completed the landing checklist, and then maneuvered the plane onto final.

"You sure you don't want to take the landing?"

"No, thanks."

"Landings are the best."

"Not right now, thank you."

Max waxed poetic. "Landings always give me a kick of endorphins. The sound of the wheels touching the pavement. The blur of runway zooming past. The satisfying sense of accomplishment that once again, I have not killed us."

"Can you please not joke like that until we're on the ground?"

A moment later, Max had parked the Cirrus on the flight line and shut down the engine. Together they allowed their cockpit doors to slide open, letting in the summer breeze.

"You have anywhere you want to eat tonight?" Max asked.

She shook her head at him as she took a swig from her water bottle—ice cubes clunking against its plastic walls. "What am I going to do with you?"

Max's phone buzzed in his pocket. He took it out and read the message.

WOLF TRAP IN ONE HOUR

"Who is it?"

"It's our surprise for the evening. I've just gotten us concert tickets. The outdoor amphitheater at Wolf Trap."

Renee's expression finally warmed. "Now that sounds lovely."

Max didn't bother to tell her that it was his CIA handler who had decided on the venue. And he would be working.

* * *

The summer concert series at Wolf Trap was one of the cultural gems of Northern Virginia. Thousands of men and women were sprawled out on blankets on the well-trimmed lawn that surrounded the amphitheater. The grass banked downward toward the concert stage area, which was covered by an architecturally stunning wooden structure. The amphitheater—known as the Filene Center, after the woman who had donated the land now operated by the National Park Authority—was constructed of

Douglas fir and southern yellow pine. It could seat seven thousand under the covered section, but on a clear night like this, Max and Renee enjoyed sitting on the lawn.

"They're good," Renee said of the string quartet on stage. Her fingers tickled the hairs on his forearm. She lay on her side, facing him, and leaned over to kiss his cheek. "Thanks for taking me out tonight. I forgive you for almost letting us crash today."

"In reality, we were in very little danger..."

He turned towards her and smooched her on the lips, then turned back towards the stage. Max rested on his back, partially propped up on his elbows.

Renee had a glow in her eye. The glimmer of unrestrained and optimistic love. While the pair had dated once before, when they were both in college, it had been so many years ago that their current reboot felt new and fresh.

The Max and Renee relationship "take two" had been going on for about a year. Since a well-publicized near-death incident on the shores of northeast Florida. Max, an ex-DIA operative, had been accused of hacking into his father's company, Fend Aerospace. Charles Fend's multibillion-dollar firm did a lot of work for the defense department, and the hacking incident had quickly turned into a national manhunt. Renee had helped Max to solve the puzzle and avert disaster. Well, with minor help from the FBI's Hostage Rescue Team. But other than that, Max's only assistance had been from the lovely French-Canadian hacker lying next to him.

Renee wore a low-cut tank top that showed off her sculpted shoulders, and a pair of skimpy shorts that revealed a pair of magnificent runner's legs. A small but elegant flower tattoo ran up her right thigh. She had been a college athlete, and while she was getting close to age forty, she kept in excellent shape by competing in road races and mini-triathlons.

On stage, the young quartet finished playing "Clair de Lune." A scatter of polite applause rose up from the crowd, silenced a moment later by the beginning of the next song.

Max checked the time on his Breitling wristwatch. The watch had been a gift from his father. A way of saying thanks for undergoing such an ordeal last summer. Max's father felt responsible for placing his son in harm's way, since it was his company that had been targeted. Hence the watch. Max thought it was enormous, but it was starting to grow on him.

He turned to Renee. "You want a beer?"

"No, thank you. I'm still nursing my wine cooler."

She really did look beautiful tonight. "You know, I'm a lucky guy."

"Trust me, I completely agree." She winked. He laughed.

He turned and marched up the grassy bowl that surrounded the amphitheater. The deep bass notes of a cello mixed with rich violin filled the air. Max weaved his way in and out of the patchwork of blankets and concert patrons.

All the while keeping an eye on his mark.

* * *

His handler was a man by the name of Caleb Wilkes—a veteran of the CIA who had built a career running agents in various parts of the world. While Max was happy to take Renee out to Wolf Trap on a nice night like this, it was Wilkes who had asked him to be here.

Max had been conflicted about working for the CIA after all that had happened last summer. It wasn't that intelligence fieldwork was an undesirable occupation to him. Quite the contrary. Max had spent over a decade under a nonofficial cover for the Defense Intelligence Agency and hadn't left of his own accord. The higher-ups had forced him to make a career change based on their needs, without asking his opinion, and without being transparent about the circumstances. Because of that, Max would probably always be leery of trusting men like Wilkes, a senior operations officer who pulled the strings from the halls of Langley. But as an experienced operative, Max knew better than to completely trust anyone, including his new handler. The world of international espionage was littered with the graves of the trusting and gullible.

Wilkes understood Max's reservations. With his experience and social stature, Max wasn't a normal asset. He was special, and Wilkes had to treat him that way.

Wilkes had given Max a few months without contact after the Fend

Aerospace incident last year. At which point he had begun paying Max regular visits. The two usually met for beer or coffee in the Georgetown district of Washington, D.C. Max was getting his MBA at Georgetown University. Wilkes often worked out of Langley, so at first, he attributed the meetings to the convenience of "being in the neighborhood."

Max knew better—he had recruited and run agents himself while he'd worked for the DIA. He knew that Wilkes wouldn't waste his time paying social calls unless there was something to be gained. By the third "friendly happy hour," Max told Wilkes to cut to the chase.

Max was a valuable agent, and Wilkes wanted him on his team. Max came pretrained and experienced, having honed his skills in Europe and the Middle East. And he certainly had access. Max's family wealth and network allowed him to recruit assets and gather information that other agents just couldn't. He was expected to eventually take a job at his father's aerospace company after he finished his MBA, furthering his stature.

But Max wasn't just skilled and reliable; he also had the most sought-after motivation a handler could ask for. It was Max's sense of national duty and his continued desire to serve and protect that motivated him to participate in the program. Max was serving his country for patriotic reasons. And perhaps for the excitement of the game. Turning foreign assets and uncovering terrorist networks could be an intoxicating thrill, as long as you didn't get burned in the process.

But there was still a level of apprehension—a feeling of slight betrayal after the way Max had been forced out of the DIA and wrongly implicated in a crime last year. The way Wilkes didn't fully divulge all of the details of the operation until it suited him. That pesky trust issue.

So the two men had come to an understanding. Wilkes would reach out to Max when he had work, and Max might sometimes decline, based on the situation.

Tonight, Max had been called up for the first time.

"I need you to keep an eye on someone. It's critical." Wilkes had said.

Abdul Syed, officially a Pakistani diplomat operating out of the embassy in D.C., was actually under the employ of the ISI. Wilkes was working with FBI and CIA counterintelligence to monitor Syed's activities, but that was proving difficult. Abdul Syed was adept at losing surveillance. He'd lost them each night for the past several weeks. But something about tonight would be different, Wilkes had told Max.

"We've received intelligence that Syed is going to make contact with one of his American agents. But he won't do it if he sees his tail. I need you to be there instead. Watch Syed. See who he meets."

Unusual circumstances. An intriguing assignment. FBI counterintelligence was supposed to have several men who would keep an eye on Syed. Wilkes was expecting Syed to give them the shake. This Syed fellow must be quite a talent, to do that. FBI counterintelligence were some of the best in the business. Why did Wilkes want Max doing this, instead of someone else? *Probably because he wants it to be unofficial. But why?*

And how did Wilkes know where Syed was going to be? He wouldn't give Max the answer to that, but somehow, Wilkes knew.

The Pakistani intelligence officer was a mere fifty yards away from Max and Renee's spot on the lawn of Wolf Trap. He was sitting alone, listening to the serene music, looking about as pleasant as someone getting a root canal.

It was crowded, and Syed could be planning to communicate with any of the thousands of spectators now listening to the concert. Maybe he already had, Max thought. After all, he hadn't seen Syed enter. It had taken Max fifteen minutes to spot him. Renee thought he was crazy, moving their sitting spot on the lawn twice. She'd thought it had something to do with his obsessive need for perfection. Like how he kept all his belongings meticulously clean and organized.

But that spot had given Max a perfect view. And the moment he'd seen Syed get up and walk to the top of the half-moon-shaped lawn area, heading towards the row of concession stands, Max followed.

3

Max walked towards the concession stand, scanning the crowd, using his peripheral vision to observe anything that might be out of the ordinary. The habits of an intelligence operative who had spent more than a decade hiding in plain sight. Syed was now pretending to talk on his cell phone, but Max could tell he was really just looking for surveillance himself. Walking one direction for a few moments, then circling back, scanning the crowd like a pro. Max needed to be careful not to be spotted.

Syed was brown-skinned, with dark bushy eyebrows. He wore gray slacks and a buttoned short-sleeve shirt, with a bright white Washington Nationals cap on his head, which Max found to be a comical addition.

Max approached the window of the snack bar and ordered a beer, paying in cash and receiving a large plastic cup foaming to the brim. Cold and tasty. Perfect on a warm summer's night. Turning around to face the amphitheater, he observed Syed walk past him and out through the concert exit.

Hmm. No one else was leaving yet, so Max couldn't just follow him without being obvious.

The exit gate was a chokepoint. A great way for Syed to be sure that he was clear of coverage before he tried to communicate with his agent.

Max had a decision to make. Follow him out, or wait? Spook him and any illicit activity could be called off. Maybe it already had been. Maybe he'd spotted Max and that was why he'd departed. The thought bothered Max. But then, through the covered entryway, past the bare metal turnstiles and roundabout blacktop driveway, Max saw the Pakistani man slow his step.

Max stayed put, half-concealed by the entrance structure, sipping his cold amber beer, eyes locked on to his target. Syed loitered across the rounded drive just outside the gate. The Pakistani man came to a stop near a park bench that rested in a mulched garden. A grove of trees swayed overhead.

Then the crowd erupted into loud clapping and whistling, and Max could hear the chatter of people rising from their spots on the lawn to leave. The concert had ended. Shit. Syed was still just standing there. Waiting. Soon throngs of people headed through the exit turnstiles, racing each other to get to their cars in the parking lot.

A flash of panic hit Max as the empty area filled with people and he momentarily lost his quarry. Lines forming at the restrooms and exits all served to block his view. A bottleneck of foot traffic formed at the concert gate. Max maneuvered, poking his head around the crowd and trying to keep eyes on his mark.

A gap in the crowd lined up perfectly. Just for a moment. But that was all it took. A split-second line of sight from Max to the park bench, and that was when it happened.

Syed moved fast.

To the untrained eye, it would have looked like nothing more than bending down to retie his shoe, or perhaps brush a speck of dirt off his pant leg. Max knew better. Syed had been standing near the park bench. When he'd dropped down low, his hand had gripped the front of the bench seat, his knuckles going white as he'd pressed down. Then he'd stood up and begun walking away, towards the parking lot. From this far away, Max could just barely make out a round white object on the wooden bench seat.

A thumbtack? A sticker? Whatever it was, it was a signal.

Max's heart beat faster as he realized that the timing had been precise. The wooden bench was now surrounded by departing concertgoers. The signal could be meant for any one of them. Max would just have to hang out and wait to see who came and sat at the bench. If the agent was really good, Max might not even pick him up.

"*There* you are." Renee interlocked her arm with his. "Were you going to come back to me? I got our blanket. I'm ready if you are..." Looking up into his face, seeing his expression, she whispered, "What's wrong?"

He kept his eyes on the bench, nudged her forward, and began walking. "I need your help. Please follow me. This is important."

Frowning in confusion, she said, "Of course."

He threw his half-drunk beer into the trash—normally an unforgivable sin—and they walked out with the crowd. Max took out his phone and led Renee under the grove of trees on the mulched area behind the park bench. He positioned Renee so that the Wolf Trap sign and entrance were behind her...along with the bench. The crowd would be directly in front of him as they departed the concert area.

"Let me take a few pictures of you. Stand right...here."

"*Really*, Max?" She sighed and forced a smile for the camera.

"Really."

She arched one eyebrow, hands on her hips, but then gave up and smiled for the camera.

One minute of picture taking later, Max caught his fish.

White male, forty to fifty years old, medium height, medium build. Every cop's favorite description. The man's eyes were staring in the direction of the bench. His gaze hovered on the thumbtack for two beats too long. Maybe he was trying to determine the color? Maybe he just wanted to confirm that he really saw his signal. Either way, it was sloppy tradecraft.

And a total break for Max.

Max slid his phone into his pocket and began walking, placing his arm around Renee and bringing her with him. He whispered, "Do me another favor? Get the car and drive around to the exit."

"Max, what's going on?" she whispered back.

"It's okay. I'll find you and meet you there. If I don't get to the car before you leave, just park on the side of the road outside after the traffic cops let you out."

"What? Max, I don't understand. It'll be dark soon. Why are you—"

"I just need to check something. *Please*."

Renee took the keys and headed towards their car.

Max kept his distance following the man, still keeping a lookout for Syed or anyone else who might be watching. The man who had observed the signal stopped at a silver sedan in the parking lot a few moments later. Max walked by the man as he fumbled for his keys. Max had placed his phone on video mode and was holding it casually by his legs, lens facing outward, positioned to capture the license plate, and then angling it up to record the man's face.

After passing by, Max continued walking towards his own vehicle. When he found Renee a few minutes later, she was waiting in the long line of cars for the exit. Max hopped in the passenger seat and threw on his seatbelt.

"Can you please tell me what we're doing now?"

Technically Max had completed his assignment. But if they followed the agent, it was possible they might learn more information. Max liked being thorough.

He turned to face Renee. "We're following someone."

"Who?"

He scanned the line of cars and located the target vehicle. About twenty cars in front of them. If Max was lucky, both cars would be let out together before they stopped traffic again.

"Who are we following?"

"Actually, I don't know his name."

The cars began moving towards the T-intersection, a traffic cop standing there with orange-lit cones.

"Go left."

Renee turned. "Which car is it?"

"About five ahead. Silver sedan. See it?"

"Yes."

For the next ten minutes, they traveled through the suburbs of Vienna, Virginia. Lots of colonial homes with finely manicured lawns, barely visible in the summer dusk.

Renee did well. She kept her distance from the silver sedan and drove past without asking when the car stopped abruptly on the gravel shoulder of the Creek Crossing Road.

"What do we do now?"

"Turn into this next neighborhood and park." Max was squinting out the rear window, trying to see in the dark.

After they parked, Max said, "You stay here. I'll only be a second."

* * *

Max crept along the side of the road, walking towards his target's parked car, headlights momentarily blinding him as cars sped by. He could feel the rush of air from the traffic. The gravel of the road shoulder crunched beneath his feet. This was poor surveillance technique, following his quarry into an unknown area by himself like this, but it was the best he could manage right now. He had texted an update to Caleb Wilkes while they were driving but had yet to hear back.

Max crept up to the silver sedan parked on the shoulder and peered inside. Empty. He turned to his left. Ten feet away, a paved path led from the road down into the woods. A buzzing streetlight above was just bright enough that Max could make out the words "Foxstone Park, Fairfax County Park Authority" in yellow lettering on a maroon wooden sign.

Max followed the path, careful to walk slow and quiet, listening for the sounds of footfalls or the snaps of breaking twigs. Instead, he heard only the summertime calls of insects and a bubbling brook somewhere off to his right.

The park wasn't big. The distant yellow windows of surrounding homes rising high all around told him that. Maybe a few football fields in length. One football field across, tops. Lightning bugs glowed every few seconds, giving the woods a magical feel.

A shoe scraped along pavement up ahead. Max's heart raced as he held his breath, straining his ears to listen.

Bzzzt. Bzzzt.

In his pocket, his phone began nonstop buzzing. Shit. He reached down and squeezed to silence it. Probably Wilkes, but he couldn't risk a look. The light would give away his position if the buzzing hadn't already. He cursed himself for the rookie move.

A whitish-blue face lit up maybe twenty-five yards ahead, and Max froze. It was the face of the man Max had seen looking at the dead drop signal at Wolf Trap. He had just turned his own phone on and was looking at the screen. For a moment, Max wondered why he would do something like that. He was ruining his night vision, for one. And if he was supposed to be here for a meeting or to pick something up, why would he need to look at his—

A deafening crack echoed through the forest, and the man's head exploded.

* * *

Renee was already nervous, waiting in the car with the engine turned off. She was checking her watch and staring in the rearview mirror, hoping to see Max's reflection as he walked back to her. She knew this had something to do with his past life. His time in Europe as an intelligence operative for the DIA would always be a part of his identity. She had known he was speaking with Caleb Wilkes about doing work for him. But she had secretly hoped that nothing would come of it.

While Renee had once worked for the CSE, Canada's version of the NSA, she did not share the same gung-ho mentality as her beau. She didn't like guns. She preferred nonviolent resolution to conflict. And she didn't concern herself with politics or worry much about international affairs.

That being said, Renee wasn't naïve. She knew how the world worked, and that there was a need for men like Max. She just didn't want him to get hurt trying to be some sort of heroic knight. Or whatever he thought he—

Renee heard what sounded like a gunshot and froze. Then she flung the car door open. Her heart raced as thoughts of the worst flooded into her mind. She stepped out onto the sidewalk and slammed the door shut.

Had Max been shot? What if Max had shot someone? *Don't be stupid.* He didn't have a gun. Did he?

Renee looked both ways on the sidewalk, tapping her foot. She had to do something. She reopened the door, leaned into her car horn and pressed down. The loud noise echoed through the night. Dogs in a nearby home, already agitated by the gunshot, barked louder in response to the horn.

She slammed the door closed behind her again and sprinted towards the parked car.

She stopped in her tracks as a tree branch cracked and someone ran out of the woods ahead of her. The dark silhouette of a man outlined by distant car headlights. The figure stopped at the sidewalk, a good ten or twenty yards away. Renee's stood in place, her heart stuck in her throat.

"Max?"

The figure didn't move.

But it wasn't him.

While Renee couldn't make out his face, this man had a shorter frame, and he carried some sort of long bag—like one of her old field hockey stick bags from college—slung over his shoulder.

The hair on the back of Renee's neck rose as the man stood inspecting her from the shadows, silent and motionless. Perhaps deciding what to do. Renee was about to run when, in an abrupt motion, the man reached down, picked up a mountain bike which had been lying in the grass, and pedaled away.

A million questions collided in Renee's mind, but only one mattered right now.

Was Max hurt?

She hurried down the paved pathway into an unlit park near the side of the road. Into the woods from which the mysterious man had just emerged.

"Max!" she screamed. Breathing fast, she took her cell phone out and turned the flashlight on to see better. Her eyes played tricks on her with every shadow. Lightning bugs blinking in the humid night air. On either side of the woods, outdoor lights were coming on, illuminating the back porches of suburban homes. She called Max's name again. In the distance, a police siren began to wail.

"Psst. Renee, over here, quick."

Max's voice. Thank God.

"Shine the light over here," he said.

Renee headed towards the sound of his voice and the blue-white glow of a cell phone on the ground.

"Max, I saw someone," she whispered. "He was running out of the forest after the gunshot."

Max turned to look up at her. "Did he see you?"

"I think so. Maybe. He got on a bike and rode away from me when he got to the street."

Max turned back to the ground. He was hunched over, working on something.

"I heard him run away," he said. "I think he was hiding in the woods, waiting. I must have walked right past him. Good thinking with the horn. I think that spooked him. He took off after you did that."

"Max, I thought...did he shoot at you? Are you alright?" As Renee got closer, she realized that Max was hunched over a man's body. "Oh my God..." She covered her mouth and fought the urge to retch. Half the man's head was missing—a mass of dark red and gray mush in its place.

"You're moving the light. Keep it over here, please." Max's voice was that of a surgeon at work. His hands glided into the dead man's pockets and shoes, searching for anything he could find. Then he scanned the area surrounding the body. He grabbed the glowing phone off the ground and pocketed it.

The blue light of the first cop car flashed in between the homes up to their right.

"Let's go. If the cops see us, we stay. But I'd like to try and make it to our car before we're seen. If we can do that, we'll leave."

"Leave?" Renee didn't like the sound of that but trusted that Max knew best in this type of situation.

Less than a minute later, they were driving away, Max in the driver's seat, his eyes scanning the rearview mirror for any sign of trouble. Then they were driving north on the Beltway, crossing the Potomac into Maryland.

"Why didn't you want to stay until the police arrived?"

Max said, "Caleb wouldn't want anyone to know we were there, if we could help it."

"Caleb Wilkes? Who were we following, Max?"

"Wilkes asked me to keep an eye on someone at the concert."

Renee had her arms folded across her chest and was shaking. "Why didn't you tell me?"

"I'm sorry."

She closed her eyes, composing herself. "Who was the man in the park?"

He glanced at her and then back towards the traffic. "The man Wilkes asked me to watch at the concert was a foreign intelligence operative. He placed a signal on the side of a bench outside the concert gate. The second man—the one we followed here in the silver sedan—was the one who picked up the signal."

"How do you know?"

"I could tell."

"And he was the one who was killed?"

"Yes."

"Why?"

"I don't know."

Max's phone began buzzing.

"Fend. Yes, Renee and I are fine. She was there too, yes. We left before they arrived. Yes, I am aware. That's right. You'll take care of it? Thank you. When? Okay, we'll see you then."

Renee folded her arms. "Was that who I think it was?"

"Yes. Caleb's going to stop by and debrief us tomorrow. I assume you're staying with me tonight?"

Renee was a mess of emotions. She took a deep breath and let out a defeated, "Yes."

Max placed his right hand on her neck, massaging it. "Are you alright?"

She took his hand, clasping it in her own. She let out a soft breath. "I will be."

4

Max awoke early the next morning to the sound of gulls and a diesel motor. He climbed up the ladder to the aft deck of his forty-foot sailboat, where he had taken to staying during the warmer weather. Sunlight reflected off the still water of Annapolis harbor. A clean white fishing boat motored out of its slip and out towards the bay. Max waved to the captain, who waved back while navigating through the channel markers.

Memories of last night ran though his head. Max had spent almost an hour on the phone with Wilkes once they'd gotten to Annapolis, recounting each detail.

Renee was still in bed. Max wanted to let her sleep in. She was understandably upset. After Wilkes's call, Renee and Max had stayed up talking in bed. The conversation veered from the murder they had just witnessed to a deep discussion around trust and relationships. After not being told the real reason they had gone to Wolf Trap, she was worried that Max was reverting back to keeping secrets like he had as a DIA operative.

Renee argued that things had changed.

"Like what?"

"Us," she had said.

If he was going to be with her, he needed to tell her everything. Max knew she was right. She was always right. It just wasn't easy for him.

Max slipped on his flip-flops and hopped over to the pier. He walked through the nearly empty cobblestone streets of Annapolis until he reached a local bagel shop, ordering a half dozen everything bagels and a tub of cream cheese. Then he walked back to his boat and sat back down at the aft deck table. A canvas tarp provided shade from the rising sun and protection from seagulls engaged in target practice.

Max smeared gobs of cream cheese onto his steaming bagel. In the distance he could hear the echoes of Naval Academy midshipmen jogging to a military cadence. Plebe Summer, the boot camp that indoctrinated Academy freshmen into the school, was in full swing.

He ate his breakfast in peace, gazing out over Annapolis Harbor and towards the distant Chesapeake Bay. A cabin cruiser motored by, its modest waves rippling slowly towards the shore. On each sailboat in the harbor, metal clips swayed on their lines, clanging against the masts in a gentle rhythm. The seafarer's song, the marina's orchestra.

Caleb Wilkes approached Max's boat, the wooden boards creaking beneath his feet.

"Mind if I join you?" Wilkes said.

"Be my guest."

Wilkes gripped the metal rail and stepped over to the sailboat, balancing a cardboard drink holder filled with clear plastic cups. Iced coffees swirling with white milk, dark coffee and caramel browns, beads of condensation on the outside of the cups.

"I come bearing gifts." Wilkes placed the drinks on the table.

Max smiled. "Why, thank you." He heard Renee stirring below.

"You mind?" Wilkes pointed at the bag of bagels.

"Be my guest."

Renee came up the ladder wearing a long tee shirt that stopped midthigh. Her hair was disheveled. But even when she was just rising, she was beautiful to Max. Red lips and alluring eyes. Seeing Wilkes, she glanced at Max, failing to hide her disapproval. Women were excellent visual communicators.

"He's here early."

Wilkes said, "Good morning, Miss LaFrancois. I apologize for my intrusion. Would you care for a drink? I brought iced lattes."

Max gave a sheepish grin. "He brought us iced lattes."

She took one of the drinks and sat down on the bench next to Max, crossing her legs. She plunged a straw into the center of her drink and snatched a bagel from the bag.

She began, "Mr. Wilkes..."

"Please, call me Caleb."

"Caleb, then. I was under the impression, until last night, that is, that Max would only be working for you as an advisor."

"That's right."

"So, you can imagine my surprise when I found him standing over a dead body in the middle of a neighborhood park in Virginia."

"Renee...," Max said, embarrassed.

Wilkes rose from his seat, examining the transparent plastic weather wall that was wrapped into a roll and tied up along the rim of the hard-shell cover overhead. He then looked around at the streets surrounding the harbor.

Max knew what he was thinking. Saturday-morning tourists had begun to walk the brick sidewalks of Old Town Annapolis. Colorful shops, restaurants, and quaint little homes lined the streets. Here in the harbor, the trio was visible from hundreds of windows that overlooked the marina. Anyone with a directional microphone would be able to listen in.

"It unwraps."

"Do you mind?"

Max got up. "Not at all. Let me help."

The men untied the plastic wall and rolled it down so that the three of them were enclosed in a ten-by-ten-foot transparent shell. Max doubted its effectiveness against a professional surveillance team with high-tech equipment, but he was also skeptical that anyone would eavesdrop on them here, unless Wilkes had suddenly become careless and been compromised. The men sat down again.

Renee sipped through her straw, then said, "If Max is going to be working for you and putting his life in danger, I want to know about it. I won't have any more surprises like last night." She turned to Max. "If you want me in your life, you need to be honest with me about these things.

You both know that I've worked in the intelligence field before. My IT security contracts require me to hold a current TS/SCI. I'm trustworthy, and I've got the clearances, so stop keeping me out of the loop. Especially if I'm going to end up doing the work anyway." Her chest heaved, and her face was flushed as she eyed both of the men.

Based on Renee's tone and body language, Max didn't think that now was a good time to point out that her work in the CSE, and as a cyber operations contractor in the US, was very different from operational work in the field.

Max looked at Wilkes. "She's right. I should have told her before we went to the concert. And Renee and I have worked well together in the past. Caleb, I would like you to consider us a team from now on." Max hoped he wasn't overplaying his hand...with either of them. How badly did Wilkes want him as a CIA asset? Badly enough to take on the risk of having another set of eyes and ears on Max's work, trustworthy or not? And how willing was Renee to go along with Max's desire to play part-time spy?

Wilkes looked back and forth between them, working something out behind his unreadable mask. His decision took about three seconds. "Very well."

Max could feel Renee straighten up in her seat a bit. A welcome victory.

Wilkes said, "First things first. I've spoken to my contact at the FBI. He'll be by this morning to ask you both some questions about what you saw last night. Your statement will be kept confidential. Officially, neither of you were at the crime scene. We want to keep both of your names out of the papers."

"Understood."

"The deceased was a man named Joseph Dahlman. He worked as a lobbyist at a boutique shop on K Street that does a lot of work on behalf of Middle Eastern and Central Asian interests."

"What makes a lobbying firm boutique?" Renee asked.

Max whispered, "I think it's a fancy way of saying small." He turned to Wilkes. "What's up with Dahlman?"

Wilkes said, "I've recently begun working on a new project with our counterintelligence division. An investigation that involves one of the Mexican drug cartels."

"Why would you be working on something involving the cartels? Isn't that the DEA's responsibility?" Renee asked.

Max said, "The CIA oftentimes gets involved in counternarcotics operations around the world. Criminal enterprises as big as the Mexican cartels influence national security. They control people, cash, and weapons. The Mexican cartels have their own private armies, often poached from Mexican special forces, some who were trained in the US."

"Why would someone in Mexican special forces go over to the cartels?"

Wilkes said, "It's not like it is here in the US. The cartels control huge swaths of territory in Mexico. Many Mexican institutions, like the police and military, aren't as well respected or well run as their American counterparts. Imagine you're a twenty-something Mexican kid who's been in the military for a few years, getting low pay and being treated like shit, and then you get approached by an old soldier buddy who'll give you a huge salary increase, women, respect. The Zetas, one of Mexico's most notorious cartels, started off as a group of bodyguards for another cartel's leader. Then they were used as a death squad—assassins who killed off rival gang leaders and middlemen, law enforcement or reporters. They began recruiting more and more former military. They had their own training centers and ran the outfit like a professional fighting force. Except for the drugs, booze, and prostitutes, of course."

Renee's eyes widened.

Max looked at Wilkes. "I've heard that some of the cartels are upgrading their intelligence operations as well."

Wilkes nodded. "You heard correctly. About a year ago, we began getting intel reports that the Sinaloa cartel had hired a foreign national to run their security and intelligence operations. That's unheard of among the cartels. Loyalty being at such a premium in that line of business, they like to keep the important jobs to a few key families within each organization."

"Let me guess, they hired someone from Pakistani ISI?"

"Not exactly. But we think the ISI may be in touch with the person they hired."

Wilkes took out his phone and tapped the screen a few times, then held it out. Max could see a tall Caucasian man sitting by a pool. The resolution was poor, and it was hard to make out facial features.

"You're right. He doesn't look Pakistani."

Wilkes said, "The name we've heard the Sinaloa cartel calling him is Juan Blanco."

"Blanco?"

Wilkes nodded. "We assume it's an alias. This is the only photo we have, taken from a satellite while he was at a cartel mansion in Durango. We've been unable to intercept any communications with his voice in them. Although we suspect he's using an echo talker."

"What's that?"

"It's where you have someone else standing next to you by the phone while you write out messages for them to read. As long as you keep changing hardware and locations, it makes it pretty tough for the NSA to find you—no voice ID to run analysis on. An effective technique, if done properly. Some of our analysts peg him as Russian, based on his contacts overseas—the contractors he uses are some of the same ones the Russian mafia uses. But we've yet to have one of our agents see him in person." He shrugged. "It's only a matter of time. We'll get better information eventually, but right now he's a mystery."

"What makes this mystery man so special, aside from being foreign?"

"In short, he's *good*. Hence why we think he's got experience from a top-level intel organization. He travels almost exclusively in the Durango region, where we don't have a big footprint. He only deals with the cartel bosses, a few lieutenants, and his own trusted team of sicarios.

"Señor Blanco has professionalized the Sinaloa cartel's security and countersurveillance operations to a level normally seen only in well-funded national intelligence agencies. The Russians, the Chinese, the Israelis. Within weeks of his arrival, DEA and Mexican counternarcotics programs months in the planning were quickly discovered and rendered useless.

"He's got them outsourcing cyber help now. The cartel's communications procedures and cyber-security became much better, making it brutally difficult for law enforcement to eavesdrop and track them. And he's taken a page out of Los Zetas' playbook—hiring away Mexican special forces soldiers and professionalizing their hit teams."

Max said, "So how does this relate to Syed and the dead man...what's his name?"

"Dahlman."

"Yes, him." Max slurped through his straw as he ran out of iced coffee. Renee shot him a look.

Wilkes said, "The man who placed the signal on the bench at Wolf Trap last night was Abdul Syed, a Pakistani intelligence officer. He works out of the embassy in D.C., and the FBI has been surveilling him as long as he's been in the US."

Renee said, "Well, then, why did we have to—"

"And he's been trying to lose the FBI every night for the past several weeks," Wilkes finished. "Sometimes he succeeded in that endeavor. Other times we only let him think he did. But last night was different. I knew he was going to meet with someone."

"How did you know?" Renee asked.

"Miss LaFrancois, as much as I am grateful for your participation, there are some things that I do not wish to share. That is one of them."

Renee folded her arms.

Max said, "So you called the FBI off because...you didn't want to spook him?"

"Precisely. It was my hope that you, with your exceptional skills, would know what to look for. And unlike the federal agents whose faces Mr. Syed probably knows by heart now, he does not know your handsome mug."

"You really think I'm handsome? Why, thank you, Caleb."

Renee rolled her eyes.

"And the FBI counterintelligence guys were okay with this?"

Wilkes didn't answer the question, which was an answer in itself. Instead, he said, "In using Max, I was able to lull Syed into a false sense of security. I was not aware, however, that Mr. Syed intended to cause harm to his own agent. If I had known that, I would have done things differently. Please accept my sincere apology, both of you, for putting you at risk. I assure you it was not my intention. I only wished to ascertain the identity of Mr. Syed's agent. Your following him and seeing where he went after receiving his signal was an added bonus."

Max said, "So Syed dropped off a message to one of his agents, Dahlman. And then the agent gets shot? Who fired the shot? Syed?"

"I doubt it. He wouldn't pull the trigger. Syed's a pro. He wouldn't take that risk. He would hire out for that."

"That makes sense."

"That reminds me—from our phone conversation last night, I understand that you didn't find anything at the scene other than the phone? I can take that now."

Max slid over the phone he'd picked up.

Wilkes pocketed the phone. "I'll bring this to the lab."

Max knew that Wilkes would take it to Langley, and that he might or might not bring this piece of evidence to the attention of the FBI, depending on what he found.

Renee said, "So the question is, why would Syed want his own agent killed? And I'm sorry—what does this have to do with Mexico?"

Wilkes said, "I have an asset in Mexico. She's close to one of the Sinaloa cartel's higher-ups—a man by the name of Hector Rojas. Rojas handles all financial matters for the cartel. He travels to Mexico City sporadically, for business. My agent spends time with him when he's there. A few days ago, Rojas made one of these trips, and my agent was able to alert us to a meeting between Rojas and a known Pakistani intelligence operative who works in Mexico City. We were able to eavesdrop on parts of that conversation."

Wilkes paused, shaking ice from his cup into his mouth and cracking it in his teeth.

"Rojas implied that our mystery man would be taking part in a meeting later this month. This meeting would include a high-level ISI representative. I assume Syed. The meeting will also include other, unnamed VIPs. They emphasized security measures and some pre-meeting requirements that had to be fulfilled. Hector Rojas indicated that our mystery man approved of an imminent operation that would meet one of these requirements. Then, the next day, an unrelated intelligence source told me that Syed is meeting with one of his American agents. A man we've been trying to identify for months."

"Dahlman."

"Correct."

"So, you think the hit on Dahlman last night was one of these 'pre-meeting' requirements?"

"I do."

"Requirements, plural. So, are we talking about a hit list here?"

Wilkes nodded. "That's my take. But it's something I'd like to confirm."

"So, the Sinaloa cartel is working with Pakistani intelligence." Max shook his head. "Strange bedfellows."

"Agreed. We can trace this new collaboration to the cartel's acquisition of Blanco as its head of security. And now they're orchestrating the assassination of Americans together. And not just any Americans. Pakistani spies."

"I don't understand why this mystery man would care."

Wilkes shook his head. "There's a lot we are yet to understand. But I know this: ordering a hit on American soil is a major risk for both parties. The ISI doesn't normally conduct active measures in the US. And the cartels usually limit their violence to rival gangs or trial witnesses about to snitch. Both organizations know better than to stir the hornet's nest. Yet that's exactly what they are doing."

Max saw now why Wilkes was concerned. "If they're willing to take a risk like this, there must be an important reason."

Wilkes pointed at Max. "Exactly. And I want you to help me find out what it is."

* * *

Wilkes went over his plan for the next hour. Personnel, operational responsibilities, communication methods, timing, equipment, locations, backup options.

When he was done, Max said, "Let me get this straight. You want us to run an operation on the coast of Sinaloa, Mexico, using your pretty female agent to lure in Hector Rojas, kidnap him while he's drunk or sleeping, and get him back to the US for interrogation. Is that it?"

"You'll need to sort out some of the finer details."

"I'll need help."

"I trust that you can put together a team. But keep it very small. One or two people tops. And you'll need to make your visit look legit. Like a vacation. Otherwise their people down there will sniff you out."

"You want me to self-fund?"

Wilkes looked around at the sailing yacht. "Money doesn't look tight."

"Having our bodies dismembered and discarded in the Sierra Madre Mountains is a higher price."

Renee shifted in her seat.

Max saw her discomfort and turned to her. "You still want to be part of this?"

"Yes."

"Fine. But if I let you come with me to Mexico, I don't want you near the actual op when it happens. We'll need to keep you out of harm's way. No offense, but you have no street experience, and just placing you in the same city is about all the risk I'm willing to take."

She started to say something but bit her tongue. "Okay."

Wilkes stood. "I'll contact you again once you're in Mexico. I'm assuming that you'll be able to find a suitable shooter? Someone with experience down there?"

Max nodded. "I have someone in mind."

"Who?"

"A guy named Trent Carpenter."

Max felt Renee's eyes on him at the mention of Trent's name. Wilkes caught the look.

"Who is he?" asked Wilkes.

"A friend. He's former Army Delta. Used to be an advisor to the DEA counternarcotics teams working down in Mexico but got out of the Army over a year ago."

"Sounds like a good pick. Just make sure he keeps this quiet."

"Of course."

"When did you see him last?"

Renee held Max's hand as he replied, "About a week ago. At his brother's funeral."

5

The day after speaking with Wilkes, Max flew his Cirrus from Leesburg, Virginia to northeast Pennsylvania. Renee accompanied him, as she had the week earlier for Josh's funeral.

During the flight, he thought about Josh. Until he'd died from a heroin overdose, Josh Carpenter had been one of Max's few life-long friends. They had been roommates all four years of prep school. Entry into the elite New Jersey boarding school had been assured for Max, son of Charles Fend, the aerospace CEO and American business icon.

It had been a different path for the Carpenter boys. Both Josh and his older brother, Trent, had attended on a special scholarship set up for the children and grandchildren of Medal of Honor recipients. Trent and Josh's grandfather had been a decorated hero of World War Two.

The school wasn't a perfect fit for the Carpenters. The prestigious high school charged over thirty-five thousand dollars per year for its boarding students. BMWs and Mercedes filled the parking lot, birthday presents for pampered sixteen-year-olds. The Carpenter boys were a different breed. They were proud of their blue-collar roots and traveled back to the family home in rural Pennsylvania on most weekends.

Trent Carpenter had been a senior when Josh and Max had arrived for their freshman year. With his father traveling for business so much, Max had become close with the Carpenter family, often spending weekends at Josh's parents' home. Together the two boys would hike, fish, play football and get into trouble. To Josh, Max wasn't the famous son of a billionaire, he was a loyal friend.

Josh's family treated Max like he was one of their own. The Carpenters had a strong family bond and three rules: work hard, be humble, and don't complain. The ethos rubbed off on Max.

Their senior year, Max was accepted to Princeton, and Josh was denied admission to West Point, his dream school. It had hit Josh hard. But he hadn't complained. Josh had decided that he would still enter the Army immediately upon graduation, just not as an officer. While he had been accepted to several excellent colleges, none of them had offered a scholarship, and money was tight in the Carpenter family. Josh had enlisted in the Army, against the recommendation of his teachers. His parents had been both proud and worried.

Josh's older brother Trent had followed a similar path. To them, heroism and self-sacrifice were a calling. Just because they had gone to one of the top private high schools in the nation didn't mean that they were above being soldiers.

Josh had excelled in the Army, rising up to Sergeant First Class and deploying around the world. After graduating from Princeton, unbeknownst to any of his friends, Max had gone to work as a covert operative for the Defense Intelligence Agency. The two friends had kept in touch over the years, but their contact had naturally grown less frequent over time.

Since he'd left the DIA last year, Max kept telling himself that he needed to reach out and go visit Josh. He had been like a brother during Max's formative years.

And now, flying towards Josh's hometown, Max again felt the pain of knowing his old friend was gone forever.

At one hundred and eighty knots, their flight time was just over an hour. Max had made sure that they departed early enough in the morning to dodge the afternoon thunderstorms of July. They landed on a short two-thousand-foot runway at Skyhaven Airport on the outskirts of

Tunkhannock, Pennsylvania. The town and airport were tucked between forest-covered mountains and the Susquehanna River.

Upon arrival, Max signed for their rental car, and they drove towards the Carpenter parents' home, where Trent had agreed to meet them. The narrow roads carved through forest-covered hills. They passed signs for Shadow Brook Golf Course and Lazy Brook Park, and an ice cream shop on the edge of a cow pasture.

"We'll need to stop there later." Renee gave a devilish grin. Max agreed.

At last they arrived at the parents' home, on the outskirts of town. As Max got out of the car, he saw that the home was still busy a week after the funeral. A screen door on the covered porch snapped every few minutes as family and friends came in and out. A smoker grill was lit in the backyard, and a balding man who Max recognized as a neighbor nodded a greeting. Max had met many of the Carpenters' friends and family last week, paying their condolences at the funeral. The support network was still in full swing. One of the town's beloved sons had passed, and they were rallying around the family in mourning.

Max and Renee went inside the home to say hello. The Carpenter parents still looked heartbroken but seemed to be on the mend. They were somewhat confused that Max had returned a week after the funeral. But they accepted that he was here to speak to Trent without asking further questions. Tina, the new widow, was also present. Her five-year-old son, Josh Junior, sat beside her, watching cartoons on her iPhone.

After Max and Renee made the rounds, they walked out to the backyard. The ranch home sat on a hill, with the rear of the property extending into a pine forest. To the south, they had a magnificent view of the Susquehanna River as it flowed through town. The surrounding mountains were dark shadows, hidden by a thick summer haze. The anvil shape of a giant thunderhead loomed in the distance.

Trent Carpenter was sitting on a lawn chair, whittling a small piece of wood with a bowie knife. He had the knotted calves and muscular arms of a football player, with close-cropped hair and manly facial features straight out of a John Wayne western.

Like his now-deceased brother, Trent was a former soldier. But while

Josh had been with conventional Army units, Trent had spent two decades in Special Forces. Max didn't know him as well as he'd known Josh. But he knew enough. Every time Josh or the parents used to speak of Trent, it was with reverence and pride.

Trent stood up when he saw Max and Renee approach, wiping sawdust from his hand and sticking it out in greeting.

Max shook his hand, and Renee went in for the hug.

"Hi, Trent. Good to see you again." Renee's voice had that perfect female touch of empathy and sadness.

Trent had the look of hard-earned life experience and the wisdom that came with it. His were the eyes of a man who knew true loss but had hardened himself against it. His brother, Josh, had died from a heroin overdose, leaving a wife and son behind. Max knew how devastated he had been at the news. But Trent also looked strong. Healthy. Resolute. He would be alright, Max knew.

Renee said, "Your family doing okay? Tina?"

"We're all doing a little better this week, I think."

Max had been shocked to learn the details of Josh's death. Josh had been off active duty for a few years, medically discharged after a bad back injury. The rest was a sad but familiar story. Josh started getting treatment at the VA hospital for chronic back pain. The VA had initially given him a bunch of very strong opioid-type pain meds. Then, as the opioid epidemic had started blowing up, the VA had changed their policies. Tina had told Max that the doctors at the VA wanted him to go cold turkey. To go get acupuncture instead. Josh had tried, but apparently, it hadn't been that easy.

Max looked over at the screen porch. Tina was running her hand through her five-year-old son's hair. A rumble of thunder reverberated in the distance.

Trent said, "Sounds like rain."

"Yup."

"So you said you want to talk. How's about we get out of here? Talk over lunch?"

"Sure thing," Max said.

* * *

Trent drove them about thirty minutes away, past Lake Winola, to another small town on the outskirts of Scranton. There was a quaint little main street that looked like it hadn't changed much since the 1960s. Max had seen many streets like this across the heartland of America. Old-fashioned storefronts with big glass windows. Rounded overhangs covering wide sidewalks. A small movie theater at the center of town, with only a few showings per day. A dilapidated family drugstore. And the insurgent hipster restaurant, with its neon chalk menu out front.

Trent parked his Ford pickup in an angled spot on the main street, and they walked into a busy bar-restaurant.

"You guys like burgers? They make the best ones here."

Trent waved to the bartender, who greeted him by name. Max surveyed the place. It wasn't bad. Hardwood floors and finished oak tables. An empty stage on one end of the diner where a local band was setting up.

Trent scanned the crowd like a pro, his eyes capturing every face, exit, threat, friend, and abnormality in view. Max followed Trent's gaze to see a few rough-looking men playing pool in a back room. A girl that couldn't have been more than twenty watched Trent with interest from a stool in the corner, playing with her tongue ring.

"Well, well...," Trent said.

"What is it?"

"I'll be right back." Trent stood and headed towards the back room.

Renee shot a curious look at Max. "Where's he going?"

Max nodded over to the billiards table. "I don't have a good feeling about this."

He couldn't hear what Trent was saying, but he could read the body language of the others in the room. Trent held the posture of an alpha male. One of the pool players—a big man with a beard, his cheeks flushed from too many pilsners—stood ominously close to Trent. The bearded man held a pool cue with both hands, his jaw clenched. The guy must have been six feet six, and three bills.

"What are they saying?" Renee asked.

Max shook his head and shrugged. "Not sure."

Then Trent walked to an exit door at the far end of the billiards room and gestured for the big man to follow. Trent's face was steady and unafraid.

Renee said, "Is he going to fight that guy?"

The big man yelled something at Trent, spittle flying out of his mouth. Heads in the restaurant part of the establishment shot over in their direction. Trent, the big man, and everyone in the poolroom headed out the door. Max got up, and Renee began to follow.

"You should stay here."

Renee rolled her eyes and kept walking. "Please stop saying that."

Max opened the rear door and saw that a small circle had formed around the two men. Trent stood still in the middle, rotating to keep his body facing the large bearded man, who was now circling him like a boxer in the ring. The big guy was cracking his knuckles and stretching his neck. Trent kept turning, looking loose and ready, his opponent in view.

"Kick his ass, Danny!" said the girl with the tongue ring. "Wasn't your fault his brother couldn't handle—"

The man with the beard took a swing at Trent. Trent sidestepped and brought up his knee into the man's stomach. Then he came down hard with his fist, knocking the large man to the pavement. His face made contact with the ground hard enough that Max winced.

Max felt a tickle on his forehead as rain began to fall. A long rumble of thunder came from the darkening clouds overhead.

Trent stood over the big man on the ground, his large chest heaving, a trickle of blood leaking out one of his nostrils. He didn't look very tough anymore. He looked scared. So did his groupies, who each took a few steps back.

"Did you sell to my brother?"

The bearded man nodded, looking away. Max recognized the type. Max had dealt with scum like this while working for the DIA. The big guy on the ground was a bottom-feeder, a low-level drug dealer. Preying on the weak, because he himself was weak of mind and morality. The big man wasn't averting his gaze because he was ashamed, but because he was afraid to finally face judgment. Life was easier that way, and men like him always took the path of least resistance.

Max glanced at Renee standing next to him. Her hair was now covered by thick droplets of rainwater. The outer rim of the storm. Renee's arms were crossed, her pretty eyes looking at Max. She was concerned about what Trent might do. Max held out his hand. His instincts told him not to interfere.

The bearded man began to get up, but Trent placed his foot on his chest, pushing him back down. Trent was expressionless, a spartan soldier at work.

"Screw off, man. What do you want me to say? Sorry? I'm fucking sorry, okay? It wasn't my fault. Leave me alone."

Trent just stared at the man. "I don't want an apology."

The girl with the tongue ring hissed.

One of the others watching said, "Then what the hell do you want, asshole?"

"Show me a bag."

The man frowned in disbelief. "What?"

"Just show me a bag."

"What the hell are you talking about?"

"You got a bag on you? Show me one."

"Let me sit up."

Trent took his foot off the man's chest. The bearded man reached into his pocket and took out a small plastic bag. Trent snatched it from the man's grasp and held it up, examining it. Max could just barely make out a gelatinous black substance inside.

The dope dealer said, "Are you...are you looking for some for yourself? I can get you better stuff, but it's not on me."

"Is this what you gave to my brother?"

The man on the ground didn't reply.

Max watched Trent's fist tighten and momentarily worried that he was wrong about the situation. That Trent really was going to kill this guy.

But then Trent calmed himself and simply pointed a finger at the man's face, whispering, "Don't show up here again. I mean that." Then Trent flung the bag back at the ground and turned away.

The bearded man picked up the bag and hustled to his feet. He and his cohort looked at each other, stupefied, then fled down the alley. As the rain began to come down harder, flashes of lightning illuminated the sky, the rumbles of thunder growing louder.

Max placed his hand on Trent's shoulder, his tee shirt getting wet from the rain. "Let's go back inside."

Trent looked up at Max. "It was black tar."

Max looked at Renee, who was biting her lip. She shrugged, not understanding. Another clap of thunder sounded nearby. "We should get out of the rain."

"Black tar?" Max asked.

Trent walked towards the back entrance of the bar. "Black tar heroin. They make that shit in Mexico. During my last assignment with the Army, this is the stuff we were trying to stop from coming into the country. It's nasty stuff. The cheapest type. And it's what my brother was getting high on when he overdosed."

Renee looked at Max again, her eyes watery. Max held open the door to the poolroom, and they were flooded with a soft yellow light as they headed back inside.

Max felt guilty for thinking it, but he realized Trent was going to be the perfect recruit.

6

———

They walked through the poolroom, the bar area. The bartender glanced at Trent. "Everything alright?"

Trent nodded back to him. "Yeah. Let me know if I owe you anything for scaring off your customers."

"Not a thing, brother. They weren't good customers."

Trent gave the bartender an appreciative smile and continued to walk with the group.

The band onstage was warming up. Country music.

Max went over to the bartender and asked if they could get the side room that looked like it was available for exclusive parties. The bartender agreed and showed them into the room through saloon doors. The band noise was muted there, and the room was empty of other patrons. A waitress approached and took drink orders.

She said, "Frank told me to make sure that you're left alone in here. Is that right?"

Max said, "That'd be great. Thank you kindly."

They sat down, and the waitress took their orders, then left to fetch drinks.

Max got Trent talking.

Trent said, "Black tar heroin is some ugly stuff. But it's cheaper and easier to make. After the cartels couldn't make money from weed, they switched their focus to heroin."

Renee said, "Why couldn't they make money off marijuana anymore?"

"Because we legalized it in the US. Criminal organizations couldn't participate in the legal marketplace. And opioid demand was rising fast. So, the cartels shifted to heroin."

The conversation seemed to be therapeutic for Trent. He got going about everything that was eating him up inside. He talked about Josh's fight with opioid addiction, and about how Josh had tried to keep it from everyone. Trent had retired from the Army fourteen months ago so that he would have more freedom to help his brother fight his addiction.

"I never would have left the Army that early. But Josh needed my help. And things went well for a while. But drug addicts get good at hiding stuff," Trent said, sadness in his voice.

Ironically, Trent's last tour with Army special operations was on the front lines of the war on drugs. Trent had been in Mexico, advising the DEA and training Mexican security forces. While he didn't say it outright, Max knew enough to speculate that Trent had also done a few black bag jobs while down there. When the head of the Sinaloa cartel had been captured in early 2016, US military special operators like Trent had reportedly been on hand. One of them might even have been Trent.

Trent said, "Sometimes the dealers lace bags of heroin with the more potent synthetic stuff. It gets 'em hooked on the better stuff so that the next time they can jack up the price. The problem is that the synthetic drugs are often ten times more powerful. Sometimes hundreds of times more powerful. And if you take it in the wrong dosage, it'll kill you. That's what happened to Josh, they said."

"Mind if I ask you something? You could have done a lot of damage to that guy in the alley back there. But you let him go. Why, if you think he's responsible?" Max needed to push the recruitment now, and to evaluate whether, after losing his brother in this way, Trent was stable enough to handle the job.

Trent sighed, staring down at his calloused hands. "It won't bring my brother back. Beating the hell out of him could put me in jail, though.

That would just cause my parents more pain." He met Max's eyes. "Men like him aren't worth it. And they aren't the real problem."

Bingo.

Max said, "What if you could go after a few of the men who *were* part of the real problem?"

* * *

The dinner conversation with Trent lasted another thirty minutes. Renee left to use the bathroom, leaving the two men alone. Max didn't finish with a hard sell. He told Trent that he could have a day to think it over. But Trent didn't need any more time.

"I'm in, Max."

Max nodded. "Good."

Trent took a swig of beer. "You know, I saw you once. When I was deployed."

"Where?"

"Syria."

"You're kidding. Why didn't you say anything?"

"Didn't seem appropriate. You were with a bunch of spooks, and it looked like you didn't want to be seen. My A-team leader was there with you in the building you were in. To be honest, I had forgotten about it until just now, when you mentioned you used to do this type of work."

"Why didn't I notice you?"

"Probably the beard, back then." Trent smiled.

Max snorted and shook his head. "So you already knew about me."

Trent nodded. "Josh had mentioned something, a while back. So you were CIA?"

"DIA, actually."

"But now you are working for the CIA?"

"Yes."

Trent looked confused. "So..."

"It's complicated." Max grinned, and then turned serious. "Hey, Trent, before we get into the details, I just want to make sure that with everything that's happened with Josh and all—"

"I know, Max. I won't lose my cool in Mexico."

"No, that's not what I mean. I mean, you know that this isn't your fault, right? Your brother."

He looked away. "I know."

"Are you going to be alright?"

Trent held up his beer. "Nothing a few of these can't fix."

"Well, make that the last one. I know your parents, and they'll kill me if I bring you back to the house drunk."

"I fear my mother too much to come back drunk." Joking. A good sign. "So what's with Renee? How is she involved in this?"

Max looked at her as she walked back into the room. "She's got a superpower, and it should come in very handy. Also, she told me that I'm not allowed to keep secrets from her anymore, which apparently includes international espionage."

Trent said, "What's the secret power?"

"Superpower," Max corrected.

Renee reddened. Max knew she disliked praise. "I'm good with computers. I believe that's what he was referring to."

The look on Trent's face told Max that this was still insufficient, so Max said, "Renee's background was with the Canadian version of the NSA, the Communications Security Establishment. She's also done cyber security for a variety of firms, including US intelligence agencies. I've worked with her on high-level assignments that were vital to national security, and I vouch for her."

Renee kissed his cheek. "You say the sweetest things."

Max had taken some liberty in his use of the word "assignments," but this information seemed to have the intended effect. Trent looked impressed.

Renee said, "So, Trent, what exactly should we expect down in Mexico?"

"Based on where Max said we're going, we'll need to be very careful. Assume that every set of eyes and ears is working for the narcos, or at least reporting to them. I'd like to check with DEA on—"

Max held up a hand. "Sorry. We're on our own on this. No one but us and my handler at CIA."

"Okay, then. Well, I would say that rule number one is don't trust anyone down there. The Mexican government and their law enforcement agencies are filled with people on the cartel payroll. Those who can't be bought are often killed. Brutally. If there's one thing the narcos understand, it's how to send a message. That's rule number two. Don't get caught."

* * *

The next morning, Max and Renee were once again at the Carpenter parents' home. They had agreed to stop by for breakfast before flying Trent down south.

Max couldn't help but flash back to the funeral he'd attended a week earlier. The town police had led the funeral procession. A column of cars had followed with their headlights on. More than two dozen had shown up from Josh's old Army unit. They'd worn crisp uniforms and drawn proud stares from the locals.

The funeral had been nice, as funerals go. Four of the soldiers had formed an honor guard and performed a flag-folding ceremony. They'd handed the flag to Tina Carpenter, who was a wreck.

The tears had flowed, especially when Mr. Carpenter had given the eulogy. He'd recalled the best of times. He'd highlighted Josh's generous and spirited personality, and the love Josh had held for his wife and son. It had been painful to hear, knowing that he was gone.

Now Max sat at a plastic table on the screened-in porch. Josh's five-year-old son was eating cereal across from him. Puddles of milk surrounded the bowl. There was an iPad on the table. Someone had put on a cartoon. But the boy wasn't watching it. He was looking at Max, chewing his food.

"My mommy said that you were friends with my dad."

"I was. Very good friends."

"Do you like Penn State football?"

Max smiled. "Your dad sure did."

"He used to watch all the games with me."

Max didn't reply.

The boy took another bite of the cereal and began watching his cartoon.

* * *

The weather was already getting hot and humid by midmorning when they had finished breakfast. Cicadas made a racket in the forest behind the home. Max wandered to the backyard, sitting in a lawn chair under the shade of an old oak tree.

Renee was playing with little Josh. They were feeding two rabbits in a homemade wooden cage propped up on cinderblocks. A thousand little pellets of food and droppings lay in the grass nearby. Renee's pretty smile and good nature had coaxed several giggles out of Josh Junior.

Tina approached. Josh's widow had lines of fatigue beneath her eyes. Her voice was weak, like she didn't have any more energy to be sad.

"Josh would have been glad that you were here."

Max just nodded, feeling numb and guilty. They hadn't spoken much last week at the funeral. He hadn't known what to say.

They both just stood there in the morning heat, watching her son pet the rabbits at the far end of the yard. Finally, Tina said, "I don't think he could bring himself to tell you. About the drugs, I mean. He was ashamed of what he'd become, I think."

"He had no reason to be."

She nodded. "He tried to hide it from everyone. At first, he thought he could keep it from me. He tried to convince me that it was just him adjusting to civilian life. There were a lot of changes. He lost a lot of weight. Slept more. Mood swings—crazy ones. When they took away his prescription, someone in town said they could help him get some black-market stuff. It started off with him getting the same thing he'd gotten at the drugstore, except now he had to pay for it out of pocket. But then he couldn't get the pills anymore, and another guy said he could get Josh some sort of patch. Like a nicotine patch, but with fentanyl. Same thing as the pills, different method. But then that stuff dried up too. And eventually he started using the *really* bad stuff, because that's all he could get. All he could afford. It was awful on our marriage. I didn't know what going on at first. He didn't want to shower when I was around, which I thought was weird. I found out it was because he didn't want me to see the needle marks in his arms. Imagine trying to keep something like that from your wife, who sleeps in your bed. I found his box one day while he was sleeping."

"His box?"

"He had a little tin box that he kept under the seat of his pickup truck. Needles inside, carefully stacked. He was always neat."

"I'm so sorry, Tina."

"It's nobody's fault." Her voice cracked, and she wiped away a tear. "I feel like we all keep saying that to each other. That it's not our fault. I don't know if any of us truly believes it. Things weren't like this when Josh and I grew up in this town. Drugs were an inner-city problem. Not here. I smoked a little weed when I was younger. Josh did too. But never the hard stuff. People like us are from good families, with good parents. Good values. This kind of thing isn't supposed to happen here. Or to men like him. Josh was one of the best men I know. And I'm not just saying that because I'm his wife. Ask any of the men from his old Army units. He was one of the good ones. But those drugs changed him. And they have ruined my life. They've killed my husband. He wanted to quit, Max. He tried. But the pull was too strong. Even for someone like him."

Max didn't know what to say. So they just stood there in silence for a few minutes. Sometimes that was the best thing to do.

Tina was looking at her son. Trent was over there now. He had gotten little Josh away from the rabbits and they were playing Wiffle ball.

Tina said, "I'm not sure what we'll do now. I guess I'll have to go back to work. We were living off his disability pay, for the most part...but now I guess that will stop."

Max said, "Are you sure that they won't keep paying you?"

"I don't know. We have a man from the VA who is helping us, but the life insurance folks already said that his drug overdose meant that they wouldn't pay out."

Max shook his head. "Tina, I can help. Let me look into a few things."

She looked up at him, alarmed. "Oh, Max, listen, I didn't mean—I know you guys are well off and all but…look, we aren't looking for a hand-out, okay? I just was telling you because—"

Max gestured for her to stop. "Please. I know you didn't mean it like that. But let me see if there isn't something we can do to help you guys out. Do you have any immediate needs? Are you okay on money right now?"

She nodded, her lip quivering. Another tear ran down her cheek. "Thanks," was all she managed to say as she hugged him.

7

Senator Herbert J. Becker of the great state of Wisconsin stared into the center of the camera lens, doing his best to imagine that it was the single representation of each and every one of his most precious voters. He had practiced his "stern-but-approachable" look in front of countless mirrors. It assured his constituents that he was the kind of man who would stick up for them in a fight but at the same time shared their family values.

"And let me just say this. Solving this country's growing heroin epidemic is my *number one* priority. That's why I cosponsored the Opioid Epidemic Act. We'll be bringing it to the floor in a matter of weeks. I believe that will have a tremendous impact on reducing opioid use within the United States."

The reporter—a slick-haired kid who was a little too cavalier for the senator's taste—followed up with, "Well, I'm glad you brought that up, Senator. Many in your party were surprised that you cowrote that bill and helped gather so much support for it. It's a piece of bipartisan legislation that many in your party don't like. Some are calling it antibusiness. Even some on the other side of the aisle are saying it will deny access to medicine to those in need. What do you say to that?"

"I would say that this country has been hurting for a long time, and I'm proud of my efforts to combat the opioid epidemic. Businesses will not be hurt by this bill, as they will end up providing consumers with better health care, without the risks of today's surplus of addictive pain medication."

"What about the people who need that pain medication? Many patients need opioids to perform their day-to-day tasks. You're going to deny them that choice? Deny the doctors the ability to prescribe it and the health care manufacturers the ability to sell it?"

"My bill—excuse me, the Opioid Epidemic Act—doesn't completely eliminate opioids as an option. Yes, it will greatly reduce how many pills are sold and used. But in the long run, it will make our country healthier and more vibrant. Now I thank you for your time, but I'm afraid I have to—"

"Senator Becker, one more thing before you go—some are speculating that you have ambitions for a presidential run in two years. Is that true? Are you going to run for president, Senator?"

The balding politician smiled demurely. "Right now, I'm just focused on doing what's right for the good people of Wisconsin. And as far as elections go, it's this year's midterms that I'm thinking about. I'm up for reelection in my own state. I've honestly given no thought to any political decisions that may lay beyond that point."

Of course it's true, you little prick, but you know I'm not going to say it here on your low-rated cable news show this far out into the future.

The kid tried one more time, probably listening to his producer humming in his earpiece. "Is there any chance you would consider a presidential run in two years, sir?"

Becker would have to tell Ron not to book him with this guy anymore. "Well, I never like to close a door fully—but I mean what I said. My focus is on the people I represent in the great state of Wisconsin and making sure that we combat the horrific threat of illegal drugs poisoning our nation."

"Thank you for your time, Senator Becker."

"Thank you."

A group of reporters stood waiting for him to finish the interview. One of them stuck a recording device up as Senator Becker walked away from the camera.

"Senator, a few questions please."

Ron Dicks, his chief of staff, said, "The senator won't be taking any more questions right now, thanks."

The senator walked away from the scrum of reporters, his entourage of aids in tow. "What's next, Ron?"

Ron scanned his notepad as they walked, their footsteps echoing in the capital building hallway.

"Sir, you have a hard stop this morning for the Senate Judiciary Committee hearing at ten thirty. Prior to that, you've got a strategy session in your office with Sarah." His chief of staff rattled off several other appointments throughout the day, finishing with, "Oh, and your daughter called, sir."

"Karen called?"

"Yes, sir."

"What about?"

"She didn't say."

They took the underground subway from the Capitol Building to the Hart Senate Office Building and then made their way to his office. His secretary, a matronly no-nonsense woman of about fifty, handed him a list of calls as he walked in.

The senator sat down behind his desk. "Give me five minutes," he announced to his staff.

"Of course, Senator." Ron stayed in the room, knowing that the senator needed time, not privacy, which he'd given up decades earlier.

Senator Becker held the landline phone to his ear, dialing the number from memory. When he was president, he wouldn't dial anymore, he thought. Only a few years away, if he played his cards right.

Aides floated in and out of the office, placing folders in the senator's inbox and removing them from his outbox. Some whispered into Ron's ear as the chief of staff waited for the senator to finish his personal call. The secretary came in and placed a china set on the senator's desk— coffee and tea biscuits with raisins.

Karen answered on the second ring. "Hello, Dad."

"Karen. To what do I owe the pleasure?"

"I got it, Dad. I wanted you to be the first to know."

Senator Becker frowned, sitting down in the chair at his desk. "What did you get, dear?"

"The Oshkosh spot. They had a dropout and chose me at the last minute. I'll have two performances. You'll be there, right?"

"You're performing at Oshkosh? Why, that's wonderful news. When is your show?"

"Two performances. One earlier in the week, and one at the end."

"And you'll dress...conservatively?"

She let out a sigh of exasperation. "Dad...relax."

Senator Becker flushed, thinking of the outfits his daughter wore when she performed. He was proud that she had reached such a high level in the aerobatics community, being invited to the top air shows in the world. But my God, did she have to flaunt her buxom figure on all those advertisements?

"Let's just make sure that any publicity you get paints you in a good light. I would hate to think that—"

"Don't worry, *Senator*. I understand. I won't do or say anything crazy. Well, not too crazy." She laughed, and Becker saw his eavesdropping chief of staff close his eyes, a pained expression on his face. A few years ago, Ron had had to pay a private investigator twenty-five hundred dollars to destroy a set of files from one of Karen's old boyfriends. The ex-boyfriend had thought he was selling compromising pictures to a tabloid. He was made to turn over all of the files and sign a nondisclosure agreement. Then the PI had scared the hell out of him with what would happen if he violated the agreement. The files had been deleted, but it would have horrified Karen had they gotten out. More importantly, it would have embarrassed the good senator, and probably cost him ten points with suburban moms ages thirty-five through fifty-four.

Karen had been a hellion ever since she was a teen. Her looks had ensured that she never suffered any lack of attention from the opposite sex, and her behavior suggested that she didn't mind.

"Well, I'm thrilled that you'll be performing there, Karen."

"You're coming?"

"Of course, you know I never miss it."

"Great. I'll see you there next week."

As soon as he hung up the phone, it chimed. Senator Becker hit the blinking light. The voice of his secretary said, "Senator, your next appointment is here."

Senator Becker looked at his chief of staff.

Ron said, "Sarah."

"Ah. Yes, please send her in. Clear the room, please. Except for you, Ron."

The aides shuffled out.

A petite woman in a suit marched in and nodded respectfully. "Good morning, Senator. How are you today?"

"Excellent, thank you."

She set up her computer on the coffee table, connecting it by wire to the monitor mounted on the wall.

"What have you got for us, Sarah? Any serious challengers pop up while I wasn't looking?"

While there was a state primary vote in a few weeks that would decide Becker's opponent for reelection in November, none of the candidates were considered a serious threat. The senator had won each of his last three elections by a minimum of eight points. And the trend was improving.

She lowered her voice. "You asked me to put some polls into the field. Widening the pool of voters past Wisconsin..."

Ron glanced at the senator. The lightbulb went off in his head. This meeting wasn't about this year's election. It was about the future.

"Ah. That time already, is it?"

Becker could see the pleased expression in his chief of staff's eyes. A kid about to peek behind the wrapping paper on the night before Christmas. Which was good, because Ron had been nothing but a worrywart since the news about Joseph Dahlman.

The monitor showed a red, white, and blue elephant on the screen. There were few things more exciting to a political junkie than new polling data. Ron and Senator Becker were about to see, for the first time, what national polls said about his prospects for the next presidential race.

"Well, don't keep us waiting."

Sarah tapped a key on her computer and began showing them a series of charts.

"Overall, the news is good. Among likely voters, your name is within the top three potential presidential contenders in your party."

They went over top-line results for the next ten minutes.

"Nationally, the antidrug message is playing very well," said Ron.

Sarah said, "Absolutely. That's what voters know him for. Taking a tough stance on the war on drugs, and helping to fight the opioid epidemic. He's going to need a message that will resonate with the base if he's going to make it past a primary. This could be it."

"Ron here thinks that's a problem," the Senator said.

Ron looked uncomfortable. "I've made my views clear, sir. I think you risk alienating the people who got you here if you appear antibusiness."

"The Opioid Epidemic Act is going to be my signature achievement. You know it's a winner nationally."

"It won't matter if we can't even get past a national primary..."

"You see what I'm dealing with, Sarah? My own chief of staff thinks my biggest legislative achievement is going to hurt me. Well, fine. Let's see if I can't come up with something a little tougher. Something that adds more meat on the bone for the people Ron is worried about losing," said the senator.

Senator Becker looked at his computer screen on his desk. His Internet browser was on a news website, showing soldiers riding in Humvees in Afghanistan. "What was that the DEA was saying last week when we went to visit them?"

"The director?"

"No. When they took us on the tour? Do you remember, we spoke to an agent that had been down in El Paso about what he needed?" They had been looking for quotes that might help them support point papers.

"He was talking about the US Special Forces down there in Mexico," said Ron.

"That's right," said Senator Becker. "He was complaining about how Mexico wouldn't let the US get their hands dirty. We send our DEA agents, military personnel, and all those other agencies down to Mexico, not to mention the billions of dollars in foreign aid...but we're still at the mercy of the Mexican law enforcement agencies. The DEA has to rely on Mexican authorities to make real progress."

Sarah said, "I'm not sure that I follow, sir. What are you suggesting?"

The senator said, "What if we were able to use American troops to really go after the cartels in Mexico? To take the gloves off. Just like that DEA agent was saying. Now, policy like that, that's got some machismo, does it not?"

"It does."

Becker said, "I like this. Let's spitball it a bit."

Ron held up his hands, as if painting it on a billboard. "Stopping the opioid epidemic in the United States means taking the fight to Mexico."

Senator Becker pointed. "And *I'm* the only one tough enough to send our military down there to do it."

"Exactly. Brilliant, Mr. Senator." Ron held up his hands like he was reading a billboard. "If America is fighting a war on drugs, then it's time we use our warriors," said Ron, tagline-testing.

"Very nice." It needed a little work, but Becker liked it.

Sarah said, "Senator, with all due respect, we would need the permission of the Mexican government. They would never go for it."

Ron and the senator shared a glance.

Ron said, "That's irrelevant. We're just discussing campaign communication strategy. It doesn't matter whether we actually *do* it or not."

Senator Becker sighed. Sarah was good at polling, but he would need to replace her once the midterms were over. If she couldn't grasp the difference between a campaign message and an actual policy proposal...

"Sarah, we'll need you to market-test it. But my gut tells me that it's going to be a winner."

He looked out the window at his office. The worker bees buzzing around the streets of D.C. outside. It was remarkable to think how far he'd come over the years. His meteoric rise since 9/11.

It hadn't been that difficult, really. Senator Becker knew he had a way with people. Politics was all about winning hearts and minds. Helping all those unsophisticated voters understand what was really good for them, so that more than half of them approved of how he spent their money. It took oratorical skill. Becker was a masterful speaker. It took intellectual flexibility. Becker was a political yoga master. He had switched parties more than a decade earlier, when he'd seen the tides changing. Becker knew that if you wanted to govern, you couldn't worry so much about ideology, but you sure as hell better care about polls. And right now, the polls told him that he needed to crack down on drugs. It was a winning bipartisan issue. The kind of platform cornerstone that could propel someone into the oval office.

Sarah was nodding. "Alright, I'll conduct some more focus groups. And perhaps run another poll. I'll send you a cost estimate, Ron."

The senator nodded. "Excellent. Thank you, Sarah. That'll be all for now." The messaging might need some work, but they could try a few things. It was still early, but the time to get his ducks in a row was now.

A minute later, Sarah was out the door and Becker was alone with his chief of staff. The chime on his phone and a blinking light told him that his next appointment was ready. He pressed the button and said, "Give us a moment, please."

Ron was taking notes in his leather binder, muttering something to himself. He repositioned his glasses and wrote some more. Becker had worked with him long enough to know to leave him alone when he was like this. This was what Becker referred to as one of his genius moments. It was the way he made his calculations. At last he looked up and took his glasses off.

"I like it. I think it will play well. The libertarians will like the fact that we're not putting our troops overseas and instead focusing on something closer to home. The base will like it because it uses our troops to damage a clear villain. And everyone will like it because it takes a strong stance in the war on drugs."

"Now I know you're lying. There's never a time when everyone likes it."

"Everyone that matters," Ron said.

Senator Becker said, "It'll be a gamble. I'll be like a peacock with my feathers out during the primary, which I know worries you."

"Maybe, sir, but—"

"I know what you're going to say. We'll need to consider the increased scrutiny we'll be under." Becker gave Ron a knowing look.

"I am sorry for any problems I've caused us, sir. I should have been more careful."

The senator ignored him. "Even the hint of impropriety can get blown out of proportion. The opposition research we've faced thus far will be nothing compared to a presidential campaign."

"The contributions were from a 501c. The FEC has no ability to link it back to—"

"You received death threats."

"Sir, they were trying to play hardball."

"Your lobbyist friend is dead."

Ron paused, choosing his words, then said, "Sir, if you want me to go to the police—let them know that you had no knowledge of any of it...I'll fall on my sword, sir."

Becker slammed his hand down on the desk and pointed at Ron. "Don't be naïve. Saying that won't make a difference in the papers."

Ron looked like a beaten dog. "Sir, you could always call off the vote. Or amend the bill to be friendlier to the...investors."

"I'm not going to be bullied. People buy into my agenda. Not the other way around."

"Sir, I never meant to suggest that your strategy wasn't the right choice."

"You leaned on me, Ron."

"Sir, I gave you sound counsel."

"Which happened to align with the direction Dahlman and his backers were pushing you."

"Sir, this bill is counter to many of your own previous stances. My advice lined up with your own—"

Becker cut him off. "Things change. Now I need to know you're loyal to me."

"Of course, sir."

"If people start poking around, this could get ugly."

"I understand."

"Your professional relationship with Dahlman can't become an issue for me."

Ron reddened. "Yes, sir."

Becker said, "You know as well as I do that those clients of his play by a different set of rules. Well, now we're not in their favor anymore. We obviously can't go to the authorities because we don't want them digging around and finding out who you've been drinking beers with at Bullfeathers." He leaned forward and whispered, "But for God's sake, they just shot someone dead. Now I need you to clean up this mess. Figure it the hell out."

8

Renee, Trent, and Max said their goodbyes to the Carpenter family and flew to Virginia. From there they were picked up by a sleek private jet.

"Courtesy of Charles Fend," said Max with a wink.

Trent whistled. "The royal treatment. Please give my thanks to your dad."

Max said, "It'll help us fit with our cover. The wealthy playboy that I play so well, my trophy girlfriend, and our private security man slash luggage boy."

"Trophy girlfriend?" Renee asked.

"Well, I didn't want to say eye candy. I thought you might be offended."

Trent said, "I'm fine with you calling me a luggage boy as long as there's some free booze on board. Hell, usually when they have me fly, the rear ramp gets opened and they ask me to leave halfway through the flight. This should be much better."

Max turned to Renee. "It's important, in the world of spy tradecraft, that you fully embrace the transformation into your cover assignment. You'll need to act like a devoted, fawning girlfriend who completely worships and adores her man."

Renee blinked. "That sounds awful. Why can't I just be myself?"

Two hours later, the jet was headed southwest. Trent slept in the rear of the cabin, aided by two glasses of bourbon on the rocks.

Renee sat in a cream leather chair opposite Max, chewing gum, her thin MacBook Pro on her lap, white earbuds in her ears. Max recognized the pattern. She was in work research mode. Hyperfocused learning, she called it. Conducting her due diligence at the beginning of a new project.

"Look at this."

She turned her computer so that he could see the screen. "Do you know that since 1999, over half a million people in the United States have died from drug overdoses?"

"Half a million?"

"Yes. And the overdose deaths are rapidly increasing—mainly due to the rise in opioid addiction."

Max had been reading up on the cartels on his tablet. Encrypted intel documents sent by Wilkes.

"You know we won't be able to solve the opioid crisis, right? That's not what this is about, Renee."

She ignored him and began typing, her fingers racing over the black keys.

"Hello?"

"Wait," was all she said.

Max did as commanded. A terrier, waiting for his master's command. He took a deep breath. Being in a relationship with a woman who was smart, opinionated, and sexy really hurt a man's ability to pretend he was in charge.

She stopped typing and looked at him. "Okay, I found what I was looking for. I'm ready to debate."

Max held his hands up in surrender. "I've learned that debating you is never in my best interests. How about you just arm me with your newly acquired knowledge?"

Renee began. "The US uses more opioids than anywhere else."

"Okay. So what? Isn't that just because of population?"

"No. This is per capita. The US leads the way, by far. Canada is number two, by the way. So I would be helping your country and mine."

Max cocked his head. "You keep telling me that you're an American now."

"I have dual citizenship. But I still like Canada better."

"Why?"

"Better beer and prettier lakes."

"We're getting better at beer, you know…"

Renee tapped on her trackpad and opened up a window. "This is the DEA's National Drug Threat Assessment. It's one of the most comprehensive annual reports on the illegal drug trade and how it affects the United States. It says that Mexico is the biggest source of heroin for the US market."

"I thought most heroin was grown in Afghanistan."

Renee said, "You're right. Most of it is. But there's a global demand for opium. And most Afghan poppy production ends up sold to European or Asian markets. Cheap Mexican heroin is flooding into the US. And look." She brought up a color-coded map of the United States. "Do you remember the name of the cartel that Wilkes mentioned?"

"The Sinaloa cartel, I believe."

"Right. They—according to this document—are the number one producer of heroin sold in North America. They control the region where it grows. Something about the climate in the warm, mountainous regions is conducive to growing poppies. And they have ultra-cheap labor. Women. Kids. Often working under slave-like conditions, growing the crops. Armed men standing watch over them. And you know how Trent was so broken up about the black tar heroin he found in the dealer's possession? He was right. His brother Josh probably overdosed on Mexican heroin—produced by the same cartels that Trent once went after. I don't know that you could ever point the finger at one person. But I certainly think that if you wanted to hold someone accountable at a high level, the higher-ups in the Sinaloa cartel would be a great pick."

Max said, "Point made."

"There's something else I found that I wanted to run by you."

"Hit me."

"I was trying to find a link between the ISI and the Mexican drug cartels. Specifically, the Sinaloa cartel, where this Blanco is."

"And?"

"I found this one journalist's blog—someone who'd been embedded with US troops in Afghanistan. One of his posts mentioned a rumor he overheard—that the Pakistani ISI are covertly running the Afghan opium trade."

Max narrowed his eyes. "It wouldn't be the first time an intelligence agency got involved in something like that. The Afghan heroin trade is a multibillion-dollar market. That amount of money would attract all the sharks in the region. And the ISI has a lot of sharks. If you've got that much cash, you can fund a whole lot of covert operations to support your cause."

"But even if the ISI is involved in the Afghan heroin trade, what's the connection to the Sinaloa cartel?"

Max looked out the window, thinking, then turned back to face her. "Heroin, obviously. You just talked about the rise in heroin use across the world since 2001. And you also said that North America has overindexed. So growth in heroin use here is higher than anywhere else, but Afghanistan still produces ninety percent of the world's heroin."

Renee said, "The Mexican cartels can't keep up. Is that it?"

"Possibly. Maybe the North American demand is outstripping the cartel's supply. So where can they go to get more heroin to sell in the US?"

"Afghan suppliers."

"And the ISI is brokering the deal."

Their jet stopped at a small executive airport on the outskirts of Dallas. They taxied next to a hangar where a small moving truck was waiting. Next to the truck stood a tall, thick man with dark curly hair and a beard. Max shook hands with the man and introduced him to Trent and Renee.

Renee said, "I'm sorry, did you say your name was...?"

"That's right, Sasquatch."

The large man's arms were folded across his chest, a wide smile on his face.

Renee looked at Max with bewilderment, not sure if this was a joke. "Why do you go by Sasquatch?"

The man lifted open the truck trailer door to reveal shelves filled with weapons and gear. "I think they call me that because of my good looks."

Max whispered, "Men in his line of work usually prefer that we not use their real name."

Renee nodded.

Trent picked up a large weapon with two hands. It was drab green and had a cylinder-style magazine. "This is nice."

"What is it?" asked Renee.

Sasquatch answered, "It's a multi-use weapon. We've got several different options for ammunition there, sir. Just take a look at the shelf above it."

"Excellent. Very nice selection," said Trent. "These rounds here—any chance you could customize them for close quarters?"

Sasquatch handed him a specially marked crate. "These here don't have the twenty-five-meter minimum engagement range. They'll arm after about seven meters. Will that do?"

"Yup."

Trent and Max inspected their gear options, made their choices, and then loaded everything onto the jet while it refueled.

"Your payment is already in your account," said Max. "And I gave you a little tip."

"Always appreciated, Mr. Fend. Just let me know whenever I can be of service."

The trio got back into the jet as Sasquatch drove away. A few hours later, they landed at an airport on the coast of Sinaloa, Mexico.

Cartel territory.

* * *

They arrived at a five-star resort on the beaches of Mazatlán. The resort had high cement walls surrounding the property. Men armed with shotguns walked the perimeter, guarding the wealthy patrons. Max wondered how many of those men also worked for the cartels part-time.

"May we take your bags, sir?"

"No, thank you, my assistant will manage fine." Max looked at Trent, who nodded and carried their luggage up to the rooms. The bags would be moved to a safe house later that night. Until then, Trent wouldn't let them leave his sight.

Their hotel room was simple, but gorgeous. Clean floors of reddish Saltillo tile, arched ceilings, and an open-air balcony with a view of the turquoise Pacific and towering palm trees.

But beautiful as it was, the hotel would have been one of Max's last choices if he were vacationing in Mexico. Outside the walls of the resort, the city streets were teeming with prying eyes on the payroll of the cartel, each of them eager to get a bonus for providing a good tip on American law enforcement—or perhaps a prime target for kidnapping.

Their cover story was simple. Max and Renee were on vacation. As many ultra-wealthy travelers do, Mr. Fend had brought along his personal security guard. While Max was well known in the US, due to his father's fame and his own misadventures, here he was just some rich gringo. This partial anonymity allowed him to assist in reconnaissance without drawing extraordinary notice.

The three travelers spent their evenings together in Max's room, with the windows closed and electronic countersurveillance equipment humming on the coffee table. Renee had carefully set up their IT network, an encrypted system that made sure no one could tap in to their phones or computers. She also scanned the room for bugs twice per day.

Still, they knew they were probably being watched. The hotel concierge. The cab driver. The airport security officials. Local police. Even some teenage kids Max had caught tailing him during his first morning stroll. One kid watching him and immediately making a call on a cheap cell phone, probably reporting Max's position to his boss. Max lost the kids during his three-hour surveillance detection route, but the fact that there were so many potential eyeballs on him was a bit unnerving.

Mexico would be harder than he thought.

The group spent the next two days making observations and adjusting plans. Max and Trent took turns walking the streets in and around the operational area. Going over potential getaway routes and choke points, and gaining knowledge of the local pattern of life. Wilkes sent gigabytes of CIA and DEA data to Renee, which the trio studied each night.

Wilkes arrived on the third night to go over the plan.

They ordered room service. Steak and grilled vegetables. Bottled waters. Max wasn't drinking a drop out of the tap. He'd heard too many stories of Montezuma's revenge.

After dinner, Wilkes pointed at the map displayed on Renee's computer screen. On it was a neighborhood block about five miles away.

"So, our break here is that we've been able to establish a new routine between Rojas and my agent. About once per month, he makes the three-hour drive from cartel leadership's headquarters in Durango to the coast here in Mazatlán. Unless something drastically changes, there is a very high probability that Hector Rojas will be in this townhome tomorrow evening, enjoying a night of drinks and carnal familiarity with my agent."

Renee frowned.

Max nodded. "Based on the pattern-of-life reports Wilkes provided us, Rojas rarely stays in the same place more than a few nights in a row. And this special meeting that Blanco and the Pakistanis are prepping for is supposed to be held within the next few weeks. So, we'll need tomorrow night to go smoothly, or—"

"Or we're fucked," Trent finished.

"Or we'll lose our opportunity to discover the location, participants, and purpose of a meeting so important that the ISI is killing American citizens on American soil before it occurs."

Renee said, "Why is the cartel headquarters in the mountains? Why don't they live here? It's beautiful."

Trent said, "It's safer for them in the villages of the Sierra Madres. The cartels live in fear of each other. If they operated here on the coast, there would be a higher chance that one of the competing cartels might try and assassinate the head family, and then steal their share of the market. There's enough going on in beach towns like this that the other cartels might be able to send in a few cars full of their sicarios without getting noticed. But not in Durango. That's flyover country, and everyone knows each other. A single stranger shows up, and they get questioned by the local hired guns."

Max said, "Doesn't sound much like a cartel. Cartels are supposed to work together, colluding on price and distribution. Not kill each other off at the first sign of weakness."

Trent said, "The drug cartels are not real cartels in the literal sense of the word. The Colombians tried to operate that way for a while, but war erupted between them. It's more like the mafia. Competing factions of organized crime families, each following a common code. They have an understanding, and each cartel's territory has been carved out through violent battles over the years. But it's a tumultuous climate. I wouldn't call it a peaceful partnership. They kill each other as much as they kill anyone else, if not more. It would be great if they really operated as a cartel. I suspect there would be much less violence. Much less chaos."

Wilkes said, "Let's talk the schedule of events. My agent will try to slip an incapacitating chemical into his drink. I've trained her on technique and risk assessment. If she can do it safely, Rojas should be passed out pretty hard by midnight. You'll just have his two security guards to handle. Will that be a problem?"

Trent shook his head. "That should be no problem."

"Are we sure it's just two men?" Max said.

Wilkes said, "He's had the same two bodyguards with him every trip he's taken for the past three months."

Trent and Max exchanged glances. Both of them knew how often mission expectations differed from the actual circumstances operators faced.

"We've been scouting the city," Max said. "I'll be parked down the street. When your agent gives her signal that tells us Rojas is passed out, Trent will take out the guards and I'll move my vehicle to the curb. Both your agent and Trent will carry Rojas down to my vehicle and we'll head towards the airport. Caleb, like we discussed, I can't use my father's jet for the extraction, so I'll be relying on one of your air assets. I need you to guarantee me that you'll have someone at the airport at the appropriate time."

Wilkes nodded. "I'll have someone there ready to fly you all back to the States."

"Where in the States? Fort Bliss?"

"No. This is completely off the books. I can't have you guys fly in to a military base. I'll give the pilot a private field to fly into, and the interrogation team will meet you there. You don't need to know the location yet. What's your backup?"

Trent said, "If things get hairy, there's a connection to the townhome next door. Max and I have set up a secondary extraction route through there."

Max said, "When are you going back to El Paso?"

"My jet's waiting at the field," said Wilkes. "I'll be watching the op from EPIC, and I'll send you updates if I spot any problems."

"Won't the people at EPIC wonder why you're having them concentrate their aerial surveillance on Mazatlán? You can't keep this thing from the DEA if they're—"

Wilkes held up a hand to stop him. "Relax. The DEA is doing recon on Rojas, and they know I have an agent involved. My presence at the EPIC tactical operations center won't be unusual, although I imagine they'll begin wetting themselves when they see Trent take out Rojas's bodyguards and your car rolls up. But even if the EPIC folks track you to the airport via satellite, they won't see where it lands. I've made sure all of our airborne tracking tools will lose the evac aircraft."

Max said, "That sounds complex."

"It will be. But really, I think hiding this operation from the DEA should be much easier than hiding it from the cartels tomorrow night."

Max winced.

Renee looked pale.

Trent shrugged. "Easy day."

* * *

Caleb and Trent left, and Max and Renee were alone in their room. He could tell that she was nervous, but also a little excited. He knew this because soon after they were alone, she finished her glass of wine in one gulp, turned out the lights, opened the balcony doors to allow the sea breeze and moonlight in, removed her dress to reveal a sexy black lace number, and began nibbling on his ear.

Latin America was known for being a land of passion. When in Rome...

Afterwards, the two lovers collapsed on top of the sheets, exhausted and covered in sweat.

"Thanks. I think I needed that," said Renee, kissing him lightly on the shoulder and nuzzling into his chest. Skin on skin, he could feel her heartbeat and heavy breathing as she recovered from exertion. Outside, the waves crashed on the beach, and a pale moon rose over the horizon.

She said, "Do you think tomorrow will go okay?"

"We've done our homework and taken precautions. We'll be alright."

"Then what's bothering you?"

Max looked at her.

"Nothing."

"Are you sure?"

"No."

"What, then?"

"I can't put my finger on it." He sighed. "It's probably just nerves. We'll be fine."

They fell asleep to the sound of the waves.

* * *

The next night, Renee sat at the suite's only desk. A "do not disturb" sign hung on the outer doorknob. Max had placed it there when he'd left hours earlier. Her laptop was in front of her, connected only through its satellite antenna. A headset hung over her ears.

She spoke into the headset's boom microphone. "Check in, please."

"In position." Trent's voice.

"Present." Max sounded like a kindergartener speaking to his teacher.

Renee, Max, and Trent were the only people who would be speaking on the encrypted frequency. If Wilkes needed to contact them, Renee would see his message on her computer. She would then notify the team over their earpieces or via a burner phone that each of them carried.

Renee had contacted one of her trusted former CSE partners—a hacker, like her. Approved by Max, this person would help her to monitor the throngs of data she was being fed and ping her with only the most crucial elements. That would free her up to communicate with Max and Trent, giving them the vital real-time information that could make or break the mission. She was also getting the same overhead satellite and drone feed that EPIC was seeing, courtesy of Caleb Wilkes and his connections at the National Reconnaissance Office.

Trent said, "All parties have arrived. With a few extras."

"Extras?"

"Yup."

Renee saw what Trent and Max were talking about. There were four guards outside the townhome, not the expected two. And instead of one woman and one man in the home—Rojas and Wilkes's agent—the rooftop patio was populated by two men and three women.

Max was right. Things hadn't even started yet, and they were already off script.

9

Hugo stood on the top floor of the seven-story parking garage at Reston Town Center in Northern Virginia. He watched as the BMW sedan crept to a halt just in front of him.

The man shut off his engine and exited the car. Ronald Dicks. The most senior aide to Senator Herbert Becker.

From the streets below came the sound of an urban outdoor luxury shopping center. The bustle of the crowd headed to chic restaurants and clothing stores. The happy hour crowd departing the bars. Young teens heading to the movies.

Up here it was quiet. Empty. Just two cars and two men. Neither man wanted to be seen with the other, although not for the same reasons.

"You're with the firm?" Dicks asked, referring to Joseph Dahlman's lobbying agency. Ron Dicks had used a back channel to contact them a day earlier. Dicks was trying to figure out a way to smooth things over.

So was Syed.

Unbeknownst to either party on the line, the ISI had listened to the phone call, provided courtesy of a Chinese communications security firm Syed had hired. Their capabilities were excellent. Within an hour, the lobbying firm had received another phone call rescheduling the meeting for a later date. The voice on the phone was computer-generated, and a perfect match for Ron Dicks.

The ISI had then reached out to Dicks via text message and orchestrated a new meeting time and place. At a discreet location, just like the Senator's chief of staff had requested.

"I am with the firm, correct. Good evening, Mr. Dicks," Hugo replied, reaching out his hand.

Dicks walked towards Hugo, his own arm outstretched. They shook hands and then Hugo motioned for him to get in the passenger seat of Hugo's own vehicle. They both got in and shut the doors.

Dicks was jittery. "We need to find a solution here. Some common ground. I assume your firm is still in touch with the Pakistanis? This wasn't what I signed us up for. There's got to be some middle ground that we can—"

Hugo's movement was swift. He swung his arm across to the passenger side, landing a strong open-handed strike to the trachea.

Dicks' mouth let out an involuntary burst of spittle and air, and then he doubled over, making a choking noise and holding his throat. Hugo leaned back in his seat and looked around the still-empty parking lot. All clear. He opened up the center console of the sedan and removed a prepared syringe. He jabbed it into Dicks' neck and depressed the plunger until it met the stop.

Dicks' eyes went wide at the sting. His body was now flooded with a neuromuscular paralytic. The same type of drug anesthesiologists used, only in much smaller doses.

With Dicks still holding his throat, Hugo started the engine and drove his vehicle so that the passenger side was right next to the trunk of Dicks' BMW. Ron Dicks was now losing control of his faculties. Hugo put on a pair of thin flesh-colored latex gloves and cleaned up his car, careful to wipe off the parts that he'd touched.

He checked his victim by pulling back on his shoulder. A wheezing noise and a twitch of his eye told Hugo that the drug was still in effect. But things were far enough along now.

Hugo grabbed the keys from Dicks' pocket and popped his trunk by pressing the button on the key fob. He shut off his own engine, got out, walked around and quickly but casually transferred the still-alive body into the trunk. From his spot on the parking garage and the time of night, there was about a one percent chance that someone could have seen this activity, and a zero percent chance that someone would see his face.

He shut the trunk and then re-parked his car so that it was in a spot, not wanting to attract attention. Then he wiped it down once more.

Minutes later, he was driving Ron's BMW north towards the Potomac. It was dark by the time he reached Riverbend Park on the south side of the Potomac. He shut his lights off, broke the gate lock, and opened it, driving through towards the water. He arrived at a small boat landing a moment later. Here he was just to the west of Great Falls, where the river turned into a roaring grinder of white water and sharp rocks.

Hugo popped the trunk and removed the body, carrying it into the water and giving it a push into the current.

Ron Dicks' body was discovered the next day, bloated and battered and miles downstream.

10

Wilkes followed the DEA assistant special agent in charge (ASAC) into the break room of the Task Force Echo ops center. The two men got a quick coffee fill-up before the long night, then walked down the hall towards the secure facility in the central part of the building.

"So your agent is on scene tonight?"

"That's right," said Wilkes.

"Hope she's careful. Sinaloa is rough."

Caleb Wilkes was nervous for his agent, Ines Sanchez. He wasn't sure she was ready for this kind of exposure, but in the field, one had to make do with the materials on hand. Wilkes had done his best to steer her away from kinetic operations involving the violent and unpredictable gangsters of her country.

Until tonight.

Ines Sanchez had grown up in Mexico City, where she had been a part-time model, part-time call girl. Her modeling career had led to a job as an actress for a syndicated soap opera shot in Mexico City, and she'd stopped taking clients for her secondary occupation.

Ines had had dreams of getting picked up by a Hollywood agent and leaving Mexico for the US to become an actress there. Wilkes had fanned those flames and offered to introduce her to a few contacts he had in the City of Stars. The promise of a better future was a case officer's best carrot.

She was young compared to most agents he ran—only twenty-six. But she was effective, relatively reliable, and brave. She seemed to get a kick out of working for Wilkes, and was quite happy with the monthly "consulting fees" that were wired to her numbered bank account on the island of Curaçao.

"Are you turning me into a spy?" she had asked him one night, early after her recruitment.

"No, Ines. You're an actress. Think of me as your director. On my stage, there aren't lights or cameras. There will be no clapping audience or adoring fans waiting for you after the show. But you'll have great rewards, if you want them. You'll help to make the world a better place. And eventually, I'll help you to become the star I know you can be."

She had liked that. The thought of doing good, and the twinkle of future fame. Sanchez, like nearly everyone else on the planet, just wanted a better life. When Wilkes had discovered her six months ago, she had been trying to sleep her way to the leading role in her soap opera. Determined and shameless, but cleverer than most girls her age. Wilkes had seen potential.

Three weeks after her recruitment, she had begun having social visits with a Russian diplomat in Mexico City, one that Wilkes had suggested could be a good person to know, if she was looking for someone to buy her drinks for an evening. From the Russian's careless pillow talk, Ines had been able to provide Wilkes with the names of three SVR officers operating out of the local Russian embassy. Two had been known operatives, confirming the accuracy of the information. But the third name was new. Not bad work for the new girl.

With a little discipline and training on her part, and some Hollywood arm-twisting on his, Wilkes truly intended to make her into a full-fledged movie star. Then he could really put her to work. Wilkes's team of spies, which included Max Fend, were among the world's most rich and famous. They had exclusive access to elite clubs and social castes. Whether they achieved that status on their own or Wilkes grew them into it mattered little to him. He was about results.

But for Ines Sanchez to blossom into the productive Hollywood star and agent of the CIA, she needed to be alive and unscarred.

Tonight, that could prove to be a challenge.

Wilkes knew that his agent would likely end up in bed with Rojas this evening, and a part of him felt bad about that. But it came with the job. If a few moments of undesirable disgust for the girl meant bringing down one of the world's most powerful drug kingpins, and uncovering a highly placed American traitor, so be it. His occupation involved deception and moral ambiguities, and he had learned to live with that a long time ago.

"You been down here before?" asked the DEA escort as they walked down the hallway.

"First time," replied Wilkes.

The El Paso Intelligence Center (EPIC) was jointly run by the DEA and US Customs and Border Protection (CBP). More than a dozen other agencies were represented there as well. FBI, CIA, NSA, ATF—you name it. There were over three hundred employees in El Paso, all working diligently to counter the Mexican cartels. It was hard work. The drug war against Mexican cartels was a furnace, and each agent stationed here was another coal in the fire.

The DEA man slid his card through the door's electronic reader, and they both entered the operations center, receiving a few hardened looks from the night crew. The mood inside the room was tense, but Wilkes got the impression that it was routine.

The DEA agent walked to his cluttered desk and sat on the front edge of his black adjustable chair. He scrolled through his messages, then brought up the surveillance schedule to show his CIA guest what was on tap for the night.

A drone flew over the Sierra Madre Mountains. A satellite pass was set up to provide live feed to this center via satellite. Several teams of human surveillance reported in throughout the region. The aerial surveillance video feeds were displayed on screens in the front of the room.

The DEA supervisor introduced Wilkes to his duty section crew. Wilkes asked which screens would show the townhome in Mazatlán where his agent was going to be. One of the DEA men pointed to the right monitor. The imagery was pretty clear but a little jumpy. One of the agents coordinating with the drone operator showed Wilkes how the high-resolution feed was able to toggle between full-color video, infrared, and night vision. The view now showed the front and rooftop patio of an upscale townhouse. A trio of petite, scantily clad women were drinking and dancing under an arbor on the roof. Two men sat at a table, beer bottles in front of them. The narcos.

"This is the drone?"

"Correct. That screen over there is the satellite. We'll have it for another hour. The NSA folks also have access to their signals intelligence during that timeframe."

"Got it."

In Wilkes's experience, the link was only so good whenever satellite comms were involved. But the sophisticated suite of sensors on board the bird would extract extremely valuable electronic data from the area, and that could drastically improve their situational awareness. The whole trade was going increasingly to cyber. Wilkes, like most from his generation, longed for the good old days of the Cold War. Give him a handheld radio and a 9mm Beretta any day.

Wilkes watched his girl on the monitor. One of the three dancing Latinas, gyrating with each other on the rooftop. The unfortunate object of one Hector Rojas's affection.

Rojas was a one-time big shot Mexico City accountant—if accountants can be called big shots. He had been scooped up by the Sinaloa cartel and promoted through the ranks when the previous head of cartel finance had been found missing his lower torso after a run-in with a competing enterprise.

Wilkes had arranged for Ines Sanchez to be introduced to Hector Rojas several months ago, at a party in Playa del Carmen. They had hit it off, but Wilkes had made sure that Ines left for the evening without giving him what he was looking for. She had flirted with Rojas over social media for the next few weeks, sending him revealing photographs and hinting that she would like to see him again.

The messages were carefully curated by a team at the CIA that specialized in psychological manipulation. Rojas could have his choice of beautiful local women. But Wilkes and the analysts calculated that the allure of bedding a semi-famous TV star would reel him in.

EPIC intelligence reports on Rojas indicated that he had several mistresses. But he dropped everything whenever Ines sent Rojas a message that she would be coming to town.

The trap was set.

Wilkes watched the girls dancing and felt internal pinpricks of stress increased in magnitude. He told himself to relax. Trent and Max were both in position. Wilkes had gotten the message from Renee. There were more people at the townhome than expected, but Max and Trent could overcome that. Everything would be fine.

A DEA agent at one of the computer terminals across the room snapped his fingers to get his boss's attention, concentrating on something he was listening to on his headset.

"What is it?" the DEA supervisor asked.

"Boss, something's up. The NSA folks are picking up some unusual chatter from the narcos."

"About?"

"Several truckloads of foot soldiers, all moving fast."

"What the hell are you talking about? Where are they going?"

The DEA man pointed at the video display. "There. The narcos are sending a shitload of guys to that townhouse."

Wilkes face went white.

* * *

Trent Carpenter sat alone in the darkness, looking through the blinds to the cartel townhouse across the street. Performing clandestine street-level surveillance was painstaking, tiresome work. He was perched like an eagle, eyeing its prey from high up, observing everything in silence.

He'd been here for over ten hours. Three plastic one-gallon water jugs lay on the floor next to him. Two were still for drinking. One was now for peeing. As the only surveillance operator with a clear view across the street, he couldn't risk leaving his post.

A high-res camera stood on a tripod next to him, its imagery uplinked to a satellite one hundred miles above the surface of the earth and then relayed down to Renee's computers. Max had helped him set it up earlier, along with a few other cool devices that could pick up nearby cell phones and activate their receivers, but Trent wouldn't touch those toys unless he had to. Renee was doing all that.

On the floor at his feet was his own set of tools. A large black canvas bag filled with weapons and gear. Trent watched the narco security guards on the street, standing outside their pickup trucks, smoking and shooting the shit. Their bosses on the outdoor patio on the roof, dancing with the full-breasted beauties—imports from Mexico City, one of whom was a CIA informant. He fought the urge to lift up his suppressed rifle from the floor and begin picking them off right now.

These were the men that had made money off the death of his brother. Josh, a father, husband, brother, son, and decorated veteran. Now a dead heroin junkie—a statistic in the war on drugs. A deep rage swelled up inside him whenever Trent thought about it. Which was often.

Trent wasn't completely sure that he trusted this CIA guy, Wilkes. But he trusted Max Fend. Fend was a good dude, and Trent had the feeling that they were both here for the same reason.

Guilt. Or justice. Or some combination of the two. Trent kept thinking that maybe if he had killed or captured enough narcos, or stopped enough drug shipments back when he was here with his special operations team, Josh would still be alive. He knew it was a stupid thought, but that didn't stop it from popping into his mind.

During Trent's time as a special operations advisor to the DEA in Mexico, he'd learned the truth about counternarcotics. The big arrests were only temporary wins. And even those were rare occurrences. Normally law enforcement didn't catch anyone of consequence. Even when they did catch one of the kingpins, if the guy was locked up in Mexico, half the time he still ran his operation from the joint. Those prisons were often nothing more than posh luxury hotels set up as narco penalty boxes. Sometimes the wardens and guards were on the cartel payroll. The guards that didn't go along with it either quit or were found dead. Suicide, with three bullets in their head. Shit.

Tonight would be satisfying. There were several more narcos than expected, but eventually the party would die down and people would go to sleep. If not, Trent and Max had talked about waiting until two or three in the morning and taking them when they were most vulnerable. There were four security guards, and two more narcos inside. Trent was pretty sure he'd have no problem with those odds, especially since he had the first-mover advantage. With Max's help, they were sure to succeed.

"Trent, come in," came Renee's voice through his headset, breaking his train of thought.

Max and Trent had told her to check on them every fifteen minutes. Trent looked at his watch. She was very precise.

"Gentlemen, Wilkes just sent me a warning. Something is wrong. The cartel is sending multiple vehicles towards your position."

Max said over the radio, "ETA?"

"A few minutes, tops."

* * *

Max was in a beat-up-looking sedan about one hundred yards down the street from Trent's position, parked in a lot that gave him a view of the townhome and surroundings.

"Renee, give us more info. What do you have?" said Max.

Renee said, "A few minutes ago, the drone picked up a spike in electronic emissions from the narcos' cellular devices. The NSA techs matched the movements to multiple vehicles moving in the area. The conversations say they're showing up at Rojas's pad. What do we do, Max?"

Dammit.

"Hold tight. Trent, be ready to evac through the rear of your building and I'll pick you up."

"Copy."

Max knew that the imagery and electronic sensors were provided by American drones based out of an Air Force base in Texas. With the quiet approval of the Mexican government, the drones flew almost nightly reconnaissance missions over areas where the cartels ran their operations.

But analysis from a drone usually wasn't that accurate in such a short timeframe. Was it possible this was a false alarm? Maybe the cartel trucks weren't really headed there. Maybe they were just going nearby.

Trent's voice. "Vehicles spotted. There they are."

Damn.

Max could see them too. A convoy of dark pickup trucks and SUVs came to a halt on the steep curb just outside Rojas's townhome.

A twinge of fear crept up Max's spine as he watched at least a dozen armed men exit the vehicles.

Shit. Shit. Shit.

Renee's voice was in his ear, saying what he was thinking. "Do they know we're here?"

* * *

Trent slowed his breathing and held still. Even though he was behind closed shades in an unlit room, his instincts warned him of the increased danger. It seemed like half the Sinaloa cartel was forming up on the streets just outside his window. Through the cracks in the window shades, he saw the lights of other homes on the street flicker on. The residents were probably nervous about the sudden influx of cartel muscle, maybe sensing that these men weren't the usual type.

"Trent, what are you seeing?"

He answered Max on the radio. "I count twelve additional narcos. They look well armed and are securing the perimeter like pros. Hold up."

Some tall white dude got out of the back of one of the vehicles. He yelled something in Spanish and pointed down the street, with men scurrying about as he did.

"There's a Caucasian male. Tall guy. Probably six five. Looks like he's in charge by the way they're taking orders from him. He's entering the house now, with several of his men."

* * *

Max's head was spinning. This was like watching a nightmare play out in real time.

One of the newly arrived trucks suddenly moved down the block towards Max. He gripped his keys and the wheel, bracing himself.

Then the truck made a hard left turn and positioned itself perpendicular to the empty traffic lanes, cutting off the townhome's street entrance. Two men stood in the bed of the truck, small machine guns slung across their chests. Another narco got out of the passenger seat and stood on the street corner. Each of the men held his weapon in a way that told Max they'd had military training. Their eyes searched the streets, alert and professional.

Max whispered, "We may need to call this off. I've got three of them about twenty yards away from me. They get any closer, and I'm made."

"You wanna abort?"

"Stand by. Not yet."

A tall white guy in charge of a bunch of armed narcos, arriving unexpectedly. Max had a good idea of who it was.

Blanco.

Their mystery man had arrived.

* * *

Renee's knee bounced under the table as her eyes flipped through the multiple windows she had open on her laptop.

On one hand, this was good news. They were finally getting eyes on Blanco, head of security for the Sinaloa cartel. But sitting here in this luxury hotel, miles from the action, she became deeply worried about the safety of Trent, Max, and Wilkes's agent inside the building.

On her computer, Renee monitored the video feed being broadcast from Trent's tripod camera. El Blanco was almost a foot taller than the others and had a long, confident stride. He barked something to one of Rojas's security men and then walked up the front steps. One of them held the door as El Blanco entered the townhome, several of his own men in tow. She could see them through the lit windows as they headed up the stairs.

"Lot of dudes," said Trent in a somber voice. "They don't look like they're here to party."

"Do we have audio?" asked Max. "Can we listen in to what they're saying?"

Renee said, "Stand by."

She typed a message to her hacker colleague who was assisting her from several thousand miles away. A few clicks and a moment later, one of her computer windows showed the audio signature of muffled Spanish-speaking voices. Renee was now using any phones that they thought were in the cartel's building as eavesdropping devices. The audio was then run through a translation program, and text was populating on another window on her computer.

Renee said, "We've narrowed it down to a few mobile devices. There are a few others that we think might be located in the home, but I don't want to clutter it up as we aren't sure. I'll tell you what they say."

On the monitor, Renee watched as Blanco appeared on the rooftop lounge area, pointing at the girls and issuing orders.

"Rojas looks pissed," said Trent.

Renee clicked on the audio options to listen to the raw data. The music on the rooftop stopped as Blanco had it turned off. Two of the girls were made to sit down at the center table.

Blanco pointed at the third girl.

Ines Sanchez. Wilkes's agent.

Renee's heart pounded in her chest.

One of the narcos walked up to Sanchez and placed a canvas bag over her head. Another man zip-tied her hands behind her back.

"Max, they're taking her. They just put a bag over her head."

Trent said, "What do you want me to do?"

Max's voice. "Continue to monitor and report. Do not move from your position."

"Roger."

"Renee, what are they saying?"

Renee was reading the translated text. "Looks like Blanco is breaking up the party. He's taking the girl and telling them to leave the building."

"Which girl?"

"Ours."

Trent's voice was intense. Begging to be set loose. "You want me to intervene?"

"Negative. There are over a dozen of them, and they appear to be the varsity team," replied Max.

On the monitor, Renee observed an intense argument between a surprised-looking Rojas and El Blanco. Clearly Rojas was not happy about losing his prize for the evening.

Renee heard Blanco say in English, "Take one of these bitches instead."

"Sounds like a British accent," Renee said.

"Who?"

"I just heard him say something to Rojas. Blanco sounds like he's from the UK."

Renee dug her fingernails into her palms, feeling horrified and helpless. She watched the Mexican men carry Ines Sanchez down the stairs, kicking and struggling with the bag still covering her head. Max had told Renee what the cartels did to people who cooperated with law enforcement. Their mutilations were usually made public—a message that ensured loyalty from the others.

Ines was pushed into the backseat of the rear SUV. Blanco and his vehicles, including the one parked near Max, peeled out and sped off.

The radios were quiet.

11

Max watched as the narco pickup truck that had been parked close to him departed with its men.

"Is Hector Rojas still in the building?"

"Affirm. He looks like he's gotten over his lost love and is now on to one of the other girls there."

Max was appalled that this Blanco character had just bagged Wilkes's agent and was now driving her away. He realized what had been bothering him the night before, when Renee had asked.

The DEA and others at EPIC knew about Wilkes's agent.

Wilkes had said he was working with the CIA's counterintelligence division. At first, Max had assumed that was just because a foreign intelligence service—the ISI—was involved. But what if there was more to it than that? What if Wilkes was hunting a mole? Blanco had to have found out about Ines Sanchez somehow.

Max couldn't do anything about a leak right now. On the other hand, he *could* do something about Hector Rojas. The senior finance executive of the Sinaloa cartel was still in the townhome, having a good time. As far as Max was concerned, the mission was still on.

Rojas was still on the roof with one of the girls. And there were the remaining four guards on street level, each one carrying an AR-style rifle.

Trent had what he needed. He'd briefed the mission. Knew all the possible options for entry and evacuation.

A buzzing in Max's pocket. He looked at his phone. It was Wilkes, sending a message to the team. Apparently he had the same idea as Max.

TAKE HIM.

Max said, "Listen up. We'll need to improvise."

* * *

Wilkes stood on the operations floor of EPIC, feeling pissed and guilty at the loss of his agent.

Unlike Max and team, he hadn't had the street-level view of the Caucasian man and still had no knowledge of Blanco's involvement. But he'd seen the beacon in his agent's phone from the bird's-eye view of the drone as she was stuffed into the backseat of the narcos' SUV.

And that definitely wasn't in the plan.

The tracking beacon was tossed out the window while they were driving on the highway. The drone had kept tracking the SUV into the brightly lit city center. The drone operators did their best to follow the girl as they brought her into a large apartment building. There were so many people and vehicles in the area that it would be almost impossible to monitor all the exits.

Which was why they had taken her there, Caleb knew.

She was blown, and they were escaping into obscurity.

Wilkes's worst fears were realized. The leak the CIA had suspected was now confirmed. He hadn't told Max or team about that aspect of the mission, because they'd needed to keep the information as tight as possible in order to catch their mole. But the fact that they'd known about Ines Sanchez drastically narrowed their list of suspects. Someone with access to a high level of intel was responsible for tonight's epic screwup. Without his agent, Max's team would have a harder time taking Rojas.

But it could still be done, which was why he'd sent his message. Sanchez was as good as gone, he knew. But right now, they needed to salvage what they could.

Wilkes waited for word of Max's movement while also thinking about what he would report to his superiors, mourning the loss of his agent, and sifting through possible leakers all at once.

"Oh shit, did you guys just see that?" A DEA agent on the watch floor had stood up, pointing at the front monitor.

The DEA supervisor said, "See what?"

"Quick, look—one of the security guards just went down."

Wilkes saw what he was talking about. The two security guards who had been standing on the front stairs of the home were now on the ground. The drone feed was back over the townhome, zoomed in and using color video thanks to the bright streetlights. A dark blur was visible on the pavement, expanding away from the head of a dead narco. The doors of the second truck swung open and two more men ran out, holding rifles.

"Those are more security men? Or did they just shoot the first two?"

"I don't know."

"They came from the second truck. I think they're just responding. Doesn't look like they know where the shots came from." The men were turning frantically, holding their weapons out, but not firing.

The two men flailed backwards and fell to the ground. The DEA agent placed her headset on and spoke to the drone operator.

"Somebody's taking them all out. They're moving on Rojas."

Wilkes leaned forward, placing his hands on the desk as he stared at the drone feed. A lone figure ran across the screen, past the four bodies of the narco security detail that now lay dead and motionless in the street.

* * *

From his second-floor window, Trent had a clear shot of all four men. Less than twenty-five yards. Child's play for someone with his experience. He fired four shots from his suppressed rifle within a six-second window. The shell casings landed silently on the soft rug at his feet. He scooped them up and placed them in a zippered pocket while he scanned the streets for movement. Nothing. He was satisfied to see that each bullet had been lethal.

"I'm on the move."

"Copy. I'll bring my car in front of the house on your word," replied Max. Trent was glad to see that he was done arguing that point. At first, Max had insisted on entering the home with him. But Trent was worried about the response time of narco reinforcements.

He grabbed the black bag filled with gear and hurried down the stairs, holding his rifle in front of him, finger pointed forward on the trigger guard. Crossing the dark street, he heard the deep bass notes of the beach resort dance clubs a few blocks away, and the distant rumble of summer storms out over the Pacific. Voices echoed from several floors above.

The sounds of drunken laughter and music. A good sign. It was the sound of targets unaware of his imminent approach.

As he moved, he calculated risk and felt the quick ticking of his internal stopwatch. It was only a matter of time before someone saw the dead men on the street. With half the city on the cartel's payroll, other narcos were sure to come. Trent didn't want to be here when they did.

He crept past the corpses still bleeding and spasming on the sidewalk, scanning the area for threats. The front door was unlocked, as he had expected. In Sinaloa cartel territory, with sicarios guarding outside, why would they lock it?

A moment later, Trent was up one flight of stairs. He could hear one of the narcos in the bedroom. Trent laid down his bag of gear, placed one hand on the doorknob, and readied his rifle with the other.

With one lightning-fast movement, he opened the door, sent a single suppressed shot through the head of the man, and ran forward to cover the mouth of the shocked half-naked woman on the bed, just as she began to scream. Trent tore off a strip of duct tape hanging from his belt and covered her mouth. Then he hog-tied her and left her on the bed.

Trent reshouldered his bag of gear and vaulted up the final flight of stairs. It had been approximately forty-five seconds since he had entered the home. Two minutes since he had killed the men outside on the street. His internal clock continued to tick.

Trent placed the rifle on the floor and removed the large weapon that had been fastened to his back, a rushing sound in his ears as adrenaline pumped through his veins. From the doorway, he couldn't see his targets, but he could still hear them, unaware. Trent stepped out onto the rooftop patio, weapon trained forward.

Incandescent bulbs hung along the outer perimeter of the rooftop, illuminating the area with a dim yellow light. Two couches and several potted plants lined the walls, and a long wooden table rested in the center of the space. An open bottle of wine with two glasses sat on the table. His target was sitting on a chair at the head of the table, with his newly appointed mistress for the evening straddling him, facing away from Trent.

Trent whistled loud.

Both of their faces snapped toward him, and Rojas threw the half-dressed Latina off his lap. The woman instinctively covered herself. Rojas reached for the pistol on the table.

Trent held an M32A1 multishot grenade launcher with two hands, the stock pressed to his shoulder and the wide barrel pointed at Rojas. It was a bulky weapon, painted a drab green, with a round ammunition cylinder similar to a tommy gun. It was designed to hold 40mm grenades, but that wasn't what Trent had loaded into the weapon just now.

As Rojas reached for his pistol on the table, Trent took aim through a holographic sight, its infrared laser designator targeting the man's hairy chest.

THUNK.

A single 40mm blunt-impact projectile round shot into the right side of the man's chest at a speed of 290 feet per second. The round mushroomed on impact, transferring all of its kinetic energy into Rojas's body. This resulted in Rojas departing his feet and flying backward into the air, his arms and legs in trail. He landed hard on his back about five feet away, a motionless heap, breathless on the tiled floor.

The woman screamed.

Trent held a lone finger up to his lips, pointing the weapon at her and advancing in her direction. Trent thought about shooting her too, but these "less-lethal" rounds had once been called "nonlethal." The company's lawyers had insisted upon the change in marketing terminology for a reason—they were known to be unintentionally fatal to a certain percentage of people they hit. Especially at this range.

Trent placed the grenade launcher on the table, walked over to his second nude and screaming woman in the past minute, removed another strip of duct tape, and went to work. He wrapped her mouth until no sound came out. She could still breathe through her nose. He tied her hands and feet together as well.

Trent could now hear Rojas wheezing from a few feet away. Thank God. He would have been pissed if this had all been for nothing.

Leaving the girl tied up, he went to work on Rojas next, quickly using the same duct tape technique to immobilize, blind, and gag him.

Trent unzipped his large black duffle bag and opened it on the floor. He fought his own disgust as he threw the mostly naked man into the bag and zipped it back up.

He brought his boom mike down to his lips. "Max, I'm going to be ready for you at the front entrance in thirty seconds."

Max didn't sound happy. "Uh, that's going to be a problem."

It was at this point that Trent heard the sound of multiple vehicles skidding to a stop on the streets below.

* * *

Max, still in the lot down the street from Trent, counted the vehicles now parking outside the townhome. Five...six...seven if you counted the police car with lights flashing.

Renee was in his ear. "SIGINT is showing massive cartel movements into the area. There are also police coming. But they're on the same radio frequency as the narcos, so I don't think that's good for us."

Max said, "Trent, can you get to the pre-positioned vehicle using your alternate exit?"

"I think so, yes."

"Do it, and let me know when you're safe in the car. If you can get clear, I'll pick up Renee and we'll meet you at the airport. If not, let me know and I'll pick you up at the checkpoint bravo."

"Wilco."

Max said, "Renee, is Wilkes's CIA plane at the airport yet?"

"He just sent me a message about that. He said that there was a problem with the plane. Something about the size. But it's there."

"What's wrong with the plane size?"

"He didn't elaborate."

Max turned on his car and slowly left his lot, turning away from the townhome. In his rearview mirror, he could see the streets rapidly filling up with vehicles.

* * *

Trent could hear the sound of car doors slamming below. Curses echoing through the street. He risked a peek over the stucco wall.

Sonofabitch.

There were too many of them to fight his way back across the street, where his primary egress path lay. Trent counted five trucks. Dozens of heavily armed men, inspecting the dead bodies and looking around.

Trent forced himself to remain calm and think through the problem. The narcos had arrived several minutes quicker than he had anticipated. An unusually fast response. They hadn't yet entered the house. Instead they seemed to be massing outside, preparing to swarm his position with overwhelming force. Wonderful.

Trent pressed the ammo quick-release lever on the grenade launcher and grabbed the other cartridge of ammunition from his bag. This ammunition had the letters "HE" on the sides. High-explosive. He twisted the new ammo cartridge slowly over the cartridge cylinder, like a giant six-shooter from an old western. It fit into place and Trent pressed it in, locking it and snapping it shut.

Trent crept atop the wall again and aimed the bulky grenade launcher at the mass of narco foot soldiers below. He pulled the trigger in rapid succession.

THUNK. THUNK. THUNK.

Ricochets of high-explosive rounds ripped through the streets as Trent unloaded his magazine. Metal fragments shot through vehicles and flesh. After the burst of chaos, the only remaining sounds were the faint moans of the injured. A putrid smell hung in the air.

Trent didn't wait to evaluate the damage. He dropped the grenade launcher where he stood, then squatted down and heaved the zippered body bag containing his prisoner over his right shoulder. Gritting his teeth under the strain, he grabbed his rifle with his free hand and jogged down the stairs and towards the second-floor bedroom.

From the pattern-of-life intel reports they had studied, he knew this was where he would find a custom-built passageway connecting to the adjacent townhome.

Trent found a door behind a standing mattress, which he nudged over with the tip of his rifle. The mattress fell to the floor, and Trent unbolted the door.

He entered the passageway and closed the door behind him just as he heard the first shouts of men entering the narco home.

Now in the adjacent townhome, Trent raced down the stairs, still performing a fireman's carry of his now-squirming prisoner. He ran past a scared-looking family huddled in the kitchen. Two kids behind their mom. A grandma next to them. Trent ignored the family, continuing down to their basement.

Towards the tunnel.

The tunnel was one of many that the cartel had created for quick escapes at several safe houses throughout the city. Human intelligence had revealed the existence of this particular tunnel to Trent's team, and it had been listed in the mission brief as an "alternate extraction route."

He flipped the lights of the basement on and looked around. Cobwebs and a leaking pipe in the far corner. And a large piece of plywood that was nailed to the wall. Trent walked up to the plywood, pounding. A dull, hollow sound.

The tunnel entrance. He pushed it forward and it gave a bit, rotating upward on a ceiling-mounted hinge.

Shouts and screams from above. The sicarios had entered the home. His shoulder-mounted passenger was now doing his best to give muffled shouts through his well-taped gag.

Trent kept his rifle slung over his shoulder and repositioned the body bag so that he was holding it in front of him with both hands. He used the man's squirming, wrapped body as a battering ram as he forced his way into the wooden tunnel entrance, lifting it and moving forward. The wood slammed down once they were through. Rojas would have a few more bruises. Screw him.

But while the tunnel allowed for a quick escape, he expected the narcos to continue pursuit. Trent grabbed a small device from his waist pack and placed it on the floor, careful to position the shaped charge so that it faced the entrance. He set the motion detector and backed away slowly. Then he once again heaved the body bag over his shoulder and ran down the dark tunnel, carrying Rojas toward a faint bluish light that he prayed was the exit.

Seconds later he was stepping through a concrete cylinder eight feet in diameter—the kind used in constructing an underground sewer—with the tunnel exit in view. He forced his way through the thin metal screen at the opening and stepped out into the night.

Trent found himself underneath the highway overpass, a scant few hundred yards from the narco home.

A detonation behind him shattered the still night.

The mine had exploded on the other side of the tunnel. Adrenaline still racing through his veins, he ran to the nondescript sedan that had been pre-positioned under the highway overpass earlier that day by Max. Trent removed the key fob from his pocket and clicked the button, hearing the unlocking sound and seeing the lights flash. Trent opened the trunk and stuffed the man inside, then slammed the lid back down.

He removed his black tactical vest with its heavy SAPI plate and left it on the ground. Then he placed a ball cap on, started the vehicle, and drove. With his spare hand, he reached to his microphone and pulled it to his lips. "I'm moving."

12

Max and Renee arrived at the airport just as Trent pulled in. They were on the opposite side of the main terminal, where only a few business jets were on the unlit tarmac, along with a tiny light-sport aircraft.

"Where's the plane?" asked Max.

Renee said, "Wilkes assured me it would be here."

Trent got out of his car, the sound of a million police sirens in the distance. They each knew that the cartel would be looking for those who had caused all that carnage and kidnapped their man.

"What the hell? What are we doing sitting around with our thumbs up our assess? Where's the CIA plane?"

Max saw a dim green flash from the cockpit of the light-sport aircraft.

"Oh crap."

Max walked over to the tiny plane and sure enough, the door opened, and a man got out.

"You Max?" the man said in Mexican-accented English.

"Yeah."

"Wilkes sent me. Said you need transportation."

The silence of the still night air was interrupted by accelerating vehicles. Max turned to see two black pickup trucks racing along the perimeter of the road.

Trent said, "Looks like they're heading towards the main terminal. We need to get out of here. They'll check here next."

Max nodded, turning back to the pilot. "How many can you carry?"

The short Hispanic aviator looked between the group. "I only have room for one."

Trent, hearing this, carried the squirming body bag with Rojas over to the pilot and dropped it at his feet.

"What...the hell...is *that*?"

"Cargo."

"Hey, man, I'm not taking it by myself. It's going to be a seven-hour flight, with a fuel stop in the middle."

Trent removed a nonaerosol tranquilizer gun from his bag, unzipped the body bag to reveal a blindfolded and gagged Rojas, stuck him in the shoulder, and then zipped him back up.

"That should last him a few hours. He might need another shot before you guys reach your landing spot."

Max looked at Trent. "What do you mean 'you guys'? We won't be able to fit. Listen, Renee and I have a cover here. And I'm...connected. We'll go back to the hotel and make a call to Wilkes and get them to get us out of here."

Trent frowned. "This is not going to be a good place for you to be. If anyone sees you come back right now—"

"We'll be alright. You need to get in and go now, before we get spotted. If Rojas starts squirming, stick him again, but be careful not to give him too big a dose."

"I'm familiar."

Max turned to Renee. "We need to get out of here and back to the hotel immediately."

She looked scared but nodded and got back into the car.

A moment later, Trent was stuffed into one side of the light-sport aircraft with his sedated prisoner sitting on his lap. The aircraft buzzed away to the north.

Max and Renee went to a restaurant near their hotel, grabbed a drink, and then came back to the hotel, laughing and hoping that the concierge got a whiff of alcohol as they made their way up to the suite.

* * *

In the room, Max whispered to Wilkes on the secure phone. Their doors and windows were locked, and Renee sat next to Max on the bed, listening in.

"What the hell happened?"

Wilkes said, "I was going to ask you the same thing. What did you see?"

Max went over the events of the evening from their point of view. Every few moments, a police siren sounded outside, and flashing lights shone through the cracks in the shutters as vehicles sped down the road.

Max said, "You've got a mole, Caleb."

He didn't reply.

"We need protection and evac as soon as possible. Do you have any teams here?"

Wilkes said, "I'm working on it. But you'll need to stay the night."

Max closed his eyes. It wasn't the news he had wanted to hear. Every moment they remained was another inch closer to someone connecting them to a street filled with dead narcos.

"Can't we just use our car and drive to—"

"No." Wilkes cut him off. "They've got road blocks set up everywhere. No one's getting out of Mazatlán tonight."

Renee cursed under her breath.

"Did you get the images Renee sent you of Blanco?"

"I did. We're running them through facial recognition software now. Good work. Just sit tight, guys. We'll have a safe transport for you in the morning."

* * *

After a sleepless night, Max and Renee walked through the hotel lobby. A car was waiting to take them to the airport. While Wilkes was supposedly working on arranging for someone to come pick them up, Max wasn't taking any chances. He'd contacted his father's assistant. A Fend corporate jet, designated for his father's personal use, was due to arrive in Mazatlán any moment.

"Hold up." Max grabbed Renee's arm as a convoy of SUVs, looking very much like the ones from the night before, pulled up outside the hotel.

"Oh shit."

A group of armed men emerged, holding AR-style rifles. Max and Renee turned around, hoping to find another exit. As Max was about to tell Renee to run, a second team of gunmen came in the back of the lobby.

"Cell phones and computers, please," one of them said, holding out an open backpack. Another had his weapon trained on them.

Max and Renee froze.

The man repeated the command, louder, and stepped towards them. Max and Renee gave them their cell phones and Renee removed her computer from her bag, handing it over.

One of the gunmen frisked them both.

At least a dozen narcos entered the lobby and walked towards the ocean view restaurant in the back of the hotel. Max noticed that the concierge didn't seem surprised or worried. Probably the one who had contacted the narcos. Everyone was on the payroll.

A British-accented voice said, "I hope you would consider having breakfast with me. I hear the menu here is excellent."

Max turned to see a very tall white man walk in.

The mystery man. Blanco.

He wore a tailored two-button blue suit, sans tie. A bright white well-starched collar. Polished brown wingtips. Sunken cheeks and piercing gray eyes.

He held out his hand. "Ian Williams. I suppose you can provide that to everyone who must be trying to find out my name right now. And you are Max Fend. Maxwell? Maximus?"

Max shook his hand, keeping his face impassive. "Just Max."

"And you must be Renee LaFrancois? Your beauty precedes you."

The cartel gunmen spread out around the restaurant, collecting cell phones from startled patrons who were eating their breakfast. Two of the narcos headed back into the kitchen. Max recognized what was going on.

Their protectee was a high-value target. They only intended to stay here for a moment and didn't want anyone giving away the location of Ian Williams.

"We were actually just leaving," said Max.

"No, you weren't." Williams's reply was thick with authority. "You were about to have breakfast with me."

His eyes darted between Max and the rest of the room. He licked his lips and scrunched his face when he talked. Some sort of nervous tic. *Something's wrong with this guy's circuit board. Beware.* Max cursed himself for bringing Renee to Mexico.

Ian Williams led them over to a spot in the covered open-air hotel restaurant with a view of the ocean. The waiter appeared at once, looking jumpy. Williams ordered in Spanish, and the waiter left with an expression of relief.

Max and Renee sat completely still. Max re-counted the number of sicarios in the room—twelve. They each carried black semiautomatic rifles and watched the crowd for any sign of a problem, with special attention given to Max. The frightened-looking patrons kept their eyes on their plates. Max could hear the distant sound of the waves crashing against the shore, tropical birds chirping outside, and light music playing over the restaurant speakers.

But no conversation. Everyone was probably too scared they might be slaughtered by whoever this cartel madman was. They knew what happened to those who showed anything but the utmost deference to the cartel kings and knights who traveled the countryside in their armed convoys.

Williams began, "You know I was made aware of your arrival a few days ago. One of my many reports—notables traveling through our territory." He smiled, his gaze darting again with the wild eyes, and a pop came from his lips.

"We've been on vacation."

Williams began shaking his head with short bursts of motion, his pointer finger slicing Max's proclamation into shreds. "People don't vacation here. Not people like you. But I said to myself, Max Fend is a fellow traveler. Let him enjoy the sweet offerings of the Sinaloa beaches.

Sip a few piña coladas. Dip his feet in the water. But then *last night* happens..."

He paused, peering into both Max and Renee's eyes, waiting for a reaction. A deafening, uncomfortable silence. But no reaction. Williams said, "It *stank* of American haughtiness. So, I did what any good investigator does. I thoroughly evaluated all of the information available to me, paying close attention to the details. The devil is in the details, you know, Mr. Fend. We've had very little unusual activity in this area, but for your arrival. That, as I said before, was notable. Not exactly what you and I, being from civilized countries, would say meets the burden of proof, if I were to accuse you of a crime. But, Max... *Max*...I hesitate to inform you and your lovely companion, lest I scare the royal shit out of you both, but my business associates here cut off limbs for much less than the coincidence of timing."

Ian Williams paused again, cocking his head. Getting no response, he continued, "So then, the proximity of your arrival to last night's horrific violence—what am I to make of it?"

The restaurant was deathly quiet. Ian Williams was the Cheshire cat, licking his lips and in need of a psychological evaluation.

"Mr. Williams, I'm sorry, but we're only here on vaca—"

Williams slammed his fists down on the table, the silverware rattling. Then he whispered, "Where were you last night?"

"We went for dinner and drinks," Max answered calmly. He turned to Renee. "What was the name of the—"

Williams clicked his tongue, his head moving side to side again in rapid tiny shakes, an ugly frown forming on his face. "No. Please. Just stop."

Max kept still as an uncomfortable silence resumed. Ian Williams's gray eyes studying his prey. He took a deep breath. "This would go much better for you if you don't play dumb. Do you know who I am?"

Max answered truthfully, "No. Should I?"

"I know who you are. I know all about you, Max Fend. And you, Miss LaFrancois. Not a 'Mrs.' yet? Tsk tsk, Max. Where's the ring?"

Max had to admit that while he was prepared for just about anything

Williams might say to throw him off balance, he wasn't expecting *that* to be a topic of conversation.

Williams smiled for the first time, revealing a crooked and discolored set of teeth. "Never mind. Excuse the poor manners. But, Renee, should you grow tired of his antics, feel free to come visit. I'll show you some proper appreciation."

Renee's face went crimson.

Max shook his head. "Sorry, buddy, but she'd eat you alive. Trust me."

Williams laughed, an awkward-sounding guffaw that revealed more bad teeth. "Let's cut to the chase. An interesting night it was, eh? I must admit that I don't quite yet know what to make of it. I show up and pay a visit to a colleague, Mr. Rojas..."

He paused to gauge the facial reactions of Max and Renee at the mention of Rojas.

"And I happen to find a woman with him who I now know was working as an informant against my employer."

He paused again, watching their expressions. Max was confident in his own poker face. He wasn't so sure about Renee's.

"Now, several events occurred after I removed Miss Sanchez from the premises, resulting in death, dismemberment, and what I suspect to be Hector Rojas's kidnapping by you Americans. Perhaps the DEA, but I doubt it. The CIA? Now why would they be involved? And how warm might I be, *Max*?"

Max shrugged. "I wouldn't know."

Ian Williams said, "But now you tell me that you were out eating and drinking and enjoying this shithole of a country. Okay. Okay. Ah. Here we are. Let us pause..."

Williams's eyes lit up as their food came. Hot plates of tortillas, beans, a red ranchero sauce, limes, and two fried eggs, sunny-side up.

Renee was silent, but Max could feel her unease. She stared at her plate, not wanting to look up.

Max couldn't help himself. "I presume that if you plan to kill me, you'll shoot me, not poison me, right?"

Renee slowly turned to him, horrified.

Williams lifted a glass of juice in a toast and winked in response. "Right you are, Max. Right you are. Eat up."

Max nodded. Then he took one of the tortillas and made it into a sandwich.

Renee looked back down to her plate and closed her eyes.

"Can I also presume that since we're still here, eating in this restaurant and not at some exclusive private residence of yours, you intend to let us go after this conversation?"

Williams nodded. "I can see that you're a man of unmatched deductive reasoning." He swallowed a forkful of food. "Max, we both understand that it is the nature of my business that there will be the occasional unpleasantries such as what occurred last night."

Max could see the two narco gunmen glaring at him, holding their weapons. They were probably friends with the dead.

"But there is a more important matter I need to resolve. I want only to find my associate. It is *imperative* that I find him. Now, my belief is that your arrival here in Mazatlán, and your past employment history, are much too coincidental. But...by the same token, I will grant you that any man of your experience, Mr. Fend, would be a complete fool to stick around after last night's fiasco occurred, if they were indeed a part of it. So, maybe you really were here for innocent reasons? Let me ask you." He looked at Renee. "Both of you. Do you know where my associate, Hector Rojas, is located?"

"I'm afraid we don't," Max answered.

Renee shook her head, "No." Her voice was soft.

Williams just nodded. "I thought so."

Williams turned to one of his gunmen and nodded towards the beach. The gunman headed through the lobby, towards the hotel's street entrance.

Max watched Williams's expression grow dark. He recognized this look. Men like him felt the need to demonstrate power. Whatever was about to happen was a warning.

Heads turned at the sound of a woman's scream. The double doors to the hotel's front entrance flung open as two of the sicarios walked back in, rifles slung over their backs. In their arms, the men carried a bloodied woman. She had deep lacerations along her back and breasts, and her dark hair was matted with dried blood. She swayed and whimpered as they carried her through the hotel lobby and restaurant area, then out towards the beach.

Renee's hand went up over her mouth, and Max noticed her eyes watering. As the men hauled the woman through the restaurant area, some of the patrons let out gasps. But many just looked away, not wanting to be a witness to whatever the narcos might do. Max moved to stand up, but the sicario behind him forced him back into his seat and pointed his weapon at Max's head.

They dumped the woman on the beach, just twenty yards in front of the restaurant, a disturbed flock of seagulls clearing the area as they did. One of the gunmen propped her up on her knees.

Williams said, "Now, I think there's a good way to determine if you are or are not working with the American intelligence or drug enforcement agencies. This woman here, Miss Sanchez. Is she a spy?"

Max didn't answer. Neither did Renee.

Williams nodded, his tone sterner. "Do you know where Rojas was taken?"

No answer.

Renee was beginning to breathe heavy as she watched the woman on the beach kneeling down like she was about to be executed. Williams saw Renee's reaction and leaned towards her. "Miss LaFrancois, I put this girl's life in your hands. Tell me where Rojas is, right now, and you can save her."

Max said, "We don't know. Is this really necessary?"

Williams nodded to one of his men, who came up behind Max fast and placed him in a headlock, pulling him away from the table.

Max knew better than to fight too hard.

Renee was crying. "I don't know. I don't know where..."

Williams used his thumb and forefinger to make a gun shape and then pointed to the girl on the beach.

Several loud shots rang out. There was a collective shudder from everyone in the restaurant, and then quiet. Anonymous weeping and cursing in the restaurant. Angry squirming from Max. But mostly just quiet. The narcos had all the power here.

Max could see Ines Sanchez's lifeless body, now filled with bullet holes. Dark crimson blood painted over white sand.

Williams stood.

"This is the way business is done in this place. There is a code which must be followed. A balance to be kept. Eye for an eye. That sort of thing. If you break the rules...if someone betrays us, this is what happens."

Max glared at Williams. "She was a girl."

Williams shrugged. "The rules apply to everyone. Otherwise we are just a pack of wild dogs." He walked over to Renee and caressed her neck, allowing his eyes to wander. He clicked his tongue. "Still, dogs need to be fed. Fed in all sorts of ways." Williams backed away from her and motioned to his men.

Max was released. The gunman trained his rifle on Max and forced him to sit back down.

Renee, her eyes red and watery, gritted her teeth, saying, "Everyone here saw..."

Williams laughed. "You think that matters here?" He leaned forward. "Now, I don't know with total confidence that you were involved last night. And...let's face it. Max, your father is famous. You can thank him for your safety. It would cause me headaches if you were to go missing. But don't think that because I show you leniency today, this can't happen to you, Max. Or her." He looked towards Renee.

Max clenched his jaw and forced himself to slow his breathing. Control his anger, before it endangered them all. He decided right then and there that someday soon, he would kill this Ian Williams fellow.

One of the guards approached and whispered something in Williams's ear. He looked up and smiled. "It appears that our breakfast has come to an end."

Max could hear a distant rumble of helicopters. Big ones, by the sound of it. Someone whistled, and the Mexican gang emptied the bag of cell phones onto one of the central tables in the hotel restaurant. Then they left the hotel, getting back into their trucks.

Williams pointed to Max and Renee. "For these two, make sure you take their phones and electronic devices with us. Don't give them back."

The man nodded. "*En el auto.*"

Williams rose and said to Max, "If you're working for him, tell Caleb Wilkes I said hello. And tell him that his agent was a delicious lay for my men."

He strode towards the door. Before walking out, Williams turned and yelled, "Max, you have two hours to leave this city. If I see you again, I'll come for Renee and feed her to my men as their next meal."

With that, Williams turned and left.

* * *

Three army-green Chinook helicopters landed on the beach. Dozens of Mexican military troops poured out, marching up to the hotel and securing the perimeter. A man wearing sunglasses, a blue polo, and khakis walked up to Max and Renee.

"You Max Fend?" he asked in American-accented English.

"Yeah."

"Phone call."

He handed Max a cell phone, which he held up to his ear.

"My God, are you two alright?" Wilkes's voice.

"Hello, Caleb. How are you?"

"I got notified you were in cartel custody there and moved as fast as I could. I had to call in a lot of favors to get the Mexicans to send in the cavalry. You're both lucky you weren't chopped to pieces. You have any idea what they do to their enemies down there?"

Max knew he was right, and he was furious at himself for letting it happen. It was reckless of him to bring Renee to Mexico, and even more stupid to come back to the hotel. Not that he'd had a choice. He looked at Renee standing on the pool patio, the wind from the helicopter rotors blowing her dark hair into streamers.

Max noticed that Renee didn't look scared.

She looked *pissed*.

And not at him, for once, which was nice. Max's intuition told him that their little meeting with Ian Williams had cemented Renee's resolve.

Max said into the phone, "We found out Blanco's name. Or at least an alias that you can look up. Ian Williams. We actually just sat down with him. I watched him execute Ines Sanchez, Caleb."

Wilkes swore on the other end of the line. Then he said, "Okay, thank you for letting me know."

"Where's Rojas? When can we get there?"

"Not over the phone."

He was right. Max was stupid to have said that. If the cartels or the ISI were able to hack into this phone call, Max would have just confirmed that Rojas was in US custody. There was no excuse for the error. Max was rattled after witnessing that poor woman's death, and seeing Renee so close to a murderer.

He tried to keep his conversation more vague. "Caleb, I want to see this through."

Wilkes ignored him. "The guy that handed you the phone is DEA. He'll see that you get out of the country safely. And soon. I've assured State Department that you had nothing to do with last night, and that my request to protect an agent in Mazatlán this morning is purely coincidental timing. Keep out of trouble. I'll talk to you when you reach the States. Goodbye, Max."

Max handed the phone back to the DEA man, who said, "I have orders to get you back to the United States. Do you have transportation?"

Max nodded. "It's at the local airport."

Thirty minutes later, Max and Renee were once again flying in his father's private jet, this time north, towards the US. The aircraft cabin was long, thin, luxurious, and empty. Two pilots up front, with the cockpit door closed. Max knew both of them by name. They had been on his father's personal staff for decades. A single steward sat just aft of the cockpit, blending in with the wall, his senses attuned to the tiniest glance from one of his passengers.

Renee and Max sat facing each other near the back of the cabin, out of earshot of the steward. Max said, "I've asked the pilots to fly us to Texas. I'm hoping to get in touch with Trent. Or see if Wilkes will let me join

Rojas's interrogation." He paused. "Are you alright? Look, I understand if you want to head home. We did what was asked."

She had been looking out the window, but now she turned to face him. "I'm with you now more than ever."

Max knew that she was thinking of the female agent executed on the beach, perhaps holding herself responsible. Or maybe she was thinking of Josh Carpenter's little boy. Josh had been killed, in a way, by the same men.

Max said, "I want to find out more about Ian Williams."

"No problem. Give me a few hours once we touch down."

"I just wish we still had our phones," said Max.

"Why?"

"Because I'm getting the feeling that Wilkes is putting us on ice. He used us for what he needed and will use other assets now that he thinks we're a known quantity to Williams."

Renee shook her head. "What's that got to do with our phones?"

"We no longer have the encrypted phones. And you don't have your computer. We needed them so that we could contact Trent and meet up with him. Otherwise we'll just have to wait for Wilkes to decide whether he wants to keep using us."

Renee gave him a funny look.

"What?"

"Max, I made a clone of each phone and uploaded it to my secure cloud storage. I always do that. Same with all of the data on my computer. Come on. What year are you living in?"

"So, we'll be able to contact Trent?"

"Yes. What do you think I'm here for, eye candy?"

* * *

J. Edgar Hoover Building
  Washington, D.C.

.   .   .

Caleb Wilkes sat in the corner of the room, his legs crossed, and mouth shut. He was still a bit groggy from the red-eye to DC, but thankfully he wouldn't need to do much talking. This was the FBI's show. Wilkes was here as a courtesy. He was, however, very interested in the discussion.

Senator Herbert Becker, a member of the Select Intelligence Committee and the Judiciary Committee, was now being interviewed after the mysterious death of his chief of staff. In his preliminary statement to the FBI, Becker had told investigators that he had information related to his chief of staff and Joseph Dahlman, the dead lobbyist.

Senator Becker sat next to his lawyer. His lawyer opened up a leather-bound case and took out a stapled document, which he slid forward on the table.

The FBI agent leading the interview said, "What's this?"

"Please read it."

Three copies were circulated, and Wilkes's eyebrows shot up when he began reading his.

Senator Becker,

If you are reading this, then the worst has happened. I can't tell you how sorry I am.

A few years ago, I became aware that Joseph Dahlman's clients were not simply businessmen representing multinational corporations, as they were initially advertised to you. Dahlman had connections to Pakistan's intelligence agency, the ISI. I should have told you, and I should have informed the FBI. I didn't, because I knew that it could ruin everything we have worked for.

Whoever reads this should know that Senator Becker is innocent of any wrongdoing. He knew nothing of Dahlman's relationship with the ISI. I was overzealous and cowardly. I take full responsibility for any improper actions.

This document serves as my insurance policy against personal harm. If I am killed, it will be sent to Senator Becker. He may do with it what he likes.

The following is a list of names, dates, activities, and bank accounts which implicate me and the ISI in illegal activity.

Ronald Dicks

Wilkes read through the document. He recognized a few of the names. No one stuck out, but they would cross-reference everything against the intelligence files of the CIA and other agencies. The FBI agent handed the document to one of his colleagues, who left the room looking grim. This would reach the director's desk within minutes.

One of the agents in the room muttered, "Seems like the insurance policy didn't work."

The lead FBI agent sat back in his chair and took a deep breath. The whole room sat on pins and needles.

"Let's start with the relationship between your former chief of staff and the lobbyist, Dahlman. Why did they meet?"

"Mr. Dahlman's firm represented business interests that were important to my constituents."

"Important to your constituents?"

"That's correct. They represented companies that did business in Wisconsin."

"What kind of companies?"

"Several types. Health care-focused, mainly. Medical device manufacturers. Pharmaceutical manufacturers. However, I fear that Mr. Dahlman's clients' interests diverged from my own policy stance in recent months."

"How so?"

"I am the coauthor of the Opioid Epidemic Act. It's the most aggressive legislation Congress has ever put forth to fight the opioid crisis in our country. But some pharmaceutical companies fear that the bill will hurt their bottom line. These drugs are very profitable. Naturally, some are upset. But it appears that I was ill-informed on just who these people were, and how upset they had become."

"You thought Dahlman's lobbying firm represented Big Pharma?"

The senator shifted in his seat, looking around the room. "Until I received this letter, this insurance policy from my chief of staff, I believed Dahlman's agency represented multinational corporations that benefited from legal narcotic production, among other things."

"Multinational?"

The senator's lawyer spoke up. "Mr. Dahlman's firm was in full compliance with the Foreign Agents Registration Act, and the senator's campaign contributions were in accordance with campaign finance law. This conversation is about the senator's recently deceased chief of staff. I would ask that we narrow the questions to that subject."

"But while you thought the clients of this lobbyist were—to use your term, multinational—you also knew they were upset with you. What made you think that Mr. Dahlman's clients were upset with your legislation?"

"Ron told me as much." The senator cleared his throat and looked at his lawyer, who nodded. "Approximately three weeks ago, Mr. Dicks received a phone call that threatened the both of us if I didn't change my vote."

Caleb Wilkes leaned forward in his chair, waiting for the FBI agent to dig.

"Threatened you? How so?"

"The man on the phone said that Mr. Dicks and I were likely to be physically harmed. I don't remember the exact wording, but it was vulgar."

The FBI agent looked incredulous. "Did you report this to anyone?"

"No."

"Why not?"

"We didn't take it seriously at first. At the time, I didn't know what was in the contents of this note. I didn't know that these people represented a foreign intelligence service. When we read that Dahlman was shot, Ron and I both were of course alarmed. Ron especially so. But I didn't imagine in a hundred years that..." His voice trailed off. Wilkes could tell the senator was upset.

"Take your time, Senator. Would you like some water?"

"No, I'm fine. You have to understand my position. If the papers get a hold of this, I'll be part of a scandal. And regardless of the fact that I have done nothing wrong, it will hurt me."

Wilkes wrote down a question and handed it to the special agent conducting the interview. The special agent looked at Wilkes and nodded.

Wilkes addressed the senator. "Senator Becker, did Ron Dicks have access to classified intelligence?" Wilkes knew the answer, of course, but he wanted to hear Becker's response.

"Of course he did."

"How often did he access the CIA's high security research room in Northern Virginia?"

"I'm on the Select Intelligence Committee. Ron was crucial in making sure that I was informed on all matters pertaining to my work on the committee. He went to that site regularly to get information and would share the top-level findings with me prior to committee meetings and hearings."

"Do you have any reason to believe he would have shared that information with a foreign national? Or with anyone who wasn't cleared and appropriately read in?"

"If you'd asked me that question a few days ago, I would have said of course not. Now, I'm not sure what to say."

"Thank you, Senator."

Wilkes stayed for a few more moments and then politely excused himself from the interview. The senator seemed truthful. He was a politician, motivated by fear and ambition. But it was Ron Dicks, his senior aide, who had been regularly accessing the classified intelligence that Wilkes now knew contained Ines Sanchez's name.

Ron Dicks had likely passed that information on to Dahlman, who had in turn passed it on to his ISI handler, Abdul Syed. Syed had gone missing two days ago, just before Sanchez was rolled up. Just before Ron Dicks was killed.

Had Ian Williams given the order to Syed to burn down that part of his network? The value of that intelligence stream to the ISI would be incredibly high. Why would Syed agree to snuff out such a valuable asset? What was worth that price?

* * *

Karen landed her aircraft on the runway and taxied up to her hangar. She shut off her engine and finished the checklist as the propeller spooled down. Then she slid open the canopy and removed her headset, long tousles of blond hair falling down over her flight suit.

A black sedan waited in the parking lot behind the chain-link fence. Her father stood next to it, waving. She waved back to him, smiling, and headed his way.

She was glad for the surprise visit. He rarely came out to see her anymore, even when he was home. Especially during a midterm election year like this, his time in Wisconsin was usually packed with town halls and visits to various groups of his constituents.

Karen's coach and agent both walked with her as she made her way from the plane towards the hangar area.

"That's your last run until we perform next week. How did it feel?" asked her coach.

"Good. How'd the spin look from where you were?"

"I think you entered it a bit aggressive."

"It was under control..."

"Karen."

"I'll ease up next time."

Her coach kept talking while she tried to signal her father through the fence. She yelled to her dad, "Give me five minutes!" The senator, who was on the phone now, nodded and gave her a thumbs-up.

Karen's agent, a woman in her late twenties who represented several singers, a touring magician, and two actors, said, "Your conference call with the reporters is tomorrow. I was going to prep you with the publicist."

"Let's do it tomorrow. I'm tired."

The agent pursed her lips. "Fine. I'll call you later."

Aerobatics pilots didn't normally have agents. Karen was the exception. Her looks and family name had gotten her a book deal, and now she was in talks for a possible documentary series. The agent always seemed put off at Karen's lack of interest in publicity. Karen saw it as a necessary evil. But it wasn't rocket science. For the crowds and cameras, she just had to smile and wink and shake what god gave her a little. Her real work was in the cockpit. The agent wouldn't understand.

In the locker room, Karen changed into tight designer jeans with a few tears in them—to make them more stylish. Karen couldn't understand why the three-hundred-and-fifty-dollar jeans had holes in them, but it gave everyone a little more glimpse of her tanned thigh. Not exactly something she wanted to show off in front of her father, but a lot of her fellow aerobatic pilots on the circuit were training here this week too, and maybe she'd join them for beers later.

Seeing her come out to the parking lot, Senator Becker said into the phone, "Gotta go, I'll call you later."

She hugged her father. "What brings the good senator to town? You weren't supposed to be here until next week, when I perform. I just spoke to you on the phone a few days ago. What gives?"

"We need to speak about something."

"About what?"

"Ron Dicks is dead."

"What?" Her mouth gaped open. "Dad, I'm so sorry. How?" Karen saw the look on her father's face. "What's wrong?"

"It's happening, Karen. Just like you said it would."

* * *

"You think it was them?"

Her father nodded somberly. "I do."

He forked a piece of rare steak into his mouth and chewed. The two were alone, other than the two local police officers who were roaming the perimeter of the two-acre property. The senator's two-story home rested on the shores of Lake Winnebago. The police security detail had been arranged after his conversation with the FBI. The authorities were taking the Senator's death threats seriously, while keeping them confidential at the senator's behest.

Senator Becker had cooked a dinner of steak, asparagus, and corn on the cob on his Big Green Egg smoker grill. Cooking was one of his hobbies from a life of calm long ago. The red juices of his steak now covered his plate. He broke off a piece of hard roll to sop them up, then stuffed it into his mouth.

Karen looked out over the lake. A summer storm brewed in the distance, brilliant flashes of lightning branching up through the clouds on the horizon.

"I'm trying not to say I told you so."

"Say it."

She shook her head, fuming. "I'm very sorry about Ron. But he made poor choices by introducing you to these men. So did that wretched woman you had with you."

"Don't bring Jennifer into this. That's not helpful."

Karen turned away. Years ago, she and her mother had come home from a shopping trip to then-Congressman Becker and one of his female staffers in a compromising situation, in this very house. That had led to a quick but painful divorce from Karen's mother.

Karen had forced herself to blame the staffer, a woman by the name of Jennifer Upton. It was easier than blaming her dad. Upton had been toxic. An easy scapegoat in Karen's mind. And while Karen knew her father had his flaws, he also had a great many gifts. He was a master politician. One of the few left who could garner support on both sides of the aisle. A true statesman with a powerful intellect. She knew in her heart that he would be president someday. And she believed he would make a great one.

But while Karen was able to forgive her father and to look past his shortcomings, the ugliness of politics had changed her. Karen had been just out of college back then. Interning on her father's congressional staff, intent on beginning a career in D.C. Then her eyes had been opened to how none of it worked the way it was supposed to. She'd found out what really motivated the people who worked in Washington. Ambition. Power. Truth and principle be damned. Her idealism was soon shattered.

Jennifer Upton and Ron Dicks were perfect examples of this. They were always conspiring together. Bending and breaking every rule. They just wanted to win, no matter the cost.

One day her father, Jennifer Upton, and Ron Dicks had arrived back from an overseas trip. Upton and Dicks acted like they'd won the lottery.

Decided right there on the spot that Becker could run for Senate the next cycle. Some new source of funding that they wouldn't talk about. But it was a game changer.

When she'd confronted him, her father had told her what was going on. He'd always been honest with her. Ron and he had made a deal. Landed a big fish. Some powerful men were going to bankroll him. She had asked if it was illegal. He'd told her no, but she'd known better. He was blinded by his own ambition, and his future was brighter than ever. The group just wanted a little help on some Afghanistan policy proposal, Ron had said.

But it was never that easy. Not with men like these. Before long, Karen had overheard signs of trouble. The mysterious power brokers turned out to have dark connections.

Karen had asked her father to break off all ties with the foreign group. Told him he should go to the authorities and tell them who they were. Jennifer Upton had argued the opposite. The funders' policies were identical to their own. What would it hurt if they were to continue to accept untraceable money?

Ron Dicks was neutral.

That was when Karen had caught her father having the affair with Jennifer Upton. She'd used it as leverage. A moment of rock bottom to snap her father out of his death spiral. She'd given him an ultimatum, demanding that Upton leave, in return for Karen's own silence to the press about the affair. She also demanded that he break off communication with the international group that had been funneling money to his campaign. Her father had probably doubted that she would ever go through with it. And he was right. But the senator was a transactional man, and he knew that he had to give something to his daughter. So, he'd cut Upton loose and promised that he would break off contact with the group.

In truth, it wasn't the affair Karen was trying to stop. She wanted Jennifer Upton's negative influence on her father gone. The next year he had become a senator, and Karen convinced herself that the dark financiers were a thing of the past.

While she'd chosen a career that had nothing to do with politics,

Karen remained politically astute. A savvy strategist, her father had for years tried to convince her to come to D.C. and rejoin his staff, or perhaps go to get a master's in public policy at the Kennedy School. He could easily get her in. But Karen had found flying, and now she wanted little to do with any of that.

"Why are they acting this way now? After all this time..."

"I've turned my back on them."

"You were supposed to have done that long ago."

"I've done it for good this time."

"And they killed Ron for it?"

"And a lobbyist that served as their intermediary."

Karen covered her mouth. "Have you told the authorities?"

"Not everything. But enough. I met with the FBI today. I've told them what they need to know, and that we received death threats. That's why I have a police escort now."

"You received death threats?"

"Ron did. He claimed the threats extended to me. He also left a note. He implicated himself and proclaimed me innocent of any wrongdoing."

Karen studied her father. "Are you?"

He looked hurt. "Of course. I didn't know the details of who these men were."

"That was intentional. Plausible deniability."

"It matters little now."

"I don't understand. Why would they kill Ron? And the lobbyist? What did they have to gain from that?"

"At first I thought they were trying to scare me. To change my vote on a key piece of legislation they didn't like."

"That's behavior I would expect from the mafia."

"You may not be far off."

Karen finished her glass and sighed. "Dad..."

"I know."

"Do you think they're going to come after you?"

"I don't know. I'm still trying to understand their motivations. I fear we aren't dealing with rational actors."

"They know you're done with them because you have no more use for them. Or no more need. Because you're running for president next year, right?"

"There's my smart girl."

"And when that happens, people will start digging into your past like never before. They'll find all the skeletons. So they're getting rid of them. That means eventually they will..." She looked up at her father, too disturbed to finish her sentence.

But her father's look told her that he'd understood. "You're reaching the same conclusion that I did."

Karen sighed, shaking her head. "I warned you that they were bad news."

"I'm sorry. I should have listened."

She shrugged.

"Have you ever spoken to your mother about any of this? Or anyone else, for that matter?"

"Never. You told me not to."

"I've asked you not to do a lot of things, and that never stopped you." Her father smiled.

She laughed. "Well, I listened this time."

"Good. We will be able to get out of this. But no one can know the truth about who these men are."

"What are you going to do?"

"I'm coming up with a plan. It's still a work in progress."

"Be careful."

13

Ian Williams sat on a stone patio, looking out over one of his boss's sprawling family ranches, ten miles from Durango. To the east, steep green slopes formed the backbone of Mexico, the Sierra Madre Occidental. A fiery sunset painted the sky a brilliant red. Williams liked this time of night in Mexico. It was muggy, but peaceful.

The Martinez family was inside, the cartel boss's wife reading to his young children. Armed men in cargo pants and tactical boots roamed the premises, carrying machine guns. Even here, on the home turf of the Sinaloa cartel, they could never let their guard down.

Especially now, when they were so close to the meeting.

As the relatively new leader of the Sinaloa cartel, Ian Williams's boss, Juan Martinez, was already a target to many. The city of Durango, along with Sinaloa and Chihuahua, formed one of the corners of the Golden Triangle, the infamous section of Mexico whose unique climate, elevation, and terrain made it the ideal place to grow most of the poppies that fed America's insatiable appetite for heroin.

Williams would have laughed if someone had told him two years ago that he would end up as head of security in one of Mexico's drug cartels.

After his forced departure from MI6, he had gone to work for a commercial research and strategic intelligence firm based out of London.

He spent six months there, doing opposition research on political candidates and potential corporate board members. But apparently it wasn't enough that MI6 had fired him from that job. The spiteful bastards had gone on to ruin his reputation outside of the agency as well. Word was out. If you hired Ian Williams, you were on their blacklist. And no one in Williams's line of work wanted to anger one of the chaps at the Secret Intelligence Service.

The official break from MI6 had been years in the making. Too many pissed-off members of Her Majesty's Diplomatic Service, and too many unexplained dead civilians.

After his firing, Williams had quickly reached out to his connections in Pakistan's intelligence service. His close collaboration with the ISI had been one of the reasons MI6 had cast him away. He was now ready to cash in on that relationship.

Abdul Syed had arranged for Williams to take a job as a security consultant in Mexico City. But that was just a seed investment. A starting point for Williams to learn the country, grow his network, and infiltrate the organizations that ran Mexico: the cartels.

A glass sliding door opened and Juan Martinez, head of the Sinaloa cartel, walked towards him, whiskey glass in hand.

A national bank vice president at age forty, with family connections to Mexico's upper crust, Juan Martinez would've had no problem continuing his successful and legitimate business career on his own. But Ian Williams had made a livelihood out of luring talented and ambitious men into his web. Martinez was the piece that was missing from the ISI's new operation in Mexico.

Together, Williams and Syed had orchestrated a remarkable coup. It was one of the most swift and complete takeovers of a multibillion-dollar company in modern history. And it was almost completely bloodless. An amazing feat, given the industry norms.

But like many achievements in the world of espionage, it wasn't something that Williams could publicize. Only ten people around the world knew anything about it.

Nine, he reminded himself. One of them had been killed last week, at a park in Virginia.

"Good evening, my friend."

"Good evening, Mr. Martinez." Martinez had told Williams several times to call him Juan in private, but he never did.

The Martinez family had been the aristocratic land owners in Durango for generations. Juan's parents had moved north, to a wealthy housing district near Mexico City, when the cartels had moved into the area. It was ironic that he would end up moving back to the area to run the cartels.

Williams, having quickly grown his book of business in Mexico City, had done work for the cartels and Martinez's bank. Williams had earned the young businessman's trust as an advisor and problem-solver in the areas in which legitimate businesses couldn't easily participate. Money laundering. Bribery. Extortion. A man like Ian Williams had no scruples about being the go-between. And Williams was happy to see that Martinez had the stomach to allow such flexibility.

With his business acumen, his Durango family roots, and his strong personal relationship with Williams, it was time for a promotion.

The Sinaloa cartel had, through a shell company, used Martinez's bank for several large real estate deals in Panama. Syed had helped to influence the bank choice through one of his ISI agents in Mexico. They'd ensured that Martinez's division would be assigned the account.

At first Martinez had wanted nothing to do with the project. He had seen enough of the cartels during his childhood in Durango. With his education and upbringing, why did he need to succumb to a life of crime? It was beneath him. Or so he thought.

But Williams had been hired by the cartel as an external auditor. Behind closed doors, he'd convinced Martinez of the benefits of taking on the job. When he'd seen some of the numbers, Martinez had realized just how obscene the profits were.

Williams had convinced Martinez that he could do better still. *Let us meet with a few of the cartel men, and see if we can't get a bigger piece of the action?* Williams was already connected with one of them.

His name was Hector Rojas.

Soon Juan Martinez, with his advanced degrees and years of experience in banking, saw what Williams had been telling him. The cartel's finances, as big as their revenues and profit margins were, were being run by amateurs. After all the articles that Martinez had read claiming that they were being run like Fortune 500 companies, he now saw what was beneath the hood and knew that he could do better.

Much better.

He was in.

Martinez and Williams soon had their hands in all of the Sinaloa cartel's financial dealings. And the higher-ups in the cartel saw their collective worth. Martinez had made recommendations for improvement that increased the cartel's profitability by billions of dollars without breaking a sweat.

Soon Martinez and Williams were taking personal meetings with the head of the cartel himself, a man named Vasquez. Vasquez liked Martinez immensely, seeing him as reliable, professional, and clean. He didn't use any of the product, he didn't drink, and he valued family. Family, and in particular the loyalty one had to family, was very important to Vasquez.

"Would you like to be part of our family?" The former leader of the Sinaloa had posed the question to Juan Martinez, with Williams standing in the background, almost two years ago.

Martinez, while disciplined and professional, was also ambitious. When he had worked as an executive in a company, he'd had the potential to rise up the food chain and one day lead that company. As a member of one of the cartels, he had now increased his risk due to the nature of the work and stepped off the golden path towards being a chief executive. He related this concern to Vasquez. Vasquez smiled.

"You know men have been killed on the suspicion that they wanted to become what I am. Yet here you are, saying it to my face."

The men had come to an agreement. Martinez would take ownership of and operate the newly formed Durango cartel, a tiny offshoot of the Sinaloa cartel. In return, he would pay a cut to Sinaloa and continue to oversee the operations and finances of both cartels. To the chagrin of Vasquez's family members and longtime partners, Martinez was effectively made second-in-command.

Heir to the throne.

Syed had arranged for Vasquez to be killed during an attempted arrest by the federales one month later.

Williams had been ready for it.

Martinez had been like a favored archbishop finding out that the pope had just died. A scramble. Posturing. Gossip and whispers. Uncertainty. Alliances and plans were made.

Martinez had been panicked. "We must flee. These people don't accept me. My family..."

Williams had forced him to hold his ground. Williams had spent months gathering loyal gunmen from the ranks of Mexican special operations, similar to the way the Zetas had formed their cadre of elite warriors. His first order of business now was to invite the upper echelon of the Sinaloa cartel—mostly members of the Vasquez family—to a meeting at the Martinez family ranch in Durango. He'd summoned them —both as an initial gesture of authority and as a way to get the upper hand.

The Sinaloa cartel was Martinez's now.

Williams had done the talking while Martinez had sat at the head of the table, trying to look unafraid.

"I understand that we are outsiders to many of you," Williams had said, "and I understand that many of you harbor hostility and mistrust towards me. So, I will tell you this: I don't care. Pledge loyalty to Juan Martinez now. Maintain that loyalty. Because I will always be watching you. And you have seen what I do to those who are disloyal. There is only one cartel now. And Señor Martinez owns it."

The meeting had broken up with glares and angry muffled voices. But Williams had been telling the truth when he'd said he would be watching. A few days later, Martinez and Williams had been given audio evidence that the eldest Vasquez brother was plotting against them. Williams had known that they could not have anyone in the family killed.

But to members of the cartels, there was a fate worse than death.

The treacherous Vasquez brother had been found hog-tied on the DEA's El Paso office doorstep. The other family members had quickly gotten the message. They might have harbored an inner hatred for

Martinez, but they understood the omniscient and omnipotent presence of Williams. No one wanted to be extradited to America.

That wasn't to say that Martinez wasn't capable of extreme violence, just like his predecessor. But he was smart about when and how he used violence as a tool. When members of the Tijuana cartel had refused to pledge allegiance to Martinez as the new head of the Sinaloa cartel, he had rightly begun a war. Three hundred Tijuana foot soldiers were dead within the first two weeks. The leader of the Tijuana cartel was found hanging from a streetlight, his eyes gouged out, a fireman's axe lodged in his chest.

Like a publicly traded company wanting to appear financially healthy to its shareholders, Martinez needed to appear strong to the masses who propped up his empire. The cartels who would join him, and the thousands of employees beneath him. Each of them feared and respected strength. It was that healthy fear that maintained order in a business enforced by violence.

Williams now sat on Martinez's patio. As the alcohol relaxed his mind, he reveled in his achievements. He was the puppet master, and his puppet was the head of the largest drug cartel in the world.

The world was his oyster.

As Williams waited for Martinez to join him, he considered his empire. It was quiet here on Martinez's ranch. Meanwhile, the violent machine that Williams had conquered continued to thrum along. Growing. Producing. Transporting. Selling. Killing. Repeat.

Men and women sweating in the fields and jungles, growing the plants. Just miles away from where he now sat, Williams had observed one of the cartel's many production fields that afternoon. He had watched as peasant farmers slowly drifted through an endless field of poppies, slicing multiple incisions into each one. From these incisions, a liquid would drip down, to be painstakingly collected by the farmers over the next few days. That was the nectar that would be transformed into heroin.

Creating and selling heroin, meth, and cannabis was a business. Williams and Martinez treated it as such. Their bustling transportation network shipped tons of product into the US each day. Williams had taken from his experience in Afghanistan to help the cartel succeed.

Working with the suppliers to the south and in Asia. Managing the sales and distribution network in North America. Paying off the police and politicians. And then there was his security and intelligence apparatus. Williams had insisted on improving the latter. Muscle was nothing without knowledge. Williams had hired experts from around the world to improve his security, and to make sure that nothing that could affect his business happened without him knowing about it.

Martinez sat across from him. Williams presented Martinez with a manila envelope. Inside was a news clipping—an article from the *Wall Street Journal*.

"Two dead?"

Williams nodded.

"Was that really necessary? It seems risky."

Williams shrugged. "A message needed to be sent."

Martinez frowned. "What of Rojas?"

"My sources tell me he is in Texas. I should have a location soon."

"Rojas's kidnapping wasn't approved by the Mexican government. I assume our politicians are raising the appropriate objections over this breach of sovereignty?"

"They are."

"Why would the Americans want Rojas this badly? Is he worth such a breach of protocol? Is this all just to get to me?"

Williams smiled inwardly. While Martinez was a very bright business-man, he was not immune to the paranoia that came from being at the top of a criminal enterprise. "Perhaps. With your permission, I would like to see if we can't retrieve him."

"On American soil?"

"It will be carefully planned. Only my best men."

Martinez frowned but nodded his approval.

Williams took another sip of whiskey, looking off into the now-darkening night sky.

14

Max and Renee had landed in Austin, Texas earlier in the day. Max got them a room at the Westin while Renee went to the store to buy phones and gear.

Max had sent a message to his virtual assistant, a high-end private service he used to keep his black book contact list updated and handle anything from transportation to confidential communications. The service had promised to have Max's beloved Cirrus SR-22 flown to Texas within the next twenty-four hours. The pilot was instructed to land it at the Austin Executive Airport, pay for parking, fill it up with gas, and find his own transportation home.

Renee had come back to the hotel with boxes of Apple products—a MacBook Pro and two iPhones. She had set up Max's phone, making sure that it had her security software installed, and then they promptly called Trent.

It went to voicemail. They tried several more times throughout the day before he finally called back in the evening.

Trent said, "Where are you guys? Wilkes told me it got a little rough."

"It did, but we're good now. Where are you at?"

"Can I talk on this line?"

Hearing this, Renee gave Max a thumbs-up.

"Renee says we're good."

"Roger. As soon as we landed, they brought in one of those HIG teams to work the guy over. The interrogation team is doing their thing now."

The High-Value Detainee Interrogation Group (HIG), formed in 2009 as a way to combat terrorism, was filled with the nation's most elite interrogators. Members were pooled from the CIA, FBI, and other governmental organizations.

Max found it interesting that Wilkes was able to get permission to use a HIG team in this situation. Was that because of the counterintelligence angle, with the ISI being involved? Or was there something Wilkes wasn't telling them?

Trent continued, "The dude seems scared shitless. Says his boss will have him and his family killed if he talks. But one of the interrogators made a bet with me after the first session that he'd crack within the first day. So it looks good. Are you guys coming down? Wilkes told me I can get out of here...but we're in the middle of nowhere and I don't exactly have a ride. One of the feds is making arrangements for us to stay at a local hotel. They've got a mobile unit set up for the interrogations but that's it. I slept in the hangar last night."

"What's your location? I'll come get you."

"We're on the coast, in between Houston and Corpus Christi. Someplace called Calhoun County Airport."

"We'll fly in tomorrow morning."

"Sounds good. This thing should still be going on. You'll see the eighteen-wheeler with the black SUVs surrounding it. Can't miss us."

* * *

Max and Renee flew to Calhoun County Airport on the coast of Texas the next morning. Trent was right. The airfield was small and desolate. Just a sheet-metal hangar, a handful of general aviation planes, and farmland in all directions. The Gulf of Mexico was a few miles to the southeast. Greenish-blue waves, the beaches filled with tourists.

They touched down and Max taxied the Cirrus to the flight line. Max threw the chocks under the wheels and walked towards the cordoned-off section at the far end of the airport. Men in black, with sunglasses and semiautomatic rifles. A miniature Area 51, right here in Texas.

"Can we help you, sir?" one of the government men asked. The other studied Max and Renee, his hand held loose outside his holster.

Max explained who he was and tried to convince them to let him pass.

The two men looked at each other in confusion. One said, "Sir, this is a restricted area. Please move along."

Max understood. To them, he was just some random stranger with a story. Their job wasn't to let people in, it was to keep people out. He thanked the guards and walked away, taking out his phone while he dialed Trent. "They won't let me in."

A moment later, one of the doors on the mobile interrogation unit swung open and Trent exited. "Gents, they're with us."

The guard swore, looking like he was debating it, but said, "I'd need to hear it from my superiors."

It took about ten minutes of phone calls and arguing. Wilkes was pissed that Max had flown out there. "Next time you better tell me what you're up to," he said. But he made arrangements for Max to enter the interrogation unit.

Walking up the ladder into the large trailer, Max asked, "Where's Wilkes, anyway? Why isn't he here himself?"

"I don't know. He said he had to take care of something else in D.C. But he's monitoring all the reports out of here."

They stepped into a dark, quiet room. Swivel chairs screwed into deck plates on the ground. Two men with clipboards and pens sat in the chairs, listening to the prisoner's interview. They glanced back at Max and Renee, shrugged, and turned back towards the show. A single two-way mirror showed the interrogation room. Sound was being pumped into this section of the trailer via overhead speakers. Rojas sat at a table across from a black man of about fifty—the interrogator.

"What else did you find out?" Max whispered.

"Shh." One of the men with a clipboard placed his finger over his mouth.

Max, Trent, and Renee scooted to the far end of the small space and watched some of the interrogation.

Rojas and the interrogator were conversing in Spanish. Max caught a few words, including Ian Williams's name, but that was about it.

Max and Trent whispered as quietly as they could manage.

Trent said, "He says Ian Williams, the tall white dude that snatched Wilkes's agent in Mexico, has his own agenda. Rojas here claims that Williams influences Martinez, the head of the Sinaloa cartel, to the point of controlling him. He lets Martinez make the legitimate business decisions on production schedules and pricing and all that...but the Brit is the one who handles the darker side of the business. I was surprised to hear he was from the UK."

Max said, "Yeah. Renee dug up some info on him. Ian Williams is former MI6."

Another shush from one of the clipboard men and Trent took the hint. "Let's talk outside for a bit. I'll get you caught up and then we can come back in." The three of them went back into the warm Texas sun, walked past the guards, and towards the flight line where Max's aircraft was parked. They walked about two hundred yards and sat near an empty picnic table on the far side of the airport's only hangar, the only place with shade. The hangar and flight line were empty. An orange-and-white barricade blocked the street entrance that led to the airport, with a state trooper's car parked next to it.

"So Ian Williams was MI6?"

"Yeah. Crazy, right?"

"And he's worked for the cartels for what, a year?"

"Something like that."

"He used to work in Afghanistan and Pakistan for MI6, but got removed for some type of scandal."

"What happened?"

Renee said, "The details weren't available. But the little I could find implied that it involved being too cozy with Pakistani intelligence."

"Very interesting," said Trent.

Max looked back at Trent. "Did Rojas know anything about the man that was killed in Virginia?"

Trent said, "To be honest, I had a hard time following that one. As you saw, the interrogator was speaking in Spanish, and mine is only passable.

You might want to ask the interrogation team or see if Wilkes will show you the transcripts. What I think I heard was that Rojas confirmed Williams has a hit list that he's working his way through before this big VIP meeting they've got coming up. Rojas thinks that this guy who was assassinated in Virginia was on the hit list."

"Why does he think that?"

"Because Rojas overheard a conversation between Williams and someone else, talking about the first name in the list being in D.C."

"A phone conversation or in person?"

"I assume phone, but I didn't catch that. Sorry, man, I'm operating on fumes here."

"I thought you were special operations," said Renee, smiling.

"I retired. Now I take naps," Trent said.

Max noticed that the silhouette of the driver in the state police vehicle was no longer visible. Odd. He had been there a moment ago, and Max hadn't seen him exit the vehicle. He made a mental note of it and pressed Trent further.

"Who else is on the list?"

"Rojas says he has another name but was negotiating for something in return. The interrogators are doing their thing, trying to get everything they can before they start promising him stuff. Rojas is trying to see what leverage he has. A few hours ago, he said he didn't have any names, and that he didn't know anything about the Pakistanis."

"So what's with the meeting? When is it, what is it?"

Trent held up his hand, his eyes squinting back towards the end of the airfield. Max heard the sound of shouting coming from the interrogation unit's trailer.

Max turned to look, saying, "What is it?"

A sudden metallic boom thundered through the air.

* * *

Trent was peering around the corner of the hangar in seconds, his pistol drawn. Max and Renee were slower, deafened and stunned from the explosion. Trent turned back towards them and mouthed something, but Max couldn't make out what he was saying, his ears ringing.

Then he saw Trent pointing towards Max's plane.

"What's going on?" he heard Renee ask, the sounds of the world returning.

Max crept to the corner of the hangar and looked in the direction Trent was pointing. The mobile interrogation unit was a burning heap. Its roof was completely missing, and most of its trailer wall was torn away. Ripped, singed metal, dust, and at least one hunk of flesh on the ground nearby.

Trent said, "One o'clock. See 'em?"

About one hundred yards beyond the blast site, three oversized pickup trucks had veered off the highway and were now bouncing over the grass field surrounding the airport. The trucks were heading towards the burning wreckage of the interrogation trailer.

Trent said, "How quick can you get us out of here in that thing?" He was again pointing to Max's Cirrus, which was only fifty feet away.

"What about the people in the trailer? Is there anyone still alive?" Renee asked. She winced as the loud, rapid rattle of heavy machine-gun fire echoed over the airfield. Men in the pickup trucks fired at the two government SUVs parked near the interrogation trailer. Pops in the metal and shattered glass as bullets riddled the vehicles. Max didn't see any return fire. At least two bodies on the pavement near the vehicles. Neither moving.

Max looked around the airfield, trying to identify all their options.

Max turned to the airport entrance and saw the state police vehicle still sitting there, its blue lights off, with no sign of a driver. Max could just barely make out a spiderweb crack in the rear window.

If anyone was left alive in the police vehicles, they were going to be killed soon. The same was true for anyone left alive in what remained of the smoking trailer. Trent had a single handgun, as did Max, but his was still in the plane. Their enemy had them outnumbered and outgunned, and they had too great of a head start.

If they were going to live through the next few minutes, they had two options. Hide and hope the attackers didn't make their way over to them, or run to the Cirrus and get airborne before the gunmen saw them.

Performing calculations and risk assessments in his head, he made a call. "You're right. Let's head to the plane."

The trio sprinted to the Cirrus. Max grabbed the chock off the pavement, opened his door and let Renee throw herself into the rear seat. Trent hopped next to Max in front. Max started it up as fast as he could.

"They see us yet?"

"Not yet, I don't think."

The aircraft's parking spot on the ramp had been near the runway midpoint. He cursed to himself. With a runway this short, three passengers and a high-density altitude, he would need to use the full field for takeoff. But as soon as he started taxiing, he was sure to draw the gunmen's attention. He didn't have a choice.

Max throttled the engine and they began rolling forward on the taxiway, towards the far end of the runway.

"What about now? Are they following us?"

"I can't tell," Trent replied, careening his neck and looking back through the side windows of the plane.

Renee leaned forward from the backseat and opened Trent's door, peeking her head out to look behind them. She immediately flung herself back in and latched the door.

"Hurry up," was all she said, her face pale.

Max tapped the brakes to slow down in the turn, then pressed forward on the right pedal to bring the aircraft around to face the runway centerline, switching his flaps to fifty percent.

To his horror, he saw not one but two pickup trucks racing towards him down the taxiway. They were still a good half-mile away, but that would change fast. Still turning, Max immediately pushed the throttle all the way forward, felt and heard the 310-horsepower engine ramp up.

The airspeed was picking up. Fifty. Sixty.

He glanced to his left and watched the pickup trucks change bearing and turn as they overshot their mark. He could make out silent yellow flashes of gunfire in his peripheral vision.

He pulled back on the stick as the Cirrus hit its seventy-knot takeoff speed.

The ground dropped beneath them, and Max banked sharply away, climbing and accelerating to safety.

Renee squeezed Max's shoulder. His heart was pounding. The geometry had been in their favor, but barely. The gunmen had been only a few seconds away from having a much better shot.

Trent put on his headset and keyed his mike. "Someone really needs to teach those mooks how to lead the target."

15

They landed at David Wayne Hooks Airport, near Houston, less than an hour later. After talking about it during the flight, Max made the decision that they would not call Wilkes to check in.

At this point, they didn't know who they could trust.

They got fuel at Gill Aviation, the local FBO, and Max checked over the weather, still deciding where they should go next. Trent used the showers and changed into a pair of spare clothes Max lent him. Renee sipped hot tea while working on her computer in an empty pilot's lounge. The two men joined her in there after a while, and Max closed the door.

Max figured that Wilkes had probably been calling and texting each of their phones after the attack, but Renee had mandated keeping all cell phones off until now. She didn't want the devices pinging cell towers along their route. Despite her confidence in the security program she had installed on their hardware, none of them were one hundred percent sure how the hit team had located Rojas.

Renee said, "I ran some checks. I'm ninety-nine point nine percent sure that it wasn't us. It's extremely unlikely that anyone could have been eavesdropping on our calls or tracking our devices."

Trent looked at Max. "How well do you know Wilkes?"

Max shook his head. "I don't see it. Why would he have us go through all that down in Mexico, just to set us up?"

"Then who talked?"

Max said, "I don't know."

"Ian Williams knew about Wilkes's Mexican agent. And now a professional hit team takes out an interrogation unit and their prisoner on American soil. Both of these events have Wilkes as the tie-in. So I ask you again, how well do you know him?"

Max shook his head. "I'm not disagreeing with you that there's a leak. I'll grant you it's possible that Wilkes was even responsible for it. But since we don't know how many people were read in to both operations, none of us can say that with any confidence."

Renee spoke gently. "What do you think, then?"

Max said, "I suspect that if Wilkes was hunting a mole, he might have let them get *some* information on purpose."

Trent looked sideways at Max.

Renee said, "Why would he do that?"

"You remember last summer in Florida, Renee. Wilkes didn't tell us the whole truth until we absolutely needed to know. As good as Caleb Wilkes is at his job, he views his assets as expendable. He told me that he wanted to find out why the Sinaloa cartel and Pakistani intelligence were working together. What if that wasn't his real objective? Or what if it wasn't his *only* objective?"

Max saw Renee's eyes moving as she worked through the problem. "You think he's purposely allowing leaks of our operation to occur so that he can achieve a different objective. What, then?"

"I can think of three reasons. One is what's called a blue-dye operation."

Trent massaged his tired eyes with his thumb and forefinger. "Enough with this spook shit...this is why I said no to the CIA recruiter when I retired from the Army. I just want to shoot bad guys. Not have to wonder if they're really bad guys or not..."

Renee said, "I'll bite. What's a blue-dye operation?"

"It's when you have a leak and don't know where it is, but you're able to see your adversary's reaction, or maybe even what information they receive. So you insert multiple variations of some important story into the information stream. Whichever variation shows up in your enemy's inbox, that's the version your mole heard. You can use this technique to narrow down your field of suspects."

"But it requires you to provide information to a mole."

"Among others, yes. Normally one would provide information that isn't harmful to an ongoing operation. But the juiciest worms make the best bait."

Renee said, "You said there were three reasons why Wilkes would knowingly leak information. What are the other two?"

"The second reason is that he may already know who the mole is. He could be intentionally leaking information to suggest to the mole's handlers that the mole is still reliable, with the eventual intention of using the mole to provide false or misleading information."

Trent said, "I'm gonna say that's not what's going on here, based on the fact that we almost just got blown up. He wouldn't have done that intentionally. Right?"

Max nodded. "Agreed. I highly doubt Wilkes would have knowingly risked an attack on Rojas."

Renee said, "And the third reason?"

"I could be wrong about the whole thing. Wilkes could be the enemy."

The group turned their attention to the buzzing phone on Renee's armrest. She had powered it up while they were talking.

She looked at the caller ID. "It's him. Wilkes."

* * *

Max lifted up the phone and answered.

"Where have you been? Are you with the others?"

Max ignored the question. "How did they know where Rojas was being held, Caleb?"

"We're working on that. We think the ISI may have access to some very high-end satellite tracking tools. It's possible they tracked our aircraft from Mexico to the US. We thought we were being careful, but if the cartels and the ISI are coordinating that closely...Syed may have passed the location along."

"To Williams?"

"Yes. The FBI thinks the Sinaloa cartel flew in a squad from Mexico to do the wet work, using local gang members as support. The gear was Mexican military-issue. They used an antitank weapon on the HIG team's trailer. Are you guys alright? I assume both Trent and Renee are with you?"

The second time he'd asked that question, Max noted. Out of concern? Or to gain intel? Max kept his voice steady.

"Caleb, I think we're just going to lay low for a while."

A pause.

"Max, there are new developments. I appreciate the danger you were in, but I'm afraid I need you guys to find someone for me."

"What new developments?"

"We got a new name from Rojas. I need this person located and brought in ASAP."

Max looked at the others in the room, both of whom could hear the conversation. Max could see that they shared his concern about going on another of Wilkes's assignments.

"Caleb, twice in the last week, we went where you told us to be. Both times, someone nearly had us killed."

The phone went quiet. When Wilkes finally spoke, his tone was softer. "I understand your concern. I hope you trust me enough to know that I value the well-being of each one of you."

"Like you valued your Mexican agent? The woman?"

Trent turned away. Renee didn't flinch.

Wilkes said, "That was unfair. Do you really think I don't regret that?" His tone showed a rare burst of emotion.

"I'm sorry. But you understand where our apprehension is coming from here. Caleb, there must be hundreds of capable people that could go find this person for you. Why do you need—"

"*Because we had a leak.* Why do you think I used you that night at Wolf Trap? Why do you think I needed you to go to Mexico? I was trying my damnedest to get this thing done without tipping off our mole. I apologize that it didn't work out so well."

There it was. Max understood why Wilkes was so frustrated. He couldn't use just anyone for this. He needed to keep the information tightly controlled. Everything that had been reported through the normal intel streams had been leaked. That was how his agent had been killed in Mexico.

But something still tugged at Max. Over a decade of instinct, telling him that Wilkes wasn't being completely transparent. He pushed the thought aside for the moment.

"You say you had a leak. Past tense. You've found the mole?"

"It looks that way," said Wilkes.

"Who?"

"The day before yesterday I sat in on an interview at the FBI. The man was a political aide named Ronald Dicks. He had access to classified intelligence, including the cryptonym and area of operation for Ines Sanchez. Ron Dicks likely passed information to Joseph Dahlman, the lobbyist you saw killed, who in turn passed information to the ISI."

"Damn. So you think Syed knew her identity before we even went down there?"

"Or at least provided Ian Williams enough information to figure it out for himself."

Max looked at the others. "Caleb, please give us a moment, I'm putting you on mute."

Max pressed the mute icon on the phone. Trent and Renee looked back at him.

"Are you guys convinced? We've been burned twice in the past two days. If either of you wants to walk away, I'll tell him to pound sand."

Renee stood with her arms folded, biting her lip. "I don't think Wilkes meant us any harm. And I assume that if he wants us to do something—to find this person Rojas mentioned—it must be important to stopping Ian Williams. If that's the case, then I think we should do it. I think we should continue to help."

Max suspected that Renee was thinking of Ines Sanchez's corpse, lying on the beach.

Trent said, "You know I'm up for it." In Trent's eyes, Max saw an eager willingness to continue the fight.

"We don't know that this will lead to Williams."

Trent shrugged. "I'll go anyway." His was a thirst that would never be quenched. A quest for revenge. One in which any satisfaction attained would be hollowed out by the sadness of loss.

Max nodded and unmuted the phone. "Alright, Caleb, we're in. But I do have one question. If Ron Dicks is the source of your leaks, and he's dead, why do you still need us to find this person for you?"

"Speed and operational security. We're on tight timeline. You know the mission details and the players involved. You've got a team read in. I don't have time to brief a new set of operators. And this is still being run out of the CIA's counterintelligence division. The more people we involve, the less secure it gets. Because of that, I want to keep this operation within a very small crew."

"What's the timing?"

"We already knew that Ian Williams and the ISI were preparing for an important meeting. This meeting, we believe, is also the deadline to complete their kill list. Rojas gave the HIG team a date. We don't know where, and we don't know with who, but he said that Ian Williams's big meeting was going to be held on the twenty-eighth. So we can assume any further hits will be executed by that time."

"That's only a few days away."

"Correct."

"May I ask why you aren't trying to find this person yourself?"

"I'm headed to Oshkosh."

Oshkosh? Max frowned. He looked at his watch to check the date. This was the last week in July. Each year at this time, the Experimental Aircraft Association hosted the largest air show in the world at Oshkosh, Wisconsin. Max's father had taken him there countless times when he was a boy.

"Why Oshkosh?"

"Rojas gave up two names before he was killed by his own men in Texas. It was a partial list, he said."

"Of Ian Williams's kill list?"

"We believe so, yes. Two on the list are already dead. Joseph Dahlman and Ron Dicks, our mole."

"Who are the other two?"

"One is a US senator. Herbert Becker, of Wisconsin. He'll be in Oshkosh this week. His daughter is one of the performers. And he's the reason I'll be in attendance. My view is that he's the highest-priority target."

"My father knows him."

"Does he?"

"Yes. They've golfed together, I believe. I actually know his daughter too."

"I see."

"You've informed him that he's in danger?"

"He was already aware. Ron Dicks was his chief of staff. It was his interview I sat in on at the FBI headquarters. He's accepted additional security but refuses to go into hiding. I want to personally monitor his security while we try and find out what Williams and the ISI are up to. If the senator is on Williams's hit list, then we know where they'll be headed. If we can take down one of their hired guns, perhaps that can lead us to one of our targets."

"What's the last name on the list?"

Wilkes said, "This is the person I need you to locate."

"Who is he?"

"It's a she. Jennifer Upton. She's a political operative. Forty-seven years old. Single. She is based out of Cincinnati, but during my cursory attempt to locate her, I've learned that she hasn't been seen during the past twenty-four hours. She was once an aide to Senator Becker, and worked with Ron Dicks. No known connection to Dahlman."

"Why would Ian Williams want to kill her, or the senator?"

"It seems that the ISI is wrapped up with some group of investors in the opioid industry. Senator Becker was once a champion of the pharmaceutical industry but has shifted many of his political stances. My analysts tell me that this is in preparation for a future presidential run. He's now the cosponsor of a bill that will gut the legal opioid industry's profits within the United States. We're talking billions of dollars."

"So Ian Williams and the ISI want to kill the Senator to what...cancel his vote?"

"Possibly."

"If they kill him, does the bill die?"

"Possibly."

"But it sounds like you're talking about legitimate businesses here. A big corporation wouldn't be involved in something like this. It would be financial suicide."

"Agreed. We don't fully know the ISI's involvement yet, or how it plays into the legal opioid marketplace. My understanding is that the Big Pharma companies are not directly involved in this themselves. The ISI seems to be working with a group of shadow investors."

"What about this woman you want us to find, Jennifer Upton? Why would Williams want her dead?"

"That's what I need you to find out. I suspect she's our missing piece. My hope is that she'll be able to illuminate much that we currently don't know."

"Does she know she's in danger?"

"I don't know, considering that we've yet to make contact. But assuming you're able to locate her, your top priority is to bring her in and get her to a safe house. Once you do that, contact me."

"Williams may already believe that we have her name, since we spoke to Rojas."

"Correct. This all assumes that she hasn't been killed already. The fact that she's out of reach right now could mean either that she's dead or that she's gone underground. Consider this me being optimistic. Please do what you can to find her."

16

The assassin had used many names over the years, but Hugo was his name by birth. He'd first killed a man at the age of sixteen. For revenge.

Hugo's father had taught him how to hunt in the wilderness of Quebec. Together, they'd shot black bear, white-tailed deer, and moose. Some of their hunting trips would last days, involving deep treks into the forest using snowshoes. That had made hauling the animal carcasses back to their home difficult. But often the most difficult tasks in life could be the most rewarding. Especially when conducted in the company of one's father.

Their town was very small. Everyone knew each other. The winters were long and harsh.

Sometimes hellishly so.

One afternoon, Hugo and his father were returning from a hunt when they heard screams coming from their home. They left the sled that carried their prize and hurried into the house.

Hugo's mother was on the bed and on her back, eyes wide and face battered. The town drunk stood over her, holding a large curved blade. The man was a thuggish brute who had been thrown in the town jail twice for assault.

Hugo's father ran to the man but was cut down, blood pouring from his wounds. Hugo tried firing his hunting rifle from the hip but missed. The drunk ran out of the home, and Hugo tended to his father's wounds. But they were too deep. His father was dead within minutes. Hugo called the police and an ambulance. They took his mother to a hospital and apprehended the town drunk.

Hugo's mother was a mess, crying hysterically at the loss of Hugo's father. The local prosecutor wanted to interview Hugo and see if he would testify in court. But Hugo had no intention of letting the courts decide the fate of his father's killer. It was a small town. And Hugo knew the cops. His killer would be transferred to a larger prison the next day, so Hugo had to act fast. When the jailer went to the bathroom, he left the jail cell master key set on his desk. Hugo took his hunting bow and seven arrows with him.

From a range of less than ten feet, he unloaded the arrows into his father's murderer. Shafts of death plunging into his flesh. The screams of pain lasted only a moment as the arrows entered his lungs and made it too hard for the man to make a sound.

It looked incredibly painful.

It was immensely satisfying.

That night, Hugo took out several thousand dollars from various ATMs—his life savings—bought a ticket from Quebec City to France, and disappeared.

A few weeks later, he would join the French Foreign Legion under an alias, and his real training would begin. Hugo spent ten years in the Legion, traveling to various parts of the globe. He became an expert soldier, deploying to Afghanistan and several nations in Africa.

It was in Africa that he'd been approached by his first private employer. Half a month pay for two hours of work, he was told.

Hugo shot a man who hours earlier he did not know. Even when he was killed, Hugo didn't know his name, only a face and an address. He placed two bullets into his chest as he entered his home. Then one bullet in his head, before he walked away.

The employer appreciated the quick, reliable work, and Hugo found that he would rather become a contract killer than stand any more guard duty for a nation he wasn't particularly loyal to, on a continent he didn't care for. But it was Africa where he stayed, for a time. Working for another two years, refining his technique and gaining experience, before being picked up by the European placement agencies. That was where the real money was. Russian, Turkish, and Italian organized crime seemed to have a never-ending desire to kill each other off. And they were willing to pay top dollar to do so.

Eventually, the Pakistanis found him, and Hugo became exclusive.

Most assassinations in first-world countries required creating as much separation from the crime scene as possible. But killing someone this close to Washington, D.C., had been a unique challenge. The security cameras and sophisticated tracking technology put in place to track terrorists meant that any movement Hugo made would be a potential red flag to American government eyes. The Ron Dicks assignment had taken twelve hours to plan, and six hours to execute. Other than that, Hugo stayed put in D.C., remaining in the same rental unit he'd secured a week earlier. Enjoying the sights. Going to bars and restaurants.

It was in this small flat near Dupont Circle that he'd received the most recent message from Syed, his Pakistani contact. The main job. The reason that the ISI had sent their most prolific international assassin to the States.

Hugo had gone to the dead drop site and picked up his message within three hours. At the dead drop, he obtained another of their special thumb drives. After returning to the flat, he connected the thumb drive to his computer and entered the passphrase, which then brought up a series of screens. A sort of timed quiz, one in which he had to answer each question quickly and correctly or else the information would self-delete, which it would do anyway after thirty minutes.

When he was finished, he read over the file. It was a mission brief. The Pakistanis were playing a dangerous game by being this bold. But that wasn't his decision to make. The fee was very good, and that was what mattered.

Hugo deleted the files and then checked his watch. He would sleep here tonight, then fly out in the morning.

To Wisconsin.

* * *

Ian Williams's convoy pulled up to the Gulfstream, his security men eying their surroundings as he walked up the ladder to the jet and got in.

His assistant handed him a phone.

"It's him."

Williams nodded. They used the best antitrace software and encryption programs. The hardware was purchased in China and flown over by Williams's men. He didn't trust American companies. Williams had heard too many rumors of NSA agents embedding their own little surprises into US-sold devices.

But even with all that sophisticated technology, Williams never spoke to Syed directly over the phone. Too high a risk of the world's intelligence agencies listening in.

For calls to his ISI handler—business associate might be a better description of their current relationship nowadays—Williams used a system of trusted voice-relay personnel. Handwriting messages, holding them up to be read aloud over the phone. Even using this procedure, phone calls were rare forms of communication for the two as the climax of their ambitious plan drew near.

A woman's voice—Pakistani with a British accent, Williams thought—said, "We are worried that recent events may bring unwanted attention."

Williams scribbled something on a pad of paper, which would be placed in a burn bag as soon as they were finished. When he finished writing, his assistant read it aloud into the phone. It was a dreadfully tedious way to communicate. But it kept the conversation secure and anonymous.

"It was regrettable but necessary."

"The meeting is imminent. Will we be ready? How many more names do you have on the list?"

"That work will be finalized on location. We are sending our best people to complete the task."

"We have received word that some of the participants don't want to go. They are nervous about travel to America."

"Please assure them that we've chosen this venue carefully. The meeting location keeps everyone safe and ensures peace during the negotiation process. Use the secure entry points and procedures as directed. Arrival inspections won't be a problem. There will be ten thousand flights in and out of this airport in a few days' time. Passenger manifests can be manipulated. Security will be lax. And tell them that if they are too scared to show up for this meeting, then they will be cut out of our new agreement."

"What about the politician?"

"It is being handled."

"Very well. Good luck."

Williams signaled for his assistant to end the call. As the jet took off and headed north, a moment of panic seized him. What if Syed was right? Had the killings near Washington been too brazen? Had it tipped their hand? That Max Fend character had shown up right in his backyard. What information had Rojas given them? It couldn't have been much. He didn't know much. What if the Americans did know more than they were letting on?

No. That was impossible. The mole had given them accurate operational details as recently as the past few days, and the assassinations ensured that there would be no further link to him or the ISI. Williams licked his lips, thinking of what lay ahead. Only a few more days of risk.

After Oshkosh, things would be easier.

17

After the call with Wilkes, Max, Renee and Trent agreed they would travel to Cincinnati to start the search for Jennifer Upton at her place of work. It would have been evening if they had flown straight to Ohio, and Renee wanted a night to do research before they arrived. So they made a pit stop in Memphis for what Max considered the most crucial elements of their success: fuel, ribs, and pulled pork sandwiches. "I'm afraid I must insist on the barbecue," Max had said. They had remained overnight in Memphis and had flown the final leg in the morning.

Max landed them at Lunken Airport, just to the east of the Ohio River, outside of Cincinnati.

"Is it always this busy?" Trent asked as Max taxied them to the ramp.

The flight line was filled with small aircraft. Mostly Cessnas and Pipers, some of which had smiling owners standing next to the planes, talking with each other as they waited. A lone fuel truck was slowly making its way through the aircraft.

"I doubt it. They must all be on their way up to Oshkosh. The fly-in starts in earnest today."

Max waited for fuel while Trent and Renee went inside. Trent's mission was to secure them a rental vehicle. Renee was in the conference room on her computer, hunting for possible hints as to where Jennifer

Upton might be. All they knew with certainty was where she lived and that she worked at a political nonprofit in Cincinnati.

"Nice Cirrus!" said a man standing beside the plane in the parking spot next to Max. He had sandy blond hair and wore wraparound sunglasses and a sweat-stained polo shirt. He stood beside two teenage boys who had trouble maintaining eye contact.

"Thanks," replied Max. "You guys headed up to Oshkosh?"

"Just like everybody else here. It's our fifth pilgrimage. Name's Jake King. These are my sons, James and Jack."

Max waved politely to the family with oddly similar names, keeping his smile to himself. "Nice to meet you."

"That Cirrus have a parachute in it?"

"I sure hope so. I hear they come in handy."

The man laughed. "Are you flying up for the air show today?"

"To Oshkosh? I'd sure love to go, but we don't have any plans to right now."

One of the sons—Max wasn't sure which was James and which was Jack—said, "We spent the last three months planning for the flight in. If you don't already know, I don't think—"

His father whispered, "You don't need to tell him that, James. I'm sure he knows all the planning required." Mr. King then looked up at Max. "Well, if you find yourself there, come see our gyrocopter. It's being shipped up by truck today. We'll be flying it on the ultralight field every day starting tomorrow."

"Well, that's pretty neat."

One of the boys said, "Yeah, but the best part is the remote-control function me and my dad built in."

The father looked proud. "Well, it's not that special. With the advancements in drone technology, it was a relatively simple upgrade."

"Yeah, my experience hasn't been the best with remotely controlled aircraft."

The man squinted. "Say, you kind of look familiar. Have we met?"

Renee was waving at Max from the FBO building, trying to get his attention. Max noticed that the two King boys saw her and gave each other looks of approval.

"Looks like I've got to run."

As he was leaving, he heard Mr. King say, "I swear I recognize him..."

Max stopped at the fuel truck and told the man operating it, "Hey, the blue-and-white Cirrus is mine. Please top her off." The fuel man nodded, and Max headed towards Renee.

"We've got a vehicle," she said. "Trent's waiting in the parking lot."

"Great. I want to run by her home and office. Maybe we can talk to someone who knows how to find her."

* * *

They drove through the heart of the city, passing the Reds and Bengals stadiums and the Procter & Gamble headquarters building. Renee had Trent take the Liberty Street exit off I-71 towards a neighborhood known as Over the Rhine.

"Well, this is charming," said Renee, inspecting the homes.

"That's one way to put it." To Max it just looked like an old inner-city neighborhood. Spray-painted graffiti art on brick exteriors. Some blocks filled with boarded-up windows. A large billboard for domestic beer. Telephone wires and power lines overhanging the street. Older-model cars in need of body work.

"Okay, well, not everything looks great, but look at these buildings up here."

Max saw what she was looking at. Some of the shops and residences had been refurbished. As they drove, he saw cleaner and more modern-looking exteriors. Their new paint jobs provided splashes of color among the old brick.

At last they came upon the central square. A clock tower stood in one corner. Large potted plants and bright red metal picnic tables were spaced out over a wide concrete sidewalk. While much of the shopping was outdoors—there was a busy farmers market on one side—there was also a great hall with several dozen shops, delis, and bakeries inside, forming the center of the plaza. The building was crowned with a turquoise-lettered sign reading FINDLAY MARKET.

"There's the office," said Max. "Drop me off here. I'll text you if I need longer than fifteen minutes."

Renee and Trent parked in a lot a block away from Jennifer Upton's workplace. They sat in the rental, engine running, air conditioning humming, Trent behind the wheel, Renee's laptop open as she continued to research Upton.

Max was going fishing, trying to glean information from coworkers on where she might be. Jennifer Upton worked for a 501c nonprofit firm based in Ohio. Max went into the office, falsely claiming to have a meeting set up with Upton. He would dangle a new and high-profile client: Charles Fend, Max's well-known billionaire father, who was known to contribute his funds to causes that would help his business. With any luck, the members of the firm would eat out of his hand, and while they were trying to make a new client happy, Max would be asking seemingly innocuous questions about Upton.

"Here he comes."

Max was walking back towards their vehicle. Fifteen minutes, just like he'd said.

Renee rolled down her window. "Anything?"

"I might have some info for you, but no obvious location." Max handed Renee a sheet of paper with keywords written down. Upton's cat's name. Past employers and clients. Things Max had noticed on her office desk.

"I might be able to use some of this for potential usernames or passwords."

Trent said, "You guys mind if we get lunch?"

"Sounds good."

Trent and Renee got out of the vehicle, and the three of them began walking towards the marketplace.

"Crowded," said Max.

Trent hummed agreement.

Findlay Market was packed. Throngs of people—families pushing strollers, grandmas shopping at the flea market, yuppies wearing athleisure wear while sipping mimosas over brunch. There were a lot of nice-looking restaurants, bars, and even freshly renovated office space.

Max elbowed Renee. "Okay, maybe you are right. This place looks pretty cool."

Renee smiled up at him, pulling him close to her in a loving gesture as they walked. He could tell she was still tense by the way she was looking around.

"How are you holding up?"

She said, "I'm alright. It's just a lot to process, all of this. The shooting in Mexico, and in Texas..."

"I know. I'm sorry. We'll be okay." He felt her arm squeeze his waist. They walked past a little row of vendor shops that were situated along the sidewalk. The corner tent had big freezers and a long line of smiling customers. A variety of delicious gelato flavors were written on a chalkboard sign standing next to the tent.

The market square was lined with colorful two- and three-story attached mixed-use units—homes, businesses, restaurants, and stores. Max didn't like the number of opaque windows looking down on their meeting spot. Or the hundreds of casuals walking every which way around the marketplace. He told himself to relax. They weren't in danger here. At least, he didn't think they were.

"I'll grab a table here and wait."

Renee came back a few moments later and plopped down in the seat across from him. She liked to order for him without asking what he wanted, and Max didn't mind. Renee took two paper-wrapped submarine sandwiches out of a bag, smiling as Max examined his lunch.

"What did you get?"

"Banh mi. Vietnamese sandwiches. Have you ever had one?"

Max opened the paper wrapping. A French baguette, pork, little slices of jalapeños, cilantro by the look of it, thin slices of cucumbers and carrots, and some type of pink spread.

He took a large, brave bite, chewing and salivating as the combination of tastes hit his mouth. "My God."

"I know, right?"

"This is so good. Why the hell haven't I tried this before?"

"There's a Vietnamese place in Charlottesville that I go to all the time. They make great ones. But this isn't bad at all..."

Trent came back with a Styrofoam plate of Greek food. Lamb, spiced potatoes, onions, tomatoes, pita, and cucumber sauce.

Renee was eating with one hand and tapping on her open laptop's trackpad with the other. Her eyes widened, and she held up a hand. "Got it!"

"Excuse me?"

"I'm done. I've found her."

"Found who?"

She looked triumphant. "Your missing woman, *mon cheri*. Well, sort of. That is to say, I know where she will be."

"How?"

"I just went on one of the overlay networks where you can buy people's usernames and passwords. You probably know this as the 'dark web.' Spooky name. I found an old email account that Miss Upton barely uses. It's not linked to her home or work IP addresses or her devices. She must have some software that she runs to avoid detection. And it's not under her name anymore. It's an alias. But this account is hers. I purchased her account data from one of the dark web sites. Max, you owe me twenty bucks for that purchase, by the way. We can work something out later." She winked. "Since no one ever changes their passwords— except for me, of course—I tried the same username and password on all of her other accounts. I also tried a few variations with the information you gave me. The winner was her current pet name, mixed with the numbers and symbols from one of her old passwords. I got a match, read through some of Miss Upton's emails, and found that she recently reserved a hotel."

"Nice work."

Trent, chewing a big bite of gyro, said, "Remind me to change my password."

Renee said, "Her check-in is at three p.m. tomorrow." Renee peered at the screen. "Hmm. Well, now, that's quite interesting. Guess where the hotel is?"

"Where?"

"Fond du Lac, Wisconsin. Which, I should point out, is suspiciously close to Oshkosh."

The table went silent for a moment.

"Really? Where Senator Becker is headed?"

Trent's face contorted into a confused expression. "Pretty suspicious that the only two names we know of on the kill list are both headed towards the same place. Why do you suppose that is?"

Max stood up and began picking up his food and stuffing it into the bag. "We'll have to ask her when we get there. Come on, we can eat in the car."

The others stood and began doing the same. Renee said, "And you don't want to just call up Wilkes and have him take care of it? Didn't he say he was going to bring a team to Oshkosh too?"

"Yeah, but the last two times Wilkes knew where we were, so did Ian Williams. How about this time, we wait to tell him until after we pick her up?"

Trent shrugged. "Works for me, man. I like air shows, and I like guns. This gives me a unique opportunity to combine the two."

An uneasy feeling overcame Max as he thought more about the situation. "If Jennifer Upton is on the kill list, then we could be facing cartel or ISI hit teams when we try to grab her."

"If she shows up," Trent said. "It's possible she made this reservation but was then taken or killed by Williams's men, right?"

Renee was looking at her computer. "Well, according to the monitoring program I now have running on her accounts, she just checked her email from her phone an hour ago. Her phone accessed cell towers in Chicago, but now it's powered off. It's *possible* that someone else is doing this. But my guess is that it's still her."

"Good. Please keep monitoring her electronic communications. Let us know if she tries to contact anyone or changes her plans. I think we should assume that our first opportunity to take her is when she arrives to check in at her hotel."

"Logical," said Renee. Renee closed her laptop, stuffing it into her handbag, and they began walking back towards the car.

Max said, "If Williams is going to send a hit team to get Upton, we need to get to her first."

* * *

Max was in the flight planning room at the FBO. It was packed. Filled with more smiling recreational aviators on a break from their cross-country flights up to Wisconsin. He recognized the two King boys, who looked like they were packing up.

"You guys heading back out to your plane?"

"Yes, Mr. Fend."

"Ah, so you figured out my name, huh?"

"Our dad did, yes, sir."

"Say, you guys mentioned it took you a long time to plan your flight to Oshkosh. I've never flown in there myself, but I was thinking about doing it today. Could you give me the two-minute version of what I need to do?"

The boys looked at each other, wide-eyed. "Uh. Mr. Fend, respectfully, it's really complicated..."

"Actually, why don't you just let me see your flight plan for a second? I'll go make a photocopy."

One of them handed a copy to Max. "You can keep it. I have three copies."

"You're a great American, my friend."

"But, Mr. Fend, if you're really going to do this, you'll need to read the NOTAMs."

Max shrugged. "No problem." The Notice to Airmen was the advisory that alerted pilots about hazards or changes along their route of flight, including the airports. It was usually a quick read, only a few lines.

"You can take my spare copy of that, too." He handed Max what looked like a small book.

Max raised his eyebrows. "Okay. Great. Thanks..."

Renee and Trent were in the lobby. Renee had caught Max's eye and was giving him a concerned look, nodding towards the TV fixed to the wall.

The national news had interrupted the daytime TV programming and was showing footage of Washington, D.C., outside the Capitol Building.

. . .

US SENATOR RECEIVING DEATH THREATS AFTER AIDE KILLED

Max walked over to Renee. "What is it?"

"They're talking about Senator Becker. A news story just broke that he's been getting death threats because of an anti-opioid bill he's sponsoring."

"Death threats from who?"

"They say there are international investors connected to organized crime who are trying to stop his vote."

"Organized crime? What's that supposed to mean? The cartels?"

"I don't know. The story's only just broken. But if it was the cartels, why would they care about a law passing?"

The newscaster interrupted their conversation.

"Senator Becker has put out a statement saying that he won't be deterred by brutish thugs who want to scare America into submission. He still intends to be in public this week, while watching his daughter perform at the Oshkosh Air Show in his home state of Wisconsin."

Max and Renee looked at each other. Max said, "Well, if there was any doubt as to where they could find him, that's gone now."

18

Trent sat in the backseat of the Cirrus, Renee and Max in front. Max had filed the exact same flight plan as the King family. In a way, it was kind of like copying someone's homework. But since he wasn't getting graded, and they all had the same destination, he didn't think it was an ethical dilemma.

They were airborne about thirty minutes after Max had filed their flight plan. After they cleared Cincinnati airspace, the three of them conversed over the internal communication headsets. Max asked Renee if she wanted to do some of the flying, and she said yes.

"You won't stall us this time?" he joked.

"I'll do my best."

Trent said, "You guys make a pretty cute couple."

"Thank you." Renee looked at Max and pinched his cheek.

Max said, "It's not all roses. She can be very tough on me. We have major disagreements on how we see some things."

Trent looked skeptical. "Like what?"

Max said, "Trent, there are two types of people in this world. Those who like Tim Tebow, and those who don't."

Renee turned her head. "I didn't say that I don't *like* him. He just didn't have an NFL-caliber arm, that's all."

"You take that back. He's flawless in every way."

Trent said, "Renee, you like football?"

Max smiled. "Uh-oh. Here we go."

She turned to Trent, pulling her sunglasses down and narrowing her eyes. "And why wouldn't I like football? Because I'm a girl?"

Trent tapped Max on the shoulder. "I see what you mean."

The flight was several hours long, but it provided some much-needed downtime for the group.

"There's Chicago," Renee said into the mike. They were flying north along the shores of Lake Michigan, the skyline at their eleven o'clock. Max looked down at his chart display and dialed up the local air traffic control frequency, checking in and requesting visual flight following as he traveled to the north. He could hear dozens of other aircraft speaking to the controller every few seconds. It was busy airspace here all the time.

Trent keyed his mike from the backseat. "Pretty cool." Renee was all smiles as well. Max was glad.

"Maybe on the way back, we can stop there and hit up Lou Malnati's."

"Now you're talking."

After getting clear of Chicago airspace, Max banked the aircraft left, ensuring that they would take Kenosha and Milwaukee off their right side as they continued north. He had pre-dialed in a set of checkpoints and was scanning his GPS to ensure that they were on course.

"Okay, this is the tricky part." Max handed Renee the white booklet he had stapled together. A picture on the front cover showed a small airplane in a shallow climb, trailing aerobatic smoke.

"What's this?" Renee asked.

"That's the NOTAM. The Notice to Airmen. I haven't had a chance to read it all yet, but I convinced one of those teenage boys to lend me their extra copy."

Renee said, "NOTAM? But you showed me those the other day when we were flying in Virginia. I thought NOTAMs were only a few words long."

"Normally they are."

She turned the pages of the booklet. "This is almost thirty pages!"

"Yeah. Well, ten thousand aircraft are all arriving at the same time. So, they probably don't want us to run into each other. Now, turn to page..." Max tried to keep his altitude while he flipped to near the end of the booklet, where he had placed a bright orange sticky note. "There. Please read that part the kid highlighted. I'm not sure what it says, but those kids seemed sharp, so we should probably read the highlights."

Renee moved her forefinger over the words as she read. "Ensure lights are on and set transponder to standby."

Max flipped a switch and scanned his instruments. "Check."

Renee kept reading the procedures, her eyes growing wider as she read. She looked over at Max. "It says find an aircraft of similar speed and type and follow them."

"Okay."

"Is that a joke? Ten thousand aircraft are flying here at the same time, and they tell you to find someone at the same speed as you and follow them?"

Max scanned outside for other aircraft. "Hmm. Well, maybe we should drop a procedural improvement into the Oshkosh suggestion box when we land. But for now, keep reading..."

Max spotted a Cessna out the window. "Traffic, three o'clock, level, no factor. He's going slower, so we'll overtake him."

More and more aircraft appeared outside, some just little white specks in the distance, others close in, and much larger. Some of the aircraft were above their altitude, some below. One little orange-and-white helicopter chugged along to their east.

They found a white Cessna at about their same altitude, and Max adjusted his speed so they wouldn't overtake it. He then fell in a loose trail position, partly making sure he was following the map in the booklet and partly making sure he followed the plane ahead of him.

The ground below was carved into an endless expanse of brown and green fields. Roads and houses, trees and barns. Grain silos and cow pastures, and a highway filled with cars headed towards the air show. Another highway filled with planes above it, doing the same. Soon Lake Winnebago appeared, shimmering in the afternoon sun off to the east.

Renee said, "Okay, we're coming up on the part where we have to talk."

"I've always been a good talker."

"I feel like you aren't taking this as seriously as you should be."

Trent said, "Are couples allowed to fly and navigate together? Should I be worried here?"

A moment later, they arrived at the main entry checkpoint, and the Oshkosh aircraft controller called out Max's aircraft. The man spoke incredibly fast. He was probably taking a break from his normal job, which Max assumed must have been as an auctioneer.

"Blue-and-white-Cirrus-at-half-mile-south-of-Fisk, rock-your-wings."

Renee said, "What the hell did he just say?"

Max moved his yoke to the right and left in rapid succession, making the aircraft roll back and forth.

"Half-mile-south-of-Fisk, blue-and-white-Cirrus, good-rock-sir, continue-northeast-bound-along-the-railroad-tracks-for-a-right-down-wind-runway-two-seven, maintain-one-thousand-eight-hundred-until-turning-your-downwind, monitor-tower-one-one-eight-point-five...*welcome-to-Oshkosh*."

Renee looked at Max. "He was talking so fast! *Merde*. What did he say? He wants us to follow railroad tracks?"

Max shushed her. "Honey, can you be quiet for a moment? I need to concentrate." The aircraft ahead of them was turning sharply. Max felt like each plane was on an infinite conveyer belt that couldn't stop. Everyone had to perform their maneuvers at precisely the right moment. Otherwise, the entire line would get fouled up, which ended badly with airborne conveyer belts.

Max could see the line of planes landing in front of them, and the giant airport itself. Enormous green fields filled with cars, pup tents, Winnebagos, and, of course, planes. Rows and rows of aircraft of all colors, shapes and sizes.

"Oh my God," Renee said. "There are so many..."

Max had switched up the radio frequency to tower. After finishing his turn, he heard the tower controller say, "Clear to land." A beautiful phrase.

The white pavement of the runway grew larger in the windscreen as they descended on their approach. The rows of aircraft already on the ground zoomed by as their altitude decreased, and the world seemed to move faster and faster.

Then, with a squeak, the wheels touched down, and Max began pumping the brakes, decelerating as fast as he could. Max turned off at the appropriate taxiway, and a guy wearing an orange vest and holding orange batons directed him to follow the line of planes inching along ahead of him.

Max exhaled.

"Nice work. I knew you could do it." Renee patted him on the shoulder. She wore a wide smile, looking pretty in her aviator sunglasses, her dark hair held back by the aircraft headset.

Taxiing the aircraft seemed to take forever. They crept at a snail's pace, past the waving crowds of people in lawn chairs, sitting in the shade under the wings of their Cessnas, past the rows of old warbirds, and past the forest of covered pavilions where lecturers were speaking about aviation-related subjects.

Finally they arrived at their parking spot on the lawn, and Max shut down the Cirrus.

Max said, "Welcome to our new home."

Trent said, "I hope we like our neighbors. They got us packed in like the parking lot of a pumpkin patch."

Max shut down the engine, and they opened the doors. It was hot—a good eighty-five degrees—but nothing compared to the Tex-Mex heat they'd been exposed to last week. The aircraft behind them had just parked, and its prop was winding down. Pup tents were scattered among the aircraft in front of them. The field behind them was clear of aircraft for the moment, but it would be filled up soon.

"So where to first?" asked Renee.

Max said, "We probably need tents, a few supplies, and a rental vehicle. Then I say we spend a few hours getting the lay of the land here. Find out where Becker is going to be, and then work out our plan to bring in Jennifer Upton without consequence."

"How are we going to find the senator? This place is huge. You want to call Wilkes, let him know we're here?"

"Not yet. They have VIP tents set up. My father used to hang out in them. We can start there." Max gave Renee a funny look. "And I might know someone here who can get us to meet with the senator."

"Who?"

"His daughter."

"How do you know his daughter again?" asked Renee, her voice suspicious.

"Well, my father and Senator Becker knew each other. You know that. And there was a brief period where..."

"Wait, did you *date* his daughter?"

Max went red. "I mean...technically...uh..."

Trent saw Max's face and said, "Hey, man, you need a shovel?"

"What for?"

"'Cause I think you're gonna need to dig yourself out of a hole pretty soon."

19

The vast majority of attendees at the Oshkosh Air Show either camped out on the airport's vast grassy plains or slept in a Winnebago or trailer. Max, having been to Oshkosh when he was younger, knew that there would be little chance of getting a hotel room now that the air show had commenced. This was why he had dispatched Trent to secure a rental car, tents, and camping supplies.

Renee and Max walked along rows of aircraft to get to the central hub of the air show. Max had fond memories of this place from when he was younger. His father made it a point to show up almost every year. As the figurehead of Fend Aerospace, Charles Fend was a fixture of the event. Sort of like Arnold Palmer taking the first tee shot at the Masters.

Fend Aerospace was also one of the biggest sponsors of the show, and they often displayed their latest and greatest aircraft in the central area, renting giant tents and schmoozing with potential buyers. The air show was a place for aviation fans and history buffs to tour, but it was also a place for aviation businesses to wheel and deal. It wasn't quite the Paris Air Show, where the focus was more on the business side of things. But there was still a lot of that.

"It's hot." Max wiped sweat from his brow.

"Maybe we can stop and get something to drink?"

Max and Renee arrived at the main static display area in the center of the air show. There were a variety of giant jumbo jets, military fighters, and old warbirds set up for viewing in the central plaza. A double-decker commercial aircraft, an Airbus A380, dominated this year's static display. An Air Force AC-130 gunship was also a big crowd-pleaser.

"There's a DC-3 over there," said Max. He pointed to another. "Oh, look. Check out the paint job on that B-17. Impressive."

Renee smiled at him. "You love this stuff, don't you?"

"Doesn't everyone?"

"It would probably be more enjoyable if I wasn't worried about people trying to kill us."

He placed his hand on the small of her back. "You alright?"

"You don't need to keep asking me that. I'm fine. Just eager to meet this old girlfriend of yours."

Max took solace in the fact that if Renee was focused on the whole girlfriend-jealousy thing, it was probably a positive signal as to her current mental health. However, it was also a negative sign for Max's.

"So...the weather...pretty hot out, huh?"

Renee smirked at his obvious attempt to change the subject. "Yes. I need to pick up some sunblock or I'll turn into a lobster."

They walked into an air-conditioned minimart and Renee purchased some sunblock. Both of them threw on gobs of it while taking refuge under the shade of the overhang outside. Next, they walked over to another vendor's tent and ordered two giant lemonades, extra ice. Max handed one to a grateful Renee, and they continued along.

Max was interested in the planes, but his mind kept turning over the problems at hand. He thought about what they'd learned about Becker's connection to Upton. About Becker's chief of staff being killed. About the cartel attack in Texas. About Ian Williams learning of Wilkes's agent in Mexico. These were all pieces of a puzzle. Clues he needed to put together before...

Before what? Before Senator Becker was assassinated? Or before the ISI and Ian Williams commenced their mysterious meeting of minds? What were they meeting about? Who was attending? Where was the meeting being held? Why would they need a list of people killed before the meeting occurred? A list that involved one of the most powerful politicians in America?

And would Caleb Wilkes really let it get that far? Was he really so bold as to use a US senator as bait? Then again, it wasn't Wilkes who had forced the senator to come here to this public stage. Becker supposedly knew that he was in danger and was choosing to flout the warnings he'd been given by attending the Oshkosh air show anyway.

Max watched Renee sucking lemonade from her straw and again felt guilty for exposing her to this dangerous world. And to men like Ian Williams.

While she had volunteered to go to Mexico, Max realized that her reason wasn't the same as his. Max felt a calling to the trade. Partially a call to serve and protect or whatever the hell you wanted to call it. But it was also for himself. This mixture of adrenaline and noble purpose was his own addiction. Max needed his fix.

Renee was different. She was motivated by selfless compassion. The tugging at her heartstrings she'd felt when Josh Carpenter died, leaving little Josh behind. The unjust killing of Ines Sanchez on the beach in Mazatlán. And more than any of that, Max knew that Renee's original and most important reason for being here was because she loved him.

That was what had gotten her on that flight to Mexico. She wanted to help keep Max safe. Walking next to her now, he realized that he felt the same way. Max loved and admired everything about her. Her infectious laugh. Her passion for life. Her love of learning and relentless work ethic.

Max looked at her now, at her dark shoulder-length hair with traces of white sunblock smudged in. Her fit yet curvy figure. Her Mona Lisa smile that seemed to come more and more often lately. The feelings he had for her made him vulnerable, which frightened him. And while he regretted that Renee was in danger, she was also proving extremely valuable to the operation.

Max once again promised himself that he would do a better job of protecting her. And when this was over...well, maybe he'd finally have that serious relationship talk he knew she wanted to have.

They sipped their drinks and walked along the crowded taxiway, which was being used mainly as a pedestrian sidewalk right now.

They came across a very old black man who was propped up on an elevated wooden chair on the side of the walkway. The set-up was official looking—the chair looked like a short lifeguard chair, complete with a large orange umbrella to keep the man shaded. A World War Two fighter plane rested in the grass behind him. Another black man of about sixty stood next to him. By their manner and proximity, Max guessed the second man to be the elder's son.

Max took Renee's arm and they stopped.

"Hello, sir. Excuse me, but did you fly that aircraft back there? The P-51 Mustang?"

The old-World War II fighter aircraft, silver and gleaming, had the word TUSKEGEE painted in blue on the engine compartment. The old man's hat read 332nd Fighter Group, TUSKEGEE AIRMEN.

The man's voice was slow and raspy with a bit of a Southern accent. "Why, yes, sir, I did."

"My father was one of the Tuskegee Airmen," said the son, a proud grin as he looked at his old man.

Max saw Renee's eyes widen. She mouthed, "Wow."

Max stuck out his hand, speaking slow and clear. "It is an honor to meet you, sir." Renee smiled widely and also shook the man's hand.

"Why, thank you both." He looked tired but pleased to be here. His smile widened at Renee. "My, my. Your wife sure is pretty." They all laughed, and neither Max nor Renee bothered to correct him.

The man's son said to Max, "Hey, don't I know you?"

Max shook the son's hand. "My name is Max Fend."

"Sure. Your father—"

"Yes, my father owns Fend Aerospace."

"I thought I recognized you. I've seen you on the news."

"Yeah, those weren't my finest moments."

The man laughed. "Well, if I recall, it all worked out in the end, didn't it?"

Max nodded. "It did." He looked back at the elderly man sitting quietly in the chair. "Are they going to let you fly that here?" Max was smiling, trying to make small talk.

"They promised me a ride on the Ford."

"The Ford?" said Renee.

Max smiled, knowing that she probably thought the old man was going senile.

The old Tuskegee Airman lifted up a shaky hand and pointed his finger down the taxiway to the south. "The old Ford Trimotor, ma'am. I come here almost every year, yet I still never rode one of them. I'm ninety-four years old now. This might be my last year. I'd sure like to fly one of them Fords."

A boxy silver aircraft rested on the active taxiway one hundred yards away. Next to it, inside the fence, was a long line of people waiting to take a ride. It was one of the first ever mass-produced passenger planes, Max knew. It had three extremely loud engines—one on each wing and one on the nose—all making puttering, scraping noises as they ran, like an old jalopy in need of a tune-up.

The nose angled sharply skyward due to the fact that the rear of the aircraft was balanced on a tiny tail wheel.

Max said, "You don't see too many passenger aircraft that are tail draggers anymore." Rides on the Ford Trimotor were a staple of the Oshkosh air show.

Renee offered the old man a big smile. "Well, that looks like it would be a lot of fun. I hope you get to take a ride."

Max and Renee bade farewell to the pair and kept walking. They headed through the central static display area, passing modern military fighter aircraft, giant commercial planes, and several large US Air Force tankers. They kept walking and arrived at the ultralight aircraft field. Small aircraft in a variety of shapes flew over that section of the airport. Some had hang glider wings. Others floated on parachutes, with rear-mounted props that reminded Max of Everglades airboats.

"Hey, look. There's the King family."

"Who?" asked Renee.

"The kids I met at the Cincinnati airport. The ones who I stole...I mean, the ones who *gave* me their flight plan."

She smirked.

The two teenage boys and their father were standing at the edge of the ultralight field, which was a few hundred yards long, south of the main exhibit, and fenced off from the crowd. Mr. King was placing a tablet computer and a joystick on top of a fold-up table. The boys were unfolding the arms of a white helicopter-like contraption about half the size of a car.

Max checked his watch. They still had another half hour before they were supposed to meet Trent near the VIP tent. They had time to kill.

"Hello, boys."

"Hey, Mr. Fend." They waved back, their teenage eyes magnetically drawn to Renee.

"Ah, Max Fend. I knew I recognized you when we met in Cincinnati." The father shook Max's hand. Max introduced him to Renee. "A pleasure."

"This your gyrocopter?"

"It sure is. Jack here was just going to take it for a spin."

The teenager wore a white helmet and was now strapping into the driver's seat. The gyrocopter had a tall, thin rotor overtop, like a heli-copter. But the rotor was much smaller than a helicopter's—it must have only been about ten feet in diameter. The rear of the contraption had a propeller that rested just aft of a small engine. There was no glass canopy surrounding the driver's seat. The pilot would be sitting in the open air. It was like a cross between a bicycle and a helicopter, with a prop in the rear.

"That motor looks about the size of a lawnmower," Renee said, then covered her mouth, hoping she hadn't said anything insulting.

Mr. King smiled wide, looking quite proud. "It was! Well, it was a big mower—a tractor—but that's what we converted it from."

Jack's brother was helping him strap in. A moment later, his brother out of the way, Jack started up the gyrocopter and began rolling along the grass, taking off in a buzz, both the top rotor and rear prop spinning.

Renee clapped her hands. "Well done."

"Thank you," said Mr. King.

"Dad, show them the RC."

Mr. King walked over to a table they had set up behind the fence. He placed on a headset and said, "Okay, Jack, now fly it back over here to where I am. We're going to demonstrate the remote-control feature."

A moment later, Jack had flown the gyrocopter in a racetrack pattern and landed in the grass directly in front of the fence before them.

"The rotors on top move very slow compared to a helicopter."

"Yes, a gyrocopter flies using a different aerodynamic principle than a helicopter. A helicopter forces its rotor blades through the air, but a gyrocopter uses a free-spinning rotor to generate lift like a glider."

"Fascinating."

"It sure is."

"So, your son will stay in the aircraft while you operate it remotely?"

"Yes. We aren't certified as a drone, so this is sort of a gray area, what we're doing. But Jack can easily take the controls and overpower the inputs I'll be making if anything doesn't look right to him."

Max turned to Renee. "Where have I heard that before?"

Not hearing the comment, Mr. King said into the headset, "Hands off, Jack, I've got it." Then he took the joystick on the table and pressed a few buttons on the tablet. The gyrocopter took off into forward flight.

James King said, "My brother and I wrote the program. We used the same code that most of the off-the-shelf helicopter drones use. You can see the readout right there."

Max watched as Mr. King maneuvered the gyrocopter forward in slow flight. It was like playing a video game. He just tapped forward on an arrow on the tablet, and he could also use the joystick to turn.

Renee said, "This is incredible. You boys did such a great job."

The kid went beet red. "Thank you, ma'am. It's also got a really cool feature that we added that will bring it right back to you if you've got it far away."

"Let's see it," said Max.

"Sure."

Mr. King used the tablet to maneuver the gyrocopter to a spot about one hundred yards away. "See this button?"

A yellow button on the tablet read "GO TO SET COORDINATES."

"Yup."

"Press it."

Max pressed the button, and the tiny aircraft immediately turned and nosed over, skimming the ground as it headed towards them at a surprisingly high speed. Just before Max was about to move them out of the way, the gyrocopter decelerated. It settled down on the grass fifty feet in front of them, with Jack once again holding the controls, a big smile on his freckled face.

Max said, "Pretty neat."

"Thanks."

"So you can program it to fly anywhere?"

"Pretty much. As long as we have a latitude and longitude, and enough fuel. But you still need a pilot at the controls to make sure we don't fly it into a tree or anything. The program is very rudimentary."

"It's impressive."

They shut down the gyrocopter and Jack ran over to the table, removing his helmet. Just then a loud buzzing filled the air as a sleek black-and-red aerobatic plane zoomed by them on one of the airport's main runways. It pulled straight up into a climb and began rolling on its longitudinal axis like a spinning Olympic figure skater.

"Is that her? Is that *her*?" one of the King boys asked.

"Yeah, it is," said the other.

The two boys took off towards the runway. Renee looked at Mr. King, who was shaking his head.

"What are they so excited about?"

"Oh, they're really interested in this aerobatic performer for some reason."

"Who is it?"

The speakers mounted throughout the airfield answered Renee's question. "Ladies and gentlemen, if you'll turn your attention to runway two-three, flying the Blonde Bombshell, may we present...Karen Becker!"

20

A spotless glass canopy covered Karen Becker's head. It was a beautiful day to fly. Bright sunshine and blue sky above. An immense crowd of several hundred thousand onlookers standing on the grass to her right, just beyond the taxiway. She wore wraparound shades to dim the intense glare of the sun. A headset fit snugly over her bleach-blond hair.

Already motoring forward on the taxiway, Karen pressed down with one of her feet, turning her black Extra 300L aerobatics plane onto the runway and aiming it down the centerline.

Her plane was adorned with the inscription "The Blonde Bombshell." Karen's likeness, wearing her signature pink flight suit, the front zipper pulled down enough to show a bit of cleavage, was painted underneath. The bleach-blond hair from her cartoon image flowed back along the length of the aircraft and was artistically transformed into bright reddish flames.

She quickly checked her engine instruments, and then the healthy whine of the engine grew into a strong buzz as she pushed the throttle forward. The grass, runway, static display aircraft, and sea of onlookers transformed into a blur as her aircraft increased speed.

The bouncing and rumbling of the aircraft changed into a steady floating sensation as she went airborne. She felt loose, light, and in complete control of her machine. Karen kept forward pressure on the stick, purposely staying low to the ground, her wheels mere feet above the runway, building speed, going faster and faster until just the right moment, when she tugged back hard on the yoke.

She flexed her stomach as the world pitched back and the Blonde Bombshell went vertical, climbing straight up, engine humming. Karen could practically hear the crowd cheering for her as she rolled hard left on the stick, and the world blurred again as the aircraft began spinning, a tornado of color.

Karen's lip microphone slipped out of place from the strong g-forces, and she stopped her turn halfway through a roll. She used her left hand to place the mike back tight against her lips, then yanked again and began her show.

Red smoke trailed from her aircraft—a red dye combined with a white smoke base. The smoke was created by pumping a paraffin-based biodegradable oil directly onto the hot exhaust nozzles of her piston engine. The oil vaporized to provide the stunning visual effect of a crimson column of cloud following along after her aircraft.

Karen kept her rapid scan flicking between the outside world and her instruments, seeking out visual cues on the ground to note her position, then forcing her eyes back inside at the instrument panel to check her airspeed, altitude, and engine instruments.

One moment she was one thousand feet in the air, upside down at the top of a loop. The next she was diving down to the earth. Then back up at eight thousand feet, throttle all the way back, using her foot pedals and yoke to send the aircraft into a spin—transforming the aircraft into a giant metal leaf, twirling as it fell from the sky.

Karen had practiced every maneuver countless times, both in the air and on the ground, "chair-flying" for hours in a windowless room, with only her coach, using hand gestures, body position, and her imagination like she was practicing a ballet routine.

That's just what it was like, in a way. Aerobatic performances were carefully scripted, and very dangerous. The g-forces alone could force a pilot into unconsciousness in the blink of an eye. Some of the maneuvers

Karen performed placed ten g's on her body, so her one hundred and twenty pounds became over half a ton.

During those intense turns, gravity tried to force her blood towards her extremities. Through practice, she had become proficient at special breathing techniques performed while flexing her legs, butt, thighs, calves, and stomach during high-g maneuvers. These techniques, and her g-suit, allowed her to keep her circulation under control. The g-suit contained water-filled tubes that ran from her shoulder down to her ankles. They would compress as the g's came on, keeping her blood pumping into the upper body and head, which allowed her to retain consciousness.

Karen had to keep in great physical shape to be able to withstand this repetitive physical toll on her body. She had to be mentally tough as well. For the past five years, she had trained like an Olympian, and now she understood the physics of aviation as well as some aerospace PhDs.

She had worked hard over the years to become one of the top aerobatics performers in the world, and now she was here, at the pinnacle of her career.

Karen pulled out of her final maneuver and touched down smoothly on the runway. Then she taxied up to the flight line next to the central static displays. Karen shut off her engine, and her propeller spooled down. She opened her canopy and removed her headset, shaking down long waves of blond hair.

All eyes were on her. And that was just the way she liked it.

Karen Becker was a marketer's dream. She climbed down from the cockpit and walked out onto the stage that had been set up for her. Karen wore ruby-red lipstick, custom steel-toed flight boots made to look like leather cowgirl boots, a bright pink flight suit, always zipped low enough that it showed off a bit of her ample bosom. Her blond hair was topped with her customary Stetson hat, handed to her by her agent. Change up a few items, and she could have easily been a Nashville country singer about to take the stage.

The aerobatics world had never seen someone quite like her. If Amelia Earhart were still around, she would probably either be blushing or shaking her head in disapproval. But as much as Karen was an entertainer on the ground, in the air, she was a professional. After leaving her father's political staff, she had enrolled at Embry-Riddle University and earned a second degree. At first she'd thought she might go into airport management. Something far away from politics. But while she was there, she'd learned how to fly and fallen in love with aviation. She'd earned a series of progressively more advanced pilot ratings and had eventually been hired as a flight instructor in Daytona. After meeting a few pilots at air shows and taking a few aerobatic lessons, she had found her passion.

Karen absolutely loved the thrill of going up and hearing the full-throated sound of her three-hundred-horsepower engine as she yanked and banked the aircraft into submission. It was like riding a roller coaster but actually being in control.

As she marched towards her post-flight reception tent, she saw that the line of fans coming to get her autograph and picture wound around the VIP tent over one hundred feet away. She noticed several old ladies in line with their husbands, eying her like she was the Leg Lamp from the movie *A Christmas Story*. Well, maybe she was. But sex sells. And she challenged anyone else performing at the air show to pull a tighter split-S than her.

* * *

"Is *that* her?" Renee asked Max.

Mr. King said, "Yup. My boys are big fans. I tried to get them to come with me to the aerospace engineering lecture that's scheduled now, but they seemed to want to get her autograph instead. I don't see why. One of Burt Rutan's engineers is going to be here."

Max said, "It's a mystery."

Renee and Max bade farewell to Mr. King and walked over towards the air show's VIP tent, watching as Karen Becker finished up signing autographs.

Karen was a stunner. Max didn't realize he was wearing a silly schoolboy smile until Renee elbowed him. He turned to face her. "What? Did you say something?"

She rolled her eyes.

Trent appeared out of nowhere. "There you guys are. Our rental car is parked in the grass lot, and I've got all the supplies we need. What are you guys looking at...?" Trent followed their gaze. "Holy mother of mercy..."

Renee said, "Well, I see we've found the Medusa of Oshkosh. Ugh. If that's what men are really looking for, then I give up. For a moment I thought she was one of those models hired by an advertising firm or something. You know, the kind that stand there smiling next to the racers at the Formula One or walk across the ring at a boxing match. Are you telling me that she was the one who was just flipping and rolling above their heads? I guess I have to give her a little respect, but why in God's name would she wear an outfit like that?"

Max said, "I'm just going to keep my mouth shut."

Renee patted him on the chest. "Good idea."

Karen Becker emerged from a crowd of smiling fans. Max tried not to look at what was probably the most marvelous décolletage ever to appear in a flight suit—if flight suit was indeed what you called the tight-fitting pink outfit that Karen had painted on her—but that proved challenging. Max remembered that she had always been a looker, but it had been a while since they'd last seen each other.

Karen had been a fling. They had been introduced by their fathers years ago at one of these air shows—her father a prominent politician and a strong advocate for the aviation industry, his father an aviation industry CEO and icon.

Karen had many such flings, Max suspected. He was just another notch on her belt. Which was a funny thing to say about a woman, he thought. But Karen was a unique woman. A wild and sexy thrill-seeker. A beautiful and buxom...

"Uh-hum."

Max realized that he was staring at Karen again, and Renee was staring at him. The damn permasmile had returned, too. The same look seemed to have afflicted all of the other men within twenty feet of Karen, most of whose spouses were rolling their eyes or shaking their heads.

"So are you going to go talk to her or what? She's your ticket to meet her father, right?"

"You know, to be honest, I'm not even sure that she'll remember me."

"Max!"

Karen waved excitedly from across the taxiway, jogging towards them, bouncing and jiggling as she did so. One man nearby was mid-sip on a soft drink and began coughing, then looked away.

Before Max knew it, he was being wrapped in Karen's arms, her chest mashed up against him. Renee stood quietly by his side, tongue in cheek, her face a mix of jealousy and amusement. Max imagined laser beams from her eyes carving into the back of his skull.

When Karen finally released Max, she shot out her hand, saying in a sweet voice, "Hello, I'm Renee."

"Oh, hello, I'm Karen. I'm sorry, I didn't know Max was with anyone."

She stuck out her hand, and Renee shook firmly, looking her square in the eye. Two female spiders, ready to fight over a mate before they killed him and devoured him for dinner.

Renee said, "And how long have you known Max?"

"Oh, we go way back. Right, Max? What would you say? Ten years at least. Was that when you were at Princeton?"

"Oh, how interesting." Renee's eyes squinted, her face bunched up into a forced smile. Max and Renee had also met while they were at Princeton. Max looked at Renee with pleading eyes, thinking he might have been safer back in Mexico.

"That's right," Max began. "Our fathers are friends, and they introduced us at one of these air shows back when they were here on business. And that's how Karen and I met...and became friends."

Trent, who had remained silent until now, stuck his thumb backward, saying, "So I got that shovel back with the camping supplies..."

Renee mercifully moved on. "So, Karen, that was you performing just now?"

Karen said, "Yes, that's right. This is my first time at Oshkosh. I've been doing the lesser-known air show circuit for years now. But this is as good as it gets."

Max said, "Renee, Karen's father is Senator Becker, of Wisconsin. Around here they joke that this is his air show. He's been a huge proponent of general aviation and the aviation industry since he's been in Congress."

"Oh, yes, Dad is famous here. But I've been hoping that maybe if I do a good enough job, I can outshine him someday."

"And where is your father? I assume he's coming."

"Oh yes, he wouldn't miss this for the world. He's back in Washington for a vote but promised to catch my Thursday performance."

They talked for a moment longer, with Trent asking such deep questions as how Karen liked being an air show pilot. Max had to admit that he was impressed. Aerobatic flying at this level was no joke. She was all at once a top-level entertainer, athlete, and aviator. So whatever he thought of her on a personal level, he respected her professionally.

Karen said, "Well, let's make our way into the VIP tent. I've got the night off, and I don't perform again for another two days. That means I'm having a cocktail."

Trent made an excuse and headed back to the campground. He whispered to Max that he wanted to scout out the area a bit more.

Renee, Max, and Karen walked into the tent, and Max saw several aviation business executives he knew through his father, a few A-list actors that he knew to be general aviation aficionados, and a lot of people in flight suits. They made the rounds, Max introducing Renee to the people he knew from his father's network.

The VIP tent was closed off from the outside and had a mildly effective air-conditioning unit, but people were coming in and out of the plastic curtain door so often that it was still quite warm. The grass floor had a thick coat of hay to avoid getting too muddy. The atmosphere reminded him of a horse race.

Except for the noise. There was always the drone of aircraft overhead. Right now, it sounded like a crazed bumblebee. Out of one of the tent's transparent patches, they could see an aircraft doing spins, one after the other, puffy white smoke trailing from behind.

Max grabbed them all drinks from the bar. They gathered around a tall cocktail table that was affixed to the grass with stakes.

"Wow. That looks pretty dangerous," Renee said, looking up at the plane. "Do you do all that, Karen?"

Karen said, "I'll do quite a few spins, yes. I have one part of my routine I'll do this week where I basically go up to eight thousand feet and spin until I get close to the ground, then I chop a ribbon in half with the prop. First time I took Max up like that, he puked all over my aircraft. He ever tell you about that?"

"Oh, you've flown together, too? No, he didn't mention it. I'm sure there's a lot that he left out." Renee shot Max another look. "If you will excuse me, I'm going to run to the ladies' room."

When Renee was gone, Max swore that Karen moved a few inches closer to him, and her tone became a bit more mischievous. "You're not exclusive with her, are you, Max?"

Max laughed nervously. "I have to admit, it is getting kind of serious."

"The single women of the world shall weep. And probably some married ones too." She winked. "Well, don't worry. I'll behave."

"I appreciate that."

Just then, the tarp entrance of the tent opened and in walked a tall white-haired man, followed by two men in suits. The members of the VIP tent gave a slight cheer.

One of them said, "There he is!"

Max's father had arrived.

* * *

Renee was delighted that Charles Fend had shown up. Max expected that he might see him here, but he hadn't spoken to his father since last week, and at the time Oshkosh wasn't something Max had planned on attending.

"Hello, son."

"Hi, Dad."

Father and son embraced, and then Charles held Renee by the shoulders, beaming at her like she was his long-lost daughter. More like his dream potential daughter-in-law. Charles's increasingly effusive worship of Renee over the last year was an embarrassing hint to Max that his father thought they should get married. Renee adored him right back, and the two had developed a sort of annoying teaming-up-on-Max relationship.

"Has he been treating you well?"

"It's been an adventure," she said. "But Max is always the gentleman."

"Good. You'll tell me if he ever hints at trouble. I'll make sure to disown him."

Renee laughed.

Charles turned to Karen. "Ah, Miss Becker, you are a vision in pink." He took her hand and kissed it.

Karen gave a toothy grin. "Good to see you again, Mr. Fend. My father will be here tomorrow. I'm sure he'll want to say hello."

"Excellent. How is your father? I've seen him on the news. Horrible circumstances, I'm afraid."

"Yes, well...he's got security assigned to him now, so I feel better about it."

Max said, "Oh yes, I saw that on the news. They say his chief of staff was killed? What happened? Is your father okay?"

Karen nodded somberly. "It's still being investigated. He asked me not to talk about it until the investigation is over."

"Oh, of course."

Charles stood erect and proper, listening closely, genuine concern in his voice. "Well, if there is anything I can do to help..."

Charles Fend's presence in the tent was felt by every one of the attendees, many of whom were clamoring to speak with him about a business proposal, or to get their picture taken alongside him. While Karen Becker might have been dazzling, Charles Fend was world-famous.

"If you'll excuse me, dear, I shall make my obligatory rounds. Max, Renee, why don't we plan on meeting up for brunch?"

"Sounds great," Renee answered, and Charles left their circle.

Renee squeezed Max's arm. "We should probably get back and set up our tent. Was there anything else you wanted to do here?"

Max turned to Karen. "You said your father is arriving tomorrow?"

"That's right."

"Perhaps I could say hello."

"Of course. Just find me tomorrow—or text me. My number is still the same."

Max and Renee said their goodbyes to Karen and then walked out of the tent. They walked through the main static display area in silence. An enormous concert stage was being set up. A crowd of thousands had gathered around it.

Renee said, "This place is impressive."

"Are you mad about Karen?"

"Do I have a reason to be?"

"No."

"Then don't be silly. Of course not. Like you said, we need her to gain access to her father."

"Although it sounds like my father will be with the senator too."

Max wondered if that was a coincidence. Caleb Wilkes had once run his father as well. Charles Fend had been a CIA asset during the Cold War, helping the American government to pass on false information to the Soviets. And as Max had learned last year, Wilkes still called on him from time to time. When Wilkes had recruited Max, he had been cast as the replacement agent for his father. The heir to the throne of Fend Aerospace. With that title came the power, access, and privileges that would be quite helpful to American intelligence. Max's background as a DIA operative was a huge plus.

Max's father hadn't looked surprised that Max was here at Oshkosh. Had Wilkes asked his father to come here? Why would Wilkes do that without telling Max?

They walked through the crowd and saw a giant drive-in-style outdoor movie theater towering over a grass field, a grove of trees in the background. Kids and families sprawled out on the lawn, waiting for the sunset movie to play.

"When do you want to head down to Fond du Lac and scout out the hotel area?" Renee asked.

"I was just thinking about that. I think we should go tonight."

21

Trent was waiting at Max's Cirrus. He was sitting in a lawn chair, whittling a piece of wood into the shape of an eagle.

"That's pretty good."

"Thanks."

Renee said, "I thought we were setting up the tents. Where are they?"

Trent rose and folded up the chair. "Probably not smart for us to camp out here. I got us a camping spot next to the rental car. It's listed under an alias, and there's no GPS installed. I checked. If we stayed by Max's plane, it would be easier for someone to locate us."

"Good thinking."

"Come on, follow me. I'll take us there."

They walked at least a mile over rolling grass fields, past thousands of cars, recreational vehicles, and tents. Campfires and little gas grills. Diesel generators motoring next to trailers. Kids playing football and playing tag. All the while, airplanes soared overhead, one giant parade in the big blue Wisconsin sky.

"Have you heard from your family at all, Trent?" Renee asked.

"No. They know me. With the type of contract work I get, sometimes I sort of go off the grid for a few weeks at a time. They know not to worry."

Max said, "You're doing private security work?"

"Stuff like that. Sometimes personal security. Bodyguard detail for celebrities, things like that. Not exactly the role you had me play." He smirked. "But I'll head back to PA once we're done here. I promised little Josh I'd take him fishing down at Harvey's Lake."

They arrived at a section of lawn with two new pup tents and a three-foot-high mound of firewood. Several grocery bags of supplies and a stocked cooler rested in between the tents.

"There's showers and bathrooms about one hundred yards that way." He pointed towards a few wooden buildings near a grove of trees. "I figured you guys wouldn't mind sharing a tent."

Max sighed. "Aw, man, she snores."

Renee pinched the skin of his tricep. Hard. Max tried to keep it together.

Trent unfolded three lawn chairs and then started a campfire. They ate cold sandwiches from the cooler and drank bottled waters.

The sun had set, and they spoke in hushed voices over the crackling fire. Max laid out his plan for how they should handle Jennifer Upton the next day. Trent and Renee chimed in with their thoughts. After an hour of working out the details, they took the rental car south and scouted out the area near Upton's hotel.

Renee dialed the front desk from the parking lot.

"Holiday Inn Fond du Lac, how may I assist you?"

Renee said, "Yes, hello, I have a reservation at your hotel tomorrow, but I need to cancel."

"Of course. May I have your name, please?"

"Yes, it's..." She read the alias Upton had used from her notepad.

The sound of fingers kitting a keyboard. "Just a moment...okay, there you go. Unfortunately, ma'am, you are within the twenty-four-hour cancellation window...but I tell you what. I'm sure that we'll be able to get someone to fill the slot. I'll see if I can get my manager to waive that fee."

"That would be great. Thanks."

"Okay, take care."

Renee hung up the phone. Max waited ten seconds before dialing the same number.

"Holiday Inn Fond du Lac, how may I assist you?"

"Yes, I was hoping to get a room for tomorrow. Do you have anything available?"

"Why, we actually just had a room open up. You're lucky. Everything is booked solid for the air show."

"Oh, what a surprise," said Max. "I'll take it."

* * *

The stakeout was tense, as they didn't know if they were the only ones who were waiting for Upton to appear. There were two possible street entrances to the hotel. Max covered one side from the car. Trent and Renee observed the other entrance from the window seat of a coffee shop across the street.

Renee, still monitoring Jennifer Upton's personal email, had promptly deleted the automatically generated message from the hotel, confirming that she had canceled her room reservation. Now Renee was using software on her computer to look for signs that Upton's electronic devices might be pinging local cell towers.

Renee wore white earbuds, and her voice was being transmitted to flesh-colored earpieces that both Max and Trent were wearing.

"There it is. Her phone is local." Renee checked her watch: 3:30 p.m.

"She could be anywhere within a five-mile range. Expect her to head into the hotel any minute now."

Trent tapped the table and rose. He would start walking around the hotel, looking for any unwanted surveillance.

Max said, "I just got off the phone with Wilkes. I asked him to get us a safe house in the area."

"What did he say when you told him you were in Oshkosh?"

"He didn't sound happy about being kept in the dark. But he also didn't sound surprised. I told him that we had an op in progress and had to go. He'll get us the safe house."

Ten minutes later, a middle-aged woman wearing stiletto pumps and a fashionable pantsuit strode into the hotel entrance. She was pulling a small rolling suitcase, its wheels bumping along on the pockmarked lot.

The automatic double doors of the hotel slid open and she disappeared inside. Trent followed her in.

Five minutes after that, she was outside again, red-faced and cursing as she pulled her car keys out of her pocketbook and walked into the parking lot.

"Okay, she's headed back to her car," said Max. "I'm moving. Renee, connect me please."

"Okay, it's going through. Remember, just speak normally. The software will do the rest."

Renee was running Max's voice through a new program being tested by a Silicon Valley–based artificial intelligence company. Renee knew one of the lead technologists, who had granted her partial access to the program. They claimed to be able to take five minutes of recorded voice data on any person and clone the voice signature.

Now, as Max spoke, his voice would be transformed into someone else's. Someone who Jennifer Upton knew very well.

Upton, feeling her phone ring, dug it out of her purse and answered the unknown caller. "Hello?"

"It's me."

"Herb?"

"Where are you? Are you at your hotel?"

"What? Yes...why are you calling me? Herb, you weren't supposed to—"

"I'm sending a car. My colleagues should be there now. I've got to go."

Max didn't want to mess around. The longer they attempted to impersonate Senator Becker, the more that could go wrong. It was a risk. He wasn't completely certain that Upton and Becker were still in touch, but they were both headed to Oshkosh, and his gut told him they were still connected. Not to mention, it was all he had to go on. He would only need a few moments' hesitation on her part.

Upton kept walking staring in confusion at her phone.

"Thirty seconds," said Max over the earpiece, now only speaking to Trent and Renee. He was driving the car into the hotel parking lot.

Trent was several paces behind Upton, having followed her out the door. He tapped his earpiece twice to acknowledge Max, the noise transmitting two consecutive thumping sounds. Trent pretended to be reading something on his cell phone while he walked a path parallel on the other side of the parking lot, following his target.

Max's car inched up behind Jennifer Upton's parked vehicle. Trent's pace sped up. Upton had put her phone back in her purse and was now in the process of collapsing the sliding handle of her suitcase. She glanced at the car now stopped just behind her.

Max rolled down the passenger window. His car was only a few feet away from her.

"Ma'am, Senator Becker sent us to pick you up. Could you come with us, please?"

"Excuse me?" She stared at Max, looking confused and worried. Her head jerked, seeing Trent approach from behind her.

Shit. She was going to be noncompliant. Max could see it in her eyes.

In one quick movement, Trent opened the rear door of their rental car, grabbed Jennifer Upton around the waist, and moved her into the rear seat. He climbed in after her, then reached for her bag, pulled it inside and shut the door as Max drove away, trying to calm her down.

"We're here to help you, ma'am," said Max, quickly making eye contact with her in the mirror.

Trent sat close, and leaned toward her, his finger over his mouth, signaling her to be quiet.

Jennifer Upton looked with wide eyes at Trent, the chiseled ex–Special Forces man, all muscle and clenched jaw, a menacing figure hovering over her tiny frame. She kept quiet long enough for them to give her an explanation.

"Ma'am, we're with US law enforcement, and we're here to protect you from an imminent threat. Senator Becker should have given you a call letting you know we were on the way." Not technically truthful, but it helped hold down her urge to scream.

Hearing Max say this, Renee shut down her laptop and headed out the door of the coffee shop. She walked quickly around the corner, and down the back alley. One block away, Max's car stopped abruptly just in front of the curb. Renee stepped out of the alleyway and hopped in the passenger seat, and the vehicle sped away.

*** * ***

Hugo's plan had been simple.

He was going to wait for the woman to enter her hotel, then pay a visit to her room and kill her. Her death would be swift and quiet. Made to look like a fall in the shower, or a tragic choking. Perhaps a suicide? It really just depended on the situation. Hugo considered himself to be a creative—like an artist or a musician. He had learned from a career of contract killings that sometimes good art just comes to you in the moment. One can't plan for all the materials available or all the external influences that might affect an operation.

Like just now.

Hugo hadn't entered her hotel. Instead, he had stayed put. Watching an unexpected team tail the unsuspecting Jennifer Upton, apprehend her, and depart. This would cost him money and time. It would also anger Syed.

Hugo had been scouting out Jennifer's hotel from an empty apartment across the street for five hours. From Hugo's years of experience, he knew a fellow professional when he saw one. He had seen the first man casing the block an hour before Upton's arrival. Hugo had taken several snapshots, which he would later show to Syed.

Not long after the first man had gone out of sight, a second man had appeared. This second man was tall and walked with a military swagger. Hugo had observed all the comings and goings within two blocks of his position. This second man had entered the coffee shop across the street from the hotel and remained inside for several hours. The fact that he had emerged just as Jennifer Upton arrived on scene could not have been a coincidence.

That left several questions in Hugo's mind. Chief among them, who was this team of operators? Their moves were quick and professional. He guessed that they were Americans, which alarmed him.

Hugo had watched most of the activity through his rifle scope. If he had wanted to, he could have executed a perfect headshot against his target while she was strolling through the parking lot. For a brief moment, he'd toyed with the idea of taking all three of them out, but that course of action would pose several problems. For one, he didn't have a clear shot of the driver, and he didn't want to risk missing one of them. Secondly, the two unknown men weren't part of the assassin's assignment. It was always possible they were allies to Syed, and that the ISI had communicated poorly. Or perhaps Williams had sent them. Unlikely, but possible. Yet the most important reason Hugo stayed still was that a triple homicide with a sniper rifle would have attracted a tremendous amount of attention. It would have required him to go into hiding, and it would have made it nearly impossible to achieve the larger objective here at Oshkosh.

So Hugo had taken several pictures with his long-zoom lens as the team drove away. Then he'd taken several more as the woman emerged from the coffee shop. A strange feeling of recognition hit him afterwards, when he reviewed the pictures of the woman on his digital camera.

Where did he know her from? Dark shoulder-length hair. Skinny and toned. Very pale complexion. The beginnings of a tattoo visible on one of her legs. Hugo couldn't place her. But these images might be useful to Syed.

Hugo packed up his rifle kit and camera, then walked out the back of the building. Within minutes, he was driving a ten-year-old Ford Focus south along I-41. Along the way he used a burner cell phone to send a text message. In code, the text message informed Syed that the mission to kill Upton had been aborted. An immediate response provided Hugo with a coded meeting location. Hugo deleted the message and powered off the phone, then threw it out the window while he was taking the highway exit.

An hour later, the assassin was safe in his hotel room. He would have more driving to do when he headed to Oshkosh to meet his handler later that evening, but for now he would rest.

Hugo kicked off his shoes and flipped on the news.

"Authorities have not ruled out whether the violent attack on a federal interrogation team in Texas several days ago, which left six dead, is related to terrorism. From the steps of the Capitol Building earlier today, Senator Becker of Wisconsin, said this: 'Whether it was terrorism, narcoterrorism, or just some thuggish drug kingpin, the people who did this will be hunted down and prosecuted. The American people will not stand for it.' Senator Becker, whose chief of staff's death has now been ruled a homicide, has himself reportedly been the target of death threats due to his strong stance against the opioid industry. While no one has claimed responsibility for these death threats, authorities believe they are tied to international criminal organizations intent on influencing Senator Becker's controversial Opioid Epidemic Bill. Experts believe that this bill could drastically affect both the legal and illegal markets for opioid pills. Senator Becker had no comment on these death threats before he left for his home state of Wisconsin earlier today."

Hugo listened carefully, changing the channel to different news outlets, still on the lookout for any sign that authorities might be tracking him after the hits in Virginia. This trip to the United States would end with quite the body count. Some of them very well known. Hugo worried that the Pakistani intelligence service was getting too careless, working with this Englishman, Williams. Hugo had met the man before. An odd cat. But very efficient at his work. And while Hugo respected that, he didn't like taking unnecessary risks. He would have to be careful there. Perhaps Hugo would take a long vacation after this weekend.

The former Legionnaire set his watch alarm, shut his eyes and slept for an hour. He then rose and drove north to the meeting location. A crowded grass parking lot at the air show. The recreational vehicle lot.

Hugo smiled to the air show staff, who happily took his money in exchange for a weekly parking pass. He then parked his car and walked through the rows and rows of Winnebagos sitting in an endless grass field.

Overhead, the sky had come alive as a squadron of World War Two bomber aircraft flew by, their deep, guttural engines droning on. Massive dark silhouettes flew in formation as the hordes of spectators watched, using their hands as sun visors.

At last Hugo came upon a smaller RV with a brown-skinned man in shorts and a tee shirt sitting just outside the door. He sat in a folding chair, under the shade of a tall beach umbrella. Hugo kept walking, double-checking the area for surveillance before he approached.

The Pakistani ISI operative couldn't have looked more out of place if he'd tried. Syed was monumentally stupid for coming here. It was very unlike him, which further concerned Hugo. Why were they taking so many risks? Was this really that important?

This security guard had on clothing that looked like he'd just purchased it off the clearance rack at a local sporting goods store, tags probably still on. He appeared grumpy and mean, not even paying attention to the air show. Instead, he was scanning the area, diligently performing his security job, and sticking out like a sore thumb.

The Pakistani man rose up, looking at Hugo as he approached the Winnebago, a suspicious look on his face.

"I'm here to see Syed."

Movement in the window of the RV, and then the thin door swung open. "Let him in," came Syed's voice from the dark interior.

Hugo walked past the security man and entered the RV. It was cramped and looked barely used, aside from an electronics suite that was set up on the small kitchen table. The Pakistani intelligence officer shut the laptop on the table and motioned for Hugo to sit in the seat across from him.

"I thought you were worried about surveillance. I understand your men needed to come here, but what are you doing here in this thing?"

"We needed to blend in. This is what people at the air show do. Besides, there weren't any available hotels within an hour's drive. This was the best we could manage for now."

"Well, call your man inside. He's not blending in with anyone."

Syed grew visibly annoyed. "I appreciate the concern. He has been in here all day and just went out to look for you. We'll only be here for a short while longer. The meeting begins soon."

Syed flinched as a twin-engine fighter jet thundered overhead. The noise was loud enough that it set off car alarms in the parking lot. Hugo still couldn't believe that Syed's organization held this meeting at an air show each year.

Well, this would be the last time.

Hugo said, "What does Williams think he is doing, killing so many in Texas like that? It's not just his own skin that he's risking."

Syed ignored the question. "What happened earlier? You weren't able to get to Upton?"

"It was not possible. There were others present. Two men and a woman. They looked American. They were very efficient." Hugo described what happened in detail.

Syed said, "Who were they?"

"I was going to ask you. I was under the impression that your operation was still clear of American law enforcement and intelligence eyes. I took a few photos."

Hugo took out his camera. He had removed the zoom lens, so it was less cumbersome. He preferred to use cameras instead of phones. Better resolution, better zoom, and most importantly—no connectivity. Hugo didn't normally carry a personal phone, only the occasional burner. He'd known too many competitors who were dead because they'd used a cell phone.

Syed's face darkened as he looked at the images. "One can never assume oneself to be completely clear of surveillance. Those who do usually wind up dead or compromised."

Hugo hummed agreement. "So you think it is the CIA or FBI?"

"Most likely, yes." Syed said something in Urdu that sounded like a curse. "You are sure that you weren't followed here?"

"As sure as I can be. Have you handled the arrangements I asked you to make inside the air show?"

Syed nodded. "Everything you asked for has been set up. My contact will meet you tomorrow morning. He'll have a spot for you here."

Syed pointed to a spot on the air show map.

"That will do perfectly. I should have a clear line of sight to the target. I will re-check when I am there."

"Good."

"I will have free time tonight. Are you sure that you do not want me to locate Upton? If it is the Americans, I assume that they've moved her to a safe house and will interrogate her. Is that a problem?"

"Yes. It is a problem."

"Then do you want me to solve your problem?" Hugo's tone was filled with impatience. He liked the fees the ISI paid him, but sometimes they were slow to act.

"No. Williams wishes to be involved now."

"I thought he was your agent. Now he tells you what he wants?"

"Our relationship has evolved over time."

"Perhaps our relationship should evolve."

"Not if you want to keep getting paid."

Hugo snorted. "He already knows that I don't have Upton?"

"He does."

"Will he now use the same men he used in Texas?"

"Don't concern yourself with that."

"The woman was my target. I don't get paid if I don't do the job. Of course it is my concern. And Williams's men will make a public mess. I don't want to deal with the hassle when I lose you as a client because you ended up in an American prison."

Syed tilted his head, smiling like he thought this was a joke. The Pakistani man rose. "I appreciate your concern. Come with me. We will go now."

Hugo said, "Where are we going?"

"To see Williams."

22

Hugo followed the Pakistanis in his car. They drove along Route 45, paralleling the shore of Lake Winnebago. They passed an inlet with a sign that read "Seaplane Base." A multiengine aircraft was visible from the road, floating in the water, its props spinning as a gathered crowd took pictures.

Ten minutes further south, Syed's RV turned left onto a long gravel driveway. The vehicle stopped at a wrought-iron gate, an eight-foot-high stone wall spreading out on either side and surrounding the property.

The gate was being guarded by two Hispanic men, who approached both vehicles and inspected them carefully. Hugo saw that the first security guard was carrying a holstered pistol. A third man stood inside a small guardhouse positioned just behind and to the right of the entrance gate. He held some sort of small Uzi-like weapon. Hugo couldn't tell the exact make, as the guard was half-hidden behind the doorway, his sharp eyes watching the new arrivals with interest.

The gate guards allowed them to pass and then instructed the drivers of both vehicles to park on a gravel lot just behind and to the left of the wall. They were instructed to walk the rest of the way to the home, a quarter mile hike down a peninsula. The home was an impressive Victorian-style mansion. Three black Suburban SUVs were parked in the roundabout driveway in front of the mansion. A handful of armed Latino guards stood next to them.

The Pakistanis and Hugo were each searched and disarmed, which annoyed Hugo. But Syed nodded for him to comply. The guards actually had a tent set up in front of the mansion entrance. Under the tent was a folding table with numbered bins to hold weapons, phones, and electronic devices. One of the guards filled out a notepad to keep track of the owners and equipment.

"You will get it back when you are done," said the humorless Mexican man who placed Hugo's pistol in a plastic bin.

Hugo shook his head but gave up his weapon. "I need to keep this," he said, holding his camera. The guard looked at what Hugo presumed was his supervisor, who nodded.

They were escorted through the main floor of the mansion and onto the back deck. Ian Williams stood in the backyard, tall and lanky, chatting with an eclectic group of men. The group sat on expensive outdoor furniture, cocktails in their hands, laughing and apparently enjoying themselves. Just a backyard cookout in Wisconsin. Surrounded by cartel gunmen. Hugo wondered what the hell was going on. Syed wouldn't tell him who these men were, but to him it looked like happy hour for the United Nations. Every ethnicity was represented, and all were dressed in expensive business casual attire.

Seeing Syed, Williams rose and walked to him. "Abdul. It is good to see you. Your men can wait inside." He yelled something in Spanish to one of the guards. "They'll take care of them." Seeing Hugo, Williams pointed. "This is your specialist?"

Syed nodded. "You may call him Hugo."

Williams said, "Ah. Please remain with us, if you would. I wish to speak with you." Williams turned to the half dozen men enjoying themselves in the sun. "Gentlemen, if you'll excuse me." Nodding heads and several held-up drinks in response.

Williams and Syed whispered to each other as Williams led them east on the property, towards the water's edge. The tip of the peninsula ended with a long wooden dock and over-water gazebo.

Williams brought them to the gazebo and had them each sit. Then he said, "What happened with Miss Upton?"

Syed recounted what he knew, and Hugo filled in the gaps. Then Hugo showed Williams the images he had taken with his camera. Ian Williams's eyes went wide.

"These were the people who apprehended Miss Upton?" His eyes locked on to Hugo.

"Yes. I assume you know them?"

"I do."

Syed said, "Who are they?"

"You and I can discuss that momentarily."

"Do you want me to retrieve the woman? Upton?" asked Hugo.

Williams shook his head, clicking his tongue. "Forget her for now. Your other work here is much more important."

"Very well."

"Have you made your preparations?"

"I have been training for weeks."

"You understand the critical nature of the timing?"

"I do."

"There will be an increased security presence. Will that be a problem?"

"It will be factored in to my approach."

Ian Williams glanced at Syed and smiled. "Good. Tomorrow, then."

* * *

Jennifer Upton barely spoke during the car ride to the safe house. This was understandable, considering the abrupt way they'd taken her in the hotel parking lot. Max had explained that she was in danger, that they were moving her for her own safety, but she looked skeptical and was hesitant to cooperate. She hadn't brought up why Senator Becker was involved, but neither had Max. He didn't want to press his luck before earning a little trust.

Wilkes had given them the address of a farm forty minutes to the west of Oshkosh. Now their sedan bumped along a rocky dirt road, beyond fields of sweet corn.

"Knee high by the Fourth of July," said Trent, looking out the window.

"What?" asked Upton, seeming more angry than scared at this point.

"Something my brother always used to say. If the cornstalks back home were knee high by the Fourth of July, it was going to be a bumper crop."

Upton looked at Trent like he was crazy.

Max parked the vehicle in the driveway of a small ranch home surrounded by weeping willow trees. An old white barn stood next to a grain elevator one hundred yards to the south. A rusty charcoal grill collected dust in the backyard. The shrubs needed to be trimmed. The front door opened, and a serious-looking kid in his early twenties stuck his head out, evaluating them while keeping his right arm behind the door. When the kid recognized Max, he placed the pistol he'd been holding down on the coffee table by the door and walked outside.

"Mr. Fend, Caleb Wilkes asked me to convey his apologies for not being able to make it here himself."

"What's he doing?"

"He's otherwise engaged."

After an awkward introduction to Jennifer Upton, Max and crew headed inside the home. The CIA kid introduced himself as Mike Barnaby. By the look of him, Max figured he was maybe a year out of the Farm, if that. Wilkes was scraping the bottom of the barrel for this op.

Mike showed them into the living room and offered them something to eat and drink. Still looking angry, Upton requested only a glass of tap water. Mike did a quick search of her person and took her phone and an e-reader device that was in her purse. "Sorry, Miss Upton, but this is for your own safety. We'll give it back as soon as we know that you're no longer in danger."

Trent and the CIA kid waited in the kitchen, watching the surveillance feed that had been set up around the house and eavesdropping on the interrogation that would soon commence.

Max asked Renee to stay with them, hoping that a kind-looking female face might help to instill trust. Renee and Max sat on the couch, opposite Jennifer Upton, who plopped down on a love seat. The room was quiet, dark, and cool. They were miles away from the drone of aircraft engines and crowds of the air show here. But the clock was ticking. Tomorrow was the twenty-eighth. According to Rojas, it was the day of Williams's meeting. Max needed to find out why Upton had gone off the grid. What had made her come up here? Was she connected to Ian Williams and the ISI? More importantly, he needed to know what was critical enough about this mysterious meeting for the ISI and the cartel to kill multiple Americans in a series of brazen attacks within the US.

Upton squinted at him, as if trying to work something out. "You're Charles Fend's boy, aren't you?"

"I am."

Her expression softened. "I've met your father."

"Did you? When was that?"

"Maybe a decade ago, at a fundraiser. He contributed to a campaign I was working on."

"May I ask who you were working for at the time?"

She hesitated, then said, "Herbert Becker."

"You were on Senator Becker's staff?" Max asked, already knowing the answer.

"He was a congressman back then. But yes," replied Upton. She looked out the window. It was getting dark now. "How long are you planning to keep me here?"

"Since we have reason to believe your life is in danger, it'll be at least a day or more, until we can find a more suitable arrangement."

"What if I want to leave?"

"We'll get you out of here if that's what you want. But you need to be under our protection. It's for your own good."

"Why am I in danger?"

"Tell me, Jennifer, does the name Ian Williams mean anything to you?"

Jennifer's smile faded. So, she knew him.

"It rings a bell, but..." She looked like she was searching her mind for a memory...or a lie. "No. No, I don't think I know him."

"Really?" Max's voice was even-keeled. His piercing blue eyes studied her face for the slightest microexpression that might give away the truth. "We received information that Ian Williams may want to cause you harm. Are you sure you don't know him?"

She shook her head.

"What about a lobbyist named Dahlman?"

"Who?" Her eyes narrowed.

"Your name was on a list. The only other name on that list was a lobbyist named Joseph Dahlman. A few days ago, he was killed in Virginia."

Jennifer went pale. "Killed?"

Max nodded somberly.

"You knew him?" Renee said.

"No," she said, her face twitching. "I'm sorry, but what is this list you're referring to?"

"What about Ronald Dicks? You knew him."

She looked down at the floor. "Yes. I knew Ron. I was very sad to read about what happened."

"They're calling that a homicide."

"I know."

"When was the last time you spoke to Ron?"

"Years ago. We've lost touch. I worked with him. That was all."

"What are you doing up here in Wisconsin, Miss Upton?"

"I...I came to see Herb."

Renee said, "Becker? You came to see the senator?"

"That's right."

"Why?"

She looked away. "It's somewhat embarrassing. A woman my age running around like this, trying to stay out of the limelight just to see a man."

Max said, "It was a social call?"

Upton said, "Senator Becker is a very high-profile individual, obviously. And unfortunately, based on our past...and the feelings of certain members of his family...we need to be discreet about our relationship."

"So you and Becker are *with* each other? In an ongoing relationship?" Renee asked, as diplomatically as she could manage.

Annoyance flashed on Upton's face. "Yes, darling."

Max said, "Miss Upton, I hope you don't mind if I pry, but it may be relevant...why do you feel the need to keep the low profile about the relationship? What do you mean about the family members? Do they not approve?"

Upton's voice grew ugly. "It's mostly just his damned daughter, Karen. She has too much influence with him. Always has. When Herb's wife found out about our little fling, she divorced him in no time. He wanted to be with me. At least the wife was reasonable. She wasn't going to make a big fuss about it and ruin his name. The senator's daughter, on the other hand—"

"Karen Becker?"

Upton nodded. "She was the one who caught us together in the first place. Our relationship had been easier to keep under wraps when we were traveling internationally, but our travel had slowed down. It was an election year, of course, and Becker was running a mere two points ahead. This was back before he switched parties. The girl said the only way she wouldn't tell the press about the affair was if I agreed to leave his staff. I mean, the nerve of that little brat. Their marriage was in shambles anyway. What the hell did it matter to her?"

Max said, "When was all this?"

"That was a long time ago. It was when I was on his staff, so...2006? Yes, that was it."

"So you are telling me that you're here in Wisconsin to see Senator Becker socially. And that you're keeping a low profile because Karen Becker still doesn't approve?"

Max could see Jennifer Upton's mind racing, trying to work out how to answer the question. Max knew this story was all bullshit, of course. If she was just hiding from the daughter, she wouldn't have kept her phone switched off for hours at a time. No one does that. Not unless they're worried about someone tracking their movements through their phone.

"Karen Becker is a very opinionated woman. And Herb wishes to keep his family life and his social life separate. There's nothing wrong with what we are doing." Another flare-up in her tone.

The conversation went on for another ninety minutes. Jennifer Upton continued to be evasive. She denied trying to avoid detection by turning her phone off. "Sometimes you just need to disconnect." She also brushed off any meaning behind making her hotel reservation with a seldom-used account, under a fake name. "I told you, I like my privacy."

Upton claimed to have no idea how Ian Williams was connected to Senator Becker, or if he even was. She said she'd never met anyone from Pakistan and laughed nervously when Max asked about foreign intelligence services. "What, now you think I'm a spy? I don't think so."

Eventually, Max suggested they take a break for the evening. It was getting dark, and they were getting nowhere with Upton. Max was ready to try more aggressive tactics, but first he wanted to check in with Wilkes.

Jennifer Upton was given one of the bedrooms for the evening, and Mike the CIA operative was joined by his partner, who had brought them all food.

On the ride back to the Oshkosh campground, Trent and Renee both verbalized Max's feelings.

"She's full of it," said Renee.

"Agreed," said Max.

"What are you going to do?" asked Trent.

"She was surprised that I knew the name Ian Williams. And she was pretty disturbed at the death of Joseph Dahlman. Rightfully distressed at the mention of Ron Dicks. I don't know what worries her more—that we'll figure out what she's really up to, or that someone might be trying to kill her. Either way, let's let her stew for the evening."

23

The next morning, Max and Renee crawled out of the tent to see Trent doing push-ups in the grass, a steely-eyed determination on his face, his muscles rippling and sweaty, huffs of exertion coming as he continued to pump out perfect-form reps.

"Morning," he said to them as he switched to sit-ups.

Renee smiled as she tied her sneakers. "We were going to go for a run. You want to come?"

"I'm good, thanks."

She glanced at Max. Renee was worried about Trent. A veteran of multiple wars who had lost his brother to a drug overdose. He was strong, but she could see that he was struggling with his inner demons.

"You sure?" Max said.

"No, it's alright. I was up early and ran around the perimeter of the field. Looks like they're going to have a 5K there on the runway. Would have liked to do that one."

"Maybe next year. Wilkes sent us a message. He wants us to meet him this morning."

Renee and Max began their jog, winding through the grass parking lots, campgrounds, and groves of trees surrounding the airfield. Droplets of dew coated the grass. A buzzing flock of ultralight aircraft skimmed the treetops on a massive morning flight, the rising sun painting them with reddish-orange light. It was a peaceful scene, and it felt good to sweat.

The pair ran for forty minutes, stretched, then showered at the campground's public showers. It felt like a vacation, but Max kept getting reminders that it wasn't. Everywhere he looked, he saw a potential conspirator staring back at him. A man leaning on his car, talking on a cell phone as he and Renee strode by. A middle-aged Latina woman, walking along the road next to the air show entrance. Everyone looked suspicious, and Max was getting twitchy.

Trent had grabbed a few breakfast sandwiches and handed them out when they arrived back at the tents. Renee was drying her wet hair with a white towel. Max sat on one of the lawn chairs surrounding the ash from last night's campfire. Renee sat on the chair next to him. She had taken out her computer again and was connecting to her sat link.

Through a mouthful of bacon, egg, and cheese biscuit, Max said, "You're working now? We've only got about fifteen minutes before we're supposed to meet Wilkes."

"I just had an idea come to me when we were running. I wanted to check it out really quick." She hit a key and said, "Bingo."

"What is it?" Max craned his head around to see her screen.

"Something Upton said to us last night was bothering me. She said that it had been easier for her and Becker to have a relationship when they traveled more. So I wanted to see where they were traveling to."

"And?"

"Afghanistan."

Trent looked up.

Max said, "Ian Williams was stationed there with MI6, right? I'd be very interested to know whether the two met. The ISI has a big presence in Afghanistan as well. Good work, Renee. We can grill Upton on this later."

Together they walked through the main entrance of the air show, under a tall blue sign with flags flapping on top. Even this early in the morning, the crowds were impressive. Groups of retirees in baseball caps, families with strollers, and young aviation enthusiasts walked over the expansive concrete walkway towards the aircraft static displays. In the distance, they heard the whine of aircraft engines starting up, then a rumble of thunder overhead as two dark F-15 Strike Eagles joined the empty runway pattern.

"Wow, they're really loud!" said Renee, holding her ears.

The twin-engine Air Force fighters were doing touch-and-goes—landing on the runway, rolling for a few seconds, and then gunning their engines and taking off again. Each time, they banked hard, exposing their underbellies in the turn, throttling their engines, tongues of blue-yellow afterburner shooting out, and then smoothly flattening out in the downwind.

"What are they doing?"

"Showing off," Max said.

"You've got that schoolboy grin again."

"Can't help it. They're magnificent beasts. Someday I've got to get a ride in one."

Trent said, "That him?"

Wilkes was standing under the nose of a KC-10 aerial refueling tanker, its monstrous nose towering over him. Seeing Max, he motioned for them to follow.

"Ladies and gentlemen, good morning."

They said their hellos as Wilkes brought them to a pair of motorized golf carts. Wilkes drove one and Max the other, and they scooted off down the taxiway, driving all the way to the opposite side of the field. It took them a good ten minutes to get to the area of the airport where the private jets were parked, but Max recognized his father's personal jet from afar.

They parked the golf carts outside the sleek aircraft and walked up the stairway. Max didn't say anything to Wilkes about his father's participation in this morning's conversation, but he was a bit annoyed. Until now, neither Caleb nor his father had said anything about working with the other at Oshkosh. Add it to the list of actions that Caleb Wilkes had taken without giving Max a heads-up.

"Renee, good to see you again," Charles greeted her at the entrance to the aircraft, holding a glass of juice in one hand as they hugged. She smiled and said hello, but Max caught a questioning glance from her as the group walked to the central area in the jet's cabin. She was also wondering how his father was involved.

The inside of the aircraft was quite luxurious, and appropriately set up as the mobile office of a billionaire industrialist. A long leather couch on one side. A computer terminal with the latest communications. Several flat-screen TVs, each tuned to a different cable news business channel.

In one section of the cabin, a meeting area had been set up. Rotating cushioned seats had been turned to face towards each other. In between them was an impressive breakfast spread laid out on a glossy maple table.

"Coffee, tea, anyone?" asked Charles's personal assistant.

"We'll be fine, thank you. No calls or visitors for now," said Charles. The cabin door was shut, and Caleb, Charles, Max, Trent, and Renee all sat down. "Help yourselves." Charles waved towards the pastries and coffee cups on the table.

Wilkes began, "Max, I read your report. So far it sounds like Upton isn't cooperating." Max had typed up a short summary of the Upton interview on Renee's computer the night before and sent it to Wilkes.

"That's my opinion. But as I wrote, I think she's hiding something."

Wilkes nodded. "She claims she's here as Senator Becker's secret lover?"

"That's it."

"And no connection to Ian Williams or the ISI?"

"Correct. According to Miss Upton," Max said skeptically. "But Renee did some research and uncovered something interesting this morning." Max filled Wilkes and his father in on what Renee had uncovered relating to the international trips then-congressman Becker had made to Afghanistan back in the 2000s.

Wilkes didn't look very surprised.

"Excellent work, Renee," Wilkes said. He turned to Charles, who was quiet. "What was your read on the senator, Charles?"

Max looked at his father, who was staring back at his son, a look of admiration in his eyes. So, Wilkes was indeed using his father to probe Senator Becker, eh? It made sense, Max thought. The senator and the CEO had known each other for decades.

Charles said, "He's worried about something, I know that much. I ate dinner with him and his daughter, Karen, last night. When I wasn't at the table, they engaged in a tense private conversation. Were you going to share that?"

"In a moment, yes. Charles, if you would, please continue to shadow the senator today. Try to keep him in your sight as much as you can, and keep your guard up. His daughter performs this afternoon. The senator's official schedule has him heading back to D.C. this evening, after his daughter's performance."

Max said, "You think they'll target Senator Becker while he's here at Oshkosh?"

Wilkes folded his hands in his lap. "I do. Max, I think it's time that I provide you with a bit more about the senator's history."

24

It began during the Cold War.

When the Soviets had occupied Afghanistan in the 1980s, they'd accused the CIA of helping the Mujahideen smuggle opium out of the country in order to raise funds. While a connection between Western intelligence agencies and the Afghan drug trade had never been proven, the various Afghan factions had increased opium production in the country after the Soviets fled in 1989. This was partially due to the loss of alternative sources of financial support from the West.

Opium production continued to flourish as the Taliban rose to power in the 1990s. That was until Mullah Omar, the effective leader of the Taliban, declared it un-Islamic in the year 2000. For a brief period, the Taliban enforced the eradication of poppy farming in Afghanistan, which resulted in a sixty-five percent drop in global heroin production during the year 2001.

Then, on a clear sunny morning in September of that year, Al Qaeda terrorists hijacked four commercial airliners and the world changed forever. Soon after the attacks, the United States demanded that the Taliban hand over Osama bin Laden. The Taliban responded that they would not extradite bin Laden unless the United States provided "evidence that bin Laden was behind the September 11 terrorist attacks."

The US military soon began deploying to Afghanistan, and the Taliban was removed from power.

Afghan farmers quickly returned to growing opium, which was much more profitable than anything else they could produce. Soon Afghanistan was supplying ninety percent of the world's heroin and expanding its production each year. Opium was the lifeblood of the Afghan farming economy. In 2007, when Afghan leader Hamid Karzai addressed all thirty-four provincial governors in Kabul, he began his speech by denouncing the drug trade. The line was greeted by a few polite claps and many looks of concern. Later in the speech, he admonished the international community for wanting to spray Afghan opium crops. The room erupted in cheers.

Wilkes said, "By the late 2000s, more than half of Afghanistan's economy—around three billion dollars—was based on the drug trade. Three billion. That's a lot of money, right?"

Max said, "Sure. It's a lot of money."

Wilkes leaned forward. "But it isn't. Not compared to what it turns into. That's damn pocket change. From there, the drugs flow across trade routes through Iran and Turkey on their way to Europe. In the opposite direction, they flow through India and by sea to East Asia and Australia. The drugs gain value every inch of the way. The closer they are to the customer, the more middlemen, the higher the risk, which needs to be built into the price. The heroin is sold on the streets for twenty times the original price. The Afghans only see a tiny piece of the action. So, who gets all that money?"

"The international criminal organizations who traffic it and sell it on the streets."

"Yes. But that's not all. Who else gets the money?"

"I don't know, who?"

"Ask the ISI. Ask Ian Williams."

Max looked at him sideways. "What do you mean?"

Wilkes smiled. "When Williams was still in good standing with MI6, he was working in their Pakistan field office, where I now believe he was recruited by our friend Abdul Syed of the ISI."

Trent said, "So Ian Williams got recruited by the ISI. That fits with what we know of him."

"Some of our sources confirmed that Williams was kicked out of MI6 for unethical and possibly illegal actions involving Afghan drug lords. He was also reportedly spotted meeting with an ISI operative, and he didn't disclose the meeting to MI6. He was kicked out of MI6 as the investigations began. But he fled the country. MI6 tells us that they think he contacted his old buddies in Pakistan and went to work for them."

"What did they have him doing?"

Wilkes said, "That's where it gets interesting. For several years now, we've suspected that Pakistani intelligence is helping to run a substantial portion of the illicit drug trade in Afghanistan. Williams was already connected to many of the players in that business. But this was back in the early 2000s. The demand for opium—both the legal and illegal demand —was only a fraction of what it is today."

"The ISI saw an opportunity."

"Exactly. The ISI knew the benefit that type of business could have for them. Behind the scenes, the ISI runs Pakistan. Taking over Afghanistan's heroin trade allows them enormous power and international influence."

Renee shook her head. "How?"

Max said, "Think about it. If Pakistan controls the economy of their neighbor Afghanistan, they own that country. And all that cash is off the books, so they can do whatever they want with it. Influence elections. Buy policy. Pay for black ops. That's why so many intelligence agencies around the world sometimes deal with narcotics traffickers. It's the darker side of the intel business."

Renee said, "The US doesn't do that, do they?"

Wilkes smiled. "We use taxpayer money to fund our black ops."

Polite laughter followed. Except for Renee, who looked slightly horrified.

Wilkes said, "And it isn't just influence in Pakistan. Remember, the trade routes for Afghan opium run through Iran, Turkey, India, and dozens of other nations. The more the ISI gets their hands in different international pots of money, the more power they have in those countries as well. The ISI wanted Ian Williams to help them grow the pie, and to make sure they got a huge piece to themselves."

Max tried to put it all together in his mind. "So what are you saying? That the ISI recruited Williams to somehow spur on the global opium market? How?"

"Pakistani influence could only go so far by itself. They needed men like Ian Williams. People with connections. Dark salesmen who wouldn't mind stuffing a politician or businessman's back pocket with illicit cash in exchange for a big favor."

"How did he do it?"

"Back in the early 2000s, after the international coalition went in and collapsed the Taliban government, the United Kingdom was put in charge of the farming and drug policy in Afghanistan. Officially it was supposed to be run by their diplomats. But Ian Williams had huge sway with them, thanks to all his backroom deals throughout both Afghanistan and Pakistan. Between Williams and a group of other ISI agents, they were able to ensure that Afghan opium farming would grow rapidly. Maybe it wasn't completely official, but there were winks and nods. And Williams and Syed didn't stop there. Recognizing the huge growth opportunity in opium, they knew that they could expand to other markets. Other regions. And we think they got involved in the legal side of the marketplace as well."

Max frowned.

"What do you mean?"

"Then-congressman Herbert Becker first met Ian Williams in Afghanistan in 2002. Becker was on a diplomatic fact-finding mission. That same year, research came out that supported the use of narcotics like opioids to treat long-term pain. This was a new development. The research was paid for by Big Pharma. A year later, Becker voted on legislation deregulating the use of prescription opioids in the United States."

Max's thoughts were a swirl of ideas and facts. "Are you trying to tell me that the ISI, along with a rogue British agent and a dirty US politician, intentionally orchestrated the opioid epidemic?"

Renee said, "That seems far-fetched."

"I thought the same thing at first. But around this time, Becker made a lot of changes. He ran for Senate. He got a ton of money from outside contributors, many of whom had ties to the drug industry."

"That doesn't mean he was working for the ISI. Every politician gets supported by some special interest."

"You're right. But you have to ask yourself, how does Afghanistan end up producing ninety percent of the world's heroin? That's a multibillion-dollar operation. You always hear about the Colombian and Mexican drug cartels and how they operated like Fortune 500 companies, right? Guess what, the Afghans *aren't* running their drug trade by themselves. There's too much money in it. A business that size needs to plan the supply chain, distribution, sales. To seed demand among millions of customers..."

"A conspiracy of this size would have to be huge."

Wilkes said, "You have no idea. Afghanistan makes a few billion dollars a year from their opioid farming operation. But the global market for illicit heroin is closer to *fifty* billion. Add in *another* fifty billion for legal opioids. Add in more money for all the treatment programs. For insurance companies. Tax dollars. Opioids are an economic juggernaut."

"And Afghanistan grows ninety percent of all of that?"

"Not quite. They grow ninety percent of the *illicit* opium. The legal stuff is grown by licensed opium producers—mostly in Australia, Turkey, India, and France, and a few other countries. These are the suppliers for the pharmaceutical companies. But the illegal and legal opioid demand is related. They feed off each other."

Trent cleared his throat. "That's how my brother got started. Josh used both. He got a prescription for pain meds. The prescription ran out, but he was hooked. Couldn't stop. And it wasn't like he was a weak guy or anything. Hell, he'd been to war."

Renee was making the same connection. "All the statistics I looked at online showed the trend of increased heroin use in the US following the increased use of legal opioids."

Wilkes nodded. "And that trend line began right after Becker met with Williams."

The group went silent for a moment.

Trent said, "How is Senator Becker in on it?"

"We don't know that he is, exactly. Our intel suggests he may have been unaware of many details," Wilkes replied. "Last night, using a device we provided, your father was able to record part of the conversation between Senator Becker and his daughter, Karen."

Charles pressed his lips together and nodded in acknowledgment.

"What did they say?"

Wilkes placed his cell phone down on the coffee table in front of him. He tapped a button, and a conversation began playing.

Karen: "I think you should go back to the FBI."

Senator Becker: "I've spoken with them already."

Karen: "Dad..."

Senator Becker: "We've had this discussion."

Karen: "I'm worried for you. I think it's time for you to tell them everything."

Senator Becker: "Let's not talk about it now."

Karen: "You made one mistake a long time ago. And that was listening to Ron and Jennifer. You shouldn't have to pay for that forever."

Senator Becker: "I'm going to take care of it."

Karen: "No more deals with Ian."

Senator Becker: "I told you I'm done with him and I meant it."

Karen: "Are they here again?"

Senator Becker: "Karen, I promise you. I have ended it once and for all."

Karen: "But Ron..."

Senator Becker: "Ron kept going without my knowledge or approval."

Karen: "And they're just...*killing people*? Now, after all this time? All for that stupid bill?"

Senator Becker: "Yes."

Karen: "Why is it so important to them?"

Senator Becker: "Money."

Karen: "Can't you just drop the bill or change your vote or something? Give them what they want?"

Senator Becker: "I could. But my career would be over, and they would have won. And our problem wouldn't end there. They would still own me."

Karen: "So what are you going to do?"

Senator Becker: "I don't want to say. I don't want you knowing any more than you have to. But they won't have anything on me after this week. Trust me, Karen."

Karen: "Fine. But if you run into trouble, you go right back to the FBI, Dad. Alright? No matter what happens, it's not worth getting killed for."

The recording ended and Wilkes picked up his phone.

Renee said, "So the senator knows Ian Williams?"

"Yes," Wilkes confessed.

Max was confused. "If they were once collaborating, why would the ISI be trying to kill Becker now?"

"Becker has changed his stance on a policy that's making them billions."

"Okay, but why? Don't politicians usually want to make the guys bankrolling them happy?"

Charles said, "May I offer a thought? In business, joint ventures often end when one party no longer needs the other. Perhaps the senator benefited from the ISI's support for a time, but now he has outgrown his britches? He has excellent name recognition and a host of donors. His eye is on the big election in a few years. He's had to make a strategic choice to part ways with some of his original fundraisers."

Renee said, "How is it even possible that foreign government agents gave him money?"

Max said, "Unfortunately, there are several ways to do it."

Charles said, "He's right. Although it is easier to do in smaller quantities. That could be another reason Becker is no longer interested in accepting money from this source. Foreign nationals wouldn't be able to give him a big enough contribution to matter in the presidential election. Not without the risk of getting caught. Those sums of money are too high. But in state races...that wouldn't have been a problem."

"Too big for his britches..."

"This assumes Becker knew about it all. He claims only his aide knew about recent contact with the foreign investors. And he knew nothing about the foreigners being tied to the ISI."

Max said, "Why would the ISI kill Dahlman and Dicks?"

Wilkes shrugged. "Perhaps they decided those sources were no longer of value."

"Why?"

"Becker wasn't playing ball. If you're a foreign intelligence service and one of your key agents stops producing for you, what do you do?"

"Try to get them producing again."

"And if that doesn't work?"

"Get rid of any evidence that can lead back to me, and put the network to sleep."

Wilkes nodded. "Some agencies have a more permanent view of what that means than others. As Renee pointed out, Upton traveled to Afghanistan with Becker. So did Ron Dicks. Senator Becker, in his conversation with his daughter, revealed that he knew an Ian. Let us assume that is *our* Ian Williams. It is quite possible that Ian Williams still has a connection to Jennifer Upton, who was—according to Rojas—on the cartel's kill list." Wilkes sighed. "Maybe the ISI wants to get rid of a rogue agent? Maybe Becker has been ignorant of ninety-nine percent of all of this, and they're just pissed off that he isn't playing ball? Either way, it certainly looks like Senator Becker is in danger. And he knows this better than anyone."

"He has protection?"

"The Capitol Police has given him round-the-clock security, even outside of D.C."

"What are the Capitol Police going to do in Wisconsin?" asked Trent.

"It's their responsibility to protect members of Congress. They've coordinated with local law enforcement. It's the Oshkosh police who are providing the senator with a protective detail. You'll see plainclothes officers here with the senator."

"How many?"

"Two to four, depending on the time of day. I also have a few of my men keeping an eye on him, but our team here is small. And I have to provide at least one body to the safe house. But I've also reached out to the FBI and notified them that there may be a threat to the senator while he's here. They have over a dozen plainclothes agents who will be close to the senator for the duration of his stay at the air show."

Max said, "This would be a lot easier if he would just go to a safe house for a few days."

"The FBI and Capitol Police have both made that painfully clear. The senator has refused to alter his schedule. He insists on seeing his daughter perform today." Wilkes frowned, "I know this is ugly. We're doing our best. For now, I think we should assume that the senator is a target, and that either the cartel or ISI may try to take him out while he's at Oshkosh."

The thought was chilling. They were leaving a highly visible target out in the open. Max didn't like this at all.

Renee said, "I still don't understand something. Rojas said that the meeting was on the twenty-eighth, right? That's today."

"Correct," said Wilkes.

Renee shook her head. "But I guess I still don't understand why Ian Williams and the ISI need to kill anyone before it occurs."

Renee's question was answered with silence.

Charles cleared his throat. "She's absolutely right. The clock appears to be ticking. Yet you gentlemen don't know what happens when the minute hand strikes twelve."

Wilkes hummed. "Yes, thank you for that, Charles."

Charles turned to his son. "What do you think, Max?"

Max let out a deep breath, searching the faces of those around him. "Upton. Now that I know more about Becker's connection to Williams, I'll know where to add pressure. She's got to know more about this meeting."

Renee said, "Why can't we just go to Senator Becker and confront him with this?"

Wilkes shook his head. "If he's doing anything illegal himself, we don't want to expose ourselves. We'll want to uncover their network. And we can't do that if they know we're on to them."

Max said, "Caleb, if you're good with it, I'll head to the safe house now to continue my conversation with Jennifer Upton."

"Approved."

Max turned to Trent. "I think you should stay here and shadow Senator Becker. Ian Williams's sicarios are military-trained. He might be using them to execute a hit on the senator. If they were Mexican military, some of them may have even been trained inside the US by our own Special Forces. You're the most familiar with how they might operate."

Trent nodded. "Sounds good."

Max said to Renee, "You can come with me. Cross-reference every tidbit of information Jennifer Upton spills on us today. And let's dig into her phone and email accounts. Maybe we can find more hints about why she really came up here, if not for a lovers' rendezvous."

The group got up to leave. As they did, Wilkes said, "Remember, no phones. Syed and Williams have access to excellent crypto specialists. If you need to communicate, we'll either be set up here at Charles's aircraft or near the VIP tent on the main side of the airport. Good luck."

25

When Max and Renee got back to the safe house, they could see that something had changed in Jennifer Upton. She appeared more nervous, and Max began to put pressure on, telling her that they already knew Senator Becker and Ian Williams were connected.

Max brought up the very real threat of her and Senator Becker's assassinations. He told her how critical she was to saving the senator's life. And he promised her that he would help her. That anything she told them would be held in the strictest of confidence. He wasn't a cop, after all. He just wanted to avoid any further violence. Whatever she had seen or done, none of it mattered to him.

"I promise to help you, Jennifer. But you need to come clean and tell me everything."

It started off as a trickle. But as she got going, the vault cracked open, and gold coins began pouring out of her mouth.

"Williams was the match that started Herb Becker's political bonfire. Ron and I were both on Herb's staff at the time. Back when he was just in the House. Herb's political career was nothing special. He barely won his seat. Then September 11 happened, and the next thing we knew, Herb was making a name for himself in the international arena. We were all flying overseas on fact-finding missions and diplomatic trips to Afghanistan. It was like the Wild West. The war in Afghanistan was still young. Nobody knew what they were doing back then. Our congressional delegation was sent there to come up with a way to stabilize the Afghan economy. To try and bring peace to the region."

"How many trips?"

She placed her water glass on a coaster. "Three? Four, maybe? I went on three, he and Ron went on four, I think."

"And that's where Becker met Williams?"

"Yes. But Ron and I quickly decided to make sure Herb stayed clear of Ian Williams. We saw that Williams's connections to international business could present us with a huge opportunity. But with it came great risk. Ian Williams was in tight with a group of investors that desperately wanted to gain influence within the US government. But we suspected Williams might not have had the cleanest record. For that reason, Ron took point on all communication with Williams and the investor group."

"What was Williams doing that make you think he was dirty?"

"There were rumors about him accepting bribes from some of the Afghan poppy growers. The British diplomats there hated him, too. Thought he was a creep, if I recall. One of the Brits gave us a warning to stay away from Williams. Said he was getting some under-the-table payments or something."

"If you thought he was dirty, why'd you let Ron keep talking to him?"

She shot Max a sly look. "You aren't in politics, are you? Honey, there's all types. We didn't see Williams do anything illegal. It's good to have well-financed friends. Williams was offering us that. If you turn away every Tom, Dick, and Harry with a speck of dirt in their past, you'd have to turn away everyone. At the time, Williams just struck me as a wheeler and dealer."

"Tell me about this investment group that he offered access to. Were they connected to Pakistan? Pakistani intelligence, maybe?"

She touched her neck and pursed her lips. "I don't think so. Not that I'm aware."

That question flustered her, Max thought.

"But it was foreign money?"

Upton folded her arms and didn't answer. Okay, she didn't want to directly incriminate herself or her friends. Fine.

"What was motivating Williams to make these introductions between Ron and the foreign investors?"

"At that time, I think Ian knew he was on the way out of the British government. He was the subject of an internal investigation—we didn't find that out until later. My guess? The money came from people making tens of billions on heroin and other drugs. Ian Williams dealt with these people in the war on terror. He was MI6, after all. I imagine with the people he had to deal with, everything turned to shades of gray."

Max knew that Upton was close to home with that assessment. When he'd been under nonofficial cover in Europe with the DIA, he'd oftentimes met with men working for criminal organizations.

"So you think Williams was recruited by organized crime? The ones moving product from Afghanistan to the sellers' markets in Europe and Asia?"

"Maybe." She shrugged. "I just know that Ian was sharp. He knew how to play the game. He knew how to influence people. He was a power broker. He spoke several languages, and he didn't strike me as the type to worry about ethical considerations."

She looked uncomfortable. "You promised me that anything I say here won't get me in trouble, right?"

Max said, "I told you, I'm not a cop."

She frowned. "Fine, then. In the end, I knew Ian Williams was dirty because of the promises he made to Ron Dicks."

Max raised his eyebrow. "What promises?"

"Now, I only know what Ron told me in confidence. I don't have any firsthand evidence. But I believe Williams wanted Becker to help push certain policy stances within the US government. Becker represented some US agricultural interests, for instance. He could help make sure the US government didn't give subsidies that would turn Afghanistan into a farming competitor."

"Why would that matter?"

"Let me ask you something. You see a big black market for corn? Ian Williams was working with people who wanted to ramp up Afghanistan opium production. While the international community would never outright go along with that, there were ways that Becker could help. Like leaving Afghanistan no other option. Ian Williams worked through Ron Dicks to make Becker sway US policy."

"And Senator Becker was okay with this?"

"He didn't know everything. Our policy was to keep Becker in the dark. It would protect him. These agreements with Ian Williams were all on Ron Dicks back then. Becker trusted Ron to give him good advice. But Becker didn't know the details, and he didn't want to know, if you catch my meaning."

"But he must have been told enough to know it was going to be beneficial for him. What did Becker get?"

"Ron said that Williams had contacts in the business world that would start contributing to Becker's campaign."

So far Jennifer Upton's story was matching up very well with Caleb Wilkes's theory. "Quid pro quo?"

Upton said, "I'd rather not be so explicit in what I say, regardless of the fact that you aren't a cop."

"How long have these investors been investing, do you think?"

"Quite a while."

Renee said, "But this was foreign money, right? Wasn't this against the law? How could this happen without people finding out about it?"

Upton shrugged. "Campaign finance is a gray area. Super PACs and certain types of nonprofits can take money from foreign entities, but there are restrictions. The beauty of it is, though, that none of these restrictions are investigated or enforced. And some of the nonprofit types, under US law, can take unlimited money from any source, without having to disclose anything about that source."

"Dark money," Max said.

"That's the buzz word, yes. But I will tell you that politicians don't get anywhere nowadays without heavy financial backing. Each one of those TV commercials cost money. We used to think that the digital revolution would be great for politics. Lower spending and make things more efficient. Then the advertising cost per click rose as the market got flooded. Everything costs more now. It's insane. The research, the advertising. It's a political arms race. My company uses social networks and online analytics to microtarget our voters. Thanks to the tech companies, we can identify everything about a person and actually calculate down to the cent how much a voter is going to cost. So each election is just a simple matter of math. Does your candidate have the money or not? Ron got Ian Williams to help Becker with money."

"And the only thing Williams got in return was help in Afghan opium farming policy? That doesn't even sound like something Becker could pull off by himself."

"That type of help might have had a huge impact on the rebirth of Afghan poppy growth. Although you would never be able to prove it. And I seriously doubt that Ron was the only one Ian Williams was working with."

Max considered that. Who else was involved with Ian Williams? How big was his circle? *VIP meeting?*

Upton continued. "Afghan policy was just how it started. Ian Williams was like the drug dealer that starts you off on pot, only to trade you up into the hard stuff later. Williams wanted Ron to taste how good it could be. Three years after the two met, Becker won his Senate seat. And that's when Williams came calling again."

"What did he want then?"

"I don't know. I was no longer on staff."

"Then how'd you hear about it?"

She looked like she was stuck. Caught saying more than she'd intended to. "Ron mentioned it last year. I saw him at the party's convention. We had a drink and got caught up. Ron told me that someone working with Ian Williams had approached him, trying to push some new policy ideas. Perhaps that person was the lobbyist who was killed?"

"Did Becker play ball?"

She looked at Max with a cynical stare. "You keep asking about Becker. Again, I don't think Herb even knew about it. You need to understand something. Senators don't do the grunt work at that level. They have staff that brings them all of the information and big ideas. With a lot of 'em, politicians are just the monkeys behind the microphones."

"So if Ron was on board, the senator was too? Maybe without knowing why?"

Upton nodded. "Yes. If Ron was sure they would get more funding, and weren't at risk, my guess is he went along with it. You know the whole system works this way, right? Money makes the world go round."

Renee shook her head. "I don't understand. What's the problem, then? Why would Ian Williams be sending Senator Becker death threats now, if Ron was still playing ball? And why would he want to hurt you?"

Jennifer's eyes darted around the room as she spoke. "I wouldn't know. This weekend was the first time I've seen Herb in a long time. My guess is that Herb found out Ron was still in contact with Williams somehow and told him to break it off, once and for all."

"Why would he do that?"

"Herb Becker is truly motivated by only one thing. Ambition. Like many politicians, he wants to be president. And Herb would do anything to become president. Herb is pushing this new Opioid Epidemic Bill. It's a political football. But it's definitely not compatible with Ian Williams's interests."

"Why not?"

"From what Ron told me, Williams's investors included members of Big Pharma as well. International companies that made billions in opioid sales in the US. So maybe Ron was still playing ball with Williams behind Herb's back? Maybe Ron told Williams or this lobbyist he was working with that everything was great. That Herb was still on board. That might have worked as long as their policy agendas were aligned. Williams thought he had a big fish in his pocket. Then Herb decides he's going to make this new bill his big signature achievement. I have to admit, it'd look great if you were running for president. Everyone wants to help stop the opioid epidemic. Who wouldn't want their name attached?"

"Do you know where Ian Williams works now?"

She shrugged.

"Let me ask a different question. Does Senator Becker know where Ian Williams works now?"

A dark smile formed on her lips. "Ask yourself why Herb is going so hard against the drug cartels now."

Max stared at her, his face impassive. So she did know. And she was implying that Becker knew too.

"You tell me," he said.

"It's because he wants to counter any problems he might have if the Williams scandal comes to light. Now let me make this clear. Herb didn't do anything wrong. But just the mere association with someone who's now involved in a drug cartel could be catastrophic to a presidential campaign. Ian Williams is toxic now. Look at where he is. Herb must be terrified at that development. Then all of a sudden, Ron isn't returning Williams's calls. He's cut Williams off. Williams feels betrayed because Herb isn't playing ball. Herb doesn't need Ian Williams's shady friends anymore. But he sure as hell will need to make sure none of those skeletons fall out of the closet if he ever wants to become president."

"You keep saying Herb. I thought Ron Dicks was the one who was connected to Williams?"

She shrugged. "Excuse me. I misspoke. Ron knows the details. He knows not to bother the senator with them, I'm sure. He did back when I worked for him. Herb's clean. But Ron, God rest his soul, may have taken a few shortcuts."

Max frowned. "Who knows about Becker and Williams?"

"Almost no one. And I'll deny it, if you ever try to make this public. Herb Becker made one mistake. He didn't report his connection with Ian Williams in the beginning. But after that, everything he did was legal. And I'll say something else. Everything he did, he did for the right reasons. We won the war on terror, in part because men like Herb made deals to keep Afghanistan stable. Keep their economy going."

Renee said, "By growing heroin?"

"Don't give me that judgmental look, missy."

Max said, "Has Senator Becker had any contact with Williams in the past few years?"

"Absolutely not."

"You seem pretty sure of that."

"I am."

"How do you know?"

"Because I have, as you say, been seeing Herb socially again, every so often. I would know if they were still in touch."

"Do you know anything about a meeting Ian Williams is about to have?"

"A meeting with who?"

"Some important people."

She shook her head. "I don't know anything about any meeting. I haven't seen Williams since the 2000s. And even then, it was only a few times."

"Why do you think Ian Williams would need to kill a list of people before this meeting?"

Max thought she looked alarmed for a moment, but then she said, "I wouldn't know. I'm sorry."

"Let me ask you the same question I asked you yesterday. Do you know of any reason that Ian Williams would want to hurt you?"

She said, "Ian Williams could care less about me."

"What do you mean?"

"The only reason he would care about me is if he was trying to get to Herb. It's not me you should be worried about. From what I've seen, Ian Williams is a survivalist. If he's at the point where he's killing people, then he'll definitely take a shot at the senator." She sighed and looked at Max. "I lied to you yesterday. I was scared, and I didn't want to put Herb in legal jeopardy or hurt his career. But I care about him. He's a good man, and he's tried to do the right thing. This is the reason I've decided to talk to you about all of this today, even if it gets Herb in hot water. Please, Max. Don't let Herb Becker get hurt. You don't need to worry about me. It's Senator Becker you need to be protecting."

Max stood. "We'll continue this later." Looking at Renee he said, "I should get back."

She nodded. He left the house, got in the rental car and drove away, leaving Renee, Jennifer Upton, and the other CIA man at the safe house. Max needed to get back to the air show to meet with Wilkes. While he didn't trust everything that Jennifer Upton had said, enough of it sounded right to him that he felt Senator Becker should be considered a confirmed target.

26

Senator Becker walked up to the grassy area where Karen was busy preflighting her aircraft before the show. Karen walked around the right wing, checking for any popped rivets or loose fasteners. She checked the oil levels and landing gear, the prop and the engine, making sure that there was no foreign object debris anywhere in sight.

"You ready?" asked her father, looking stiff and artificial in his creased button-down shirt.

Her coach was nearby, still within earshot. "Could you give us a moment?"

The coach pointed at his watch. "Two minutes and you gotta start up."

She nodded, mouthing, "Thanks."

On the nearby taxiway, people were staring at both Karen and her father as they spoke, close and quiet beside her cockpit. Karen could see at least three security men, watching the crowd through their sunglasses.

"Have you decided what you'll do?"

Her father nodded. "Yes. I've made arrangements to speak to someone representing the group. I think we'll be able to work something out."

"How can you trust them after what they've done? What makes you think they'll ever leave you alone?"

"Don't worry about that now."

"You made a mistake. But you were trying to do the right thing. People will understand that. You might not be able to run for office again, but you don't need that. Tell them you're done, Dad. They'll just keep coming after you for more."

"I know, honey. You're right." He looked into her eyes, giving her that same warm smile that had soothed her as a child and annoyed her as an adult, when she realized he gave it to everyone on the campaign trail as well. "I'll end it. Once and for all. Everything will be alright. Why are you crying? Honey..."

She shook her head. "Dad, I can't be doing this right now."

"It's fine. We'll talk later."

Karen nodded. She wiped away a tear and hugged her father.

"Now good luck today."

Karen smiled and climbed into her plane.

* * *

Max walked under the air show entrance gate and towards the VIP tent area. Once there, he saw the other CIA guy, Mike, standing behind a vendor stand that was selling airplane vacation tours in New Zealand. A red "Display Closed" sign sat on the desk in front of him.

"How's everything going?"

Mike looked up at Max and motioned him to come closer. He pulled out a drawer and handed him an earpiece, which Max promptly put in.

"Trent and Wilkes are both up on our closed circuit. FBI and local police have about twenty personnel doing roaming security, most of them close in to the senator. They're both on separate comms freqs. They know we're here. Your father opted not to wear one of these since he'll be in the VIP tent. Have you heard the news on timing?"

"No, what?"

"Our SIGINT techies said they picked up some chatter. They think Williams has someone on the move right now."

Max's eyes went wide. "Shit. Where's Wilkes?"

Mike pointed towards the grove of trees behind the VIP tent. Max walked over there, tapping his earpiece as he did. "Comms check. Max is up."

"Trent hears you."

Max could see Wilkes give him a thumbs-up as he approached. Caleb Wilkes had a pair of binoculars wrapped around his neck but was using them to scan the crowd, not the five aerobatics planes flying in formation above them.

Max filled Wilkes in on what he'd learned from Jennifer Upton.

Wilkes cursed softly. "This is crazy. I don't care what the guy wants. We should move him. With this and the intel we received earlier, I think it's now too much. I'll get on the phone with my contacts at FBI and the Capitol Police. It might take a few minutes, but they'll put the word out to the security he's got stationed here. I expect they'll insist on pulling him out. You and Trent keep your eyes open until that happens."

Max said, "Trent, you got all that?"

"Copy."

Max could see his father and the senator through a plastic window of the VIP tent. They were holding drinks and talking with their hands, telling stories to a captivated group around them. The senator looked completely unaware of the danger he was in.

* * *

Trent walked along the alleyways and vendor tents of the air show, scanning for anything out of place. It felt weird to be using these skills here. In Middle Eastern and African countries and, during the final years of his Army career, in the streets of Mexico, he had grown used to having to blend in. But operating at an air show in Wisconsin was a first. He'd spent more than half his adult life deployed overseas. Where had the time gone? Just yesterday he and his brother had been teenagers, having pushup contests in the backyard and watching old Rambo movies on the VHS.

The thought of Josh brought a sting of sadness. He missed his brother like hell.

He shook off the thought and continued to walk the air show exhibits near the VIP tent, evaluating each face in the crowd through his sunglasses. This wasn't the kind of place where he wanted to get into a firefight. Way too many civilians around. He looked for possible IEDs, sniper locations, ambush spots. He profiled everyone he saw, paying particular attention to the younger, fitter men, anyone with Latin or Central Asian features. He also scanned anyone with clothing or bags capable of hiding a weapon.

He took a turn and saw Max walk by, evaluating the crowd in the same fashion. They gave each other barely perceptible nods and kept at it. Max looked tense. Trent had a hard time believing that the cartels would try something here. Especially against a US senator. Trent had worked in Mexico. He knew that the cartels could be brutally violent, but they also had rules. And one of them was not to poke the bear to the north. Assassinating a senator was definitely against the rules.

He checked his watch. Almost time for Karen Becker's performance. After that, Senator Becker would leave the air show, and protecting him would get a lot easier.

Trent flexed his fingers together against his palms, his eyes darting from one end of the central plaza to the other. Everywhere he looked, there were people. The atmosphere was jovial. Kids licking ice cream cones and holding their grandparents' hands.

Trent realized that the crowd was now moving en masse, migrating the hundred-yard distance from all the aircraft exhibits toward the sprawling grassy plain situated just next to the runway. People were setting up their lawn chairs and blankets, grabbing the empty spots and looking up at the sky, which was, for the moment, silent.

Today's highlight was about to begin.

Karen Becker's show.

A golf cart bumping along in the opposite direction of the crowd caught his eye. Two men wearing gray flight suits with plenty of pockets. Sunglasses and dark blue ball caps. One white guy, one looked...Indian or Pakistani, maybe? Both looked to be in their thirties or forties. Neither spoke, and both looked deadly serious. Their uniforms made them look like they were part of a performance crew—maybe maintenance men or part of the air show admin team? But something seemed off about them. They didn't have those keycard IDs around their necks, for one. And he hadn't seen any of the other aircraft maintenance crews driving in pairs, only by themselves.

He kept watching them as their golf cart passed by the vintage air exhibit and came to a halt next to the now-deserted outdoor movie theater in the woods.

An odd destination.

As Trent had learned in the past day, nothing went on there until after sunset. His instincts tingling, Trent tapped his earpiece and said, "Max, meet me in the woods by the vintage aircraft hangar ASAP."

Max's reply was drowned out by the loudspeaker, which was fixed to the tree above Trent's head.

"Ladies and gentlemen, please turn your attention to the south side of the runway as the Blonde Bombshell, Karen Becker, begins her takeoff roll!"

* * *

Renee sat in the living room of the safe house. Jennifer Upton was on the couch. She had the TV on and was watching bad reality TV. Renee had given her a questioning look, and the woman had actually hissed at her. There was something off about Jennifer Upton.

Renee had been sitting feet away from Upton while researching her testimony on the computer.

"Why can't I have my phone back?"

"It wouldn't be safe," answered the CIA kid from the kitchen. Upton rolled her eyes and heaved a hearty sigh like a teenage girl angry at her father's rules.

Renee had just connected with one of her hacker friends on an encrypted chat. He was helping her get access to the previous locations of Dahlman, Dicks, Becker, and Upton. They accessed the cell phone GPS coordinate archives of each person and overlaid that information with any known locations where Ian Williams or Abdul Syed had been stationed and associated dates.

Information about Williams and Syed was scarce. And what little they did have turned out to be a dead end.

But after about fifteen minutes, Renee saw a definite trend. When she looked at the four Americans' information and took the timestamps back three years, they were in the same location at the same time each year.

Oshkosh.

All four of them at Oshkosh?

They must have been together, which was not consistent with the story Jennifer Upton had just told them. She'd said she hadn't seen Ron Dicks in years, for one.

Renee thanked her hacker friend and signed out of the chat room. She glanced at Jennifer Upton to make sure she wasn't watching her. Upton was still busy messing around with her watch, only half-paying attention to the trashy TV show about whiny brides and wedding dresses.

Renee locked her computer and went into the kitchen, where the CIA operative was watching the security monitors.

"Anything going on?" Renee whispered.

"Nothing," the young man said.

She kept her voice very quiet. "I need access to her phone."

He nodded and opened up the safe under the kitchen counter. He removed Upton's cell phone and handed it to Renee. "You need a cable?"

"Won't be a problem."

Renee powered up the device and slid it into her pocket. Thankfully it wasn't an iPhone. Those were harder to crack. Sitting on the couch across from Jennifer Upton, Renee used her computer's near field communication and some special software to access the phone. She then searched through pictures, text messages, and any other data from the time period that overlapped each annual Oshkosh visit.

There wasn't much. It was almost like Upton was purposely not communicating or taking pictures during those time periods. The fact that all three of them were together at Oshkosh meant something. But now that Renee had that morsel of a clue, she was determined to find the missing puzzle piece.

She looked up again. Upton was looking at the TV.

Renee looked at the map on her screen again. The one with the overlay of locations. She frowned. It wasn't exactly at Oshkosh, was it? No. It was southeast. Near the water. Renee decided to try something else. She dug into Upton's cloud storage accounts. Sometimes they synced up photos without people realizing it, keeping images that were thought to have been deleted.

Nothing. Upton wasn't a big social media person. Neither was the senator, which made sense.

Renee typed to her hacker friend again. With his help, Renee was able to search through hundreds of thousands of images stored online with GPS stamps near the same time and location she was interested in. They put the images through facial recognition software and came up with several hits. One of the photos was particularly interesting. There was water on the lower half of the image. It might have been taken from a boat or across a small inlet, but the resolution was good. Renee was able to zoom in on a gazebo where a group of people were having some type of gathering. The photo was dated three years ago, and the GPS tag was within five miles of Oshkosh.

In the image, Senator Becker was standing next to Jennifer Upton and Ron Dicks. They were outdoors, drinks in hand, smiling. They seemed to be unaware the picture was being taken.

Ian Williams was in the background, on a cell phone.

They *were* all together at Oshkosh.

Becker, Upton, Dicks, and Ian Williams. Only three years ago. What did this mean? She needed to tell Max.

Renee got up from the couch and walked into one of the spare bedrooms, closing the door and locking it behind her. Damn the security procedures, she had to call Max. She dialed his phone, but it just went straight to his voicemail.

Renee left him a voicemail anyway.

Short and to the point. Hopefully he would get it soon.

Then she walked into the living room and sat back down on the couch. Renee looked back up at Upton, who was still playing with her watch...

But it wasn't just a watch, Renee realized.

It was a smart watch.

A connected device.

They had confiscated her phone but didn't notice the watch. The design hadn't looked like a typical smart watch. They had glossed right over it.

She was communicating.

Jennifer Upton glanced up at Renee, and their eyes met.

Renee's heart pounded in her chest. She could feel herself breathing.

Renee turned at the sounds of the CIA man swearing from the kitchen. Then she heard the sound of vehicles arriving out front. Tires grinding to a halt on the gravel driveway.

Renee shut her computer and ran into the kitchen. The CIA man had his gun drawn.

On the security monitors, Renee saw several SUVs parked outside. Men wearing masks and holding assault rifles approached the home.

27

The same announcer broadcasting over the air show speaker system was on frequency with Karen as she began racing down the runway.

"Can you hear us, Karen?"

"I read you loud and clear! Good afternoon, Oshkosh!"

The crowd cheered and hollered as Karen gained speed, pulled back on her stick, and shot straight up into the air.

Karen's heart was beating fast. Adrenaline pumped through her veins. This was her Super Bowl. Nothing compared to performing at Oshkosh. It was her time to shine in front of hundreds of thousands of screaming fans. To leave behind the angst she felt about her father's mistakes and her own insecurities. Up here, she was alive and in her element, doing what she was meant to do.

She went through her routine with expert precision. She got on altitude and airspeed, checked her instruments, ran through her silent checklist, then jammed the stick hard left, cut the throttle and pulled through her dive upside down and gaining speed, the ground coming closer and closer, the spectators' mouths opening as they clicked pictures. Then she came to the bottom of her dive, airspeed rocketing upward, the g's hitting her body, flexing her legs and grunting and pulling in a bit more backstick, then slamming down one pedal and putting her aircraft into a sideslip, practically hovering over the ground at an impossible angle.

Her engine buzzed loud, its pitch changing to the ears below along with the dynamic stresses and speeds of her maneuvers, and she demanded all the power it could muster without redlining. Then she centered her pedals, dipped her nose, and began gaining speed again, diving towards the earth.

"How's it going up there, Karen? Ready to cut the tape?"

"Sure am, Oshkosh!"

Her eyes scanned her instruments again. She leveled off at eight thousand feet, the clear runways and colorful crowd huddled below her. Blue sky above. Each pull of the stick put enormous g-forces on her body, and she huffed and flexed to stay conscious as she performed loop after loop. Roll after roll. She couldn't hear the cheering below, but she knew that they were getting one hell of a show.

Now she would start her spin. Full left pedal, full back and slightly left stick...enter the stall...feel her stomach floating up, and then the green and red and blue outside the windscreen swirled into a blur as her aircraft departed controlled flight.

This was her most challenging maneuver.

An eight-thousand-foot controlled drop, plummeting and twirling seemingly out of control, like a maple leaf falling in the air, spinning and spinning towards the ground, all the while she was in control, taking a scalpel to the air and carving it up exactly how she intended.

Her spin would transform into a steep dive below two thousand feet, and she would once again pull herself out just feet over the runway, using her propeller to cut a thin plastic ribbon which had been set up just in front of the crowd.

* * *

The two men in gray flight suits were just waiting there.

"What are they doing?" asked Trent.

Max spoke into his earpiece. "Caleb, if they're armed, they could be at the VIP tent in about thirty seconds. Trent and I are going to head over there. Has the senator been alerted to the threat?"

Wilkes shook his head. "Local law enforcement is passing on the warning now."

Max looked back and saw a man he knew to be a plainclothes police officer assigned to the senator's security detail. He was speaking into the senator's ear, with Max's father looking concerned next to them. Max's father also had a bodyguard, but if these guys had the same equipment they'd used down in Texas and Mexico, the best course of action was to evacuate the VIPs immediately and notify the police.

Overhead, Karen's aircraft was looping and swirling, a bright red stream of smoke trailing behind her.

* * *

Hugo had spotted several plainclothes security personnel during his time on the air show grounds this morning, but his risk would soon be minimal.

He had a clear line of sight to his target from here. Hugo fished into the navy-blue maintenance bag on his lap and took the black plastic transmitter in his hands. He had powered it up moments ago, making sure that the LED lit up green. Now he had to wait until his target was in just the right position.

He had trained for this for the past few weeks, working with an explosives expert to custom-design the charge and ensure that they had just the right weapon for this job.

There. His target was at the perfect spot.

Hugo flipped up the transmit switch and watched Karen Becker's plane.

* * *

Just as she was about to take herself out of the spin, Karen heard a sharp mechanical pop underneath her, and her controls went slack in her hands and under her feet.

All the resistance pushing back against her right hand, which gripped the yoke, and against her boots on the pedals was now completely gone. Karen rapidly moved the yoke as far as it would go in all directions, alternating pumps with each foot. Moving it around in a big square. Slow at first. Then fast. Both directions.

Nothing.

A terrifying chill ran up her spine as her aircraft continued to spin, plummeting towards the earth.

What she didn't know was that Hugo and his ISI assistant, who had been trained by the Pakistani Air Force in small aircraft maintenance procedures, had accessed Karen Becker's plane at three a.m. local time. Together they had placed a trace amount of plastic explosive at three critical points that connected the plane's flight controls. A silver-colored patch was placed over the control rod, encasing a small receiver, trigger, and detonator. The charges had been painstakingly planted in a ring-shape around the control rod. The explosions would be small, but quite effective, snapping apart the linkage from the flight controls to the aircraft's control surfaces.

The work was almost invisible to the naked eye and had not been noticed by the maintenance or pilot inspections, as it was located inside the aircraft—a position only checked during scheduled maintenance tune-ups.

"Tower," she began, her voice strained.

"Say again, Bravo Sierra..." A different voice over the radio now. Deeper, and this man had used her call sign, all pretense of showmanship gone.

She tried again, moving her yoke in one big square, attempting to fix the problem. She pushed and pulled both foot pedals all the way forward and backward, to no avail. Nothing was giving her control back. It was like the mechanical connections had all been severed.

Her altitude wound down with sickening speed, the colors of the spectators still swirling together as the ground rushed up to meet her.

"Tower, Bravo Sierra. Declaring an emergency. Loss of flight controls..."

* * *

Max and Trent made their way through the grove of trees towards the two men in gray flight suits. They were watching the aerobatics demonstration.

"Hold on," Wilkes said. "Are you guys listening to this?"

Trent and Max were farther away from the air show loudspeakers. The two men stopped and turned to see where the crowd was pointing.

One woman near Max was hugging her husband and wincing, saying, "Oh my God..." Another man was swearing over and over, seemingly unaware of the children next to him. Both were looking up at Karen Becker's aircraft.

What had Max missed?

Then he heard Karen's radio call, still being broadcast over the speaker.

"Did she say loss of controls?"

Trent looked alarmed, his head on a swivel, careful not to lose the men standing by the outdoor theater.

Max looked up towards Karen Becker's aircraft. Red and black, spiraling downward, lower and lower. His eyes widened as it became obvious she was in real trouble. She was too low. She should have recovered from that spin by now...

Max looked towards the VIP tent. He could just make out the figure of Senator Becker pressed up against the translucent plastic of the tent, looking up at the plane, and then away at the ground.

Max looked up at the aircraft again.

"Something's wrong," Max said. "Something is very wrong..."

* * *

The last hundred feet felt like the aircraft was flying straight down.

Screams from the crowd the closer it got.

And the chilling cries of Karen herself, still broadcasting over the outdoor speakers as the aircraft slammed into the hard pavement of the nearest taxiway. A gaseous yellow fireball erupted from the concrete, transforming into plumes of thick black smoke.

A collective gasp of horror from hundreds of thousands of spectators, holding their mouths and picking up crying children. Men and women stared at the wreckage, held captive by their own morbid curiosity.

Sirens blared from a mile away as the crash crew activated. Giant versions of fire engines and heavy-duty ambulances raced to the scene. They sprayed water on the fires, but there was nothing anyone could do for Karen Becker now.

Max looked at the senator. He was on his knees, one hand still holding the plastic of the tent window, the other over his face.

"Hey." Trent tapped Max on the arm to get his attention. "Look."

The men in gray flight suits were on the move, riding their golf cart away from the scene. Max watched as they rolled through the nearest exit and headed for the massive parking lot area.

"They're gone."

* * *

Bullet holes filled the door.

Renee watched in horror as the CIA man standing behind it collapsed to the floor, his chest covered in crimson. Three men in black tactical gear stormed through the entrance, fanning out through the living room, their weapons trained on the two women.

Within seconds, Renee and Upton were on their stomachs, a boot in each of their backs, the barrel of a submachine gun aimed at their heads.

More men entered the house, including two who carried in a large plastic tarp roll. One of the gunmen flipped up the coffee table and threw it into the corner of the room, picture frames and glass shattering. Two other men pushed the couches and chairs so that the space became open. Then they unrolled the plastic tarp on the floor.

Renee became nauseous as she realized what was going on.

A tall Caucasian man appeared in the doorway, a thin smile on his face.

"Hello, ladies," said Ian Williams in his thick British accent. He said something in Spanish, and both women were hiked up off the floor.

Jennifer Upton said, "Ian, would you please tell your men here to release me? I'm the one who called you here, for God's sake."

"Yes, and it's much appreciated." One of the men set a toolbox down on the floor next to Williams.

"*Gracias.*" He opened the toolbox and removed a pair of pliers, a vise, and a small power saw, which he plugged into the wall.

Williams walked over to Renee and caressed her neckline up to her cheek. His face twitched, and he pressed his lips forward and together like a deranged kiss. Renee turned her head away, shivering in fear and revulsion.

Where was Max? Wilkes must know that something had happened here. They would come for them. But how long would it take? The air show was more than a half hour away.

Williams seemed to be reading her mind. "Don't worry, dear, I'll have you out of here before your friends begin to worry. They're busy cleaning up another mess right now."

He kissed her on the neck and walked around her body, sliding his fingers over her bare arm. Renee wanted to lash out. She could feel her blood pressure rising and her face heating up as anger overcame all her other emotions. But there must have been six of his attack dogs in the room, each one holding a large black machine gun. Renee hated guns. But what she wouldn't give to get her hands on one of them right now.

"Renee. You don't know how happy it makes me to see us united again. If you please, my dear. Go wait in the car. I will join you momentarily."

He gave another command in Spanish, and she was escorted into the back of a large SUV outside, a gunman sitting on either side of her. They didn't even bother to tie her hands. She had no chance against men like these. They left the door open, allowing the airflow to cool them in the warm summer day. Through the open door, Renee heard the high-pitched sound of the power saw. Then she heard screaming. A loud, blood-curdling scream. Then nothing for a few moments. Then more power saw and screams, and an awful gurgling noise. Then nothing.

Renee dry-heaved in the backseat of the car and one of the men guarding her laughed.

The whole thing took ten minutes, and then the men marched back out. This time the tarp was significantly thicker and heavier, with ties around each end as they shoved the remains of Jennifer Upton into the empty back of the lead vehicle.

Ian Williams sat shotgun in Renee's SUV. He looked back at her. "We're in good shape. Now let's go show you the lake house, shall we?"

He smiled at her, his white teeth contrasting with the rest of his face, which was covered in tiny crimson dots of blood.

28

Max, Trent, and Caleb Wilkes stood talking in the CIA's faux vendor booth near the VIP tent. Charles had retired to his private jet after Senator Becker had left. Becker had wanted to mourn his daughter's death alone, and Charles Fend had to agree.

Max was still in shock after witnessing Karen Becker's crash. It had affected everyone watching.

Max spoke in a hushed tone. "So what do we think happened here? Was this another attempt to intimidate the senator? By targeting his daughter?"

Wilkes nodded. "It fits with the profile thus far."

"This seems different than the other killings."

"Are you sure it wasn't an accident?"

"Yes. It's too much of a coincidence not to be intentional. And with the men in the gray flight suits you saw disappearing after the crash...it's got to be foul play."

Max looked out at the wreckage, rubbing his chin. The thick plumes of black smoke had ceased, but there were still wisps of white and gray rising up into the air. The air show, being as large as it was, had a policy in the event that a crash occurred. All flight operations stopped, and a new tentative schedule was announced. There was to be a four-hour delay before flights would continue. The taxiway where the accident had occurred would be closed while safety and investigation crews did their jobs. When the day's events resumed, they would begin with a moment of silence.

Wilkes picked up his phone. "Go ahead."

His face went from annoyed to panicked. "When did you get there? Son of a bitch. Do another sweep of the place, then call the local police and notify the FBI. You'll have to stay there. Call me when authorities arrive. Don't provide any info on our ongoing operation. I'll contact my man at the FBI and give him a heads-up."

Wilkes hung up and looked at Max.

"What is it?"

"Mike just got to the safe house. Someone hit it."

"What?"

Trent shook his head and cursed.

Max said, "What the hell do you mean? Hit it? Where's Renee?"

"She wasn't there. My agent was dead at the scene."

Max felt dizzy.

"No sign of either Jennifer Upton or Renee. But there were several bullet holes near the door, the furniture had been kicked around, and there were a few traces of blood spatter on the walls."

Max's mind was on fire. Caleb kept talking, but he couldn't hear him. Max turned and walked away, fists clenched, breathing heavy through his nose and flexing his jaw.

Renee was gone.

Ian Williams had taken her. Was she still alive? If so, how long did she have?

Trent had placed his hand on his shoulder. "Max, you alright?"

The world was spinning all around him. Conversations and memories of the past week flashed through his head in a vortex of images and emotions. Joseph Dahlman shot in the park. Breakfast with Ian Williams. Ines Sanchez killed on the beach. The attack in Texas. Flying in to Oshkosh. Karen's crash. Now Renee had been taken by these murderous madmen.

Then the flood of thoughts froze as he felt his phone vibrating. After the crash, he had turned it back on in hopes that Renee might have left him a message—before he knew she had been taken.

He hoped that she had been taken, and not worse.

There it was. A single voicemail. Max pressed the play button and held the phone up to his ear. Renee's voice was a mousy whisper, quick and nervous.

"Max, I know I'm not supposed to call, but this is important. What did Karen Becker say to her father in the conversation your dad recorded? She asked him if they were *here again*? That kept bugging me, the way she said that. *Here again.* I didn't think anything of it at first. Like maybe just that the bad guys were back. But now I think she actually meant that *literally.* Like here in Oshkosh. I found a picture from the internet dated three years ago. Get this. Senator Becker, Ron Dicks, Jennifer Upton, all smiling, and Ian freaking Williams is in the background. Max, they were at Oshkosh. Becker and Williams, Upton and Dicks. Oshkosh. Three years ago. Call me."

Max was stunned. He pressed the play button and listened the the message again. Thoughts racing through his mind.

When the message finished, he looked at Trent, who was watching him with a concerned look. Max said, "Karen Becker was killed right when they hit the safe house."

Trent said, "Yeah, I know, Max. Hey, maybe you should sit down, man?"

What had Senator Becker said to his daughter? *They won't have anything on me after this week.*

This was part of his plan.

"He knew about it," Max said.

"Knew about what?" said Trent.

"Senator Becker knew. That bastard knew his daughter was going to be killed. Becker didn't have a plan to escape Ian Williams and the ISI. He has a plan to cover up his involvement with them."

* * *

Renee was shoved out of the SUV by Williams's gunmen and made to follow him up the large flat steps and through the mansion's entrance. The opulent home was empty inside, but Renee heard raucous laughter coming from the rear garden area. Through open French doors, Renee saw a group of six men sitting around an open fire pit.

A dark-featured man walked up the expansive lawn towards them. He looked at her with surprise and fear.

Syed, Renee realized.

"What is she doing here?" he whispered to Williams.

Williams, who was nearly a foot taller than the Pakistani man, craned his neck to look at him as he spoke.

"Don't worry about her. What happened at the air show? I heard on the radio there was a crash."

Syed looked at Renee.

Williams snorted. "I told you to relax. Say what you want. Did your man Hugo have any problems?"

"No, I didn't," came a voice from behind them. Renee turned and saw a younger man in a gray flight suit, two-day old stubble on his face. She thought she recognized him. Evidently, he was thinking the same thing, staring her down with menacing brown eyes.

Williams said, "She's dead?"

"Yes."

"You're sure?"

"One hundred percent. Now I need to clean up and collect my payment. Then I'll be gone."

Syed said, "I'll be leaving with you shortly. Mr. Williams and I need to take care of something first. You will need to remain in the house. Out of the backyard." The tone and look Syed used were ominous. The men in the room exchanged glances.

Williams said, "You can babysit her." He pointed to Renee. "Have a seat, darling. We'll be a few minutes."

Syed and Williams walked outside. The group of men around the fire pit were smiling and holding up their drinks. They were trying to get them to come join them, but the two men kept walking, out towards the lake. They walked down the dock and sat in a little wooden gazebo that stood over the water.

It was just the two of them now. Renee needed to find out what was going on. Understand who she was dealing with. Figure out more options. She was scared, but she was also raging inside.

She looked at the man standing in the room and said, "You were in Virginia, weren't you? Two weeks ago. In the park. I saw you get on your bike and ride away."

The man looked at her, expressionless. "Why has he let you live? Williams?"

"I don't know."

"I would be concerned about that if I were you. He's not a nice man."

Renee let out a scoff. "You killed someone. You're not a nice man."

"I've killed a lot of people."

"Why?"

"Money."

She spoke softly. "I can get you money. Help me. They're all outside. You could help me get away right now. I..."

He shook his head, looking at her with a skeptical eye. "Don't waste your time. If I betrayed them, I would be hunted down and killed. And I wouldn't be paid. Nor would I get any more work. No offense, but your proposal is illogical."

She exhaled, looking outside. "*Baptême.*"

He turned and looked at her with renewed interest. "You're from Quebec?" he asked in French.

"Yes. I lived there until I was eighteen," she said, also in French. "You?"

"I've spent time there. Also in France."

For a moment, Renee thought she saw an opening, but then he switched back to English and turned away. "But that was long ago. What do you think is going on here?"

"I assumed you knew more than me."

"They only tell me what they need to."

"And you trust them?"

"No. But I trust money and leverage. Both of which are working in my favor. Syed knows what will happen if he double-crosses me. And I know the same. It's a healthy relationship."

Outside on the gazebo, Ian Williams and Syed were standing up now. It looked like they were talking to someone on some type of oversized phone.

* * *

The senator was numb, but he remained focused on the task at hand. Charles Fend had wanted to accompany him home, but Becker had insisted on being alone. Only the local police security detail had accompanied him back to his lake house after the crash.

The maid was in tears when he entered, and the police officers stood by the door with awkward and curious looks. Not wanting to intrude, but also keenly aware that the man they were tasked to protect was still at risk and shouldn't be left alone.

"Gentlemen, you can stand watch in the front yard, but I don't wish to be disturbed. Please keep off the property for the evening."

The police officers nodded and kept their vehicles where the long drive met the main road. The senator's backyard was on Lake Winnebago, so that was secure. The policemen figured as long as they monitored the entrance, the security risk was low. The man was in mourning. Anyone could see the despair in his eyes. He deserved his solitude.

"Your wife called, Senator."

The maid had been with the family for decades, although she was only asked to come occasionally now that the senator spent most of his time in Washington. She knew Karen's mom from before the divorce, and Becker suspected that she liked her better than him.

"No calls for now."

Senator Becker walked up the creaky stairs into his office, which overlooked the lake. He closed and locked the office door.

Alone at last, he allowed himself a moment of reflection. His daughter was dead. It wasn't his fault. It was her own. If she hadn't been so stubborn and nosy, like her mother. He told himself that the feeling of guilt would pass. He willed it to pass. This had been the only course of action, he told himself. His was too important a career to sacrifice.

Thankfully Karen hadn't told anyone else about the annual meetings with the cabal. While this was her first performance at the show, Karen was at Oshkosh each year, often in his presence. Because of that, she had seen things she shouldn't have. She had seen Dahlman, Dicks, and the senator together with Ian Williams. She might have even seen Syed there, once.

Four or five years ago, Ron had told the senator about a conversation he'd had with Karen. After witnessing the group at Oshkosh, Karen had privately admonished Ron for the continued relationship with the international investors. Senator Becker had gone to her after that and apologized. He'd assured her that it was only a meeting. That no further partnership was underway. Becker partly blamed himself. He never should have told Karen so much. For a long time, Becker thought that Karen was like him. A future politician, sharp as steel and able to look past the rough spots of the game. But for that damned afternoon where his daughter had caught him with Jennifer Upton. The girl had changed after that.

After Ron's warning, Senator Becker had made Karen promise to keep what she had seen at Oshkosh to herself, and she had. But if scandal broke during a presidential election campaign, Becker couldn't risk her stubborn streak showing itself again. Perhaps if she hadn't threatened to go to the press about Jennifer Upton years ago, he would have been able to trust her. But no.

That was why Becker had had dinner with her last week. One final check to make sure Karen hadn't told anyone anything she shouldn't have. Her accident wasn't originally supposed to occur during the Oshkosh airshow. Until recently, it was to have been a target of opportunity. Scheduled to occur during any number of her summer air shows. But then Karen had been selected for this performance at Oshkosh. The other members of the cabal were to be eliminated at that time. So with all of Syed's assets in the area, taking care of Karen here had been the most efficient solution.

While he tried not to think about it, Becker couldn't help but wonder how the sympathy vote might impact him in the years to come. His beautiful daughter, lost in a tragic accident. Tearful interviews recalling how much she had meant to him. Even better would be if Syed's explosive residue was discovered by investigators. The cartels or some of the rogue agents the ISI was cutting loose would take the blame. Then her death would be seen as a horrific attack on the senator. A man beyond reproach, having paid the ultimate sacrifice in the name of our country.

A grandfather clock ticked behind him. The sands of time. The endless prompt of ambitious men. As he grew older, the scarcity of time filled him with fear. Fear that he would not achieve his goals. Fear that he would not be seen as great. Fear that his competitors would discover him and take from him that which he had worked so hard to achieve.

Senator Becker walked over to the liquor cabinet and poured himself a tall glass of Bombay Sapphire gin. He then took a large cube of ice from the mini fridge, dropped it in, and poured in a splash of soda water. He sipped it and looked out over the darkening lake. Here he would be alone with his pain.

And with his relief.

The hard part was finally coming to an end. The witnesses were being removed. The loose ends tied up.

Senator Becker took another sip from his glass and then placed it on the top of a knee-high black safe that rested next to his office desk. He spun the dial back and forth several times from memory, hearing a click as the final digit in the combination unlocked the safe. Then he slid the latch downward and pulled open the sturdy door. He reached inside with two hands and removed the small black device that the lobbyist, Joseph Dahlman, had given him three years earlier.

The point-to-point laser communication was very secure, and the device wouldn't store any traceable information.

Dahlman had been Senator Becker's only contact in Washington. They had rarely met face-to-face in the past year. Even the annual cabal meetings at Oshkosh were coming to an end now. Becker was getting too high up on the food chain. People were getting suspicious. Ian Williams had warned him that this might happen eventually if things went according to plan. Too much attention. Too many questions.

Too many loose ends. Even Karen.

He finished the drink and wiped his eyes, then poured some more gin in the glass. He took another sip, then put the glass down on the desk.

Senator Becker placed the black box on his desk and opened the window the way he'd been trained, making sure that the transmitter was aimed at the gazebo across the small bay. The cabal acquired the property through a cutout over a decade ago, using it as a vacation spot for visiting members during the annual meeting, and renting it out during the rest of the year so as not to look suspicious. The communications device connected to the receiver and began flashing, and Becker was prompted to place his finger down on the scanner and enter a passcode. The double verification allowed the encryption key, stored in the device's hard drive, to be transmitted to a similar device that had been set up on the gazebo.

Becker picked up his binoculars and looked towards the gazebo. There were only two men sitting there, as he expected.

Williams and Syed. Their final meeting. Risky, but they would have called it off if there were a problem.

The link established, Becker put on the headset and listened to their voices for the first time in a year.

It was Syed who spoke first. "We are sorry for your loss, Herbert."

"Thank you, Abdul."

"But your sacrifice and determination have once again proven to be unmatched."

"Yes."

He fought back the taste of bile in his throat, taking a moment to maintain his composure. "So, we are done now?"

"Almost."

"Almost?"

"Your government is under the impression that you are a target. Ronald Dicks is seen as the source of the intelligence leaks. But there is a complication. The CIA was interrogating Upton."

Senator Becker's eyes went wide. "What?"

"The CIA has a team here in Wisconsin."

"But I thought...how is that possible?"

"Herbert, be calm. It has been taken care of. We instructed Miss

Upton on what to say. After speaking to her, we can confirm that the CIA is unaware of our true relationship. They are now under the impression that Ian Williams worked through Ronald Dicks, and that you had no knowledge of illegal activities. All others with knowledge of our relationship have been terminated, with the exception of a few members here with us now. Upton is no longer a problem. She is dead, and her body will not be found. You shall continue to say that Ronald Dicks was your only contact with Dahlman, and that you had no inappropriate foreign contact."

Becker simply said, "I understand."

He ran through the plans and possible options in his head. This was always going to be a complicated exit strategy. He simply had too many coconspirators and witnesses that were close to him.

Jennifer Upton had been naïve enough to think her personal relationship with him would protect her. That was what Becker had promised her. Syed had taken care of her now.

That she had spoken to the CIA was very worrisome. He should get off this device soon and get back to D.C. Syed would send a team into his house to empty his safe and clean up any evidence.

There still remained members of the inner circle across the bay that knew of his participation, however. The group of executives and politicians, of lawyers and executives from around the world. The men who had helped to orchestrate the opioid boom and reaped the rewards. Cash payments to numbered accounts, with a final large bonus payment expected today, as the new contract terms were settled. Williams could just make out some of these men, sitting across the bay in the backyard of the Pakistani mansion. Surrounding a fire pit. Drinking and laughing.

The final names on Ian Williams's list of participants. The last of the loose ends that must be dealt with.

Now it was Ian Williams's voice. "Herb, it's likely that you'll be interviewed by American counterintelligence."

He took another gulp of his gin. "I thought we were doing all this so that we could avoid—"

"It will be crucial that you maintain a consistent recollection of the facts. If you do this, you'll come out of it unscathed. You knew nothing about any quid pro quo on campaign contributions. You only met me briefly in Afghanistan. You didn't characterize your conversations with me as a recruitment, and you don't recall the specifics anyway. It was almost fifteen years ago. Even if we did speak, you never went along with anything I said. Anyone who says anything other than that is a liar. Ron Dicks was the only one we ever worked with, and he didn't tell you what he was doing."

"So that's it?"

"Yes. We have some housecleaning to do here tonight. But once that's complete, you will be in the clear, Herb. We will no longer contact you through unofficial channels."

Becker rubbed his hands together. This was good. Finally, he would be free. With no ties to this cabal, he could run for president without fear of scandal. The deaths of those near to him were tragic, of course. But they wouldn't be in vain. He would win the presidency and make this the greatest nation on earth. That was what mattered.

And if he was unable to attain the presidency, whether it be due to scandal or luck, he would still have the hundreds of millions of dollars piling up in several numbered accounts around the world. The investors' secretive dividend payments. Those financial updates were another reason the cabal met each year.

Senator Becker had made a pact with Ian Williams and Abdul Syed years ago. Together their fortunes would rise or fall.

Now it appeared their fortunes would rise higher than any of them had imagined.

"When will you two be gone?"

"In a few hours. We'll wrap things up here and clean up. This will be the last time we speak. Good luck."

Becker didn't need a handler anymore. He knew what Ian Williams and the ISI wanted. And they knew that if he ever decided to go back on his word, they could ruin him by bringing certain elements of the conspiracy to light. Perhaps someday, the other two would become leaders of their own nations. Someone always had leverage on you, Becker had learned over the years. But if your interests were aligned, it didn't matter.

Becker wouldn't double-cross them. He was getting what he wanted and would push policy that helped them all. It took ambitious men like him to change the world. Bargains and sacrifices had to be made. Too many people saw the world in black and white. But not him. He was a visionary, and he was willing to do whatever it took to win.

* * *

Max now stood in front of Wilkes under the CIA's faux vendor tent. "You said Senator Becker went back to his home here in Oshkosh."

"That's right."

"Where?"

Wilkes narrowed his eyes. "Max, the man just lost his daughter. What are you going to do, barge in there and confront him?"

"At this point, I think that's the best idea."

Max dialed up his voicemail and played it on speaker phone so both Trent and Wilkes could hear. They looked at him, shocked.

"I think Becker knew his daughter was going to be killed. And I think this meeting might be here in Oshkosh. You said Syed disappeared. What if he's here?"

"He could be anywhere."

Max played the voicemail again.

"Karen Becker asked her dad if they had come back here. *Here.* As in, Oshkosh. Ian Williams is here, Caleb."

"That's insane. Why would they take that risk?"

"Ten thousand planes and nearly a million people all coming in and out of the same place, at the same time, once per year. Sounds like a great place to hold a meeting you don't want discovered."

"I don't know..."

"They took Renee, Caleb. Some of them must be here. Becker might be able to tell us how to find her. You said yourself that Ron Dicks was only a possible source of the leaks to Ian Williams. What if it wasn't him? What if it was really Becker?"

Wilkes lowered his voice. "The counterintelligence investigation is ongoing. It could have been twenty other people. We just don't know yet."

"Let's consider it," said Max. "What if Upton only gave us half the truth? What if Williams and Becker met, just like she said, but Williams actually bought in? He's been working for the ISI for more than a decade. He isn't a target. He's the mole. A traitor to our country."

"What about Ron Dicks?"

"A fall guy. Someone types up a bogus letter and mails it to the senator, right after they kill him."

"Why would Ian Williams and Becker both be coming here? That's crazy. And why would he let his daughter be killed?"

Max said, "You said that Senator Becker is going to run for president next election cycle, right? What if this big meeting is to get rid of witnesses? They're cleaning house so that they can get their man elected. Hell, even if he doesn't win the presidency, running alone will give him huge political influence."

"And this secret society decided to meet here at Oshkosh? Why?"

"I don't know. But Becker would. And I bet he knows where Ian Williams is. We get to Becker, we get to Williams. And to Renee…"

Wilkes looked unsure. "I can give you Becker's address, but—"

Max said, "Caleb, this isn't me operating on your behalf. I'm doing this whether you want me to or not."

Trent said, "I'm coming."

Wilkes said, "Very well. But it'll take you a while to get there. The traffic to exit this place is awful right now. Everyone wants to leave after witnessing that crash. There must be a hundred thousand people trying to drive out."

He was right. Max could hear the horns of static traffic in the distance.

The overhead speakers came on with an announcement. "Oshkosh flights will resume at six p.m. Aircraft are allowed to conduct maintenance ground turns prior to that time. Contact Base Ops for questions."

Max looked at Trent. "Follow me. I think I have an idea."

29

The gyrocopter controls took a little getting used to. And Max was pretty sure that the King boys were going to catch hell from their father when he realized they'd allowed Max to take it. Max had received a five-minute orientation from the two boys.

"It's super easy," said Jack.

Then they set the destination GPS coordinates in the iPad, and Max and Trent strapped in. Trent had a bulky black duffle bag on his lap, which he had retrieved from their car. Max promised the boys he would get them a private tour of Fend Aerospace headquarters someday, and they were off.

Max started it up and saw Trent shaking in the seat next to him. "Will this thing really fly?"

Max shrugged and yelled back, "Think so." He pushed the throttle lever forward to add power, and they rolled forward in the grass, gaining lift at a very slow speed. Max banked left and headed towards the east, then tapped the button on the iPad to allow autopilot to take over steering.

An Oshkosh air show official was waving and yelling at Max as they overflew the runway. It was still an hour before the airfield reopened, and they were breaking the rules. Max realized that there were probably fifty thousand people watching him, including FAA officials who could take away his prized pilot's license. But he didn't care. Ian Williams had Renee, and Max had to get to her.

They puttered along, only feet above the power lines and treetops east of the airport, headed towards the huge lake on the horizon. Max scanned the iPad, careful to keep his hands on the controls in case the autopilot did anything unsafe. Even at the slow speed the gyrocopter was going, this trip would be much faster than driving.

"Where are you going to land it?" Trent yelled.

"There's a farmer's field about a half mile to the east. It looks like I'll be able to land it unseen if that grove of trees is thick enough." Max pointed at the map on the iPad. "I'll put you down and give you five minutes before I approach the security detail. If it doesn't look doable, just meet me out at the street and we can try to negotiate with them. If all else fails, I'll call Wilkes and see if he can pull some strings with the cops."

"That won't be necessary," Trent said with an air of confidence.

Max gave Trent a look, then turned his attention back to the landing, the rotor whomping above them as they passed a flock of surprised-looking geese headed in the opposite direction.

Ten minutes later, the dark blue expanse of Lake Winnebago spread out before them. A grassy peninsula jutted out to the left, with a two-story mansion capping the point. A row of nice lakefront homes was spaced out along the adjacent bay, each with long driveways and carefully manicured lawns. The street below had two police cars—one unmarked—parked at the gate of one of the homes. Max flew past them, hoping he was high enough that they wouldn't recognize faces, and if they did, that they wouldn't think about the fact that there were two passengers.

He saw the farmer's field, his intended landing spot, and maneuvered them around into the wind, lowering the throttle and making his approach on a flat patch of grass just next to the tree line. He quickly shut the engine down, and Trent disappeared into the woods with the duffle bag over his shoulder. Max walked along the field until he reached the street, then headed towards the senator's driveway gate. He kept an eye on his watch, making sure that he gave Trent at least five minutes to make his way through the woods and towards the house.

Eventually Max walked up to the police car outside Becker's property and waved. "Good afternoon." He must have looked like a drifter, coming down the street without a car.

"Can I help you?" asked the uniformed cop, approaching from the nearest police vehicle.

"Sir, my name is Max Fend. My father is Charles Fend. Perhaps you've heard of him? He's the CEO of Fend Aerospace and a good friend of Senator Becker's. I know the senator is in, and I wished to pay our respects and offer our services."

"The senator told us he didn't wish to be disturbed."

"Of course, I understand that, sir. However, my father and I have a personal relationship with the senator—"

The second cop got out of his vehicle and approached, this one in plain clothes. Good. Two cars, two cops. No one else watching the house. Max could make out a shadowy figure in the distance, walking fast from the woods towards the house, a black duffle bag over its shoulder. Moving quick enough to make up the ground at a good pace, but slow enough not to draw the eye's attention. Just another few seconds.

"What's going on?" asked the second officer. Max surmised that this was the senior man, based on the way he was posturing. Max relayed his request to pay Senator Becker a visit, adding, "Officer, our family is very close with the senator. My father, Charles Fend, owner of Fend Aerospace, is a good friend. I will only be a few minutes. My father wants to offer him a flight on his private jet back to D.C., where the funeral will be held."

The last part was total BS, since the funeral likely hadn't even been discussed, but Max figured where there was confusion, there was opportunity.

The two cops looked at each other. Max heard one whisper to the other, "Well, his dad is famous. I mean, what's he gonna do? I say let him at least go to the door."

The plainclothes cop shook his head. "I'm sorry, Mr. Fend. But the senator said—"

A yell from the home interrupted them, and for a moment Max panicked, thinking Trent might have run into trouble.

But it was the senator, standing in the doorway, waving. "Let him in, gentlemen! Thank you."

The police officers tipped their hats to Max, and he walked the fifty yards down the paved driveway and up the steps to the front entrance. The door was left cracked open, and the senator's face looked much less peaceful this close up.

"They still looking?" Max asked.

"Yeah," replied Trent from the dark hallway.

The maid was on the floor, her wrists and ankles bound with zip ties and her mouth covered with duct tape. Trent stood next to her holding a pistol, its suppressor nuzzled against the senator's back.

Max shut the door behind them.

"Hello, Senator. We'd like to have a quick word."

30

From inside the home, Renee could see Ian Williams's men moving closer to the group in the middle.

She spoke quietly, still trying to dig for information. The man was holding a weapon. A small black pistol. "Who are the men here, do you think?"

The assassin said, "I don't know exactly. But I don't give them much longer to live."

Renee gave him a concerned glance.

One of the men sitting on the patio furniture called out to Williams. Renee could hear him speaking Spanish and laughing. Then Williams nodded to one of his gunmen, and the rest happened quick.

She cupped her mouth as the gunman wheeled around and unslung his submachine gun. One of the tiny black ones, with a long cylinder on the end. A rapid spray of flame, and the group of men around the fire pit were cut down in a burst of red, their bodies littered with bullet holes.

Everything went quiet as the shooters surveyed the scene. Renee was horrified. She saw two of the gunmen rolling out the same blue tarp that they had used to wrap up Jennifer Upton's body. It looked like they were about to start cleanup.

The French-speaking assassin standing next to Renee suddenly cursed.

"What's wrong?"

He had been calm during the gunfire but was now agitated. He stood up quickly and moved towards the window, holding his weapon in both hands.

"What's wrong?" asked Renee again, wondering if he would go outside, leaving her alone in the room.

A chance to escape.

"Shhh."

The men outside were now upset as well, she saw. One of Williams's Mexican gunmen was down on the ground, dead and bleeding from his head. She heard Williams swearing at his men.

"Well, one of you must have bloody shot him! It couldn't have ricocheted from there! How the hell...?"

Then another gunman's face went missing, his body dropping to the brick patio.

For a moment everyone was frozen in confusion. By the time the third gunman was hit, they were scattering like ants. Williams and Syed sprinted towards the house, heads tucked low. Loud cracks of gunfire rang out as some of the sicarios began shooting towards the inlet.

At what, Renee couldn't see.

* * *

The senator hadn't known who Renee was or whether she was in captivity. But after Trent had held a gun to his head, Becker had done two things rather fast: wet his pants, and revealed Ian Williams's location.

Williams was—incredibly—just across the bay, at the mansion on the peninsula. Within Trent's rifle range. The senator's window was the only spot with a view over the stone wall of the peninsular property. Just as Max and Trent looked out the window, they witnessed several men in black gun down a group sitting on a patio.

Trent had taken out his suppressed rifle and gone to work. Max ran down the stairs and out the senator's front door, towards the police vehicles in front of the house. He had quickly called Wilkes, frantically filling him in. Wilkes promised to contact local law enforcement.

Now Max watched as the black-and-white police car put its lights on and sped out of the driveway, heading north on the main road. The plain-clothes officer was halfway into his vehicle when he saw Max.

"We just got a call from our chief. It seems you misled us, Mr. Fend."

"Sorry about that," Max huffed.

They both turned as the sound of popping gunfire erupted in the distance.

"It was suggested to me that I let you tag along. You've got some three-letter agency affiliation."

"Please..."

The cop rolled his eyes. "Get in. Get in. We got to go."

Max hopped in the passenger side and the police vehicle accelerated down the road.

"Does Oshkosh have a SWAT team?"

"Yes, we do."

"They on the way?" The speedometer got up to eighty on the tiny road, the trees flying by. Then the police officer decelerated rapidly and took a hard right, following the lake road, the car bouncing as they drove.

"Most of them are on duty at the air show. But they've been notified to get here as soon as possible."

Ahead of them, Max saw the other police car parked outside of a stone wall with a wrought-iron gate. The cop had his pistol drawn and was standing behind the car. Max's vehicle came to a halt right behind the first vehicle, and both he and the plainclothes officer got out.

The gunfire was louder now that they were here, coming in rapid bursts. But they couldn't see anyone manning the gate. The whole property was surrounded by a tall stone wall. All Max could see through the wrought-iron front gate was a row of fancy SUVs parked on the lawn just inside the stone wall, and two more SUVs parked in the roundabout driveway in front of the mansion.

"What are you doing?" asked the cop.

Max was feeling his way up the stone wall, finding a grip and placing his shoe on a foothold.

"I need to get in there. I suggest you two wait here for your SWAT team. There's at least one hostage inside—a woman. Tell them to be careful when they arrive."

Max didn't wait for a response. He flung himself over, scraping his leg and ignoring the pain, landing on his feet on the grass. He then removed his pistol from his concealed carry holster and jogged towards the entrance of the house.

* * *

Trent had picked off seven of the twelve gunmen from the senator's office window across the bay when he'd decided to move his position. By then, some of the gunmen had located him and he was drawing fire.

He placed his weapon on safe and tucked it back in the duffle bag. Then he headed down the stairs. The senator and maid were both still tied up, sitting in the front hallway. The duct tape had been taken off the maid's mouth and placed over the senator's.

A knock at the door made Trent reach for his pistol. Mike, the young CIA operative, stuck his head in.

"Wilkes asked me to give you a hand here."

Trent looked at the senator, who was avoiding eye contact. "You babysit them. And give me your keys."

"Wilkes is outside. He'll drive you."

"Fine."

Trent jogged to the car and got in.

"Everything go alright?"

"For me. Not so much for them."

Wilkes hit the gas and they headed towards the fight.

Wilkes said, "Any word from Max?"

"I couldn't see him, but he should be there by now."

"How many?"

"At least five of them were left."

"That's not great odds."

* * *

Renee was wired with adrenaline and sheer terror as she witnessed the gunfire. Williams and Syed were now inside the room, both looking out at the carnage in the yard. The assassin was also looking that way, but he'd moved to an adjacent room, still holding his gun.

She decided it was now or never, and she bolted.

Renee raced towards the mansion's front door, pumping her arms and gritting her teeth, her limbs feeling like they were twice their usual weight. She was scared half out of her mind as she braced herself for a bullet in the back.

"Hey!" someone shouted from behind, and she heard the fast squeaks of footsteps on hardwood flooring.

Her sweaty palm pushed down the ornate door latch and pulled, but she felt resistance. She cursed, then flipped the deadbolt and repeated. The door flung open, and she could just barely make out a man running towards her with a gun in his hand. She almost panicked but then realized who it was.

She screamed, "Max!"

As she started to run out the door, what felt like a locomotive hit her from the side, knocking her out of the way and to the floor. The sound of gunshots and a slamming door and then more yelling and a searing white-hot pain in her temple.

"Take her with you."

Her vision was blurred, but somewhere in her mind she knew the voice belonged to Ian Williams. She felt herself being dragged away. She tried to squirm and fight, but the strong grip and multiple hands on her were too much to overcome.

Renee blinked away the haze and realized she was being carried into a garage, then thrown in the backseat of a car. The cough of an engine turning over and the familiar creak of a garage door opening. Then a lurch as the car accelerated and the deafening roar of gunfire coming from inside her vehicle. Ears ringing and a clang as the car must have hit something.

Then everything got quiet. She looked up, and Ian Williams's face was smiling over hers. Licking his lips in his disgusting way.

He whispered, "I told you that I would take you myself, dearie."

31

Max cursed from his hiding spot in the hedges in front of the house. He'd seen Renee at the door, screaming his name. She was so close, but then someone had tackled her from the side. Max had shot one of the gunmen square in the chest before the door had slammed shut. He was getting ready to break through a window when an SUV had emerged from the garage. Max was sure he could make out Renee's face in the backseat.

Someone from the getaway vehicle had fired at the now-substantial police presence on the main street in front of the home as it barreled through the wrought-iron gate.

Max got up, tucked his gun into its holster, and ran the fifty or so yards towards the police vehicles, hoping no one would mistake him for one of the cartel gunmen. He heard a pop shot behind him and the snap of a bullet going past but kept running, knowing it was his best course of action.

As he arrived at the now-bashed gate entrance, a man in SWAT tactical gear grabbed him and pulled him behind the stone wall. A few of the police cars were starting up, looking like they were getting ready to pursue the fleeing SUV.

Someone yelled, "It's okay, he's with us!"

A sedan came to a halt in the middle of the street and two men got out. Trent and Wilkes.

Max pointed down the road as the SWAT man released him. "Trent, they're about a half mile ahead. Dark SUV. They've got Renee."

Trent nodded and grabbed the keys out of Wilkes's hand, jumping in the driver's seat. Max opened the passenger door and threw himself inside.

Wilkes stared at the two from the street as Trent accelerated, and the world spun past. Max's mind raced as he thought of what Renee was going through. Of where she was headed. Of what they might do to her...

* * *

Renee felt the SUV jolt as they drove through a chain-link fence. She was sitting up in the center of the backseat, a Latino gunman to her left, Williams to her right.

"There," William yelled. "That's ours."

The SUV zoomed along the flight line, where the private jets were parked. It came to a halt outside a sleek white Learjet.

Williams talked to one of the pilots out the window, speaking rapid Spanish and getting angrier by the moment.

"He says we can't take off. Several of the private jets have been defueled by airport operations, this one included. They say the order came from the Department of Homeland Security. We need another way."

Syed said, "If we can get to Fond du Lac's airport, my aircraft is there."

"How do you know we won't face the same issue?"

"My men will not have allowed this to happen. If we can get there, we will be able to leave without problem."

"Well, we can't drive there. The police are everywhere now."

The younger man—the assassin—was in the front passenger seat. He pointed out the front window. "That aircraft over there across the runway has started up. We can tell the pilot to take us to Fond du Lac."

"That thing is a relic. It's for tourists."

"It doesn't matter, it flies," spat Williams.

He said something in Spanish, and the driver raced across the taxiways and main runway as fast as the SUV would go. The vehicle slammed to a stop just in back of the running aircraft.

Renee recognized the plane. She realized it was the Ford Trimotor. The one the old Tuskegee Airman had been telling her about. A short line of passengers stood at the gate. Renee was forced out of the SUV at gunpoint, and the group began walking towards the old aircraft. Three loud external motors, each the size of a man, sputtered and rattled, their propellers spinning, angled upward.

The crowd in line for Ford Trimotor rides looked alarmed as the menacing group walked towards the plane. Some noticed that they were carrying weapons, and someone yelled, "Gun!"

A police officer wearing a bike helmet and a neon-yellow-and-black uniform shouted and began to draw his weapon. Ian Williams lifted his pistol and shot the man twice in rapid succession, the dark red holes appearing in the neon yellow uniform as the man fell backward.

Renee cringed and let out a yelp, the crowd around them screaming, running away.

As she was marched towards the plane, she saw the assassin get on first and point a gun towards the pilot. She walked up a short staircase and ducked through the entrance. Renee was made to sit in the front of the cabin. The rear door slammed shut, barely audible over the noise, and Williams and Syed sat in the seats behind and next to her. Then the engines roared louder, and she could barely hear a thing. She looked up at the cockpit of the plane, high up another set of stairs, bright white daylight from outside the cockpit windscreen contrasting with the dark cabin. The assassin stood there, pointing a gun at the head of the pilot in the right seat.

She realized the man in the left pilot seat was the little old Tuskegee Airman. For a brief moment she thought she was hallucinating, yet there he was, his wrinkled face looking up at the assassin's eyes and then down at his gun.

Renee felt a jolt as the aircraft's engine power overcame the friction of its own chocks, and they began moving slowly forward down the taxiway.

* * *

Max's vehicle raced across the runway as the Ford Trimotor began taxiing.

"We've got to stop them from taking off."

"How?"

"I don't know. The plane's passenger door is on the rear right side. See if you can get me on board."

Trent glanced at Max quickly. Maybe seeing if he was kidding. Then he looked forward, gripping the wheel tight, the gas all the way to the floor. "Roger. Get in the backseat."

Max hopped in the back-left seat and lowered the window.

Trent kept the speed up and stayed wide, maneuvering his vehicle around the aircraft's tail and then pulling in left, slowing and getting snug up to the aircraft.

Because the aircraft rested on a tail wheel, the fuselage angled up sharply. The cabin windows were just forward of the rear passenger door. Trent had the car positioned in a blind spot, just aft of the passenger door. Right now, Max and Trent couldn't see any of the passengers, and the passengers couldn't see them. But the vehicle would need to come forward in order for Max to reach the door.

"Get ready," said Trent. Max saw that he had his silenced pistol in his right hand, relying on his left hand to drive.

Max stood on the rear seat and prepared himself to exit out the window. They were only going about forty miles per hour, but looking at the pavement below, it still seemed fast. But they were running out of time. Max's best guess was that they had about twenty seconds before the plane turned sharply left onto the active runway and he missed his chance.

He stuck his head out the window and the wind met his face. Max looked forward along the length of the plane and could make out the pilot's eyes through the reflection of the aircraft's right side-mounted mirror. The pilot's mouth opened, and then closed as he saw the car driving along next to them and recognized what was happening.

Max continued climbing through the window, grabbing on to the car's "oh shit" handle with his right hand, balancing himself on the door frame and reaching with his left hand for the door latch of the Ford Trimotor.

Trent began moving the vehicle forward. Here it came. The leap of faith. Hot exhaust and deafening noise all around him. The taxiway pavement whizzing by below. A two-foot chasm waiting to break his bones.

Remarkably, the door opened from the outside without much effort. But keeping it open as the wind pushed against it was a challenge.

Then the gunshots sounded. The passengers had seen Trent. He was firing with one hand on the wheel.

Shattering glass and muffled yelling.

Time to commit. If any of the gunmen were looking back this way, he would be a dead man. But this was his only chance to save Renee.

Max pulled open the door with his left hand, reached out with his right, and dove forward. He landed with a sharp pain, his chest now on the floor of the aircraft cabin, then felt the terror as his legs began to fall, their weight starting to pull him back out the door.

Max dug deep and swung his legs up, pulling his body over the precipice. Then he used his arms to wriggle forward the rest of the way through and onto the aircraft cabin floor.

He was on board, heart pounding in his chest.

Max looked up to see one of the gunmen standing over him, aiming a submachine gun at his face. Then the man's chest popped with two red holes and he fell backward toward the cabin wall.

A burst of gunfire forward and a lurch as the aircraft veered left and Trent's vehicle slid away.

Yelling and cursing in Spanish. Max realized Trent had shot several of the men on board through the windows. Max reached across the aisle and picked up the weapon of the now-dead sicario from the floor. Then he craned his neck around the seat that had been concealing him from the front of the plane.

Max took a mental snapshot of the aircraft interior, then hid back behind the rearmost row.

The aircraft had a narrow column of seats. One seat on either side of the aisle. Five rows, ten seats total. An incredibly steep incline up toward the cockpit. No door between the cockpit and cabin. Max guessed he was looking at a twenty-foot ramp towards the bright white light of the cockpit windows. A difficult length to ascend.

Renee sat in the forwardmost left cabin seat, looking unharmed.

Williams stood in the center aisle just aft of her. He was holding his hands to his face, bright red blood dripping through the cracks in his fingers. Glass from the window, or a graze, maybe.

Max saw two men on the ground, injured or dead, he couldn't tell which yet. But one looked like Abdul Syed. There was a white guy gripping the back of the right-side pilot's seat, holding a gun to the man's head.

Now all Max had to do was get past the gauntlet and tell the pilot to halt his takeoff.

Max felt the aircraft make another sharp left turn onto the runway. Then the engines roared to full power, and both of the remaining men in the cabin—Ian Williams and the man holding the gun to the pilot's head—tumbled backward along the steep aisle as the aircraft accelerated forward on its takeoff roll.

* * *

Renee felt her head press back into her seat as the aircraft throttle was moved to takeoff power. She felt like she was launching in the space shuttle the way she was angled up so sharply.

The assassin who'd been pointing his gun at the pilot hadn't been prepared for the force of the acceleration combined with that steep an angle. His only grip had been one hand on the pilot's seat, his other hand holding a pistol. The man fell backward through the air, landing on his back halfway down the aisle, rolling and then sliding towards the aft end of the aircraft. Renee saw the flying pilot look backward, the aircraft still rumbling through its takeoff roll.

A decisive moment. Would he abort the takeoff with two gunmen still on board and remaining runway disappearing before him? Renee hoped he would, but even she was fearful of the repercussions.

Her hopes were dashed seconds later when they became airborne, gliding up and banking slightly to the right, the air now rushing through cracked and broken windows on the right side of the cabin. Renee let out a breath of defeat. Out her window were thousands of planes parked next to each other in the grass. Rows of tents and the massive static display of jumbo jets and military aircraft in the center of the air show.

And Max.

He was down there. She hoped she would see him again.

Then she turned around and did.

Impossibly, Max was now locked in a wrestling match with the assassin who had just fallen backward from the cockpit. They were fighting for control of a gun.

She reached down and unlatched her seat belt. Taking a quick breath, she forced herself out of the seat, ready to vault down the aisle, past the bloody bodies on the floor, and pummel the man who dared hurt her beloved Max.

Then Ian Williams rose up from his seat. One of his eyes was a mass of crimson. His face was smeared with wet blood. His other eye was wide and crazed. Mouth open with white teeth clenched down in a mad rage.

Williams raised a black pistol towards Renee and fired.

* * *

Max heard a gunshot and involuntarily snapped his gaze towards the shooter. Ian Williams had fired up near the front of the aircraft. Renee had been up there, but Max couldn't see her now. A single shot rang out. Max kept trying to spot Renee but then felt a fist pounding him in the kidney.

He forced himself to fight one problem at a time.

The man was wrapped around him, off balance but trying to gain leverage. Max elbowed his opponent in the face twice and felt him go limp. Then Max got to his feet and brought his knee up hard under the man's chin, breaking his jaw and sending him to the floor, motionless. Unconscious.

Renee.

Max turned back towards Williams. The Englishman had dropped his pistol and was searching around on the floor for another weapon. Max sprinted towards him and tackled him from his blind side, putting all his force into his right shoulder and wrapping up the way he'd been taught to tackle playing football as a boy.

Williams slammed forward with a grimace, landing on his chest and already-bloodied face.

"Max!"

Max looked up from the floor and saw Renee standing at the front of the plane. Then she began to have trouble balancing herself as the aircraft tilted sideways.

Max looked beyond her. The pilot was hanging lifeless from his seat.

* * *

Renee watched a squirming Ian Williams as he tried reaching for a weapon on the floor. Renee had sent her forearm into Williams's shooting hand moments ago as he was trying to fire his weapon. He was half-blind from a vicious eye wound, and in his disorientation, she had managed to throw off his aim.

But while she was unharmed, it appeared that Williams had shot the pilot.

"Help the pilots!" Max shouted, pointing with one hand.

Renee frowned and turned around, still holding on to the edges of the aisle seats so she wouldn't fall over, the aircraft now in a sharp turn and an unusually steep climb.

The pilot was dead. Ian Williams's gunshot had hit him in the back of the head. Renee panicked as she realized the copilot was the ninety-something-year-old Tuskegee Airman. She climbed up the stairs as fast as she could, fighting the pull of the earth's gravity that seemed to want her to lie on the wall.

Renee heaved herself up to the pilot's seat and grimaced as she unstrapped the dead man and pulled his body into the center aisle. Then she got in the seat, strapped in, put on his headset and grabbed the... steering wheel?

The plane had a steering wheel.

She said over the headset, "Can you hear me?" Then she tried to do what she thought Max would tell her to do during one of her flight lessons.

"Yes, I can hear you," said the Tuskegee Airman. "I'm afraid I'm having a hard time seeing everything. I don't have my glasses." His hands were on his steering wheel.

"It's alright. I'm going to try and level us out. I think I should just turn the wheel left. What do you think?"

"Yes, I think you're right."

Renee turned the wheel to the left, feeling a good amount of resistance. But sure enough, the wings banked over to the left and now they were only in a climb, not a turn.

The Tuskegee Airman said, "Now I think you need to push the stick forward."

"Okay."

Renee pushed forward on the steering wheel and the nose tilted down until they were flying almost straight and level.

She looked at the Tuskegee Airman and smiled. "We did it!"

A series of gunshots rang out from the rear of the plane.

* * *

Max had seen it coming. The man in the back, whom Max had thought was unconscious, rose up on his elbows and reached for a submachine gun that had been resting underneath one of the dead sicarios. Max released Ian Williams from his wrestling hold, reached out for the handgun four feet down the aisle, turned, and fired, single-handed.

Both shots missed, but they helped him gain the advantage over his opponent.

The man was now hunkered down behind useless cushioned seats. The only thing they did was put him out of sight. But Max knew exactly where he was. This was a thinking man's game. The one who solved the problem the fastest won.

Max drew himself up from the floor and balanced his weight between his left foot and his right knee, holding the pistol firmly with both hands, steadying his aim as much as possible in the maneuvering aircraft...

And pulled the trigger.

He saw a quick jerk in the shadows beneath the seat. Then the man's body collapsed into a heap on the floor.

Now it was just Ian Williams. Max saw Williams rise up in the middle of the aisle, standing defiant and unarmed. He started to turn and walk aft.

"Don't move!" Max yelled above the howling wind.

Williams turned and stared at Max with one eye, his other just a swollen slit now. "Shoot me, then." He slowly stepped backwards, holding on to the tops of the seats for balance. Looking Max in the face, daring him to fire on an unarmed man. And getting closer to the other weapons on the floor that had slid to the aft part of the aircraft.

Fine, Max thought. *He wants to go this way? He deserves it.*

Before Max pulled the trigger, he did a double take, looking down at the weapon in his hands. In the excitement of the moment he had missed it. The slide of his pistol was all the way back, the chamber empty.

He was out of bullets.

* * *

Renee had her head on a swivel. Just like playing defense on Princeton's field hockey team. Except now she was trying to fly an ancient plane and make sure that the love of her life wasn't being shot at.

"What is he doing back there?"

"What do you see?" said the Tuskegee pilot. He was holding the airplane's controls with her. She could feel his inputs every few seconds. Flying by sight, judging the horizon. Unable to read any of the dials, but his decades-old aviation instinct helping nonetheless.

"Max isn't shooting. I think the man who hijacked the plane is going for a gun. We need to do something."

Renee looked forward again, making sure that they weren't aiming towards the ground. They were probably thousands of feet off the altitude they had started at. Indeed, the air seemed cooler and hazier than a few moments ago. But her only real goal was to make sure they didn't crash until Max could come help.

But he wouldn't be coming to help if Ian Williams shot him.

"What can we do?"

"Land," the old man offered.

"I mean right now. Is there something we can do to help shake things up back there?"

The old man looked at Renee and said, "We could try some maneuvers."

She said, "What if we stall the aircraft? Maybe we can shake them up enough back there that..." Renee wasn't sure if it would work, or help. But she didn't have any other options. There was only one problem. "I have no idea how to stall this thing, do you?"

The old man said, "I would try to pull those levers right there. The throttle levers. No, not that. Yes, those ones. All the way...well, maybe not all the way..."

Renee pulled the three levers back to about one quarter of where they could be set. The engines wound down and became much quieter, and thankfully the propellers were still spinning.

"Now pull back on the stick as hard as you can. Don't let go. After we go through the stall, push forward hard. Then, when we get speed back, pull up hard."

Renee pulled on the steering wheel with sweaty hands. She reached her forearms around it to help. The nose of the large aircraft went up, and she could see the airspeed sliding back. A high-pitched whine sounded through their headphones.

She turned her head back and yelled as loud as she could. "Max, hold on!"

The airspeed slowed, the sun came into view, and then the bottom dropped out.

* * *

Max started running towards Williams but was going to be too late. Then he heard a female voice screaming about something, and Max realized the aircraft had changed configuration. As Ian Williams raised up the submachine gun from the floor, Max grabbed on to the metal base of the seat nearest to him and held on tight.

The next few seconds happened in slow motion. Ian picked up the weapon just as the stall began. As the nose of the aircraft dove down and they passed through zero g's, Ian Williams floated up into the ceiling. Then the g's came back on and he slammed to the floor, hitting it hard enough to stun him.

Max was crouched and holding on to the seats. He took two quick steps towards the rear of the aircraft.

Ian was now sprawled out right next to the exit door.

Which was fluttering ever so slightly.

The latch had taken gunfire, Max realized.

The only thing holding the door shut was the airflow over the fuselage. Which was considerable at this speed. But no match for the force of a man being kicked through it.

Before Williams could regain his balance, Max grabbed on to the two metal handles atop the rearmost aisle seats. He swung his legs forward and aimed his heels towards Ian's sternum, extending himself, kicking and squatting with all his might.

The result was Ian Williams flying backward, slamming through the unlocked exit door, screaming as he disappeared into the wild blue yonder.

* * *

Max took Renee's seat and contacted Oshkosh tower on guard, the emergency frequency for all aircraft.

The tower air traffic controller got one of the other Ford Trimotor pilots on the radio, and while the landing was definitely not Max's finest, they were able to talk him down to the runway safely.

Max taxied the aircraft up to the central display area of the air show and shut off the engines. Renee embraced him and kissed him on the lips.

Then she did the same to the Tuskegee Airman, who was smiling, despite the chaos.

Firetrucks and ambulances converged on the scene. Police cars and news crews. Crowds of people, stunned and taking pictures and clapping and pointing. Max, Renee, and the Tuskegee Airman were helped out of the aircraft and taken to the hospital under police guard.

Max's father Charles, Trent Carpenter, and Caleb Wilkes all met him there. After all the official interviews and medical treatment, Max asked Trent what had happened to the senator.

Trent gave him a look and said, "Later."

Max understood enough to be patient.

32

Max and Caleb Wilkes sat across from Senator Becker, a recording device resting on the table between them. They were in the senator's home. The investigators were done with it, although they were still evaluating evidence at the mansion property across the cove. That was a crime scene, still being investigated several days after the events of last week.

No charges had been filed against Senator Becker yet. The problem was witnesses. For all of Ian Williams's faults, he had done a good job of covering their tracks. Almost everyone who could point to Becker's participation in the cabal was dead. Those who were thought to be alive were outside the country, being protected—or eliminated—by the remaining coconspirators.

But the digital and financial trails would eventually be uncovered, the FBI investigators had assured them. It was just a matter of time, now that they knew what they were looking for. And Max and Renee could testify to what they had seen.

Becker's only hope to avoid a life in jail was to cooperate wholeheartedly. The news media had already begun putting the pieces together, and the cable news channels were featuring wall-to-wall coverage of the senator's international conspiracy. Each night, the *Washington Post* and the *New York Times* tried to outscoop each other on another major revelation.

Wilkes had gotten about all the information he needed from the senator. It confirmed what Max had hypothesized. Becker was an agent of the ISI, and a coconspirator in Williams's cabal, which had started as a product of the ISI but had morphed into something more. Becker had been feeding Ian Williams and Abdul Syed classified intelligence for years. But now the mole had been caught and the network had self-destructed.

Both were big prizes for Wilkes.

After almost six hours, the senator's debrief was finally wrapping up. The politician's chin was still held high, despite everything that had happened. But there was worry there as well. Having reached the point where he had given up all of his secrets—Becker's only real leverage—his eyes were now searching Wilkes's face for some sign of what would happen next.

Wilkes gave him nothing. He rose from his chair, telling Max, "I need to make a call." Trent entered the room and stood by the wall, arms folded.

Becker vociferously denied having anything to do with his own daughter's death and looked offended at the suggestion. Max didn't believe it.

The conspiracy had been vast, and well planned. Most of the agents inside the US were unwitting. The politicians who had voted with Becker were influenced by their donors, not by foreign spies. But many of their donors were influenced by the cabal. Becker had simply used his inside knowledge to steer the cabal network money to the right politicians. Big Pharma executives around the world were already paying lobbyists and contributing to policies that would help their bottom line. The overt crossover between the legal opioid businesses and illicit industry was almost nil.

But there was coordination.

As Senator Becker admitted, the combined industry growth had been planned and fertilized by Ian Williams and Abdul Syed.

Becker turned to Max. "You don't understand why I did it, do you?"

Max didn't respond.

The senator said, "We won the war on terror thanks to my actions. I was the one of the few people who were willing to do what it took. To get my hands dirty. Come on. You can figure it out. It all comes down to economics. If the poor people in Afghanistan didn't have money and jobs, they would have been just as susceptible to the siren song of the Taliban and others. By keeping their economy going, we made sure that Afghanistan wouldn't transform back into a haven for terrorism. The Pakistanis wanted stability in the region. So did we. I simply made a deal to keep the peace."

"By using heroin as an economic growth tool?"

"It worked. It kept money flowing in. Do you know how much worse Afghanistan would be right now without those jobs? Growing poppy is perfect for Afghanistan. It needs little capital investment, it grows well in their climate, and the profits are enormous. We helped feed and employ the people of Afghanistan by growing those opium plants."

"You made a deal with foreign intelligence operatives and drug cartels."

"You don't make deals with your friends, Max. I did what needed to be done to protect American interests."

"You mean to protect your own interests. Didn't you know that these drugs would be sold in the US? Didn't you think about the consequences?"

"Most Afghan heroin ends up in other countries."

"Is that what you told yourself? Don't be naïve. It's a global market, and Afghanistan makes ninety percent of it. Afghan heroin might not all end up in the US, but it still affects Americans. You also helped facilitate laws that loosened regulations on opioid sales in the US—"

"Regulations kill the economy—"

"Save your political speak. Your actions were calculated. With one hand, you guys opened the valve for heroin coming in. With the other, you made sure that there was a growing customer base. In your own back-yard, for God's sake. You made money off narcotics so that you could win elections."

The senator's mask of confidence began to crack. "The people that use that stuff are the scum of the earth. They're leeches on society. So what if they get high? Keep them in the slums. They'll shoot themselves up into oblivion and we'll all be better off for it."

"Decrease the surplus population, eh?"

Becker rolled his eyes. "Spare me. You don't see me out there using drugs on the street. Some people are just weaker."

Max turned to Trent. The veins in his forearm pulsed as he clenched and unclenched his fists. His eyes burned holes into the senator as the muscles in his jaw flexed.

Just then Caleb Wilkes came into the cabin, looking annoyed. "Time to go."

"What's wrong?"

"Nothing. We're done with him."

Max, Trent, and Wilkes departed the home, leaving the senator inside.

When they were alone, Wilkes said, "I just talked to my buddy at the FBI. He says they'll nail him eventually. But he'll spend the next few years in and out of court. Appeals. All that jazz."

Max shook his head in disgust.

"Why did the ISI and Ian Williams go to all this trouble?" Trent asked. "Why clean house with their network? Becker's the only beneficiary."

Wilkes said, "Maybe not. You know that Opioid Epidemic Bill that Becker was pushing? This ISI-sponsored group of investors stood to earn huge from that. Becker and the remaining members each stood to gain financially."

"How?"

"The Opioid Epidemic Bill would greatly reduce the number of legal opioids in the US. But Ian Williams and Syed's group were planning to capitalize on the black market it would create. Some of my intelligence sources told us that the Sinaloa cartel was going to start buying over three hundred percent more heroin than it ships today. They were going to get it from Afghan suppliers next year to feed the new demand. The cartel would make a fortune. The ISI's investor group was also going to buy a lot of the extra supply from the legitimate international opioid suppliers around the world and make their own unlicensed pills to sell on the black market."

"Who were these investors?"

"Businessmen, criminals. Shady financiers. People the ISI grouped together to help them make money and influence national policy in their favor."

Max nodded. "And Syed and Williams thought they had the perfect American politician in their pocket to provide them cover. One with very strong presidential prospects. They just had to get rid of any remaining connections to him before he got too famous."

"They couldn't really pick someone to become president that far out. Too much uncertainty."

Wilkes said, "The FBI investigators think he's got accounts that they were transferring money into. Sort of a backup payment. Like I said, it'll all come out eventually. Maybe he would get elected president? Maybe he wouldn't. Either way, he was valuable to them."

"Not so valuable anymore, though."

"No, not anymore. He's a wounded animal now."

"But not dead," Trent said. Max exchanged glances with both men.

They walked to the CIA vehicles that remained at the entrance gate. It was dark out. Max and the others watched as the senator, who had been looking at them out his front window, disappeared into the house.

Across the water, they could see floodlights set up in the backyard of the cartel mansion. Yellow tape marking off areas of past violence. A few FBI agents in blue coats scavenging over the yard, looking for clues to assist the forensic investigation.

"Becker's law enforcement detail got called off?" asked Max.

Wilkes said, "Yes. Once it became apparent there was no longer a need. Once they indict him, he'll have another type of police escort."

The men gave a dark chuckle.

Wilkes got into his car, bade them farewell, and departed down the road.

Max and Trent stood alone by their car. A streetlight buzzing above them.

Trent said, "He killed his own daughter and helped encourage a plague of drug addiction around the world, all for his own benefit. Prison is too good a fate for him."

Max got into the driver's seat. "Come on." Trent got in and they drove a half mile down the road, parking behind the same grove of trees near where Max had landed the gyrocopter a few days earlier.

Trent said, "You wait here."

"No. I want to come."

They walked into the woods adjacent to the senator's home, surveilling their prey. The senator had gone out onto his back patio. It was near 11 p.m. He was drinking by himself. Very few lights on in the home. No guests.

"Ready?" Trent whispered.

Max didn't reply. He watched Becker sitting there. A despicable waste of a man.

"I don't think I can."

Trent looked at him.

Max said, "Everything he did. In his mind, he justified it. He tried to say he was helping Afghanistan. Helping fight the war on terror. Everything he did, he had an excuse. A rationalization for why he could make such an immoral choice."

"He killed his own daughter. Or at least knew about it. Didn't stop it. He helped flood our country with opioids. Guy's practically a mass murderer."

"Yes, he did. And he deserves to die for that. But it's not our place to kill him."

"I killed people in Mexico. What's different?"

"Because here he'll face justice. Our country is what's different. The rule of law. We need to let him face justice the right way. Let's not tell ourselves the same thing he did. The ends don't justify the means. We are honorable men, and we should make the less satisfying choice, because it is righteous."

Trent didn't say anything for a long time. Max began to worry that his words hadn't mattered.

Then Trent said, "Can we at least go in and scare the shit out of him? Maybe slap him around a little?"

Max thought about it. He shrugged. "I don't see why not."

A few moments later, they both approached the senator wearing black masks. When Trent's hand came up over Becker's face, he was half-drunk.

The old man struggled at first, but he was no match for Trent's brute strength. Max turned the last remaining light out near the rear of the home, and they were engulfed in darkness.

Trent held him nearly upside-down, and Max whispered into Senator Becker's ear.

"You called them weaklings. I knew one of those weaklings. He was thirty-six years old. An Army veteran. He left behind a wife and a little kid. This guy here? It was his brother."

In the moonlight, Max could see the senator's eyes go wide with fear.

Trent whispered, "You made a deal with the devil, Senator. And he always collects."

Max had placed a zip tie around the senator's wrists, holding his arms behind his body. They placed a gag over his mouth, then carried him towards the water and down a short dock. Trent kneeled down and lowered the senator's head into the water, upside-down, holding him there for a moment, then lifted him up.

Max said, "The next time you speak to investigators, you better tell them everything. Because we know the truth. And we'll come back for you if you don't."

33

A week later, Max and Renee were back in the Poconos. Max had rented a lake house near the Carpenters' home. He decided that Renee and he could use a vacation—a real one. Max stood on the upper deck, directly above a boat slip. He could hear the sound of water sloshing around below. Waves from the Jet Skis and pontoon boats motoring by.

Renee sat in a lawn chair, wearing a bikini, a towel wrapped around her bottom half. She was sipping a cold beer, a lime wedge tucked in the long neck of the bottle, taking in the carefree scene below. The setting sun cast long shadows over the surrounding mountains. This was the only time of day she partook in sunbathing her fair skin.

Trent had brought Josh Junior to meet them for the afternoon. He and his delighted nephew had spent most of the time jumping off a ten-foot deck into the water. Now they were fishing for sunfish, using mushed-up Wonder Bread as bait.

Renee was reading him an article about the senator's recent confession. "The Justice Department has been very pleased with how cooperative the disgraced former senator has been, however disturbing the details. He has confessed to multiple counts of espionage, bank fraud, and conspiracy to commit murder."

"Nothing else? Any complaints from the senator or anything?"

"What were you expecting?"

"I don't know. Two men. Head dunking. Nothing. Just curious."

Renee frowned. "What will happen now?"

Max used tongs to turn over bratwurst, making sure each one got an even brown. "With what?"

"With the drug ring? All those people, involved in that conspiracy..."

"Many of the ones responsible are already dead. Williams and the ISI saw to that. But there will be countless investigations, I'm sure. Senator Becker was a politician, so Washington will be chewing this up for the next few years. Caleb and his team are already moving on some of the information they uncovered. My understanding is that there are a whole host of punishments waiting to be dished out. The State Department will be announcing sanctions against Pakistan. The Treasury Department is freezing assets of several lobbying firms and Jennifer Upton's political nonprofit."

"Oh, I did read about that. It was Jennifer Upton's nonprofit that much of the foreign political contributions were coming through."

Max nodded. "There are also more than a dozen executives in some overseas pharmaceutical companies that are being brought up on criminal charges."

Max placed the brats on a paper plate, next to a tinfoil-covered plate of roasted peppers and onions.

"Dinner's ready," he called down to Trent, who gave him a thumbs-up.

Renee said, "What about the cartels?"

"Ironically, that may be one of Senator Becker's only lasting policy ideas. There's talk that our military may start deploying larger numbers of special operations personnel into Mexico to crack down on some of the cartels. From what I understand, Becker had proposed it to a few congressmen, and they've begun drumming up serious support after all this mess has come to light."

"That sounds like it'll be even more messy."

"It probably will be. But we've got to do something."

Max grabbed a beer out of the cooler and sat in the lawn chair next to Renee. He leaned over and kissed her, then rested his head back in the chair, enjoying the view over the lake.

Max smiled at Renee. "You know, we really should teach you how to land."

* * *

Sign up for the Reader List and be the first to know about new releases and special offers from Andrew Watts.

Join Andrew Watts' Reader List at AndrewWattsAuthor.com

ABOUT THE AUTHOR

Andrew Watts is the USA Today bestselling author of The War Planners series. He graduated from the US Naval Academy in 2003 and served as a naval officer and helicopter pilot until 2013. During that time, he flew counter-narcotic missions in the Eastern Pacific and counter-piracy missions off the Horn of Africa. He was a flight instructor in Pensacola, FL, and helped to run ship and flight operations while embarked on a nuclear aircraft carrier deployed in the Middle East.

Today, he lives with his family in Ohio.

THE WAR PLANNERS: Books 1-2

From a secretive jungle-covered island in the Pacific, to the sands of the Middle East. From the smog-filled alleyways of China, to the passageways of a US Navy destroyer. The War Planners series follows different members of the military and intelligence community as they uncover a Chinese plot to begin a world war, and attack America.

Book 1: The War Planners

A CIA agent and a group of American defense experts are part of a secretive CIA Red Cell. They are tasked with stopping a Chinese invasion - but not every one of them intend for America to win...

Book 2: The War Stage

A US Navy destroyer sinks an Iranian patrol craft during a controversial exchange in the Persian Gulf. With tensions soaring between the two nations, an Iranian politician secretly contacts the CIA with a chilling revelation involving the Chinese.

Get your copy today at AndrewWattsAuthor.com

ALSO BY ANDREW WATTS

Firewall

The War Planners Series

The War Planners

The War Stage

Pawns of the Pacific

The Elephant Game

Overwhelming Force

Global Strike

Max Fend Series

Glidepath

The Oshkosh Connection

Books available for Kindle, print, and audiobook.

*Join former navy pilot and USA Today bestselling author Andrew Watts' Reader Group
and be the first to know about new releases and special offers.*

AndrewWattsAuthor.com

Made in the USA
Coppell, TX
14 November 2020

41357459R00340